LOOSE AND EASY

"Hot, fast, and sexy." —CINDY GERARD,
New York Times bestselling author

"Sexual tension crackles and snaps....Crossing and double-crossing is on most of the characters' agendas, which keeps the pace fast and the action sharp....Janzen's place in the romantic suspense pantheon is assured." —*Romantic Times*

CUTTING LOOSE

"Bad boys are hot, and they don't come any hotter than the Steele Street gang. This high-octane chase drama accelerates out of the starting gate and doesn't look back.... This novel is smoking in the extreme!" —*Romantic Times*

"*Cutting Loose*...is a wonderful, fast-paced, and exciting read." —*Fresh Fiction*

"Tara Janzen once again takes readers on a nonstop thrill ride.... An exciting and engaging story. Don't miss *Cutting Loose!*" —Romance Reviews Today

ON THE LOOSE

"[A] wildly romantic thriller." —*Booklist*

"Nonstop action, a mysterious mission and a rekindled romance make *On the Loose* a winner."
—Romance Reviews Today

CRAZY HOT

"A cast of memorable characters in a tale of fast-paced action and eroticism." —*Publishers Weekly*

"Edgy, sexy, and fast. Leaves you breathless!"
—JAYNE ANN KRENTZ, *New York Times* bestselling author

CRAZY COOL

"Wild nonstop action, an interesting subplot, a tormented-but-honorable and brilliant bad boy and a tough girl, and great sex scenes make Janzen's... romance irresistible." —*Booklist*

CRAZY WILD

"While keeping the tension and thrills high, Janzen excels at building rich characters whose lives readers are deeply vested in. Let's hope she keeps 'em coming!" —*Romantic Times*

CRAZY KISSES

"The high-action plot, the savage-but-tender hero, and the wonderfully sensuous sex scenes, Janzen's trademarks, make this as much fun as the prior Crazy titles." —*Booklist*

CRAZY LOVE

"Readers [will] instantly bond with [Janzen's] characters. Driving action and adventure laced with hot passion add up to big-time fun." —*Romantic Times*

CRAZY SWEET

"Exciting and adventurous suspense with nonstop action that will keep readers riveted. I highly recommend it, and can't wait to read more."
—Romance Reviews Today

BREAKING LOOSE

TARA JANZEN

 A DELL BOOK

Breaking Loose is a work of fiction. Names, characters, places, and incidents either are the products of the author's imagination or are used fictitiously. Any resemblance to actual events, locales, or persons, living or dead, is entirely coincidental.

2009 Dell Mass Market Edition

Copyright © 2009 by Glenna McReynolds

Published in the United States by Dell, an imprint of The Random House Publishing Group, a division of Random House, Inc., New York.

DELL is a registered trademark of Random House, Inc., and the colophon is a trademark of Random House, Inc.

ISBN: 978-0-440-24470-7

Printed in the United States of America

www.bantamdell.com

2 4 6 8 9 7 5 3 1

BREAKING
LOOSE

PROLOGUE

Elegant.

The woman sitting across from General Richard "Buck" Grant in his office absolutely, positively owned the word—lock, stock, and barrel.

It was impossible for a guy to keep his eyes off her, so Buck didn't even try. What he did do, what he always did, was try not to let his gaze drop below her chin. If she was fascinatingly beautiful from the neck up—and she was—then she was nothing but trouble with a capital "T" from the neck down.

Dangerous, dangerous territory—he let the thought cross his mind with just the slightest downward glance.

Hot damn.

She did it on purpose—a hint of cleavage, the curves of her magnificent breasts always draped in some kind of soft material, her clothing perfectly fitted to a waist he knew he could nearly span with his hands. Any further than that, he never went, not unless she was walking away from him. The last thing he could afford, under any circumstances, was to get mired in the fantasyland of Suzi Toussi's hips. She was just too damned important, his secret weapon.

"Stargate?" she said, repeating the word he'd dropped between them like a small atom bomb. "Sure, Buck. I remember Stargate, the Defense Intelligence Agency's experiments in remote viewing, the psychic spies, the ones trying to gather intelligence using ESP."

She, at least, could say it with a straight face. That was the great thing about Suzi, her smooth coolness. She was always gracious, always unfazed, always somewhat imperious.

Okay—he paused and backed up to his last thought—she was always *damned* imperious. She knew the effect she had on men—which was the point, one of the reasons Christian Hawkins had recruited her five years ago to do a piece of contract work in Eastern Europe for Special Defense Force, SDF, Buck's unit of black-ops shadow warriors based in Denver. She'd done good, damn good, so he'd used her again and again, until one day she'd turned the tables on him and started using him.

Smart girl like her, he should have seen it coming. No complaints, though. She was a topflight paid asset, his sleeper, and the tasking that had landed on his desk last night had been tailor-made for her. Personally, he thought the whole Stargate thing was a holy crock of crap and a criminal waste of the American people's tax dollars and the military's budget, but nobody had asked him.

Nobody ever asked him anything—except when it came to doing the deed. Then they asked plenty of him, and especially of his team. They asked for guts and gave no glory—and his operators wouldn't have had it any other way.

"The DIA initiated and performed another set of experiments associated with the Stargate program," he said. "Moonrise, as they called it, is still classified." And in his opinion, if Stargate had been a holy crock of crap, Moonrise had been an *un*holy crock.

He picked a folder up off his desk and leaned forward, handing it over to her.

"Moonrise dealt with the use of . . . *special objects* to achieve the same goals," he said, knowing that wasn't quite as descriptive as it might have been, but finding himself stumbling over the more accurate word. To his way of thinking, the words "military" and "magic" were diametrically opposed, nonexistent on the same plane, nonsensical to the point of absurdity. "To that end, the program had an inventory of these . . . uh, special objects, and one of them, in particular, has gone missing."

"Missing?"

"Disappeared," he clarified . . . sort of.

"Stolen?"

"Teleported." He cleared his throat. "Officially."

Even the cool Ms. Toussi lifted an eyebrow at

that—thank God. He'd known he could count on her.

"Are you sure you don't want Skeeter on this?" she asked. They all knew SDF's blond bombshell, Skeeter Bang-Hart, had more...psychological empathy, Buck liked to call it, than the other operators.

"No," he said. "We have a line on it. Regardless of how it might have gotten there, telepathically or airfreight, two days ago the DIA intercepted some chatter that leads them to believe the object has surfaced in Paraguay."

Both of the lovely Ms. Toussi's perfectly arched eyebrows rose this time. "It seems a lot of things are surfacing in Paraguay lately."

She shouldn't know that.

"Do I have a security breach at Steele Street you need to tell me about?" Steele Street, an alley in Denver's lower downtown, was where the SDF team was housed in a state-of-the-art, steel-reinforced old brick building, along with every techno gadget and classic American muscle car known to man.

"No." She shook her head, sending a fall of richly auburn hair sliding over her shoulders. He shouldn't have noticed, but he did. "Dylan had me do some legwork for him the last time I was in San Francisco. Contact some people, strictly off the books. Paraguay came up over lunch, very casual, that's all. It's in my report."

Strictly off the books.

Right.

Everything Suzi did for the team was strictly off

the books. It was the reason he used her. No one on either side of the Potomac knew the drop-dead-gorgeous art dealer reported to him, or in the case of her lunch dates, apparently, to his second-in-command, Dylan Hart.

Hell, he only knew the simplest, most basic, least damaging parameters of how Dylan was conducting SDF's current top-priority mission, and that's the way he needed to keep it. If Suzi had written a report to Dylan about some "casual" lunch in San Francisco where the word "Paraguay" had come up, it was the last damn thing he wanted to read. To the very best of his ability, he didn't want to know Dylan had been going in and out of South America, and in and out of Paraguay in particular. Hawkins had been doing the same damn thing, and Buck didn't want to know that either, and all he could hope was that one of them knew where in the hell Zach Prade was going in and out of—Buck sure as hell didn't. And if anyone knew where Creed was, well, hell, Buck actually did want to know that. The jungle boy hadn't shown up on SDF radar for three weeks, which was just about two weeks and six days too long in Buck's book. *Crap.* What a way to be running a command. All he knew for sure was that everybody knew where in the hell he was, where in the hell he *always* was, next to the damn boiler room in the hell-and-gone Marsh Annex, and if anyone needed him, the codes were in place and the gloves would come off.

The CIA had certainly known where to find him, and they'd known he had guys already in place in

Paraguay, which told him plenty about whose hands were in this Moonrise-and-magic cow pie. He didn't know why they'd sicced the DIA on his ass, when his team was cleaning up one of their messes, a rogue agent the CIA had not been able to bring to heel, but he was sure they'd gotten something for the trade—and that would probably bite him in the ass, too. Both agencies would have been better off sending this mess somewhere else. Dylan and Hawkins were in too deep to break cover over a damn crystal ball or whatever the DIA thought their "teleported" knickknack was—but if Suzi could find it, his boys could snatch it, done deal, everybody happy. Of course, the whole damn request begged the question of why the Moonrise geeks didn't just have their own psi guys "teleport" the damn thing back to their lab. Which, of course, was no question at all, not in Buck's mind. Teleport, his ass. Somebody had plain old stolen Moonrise's hocus-pocus doodad.

"All I want you to do is go down there and verify the rumors," he said, getting the conversation back on track. "If it pans out, and if you can locate the item, I'll send in a team to retrieve it."

Tele-freaking-ported, *geezus*. What in the hell was this man's army coming to, Buck wondered, when teleportation became an officially acceptable designation for theft? The quacks over at the DIA must have pulled strings from here to Langley and back to get this landed on his desk, because if there was one thing he'd learned in his fifty-four years, it was that things didn't simply disappear—not without somebody's hot little hands on them. If Suzi could find the object, Dylan and Hawkins would damn well find those hands. Then, whoever had screwed up over at the DIA would find themselves "teleported" into the psychic unemployment line.

"I'll do my best, Buck," the beauty across from him said, turning her attention to the folder and opening it.

One perfect auburn eyebrow arched again, and yeah, he understood. The DIA's hootchie-kootchie was a weird-looking thing, spooky, and that from a guy who didn't spook, easily or otherwise.

"It's called—" he started to say.

"The Memphis Sphinx," she finished for him, her voice slightly confused, her gaze fixed on the first-page photo. "What the hell, Buck. This is the Maned Sphinx of Sesostris III, Twelfth Dynasty, Middle Kingdom, supposedly found by Carter in the Valley of the Kings during the excavation of King Tutankhamen's tomb, though some accounts have it recovered much earlier and from either Memphis or Tanis." She lifted her gaze to meet his. "This is a photograph."

Obviously, he thought, and a damn fine one, full color, with good lighting to reveal every detail of the thing.

"So you're familiar with the object," he said.

"No," she corrected him, shaking her head, her attention shifting back to the open folder, her brow furrowed. "I'm familiar with the *rumor* of the object, the *myth* of the object, and the *stories,* most notably of the Theban dynasty using it to expel the

Hyksos from Egypt at the beginning of the New Kingdom, and the twelfth-century slave kings of Delhi subjugating the people of northwest India with its powers. In this century, it was supposedly in the hands of the Nazis, who apparently had quite a bit of trouble controlling the forces they un-leashed, but this...this is a photograph of an ac-tual statue, a sphinx of about the right size, five by five by seven inches, sculpted out of black granite with a gold death mask, a gold and lapis lazuli lion's mane in place of a royal headdress, and clear crys-talline quartz eyes, which fits every description I've ever come across of the Memphis Sphinx, and in my business, a person comes across quite a few. There are people who would kill for this thing, Buck."

There usually were in their business, but that was no reason to back off, ever. Suzi had been play-ing with the big boys since he'd first sent her into Eastern Europe.

"So you've never actually seen it?" he asked.

She gave him a brief glance before rising to her feet and moving a step closer to his desk.

"No one has," she said, leaning forward and holding the photograph under the desk lamp, let-ting the light fall on it. "Not ever, not publicly. It's a legend, four thousand years' worth of hearsay, a rumor, but a damned persistent rumor. No one has ever published a paper on it. It's never been exhib-ited, or documented, or authenticated, or anything. The only proof of its existence was a drawing re-portedly from Howard Carter's notebook, along with a few notes on its supposed powers." She turned the photograph this way and that under the light.

"So maybe this one is a fake?" he suggested. And that would certainly solve his problem of finding it. He could just have the whole mess couriered back to the DIA. Except, of course, however unorthodox the mission felt to him, the DIA was a damned serious piece of business. If they wanted him to find the thing, it didn't matter if the Sphinx was a fake or not. And honestly, if anyone could have come up with a four-thousand-year-old Egyptian statue with magical powers, it would have been the Defense Intelligence Agency of the United States of America.

"I doubt if the folks over at the DIA would get this excited about a fake," she said, echoing his sentiments. "But I'd have to see it to know. Check with some people, have them run some tests." She bent further over the photograph, and Buck just completely ignored what that did to his view of her cleavage.

Just completely ignored it.

Completely.

"Good Lord, Buck," she murmured, her gaze going over the picture. "The Memphis Sphinx, the *Maned* Sphinx of Sesostris III." She gave her head another small, disbelieving shake. "How long has our government had it?"

"I don't know, but they lost it four months ago, and they're damned serious about getting it back."

She nodded. "I would be, too. This looks good.

Real good. But I'd have to get my hands on it to know for sure."

"Your job isn't to get your hands on it. If you can confirm the object's location, your government will be grateful."

"To the tune of?" She glanced up from the photograph.

"An all-expense-paid vacation to Paraguay."

"And?" she prompted.

"You don't do this work for the money any more than I do, Suzi."

"No," she agreed. "But I still like to get paid, in cash, and the next time I need help with one of my Czech couriers, I'd like to know I can continue to count on you."

Her "couriers," right. The girl was single-handedly moving art and women out of Eastern Europe at the rate of twelve paintings and six "couriers" in the last two years. The paintings were legitimate purchases and went on to galleries or private collections. The women were pure contraband, trafficked from the United States into prostitution, virtual slaves who'd been lucky enough to show up on Suzi's radar. He never asked about her couriers, but he knew of at least one occasion where a girl had been returned to her family in South Carolina. Another girl, he knew, was working at the Toussi Gallery in Denver as an assistant, and he knew about Lily Anne Thompson, the girl who had not made it out of Ukraine three months ago.

Papers were what Suzi usually wanted from him, and transportation, if something was available, along with the necessary documents to get her courier on whatever secure plane or truck he knew was moving through the right area at the right time.

Fair enough.

She needed to save somebody, to make up for someone she'd lost a long time ago, and she'd found a bottomless pit of girls in Eastern Europe who needed to be rescued. He wasn't going to begrudge her, not when she did good work for him.

"Ten thousand."

"Twenty," she countered. "The Sphinx is worth millions, if it's authentic. Twenty is a tenth of what I'd charge a private collector."

"Twelve. You don't have to recover it, just find it."

"Fifteen. Paraguay, Buck. It's dangerous down there."

"Fifteen," he conceded.

"Deal," she said and smiled. "So, where exactly are you sending me? Asunción?"

Asunción was the capital, a logical supposition, but no such luck.

"Ciudad del Este." *City of the East*—to the best of his ability, he said it without any inflection. Truth was, though, that particular name didn't need any inflection.

Her smile faded, and for a long moment, she just looked at him.

He understood, and for a moment of his own, he wondered if he was expecting too much this time.

Drugs, guns, money laundering, rampant smuggling, and every form of vice and corruption in between—the City of the East seethed with them all. No street was safe. Millions of dollars of illegal trade took place in its markets and warehouses every day, billions of dollars a year. It was a haven for criminals, from street hustlers to cartel heavyweights. After World War II, Paraguay had granted sanctuary to the worst of the Nazi war criminals. These days, terrorists from Hezbollah to al-Qaeda had cells of true believers in the city.

And he was sending Suzi Toussi into the middle of it, into one of the most depraved and violent cities in the world.

"Twenty thousand, and that's if I'm back in five days or less," she said, when she finally spoke. "It'll be a thousand a day every day longer that I'm there, and don't even think about quibbling on the price. Ciudad del Este is a hellhole, and you know it."

Yes, he did, and he didn't like it either, but it was what it was.

"Twenty," he agreed. "And you don't have five days. The DIA needs their Sphinx secured by Sunday, which means our courier either needs to have it in a lockdown situation or be on a plane out of Paraguay with it in hand. Factor in a minimum of twelve hours for our team to recover the object, and it means you need to do your part in one day or less, preferably less, which means you leave tonight. I've got you booked on a seven-thirty flight out of Dulles."

"That's pretty damn short notice, Buck, for me and your team. What's the rush? Why Sunday?"

It was a legitimate question, but the answer was definitely filed in Buck's BS deck.

"Things are lining up Sunday night, some planets and things, like meridian lines and the tides, and some...uh, energy planes, and the guys over at Moonrise want the Sphinx back to...uh, channel some kind of astral...uh, shield to...uh—oh, hell, Suzi, it's all in the file. Read it on the plane."

"You're not on board with any of this, are you?"

Actually, that was putting it mildly. He was royally teed off by the whole damn thing, that he was putting one of his assets and two of his operators in the line of fire for some damn piece of junk.

"I do my job," he said.

She held his gaze for a moment before returning her attention to the photograph. "And I'll do mine. You can count on it, Buck."

He knew that. She was good, a certain edgy part of her always rising to the challenge, thrilling to the game, to the win, and she was tougher than she looked, far tougher. She'd needed to be for as long as he'd known her. He knew what drove her, the same way he knew what drove Dylan, or Kid, or Skeeter. So he kept hiring her, and she kept working for him, and if she kept saving lost girls on the side, despite her setbacks, good for her.

Hell, life was hard all over.

"We've arranged an introduction to a man named Jimmy Ruiz. We own him, to some extent, which means you'll have some leverage, but watch your back."

"I always watch my back."

"Good. As usual, you'll be traveling as Suzanna Royal," he told her, "a rich American art dealer

working for an even richer client, a U.S. congressman this time, who is looking to round out his collection of pre-Columbian goldwork and whatever
else you can find on the side, like Twelfth Dynasty
Egyptian statuary. There's a shop down there, in
the market, *Galeria Viejo,* the Old Gallery. Ruiz will
vouch for you. The man who owns the gallery,
Remy Beranger, came up in the DIA's intercept,
and he has a confirmed reputation for trading in il-
legally acquired artifacts. You'll start there."

"And find the Memphis Sphinx in one day?" she
said, lifting the photograph closer into the light,
not sounding too daunted by the task, which was
why she was standing in his office—and he'd bet
the damn Sphinx that she knew it as well as he did.

"I need someone who knows a real four-
thousand-year-old statue from a fake and can hit
the ground running."

"Then I'm your girl, Buck. Assignment accepted." She bent further over the eight-by-ten
glossy of the Memphis Sphinx again, and suddenly
Buck was staring at her cleavage—again.

Yeah, she was his girl, all right.

But he was ignoring her cleavage.

Just completely ignoring it.

CHAPTER **ONE**

Ciudad del Este, Paraguay—Saturday afternoon

Sitting at an outside table in front of the Mercado cantina, possibly the slummiest bar in the southern hemisphere, Dax Killian made one more careful check mark in his notebook, right next to the word "asshole." It was the third such mark he'd made in the last hour—sixty minutes, three assholes.

Not bad.

Things were heating up.

Taking a short swallow of beer, he keyed a number into a small receiver and held it to his ear, tapping back into one of the transmitters he'd planted in the Galeria Viejo down the street.

Three days in this hellhole of a city, with one day left to go, and all Dax really had to show for his efforts was the notebook, and his check marks, and an appointment for later tonight that he hoped to hell panned out.

He was ready. More than ready with the deadline looming ever closer—Sunday, tomorrow. Do the deed by then, or have the rest of his life to nurse his regrets. It was a helluva deal. He'd been handed an opportunity here, and he didn't want to fuck it up.

He took another swallow of beer, then popped the last piece of his empanada into his mouth.

Asshole number three was dawdling, taking his sweet time getting to the gallery. Short and dark-haired, dressed in black slacks and a brown polo shirt, he stopped at one of the market stalls bordering the street and looked at a couple of cheap-ass nylon duffel bags.

Maybe he was a guy looking for a deal on cheap-ass nylon duffel bags, but Dax was betting not. He knew a wiseguy when he saw one. A few more moments passed, with the guy moving a couple of stalls closer to the gallery, then he knelt down to tie his shoe, and Dax figured that maybe his ship was about to come in. The man was signaling somebody—somebody with three potential bodyguards now in place on the premises.

Lucky, lucky day, if this thing actually turned into a party.

The two earlier arrivals were still in the gallery's back office with the owner, a thin, harried-looking man given to crumpled linen suits and Panama hats named Remy Beranger. The men were still regaling the French expat with an account of their latest debauchery and the superior quality of the new crop of whores at the club down the street, *La Colonia*, The Colony.

Whatever. Dax pulled his phone out of a cargo pocket on his pants and pressed a couple of buttons. He could see The Colony from his prime spot in front of El Mercado, and the girls looked as tired and lifeless and bored as any he'd seen, maybe even worse. Regardless, nothing of relevance to the problem at hand had been said in the office since the first two guys had gone in, and Remy Beranger had hardly said a word at all, relevant or otherwise, but that was the nature of surveillance—hours and days of next to nothing, and then bingo.

Lifting the phone to eye level, Dax took a look at the screen, zoomed in, then took the polo shirt guy's photograph. Keying in another sequence sent the photo to his computer in his room at the Posada Plaza, two blocks away. He had quite a little yearbook of gofers, traders, tourists, and customers accumulating on his hard drive in the dumpy room, but no kings, no real movers and shakers, and if they didn't start showing up here pretty damn quick, then he was in the wrong place at the wrong time, and his appointment with Remy Beranger later tonight was going to be one big bust, just him and maybe a couple of no-name hustlers playing patty-cake in Beranger's back room.

He couldn't afford that, to be in the wrong place at the wrong time, not this week. Time was running out. He'd been chasing this damn score for months.

With the photo sent, he returned his attention to his handheld receiver, just in case somebody decided to talk about something, *anything*, besides nooky. He'd wired the gallery his first morning in town. Nights in Ciudad del Este tended to be extremely busy, the streets and alleyways rocking and rolling with the transport of illegal everything, but in those quiet couple of hours before sunrise, things settled down, and that's when Dax had accessed a small rooftop patio tucked into the back of the building and broken into a second-floor window to go to work inside.

He took another short swallow of beer, and when the guy stood up and looked down the street, Dax followed his gaze. A black Range Rover bristling with antennas was nosing its way through the crowds, heading for the Old Gallery.

Bingo. Game on.

Dax knew the Range Rover. It belonged to Esteban Ponce, the youngest son of a large, obscenely wealthy family based in Brazil, with Ponce money fueling businesses from one end of South America to the other. According to Dax's intel, Esteban Ponce's "moving and shaking" included a lot of low-end women and upper-end antiquities, especially anything connected with the occult, like maybe something from Egypt's Twelfth Dynasty, possibly a sphinx with rock-crystal eyes that enabled a viewer to see the past, the future, and the present at locations far removed from the statue itself.

Or not.

Dax was a little on the skeptical side of the hocus-pocus equation, but he didn't have to believe. He just had to get the damn thing and deliver it to São Paulo, Brazil, by Sunday night, where one crooked piece-of-crap German named Erich Warner was waiting for it, and for his trouble, he'd been guaranteed two names.

That's all he needed, two goddamned names, one of a man, the other of a place, somewhere in Texas, and he'd be good to go. He could call his old Special Forces commander, Colonel Hanson, who'd been kicked up to the E-ring at the Pentagon, and rest a little easier at night, knowing the good guys could chalk up one more win in the war on terrorism.

So here he sat, waiting for his chance with Remy Beranger, hoping to gather some workable information from the afternoon, or some actionable intelligence. Cut a deal or steal the guy blind, either option worked for Dax. He just needed to know the Memphis Sphinx was in play and where it was—at the gallery, or stashed elsewhere, or worst case, not within a thousand miles of this damn place.

He sure hoped to hell not on that last scenario. There wasn't time to put together another search, and he'd all but guaranteed Warner that the damn thing would be here, this weekend, in Ciudad del Este.

Fortunately, he worked well under pressure... quite well.

No, no, no. No sales, not today, and not tomorrow, Beranger had said, when Dax had shown up at the gallery, flashing his cash. *Later, monsieur, in two, maybe three days.*

Two or three days hadn't cut it for Dax, though,

not on this deal, so he'd pushed until he'd gotten a more workable schedule on the table, knowing guys like Beranger didn't turn down cold cash in U.S. dollars, not unless something was up, like an even bigger score.

Tomorrow night, then, late, Beranger had finally agreed. *I have some very nice Moche ceramics I can show you, very nice, the erotic style, just as you wish.*

Eighteen-hundred-year-old erotica—Dax couldn't remember ever being in the market for anything stranger, but apparently, for those in the know, Galeria Viejo in Ciudad del Este was the place for acquiring a little ancient pornographic pottery.

He slipped his hand into the cargo pocket again and pulled out a pack of cigarettes. His lighter came next. Settling a little deeper into his chair, he lit up, and through a thin veil of smoke, watched the Range Rover muscle its way through the crowds of people and vehicles, until it reached a spot in front of the gallery.

Lowering the cigarette, he flicked off the ash and readied the phone in his other hand. One, two, three more bodyguards exited the Rover. Then the boy from Brazil stepped out—Esteban Ponce, tall and noticeably thin, dark hair hanging in a long braid down the middle of his back, expensively dressed with lots of flash, black slacks, white sports coat, red silk shirt, and sporting a long gold chain strung with a crucifix, an Egyptian ankh, and a pentacle, and yeah, Dax figured that should just about cover all the other-world crap that could ruin a guy's day.

Geezus.

Every overrich, inbred family Dax had ever worked for could lay claim to one of their own as the resident fuckup, and Esteban was the Ponces'. No guts, no brains, no glory, but plenty of time and money on his hands, most of it spent trying to carve a niche for himself in a pack of world-class wolves and jackals.

Personally, Dax doubted if there was much competition for resident Honcho of the Voodoo Hoodoo in the Ponce clan. He took everybody's picture, including a couple of group shots and a zoomed-in close-up on the Range Rover's license plate. While he forwarded all the photos to his computer, the Brazilian contingent moved inside the gallery, leaving two guys to guard the door.

Clamping the cigarette between his teeth, Dax typed in a brief, coded text to São Paulo, then returned the phone to his pocket and went back to listening to the handset.

"Señor Ponce, my pleasure. So pleased, so very pleased..." Remy Beranger finally came to life, his words verifying Dax's identification of Esteban Ponce, not that he'd needed much verification. He'd started doing his South American homework as soon as he'd realized where the game was heading. *"Oh, yes, señor, the others will be here very shortly. Very shortly, indeed."*

Others? Dax thought.

Good. Maybe this thing was going to roll.

He took another drag off his cigarette and checked both ends of the street while he exhaled. A silver Mercedes was heading his way, looking promising. The luxury sedan passed him by and kept going almost the length of the block, before it pulled to a stop a couple of cars down from the Range Rover, in front of a bar so seedy it almost made the Mercado look like it had some class. Two men got out of the front. Only one got out of the back—Levi Asher, short, balding, narrow through the shoulders, rumpled, potbellied in a pale blue suit, and sweating like a pig in the heat.

Perfect.

Under any circumstances other than a stakeout, Dax would have grinned. The day was definitely looking up. Levi Asher was exactly the guy Dax had wanted to see in Ciudad del Este, the same way he'd seen him in Milan, and in London, and in that nondescript little spot on the road north of Washington, D.C., the two of them on the same damn trail.

Sonuvabitch. Third-rate Remy Beranger and his fourth-rate gallery had actually scored the Memphis Sphinx, and in the nick of time. Everybody had heard the stories, they knew the legend of what was supposed to happen Sunday night. They'd all just been waiting for the damn thing to show up somewhere, and to a man, everybody Dax had met or dealt with over the past four months of his investigation believed that what was supposed to happen Sunday night would happen, that the Gates of Time, whatever the hell those were, would open and reveal the secrets of the ages, possibly even the secrets of immortality.

Everybody believed, that is, except Dax. But he got paid to be skeptical. Fortunately, he was very good at that, too.

Yeah, that was him, just one damned fortunate guy.

Erich Warner sure as hell believed in the Sphinx's powers. The guy was desperate to get his hands on the Maned Sphinx of Sesostris III, which in Dax's book made him more than a little unstable on top of already being a psychopathic asshole.

He dropped his cigarette to the pavement and ground it out with his boot, all the while watching a dark blue Land Cruiser ease its way down the street through the crowds.

The Cruiser came to a stop next to Levi Asher's silver Mercedes, and a minor player named Jimmy Ruiz got out from behind the wheel and crossed in front of the car. Dax recognized him as an associate of Remy Beranger's from the file he'd compiled on Galeria Viejo. When Ruiz stopped next to the passenger door and started to open it, Dax set aside his handset and pulled his phone back out of his pocket. Then he reached for his beer.

There were three things he knew for certain about the Memphis Sphinx: Erich Warner wanted it; Dax was going to get it; and there wasn't a nutcase from here to Cairo who wasn't after it. He already had Asher and Ponce. That was enough to assure him he was in the right place at the right time. Anyone else was either a pure bonus or an unnecessary complication.

Or both.

In spades.

He paused with the beer bottle halfway to his mouth, his gaze riveted to the navy-blue-and-white-striped, peep-toe spectator pump descending from out of the passenger side door of the Land Cruiser. The shoe was elegant, expensive, leather, and handmade, and it encased a sweetly feminine foot whose arched lines extended up a delicate ankle, a silken calf, a slender, cream-colored thigh that hit him where it hurt, all the way up to the leading edge of a tight navy blue dress that wrapped and swirled its way up the most dangerous set of curves Dax had seen since...since he didn't remember when.

On second thought, he did remember when.

His gaze narrowed, zeroing in on the woman and cataloguing every square centimeter of her lush female form, every brass button marching down the front of her short cropped jacket, every perfectly tailored fold and sweep of the navy blue dress so lovingly molded to her body, every inch of blindingly white piping accenting the suit, right up to the tortoiseshell sunglasses on her face and the elegantly broad-brimmed white Panama hat set at a rakish angle on her head. Her richly colored hair was swept up under the hat, but there were enough silken auburn strands drifting down the nape of her neck to tell him he was in way more trouble than he had bargained for—more than a boatload, more than made sense.

He carefully set his beer back on the table, untouched. There weren't many women built like the one getting out of the Land Cruiser, but he knew one. He knew one with that exact set of cyclone curves and auburn hair.

Geezus.

He didn't believe in the impossible, any more than he believed in the immortal powers of the Sphinx. But there she was, straight out of his dreams, the headliner of his fantasies, the girl who'd stood him up at Duffy's Bar in Denver six months ago, the one whose presence here told him more about her than he'd unearthed in all his months of investigation—and everything it told him set every nerve ending he had on full redline alert.

He didn't take her picture. He didn't need to take her picture. He knew exactly who she was, and he knew it because the first time he'd laid eyes on her, she'd lit him up like a flare. It had been pure, unadulterated lust, and in six long months, he hadn't recovered from the smackdown, not even close—Suzanna Royale Toussi, born and raised in San Francisco, educated at the University of Southern California in Santa Barbara, lately of Denver, Colorado. Hell, he had copies of her résumé, her biography, her birth certificate, and her college transcripts. He even had a copy of the application for her first Small Business Administration loan for her first art gallery. He knew her GPA, her favorite color, the name of her first husband— some guy in Australia—and her second, the dates of her divorces, and her shoe size. What he didn't know was what she was doing in Ciudad del Este, in front of the Old Gallery, with damn Jimmy Ruiz.

But he had a pretty good idea, and it set his teeth on edge.

Sonuvabitch.

He was unbelievable. Out of all the girls in all the world, he'd had to get himself just a little bit fixated on one who was on the wrong side of the game. It didn't matter that in the case of the Memphis Sphinx, he was working out in left field, too. He had his reasons, and sweating it out at a hundred and one in the shade in Ciudad del Este, he didn't care one way or the other about the twelve-to-one odds piling up in the Galeria Viejo, or what really happened to the friggin' Memphis Sphinx, or whether or not it really had any occult powers—but he cared very much about the information Erich Warner had used to rope him into this deal.

He also—*dammit*—cared about the drop-dead-gorgeous redhead shrink-wrapped in that damn sailor suit.

He shouldn't.

She'd gotten herself here. He was sure she could get herself back out. Without a doubt, she knew a helluva lot more about what she was doing in this scrap heap than he did, and it pissed him off to think he had read her so wrong. He wasn't here to save a wayward art dealer who was putting her ass on the line to dabble in illegal antiquities.

But, *geezus*, what an ass.

Her second foot hit the pavement, and with just

the slightest wiggle, she readjusted the skirt of her dress.

Slight.

Right.

He felt that little wiggle from his heart to his groin.

He knew better.

So help him, God, he knew better.

So why in the hell was he dropping a wad of bills on the table and getting ready to cross the street?

CHAPTER TWO

Well, things were going just great, Suzi thought, standing at the entrance of the notorious Galeria Viejo, possibly the dumpiest, dirtiest, most squalid place she'd ever stood in her life. Or at least things had been going great—spectacularly great. She hadn't had any delays on the flights getting from Dulles to the Guarani International Airport in Ciudad del Este. Her hotel, the heavily guarded Gran Chaco, was first-class, her suite gorgeous and overlooking the luxury establishment's tropical garden and courtyard pool area. The light lunch she'd had delivered via room service had been impeccably prepared. Jimmy Ruiz had shown up on time, nervous and unkempt, but also well armed and accommodating. She hadn't had a single problem since she'd left General Grant in his office at the Marsh Annex in Washington—until now.

This was a problem.

"No," she said, very clearly, lowering her sunglasses partway down her nose and giving the ape blocking the door of Galeria Viejo her steeliest gaze. He wasn't frisking her, not this side of the grave. Oh, hell no.

Next to her, Jimmy Ruiz was talking a mile a minute to ape number two, but without getting much affect, despite the addition of dramatic hand gestures.

He needed to get some affect.

She understood that he'd brought her here under duress. She hadn't been shy about threatening him with certain agents of the U.S. government, who had been investigating his dealings with a U.S. Treasury agent recently transferred out of Paraguay and currently under indictment for charges ranging from tax evasion to treason.

But Ruiz needed to make her position clear, crystal clear, or he wouldn't see the light of day for another twenty years, if then.

"Who do they work for?" she asked in English, interrupting his tirade. Ruiz had short dark hair, a medium build, a cheap brown suit that fit him like an old paper bag, and a rap sheet a mile long.

"The two out here, for Esteban Ponce," Jimmy said, meeting her gaze with a brief glance. "The one just inside the door, staring at us, for Señor Levi Asher."

Yes, she thought she'd recognized the hulking man standing in the shadowy interior of the gallery. His name was Gervais.

"Señor Asher is from New York," Jimmy was saying.

New York, London, Athens, Cairo, she thought. She and Levi the Pervert went way back in the art trade, and the minute she'd seen that photograph in General Grant's office, she'd have laid a thousand dollars down on Levi being in Paraguay. That boy had been after the Memphis Sphinx for as long as she'd known him.

"Esteban Ponce is a very important man from Brazil," Jimmy finished up.

Actually, Esteban Ponce was an idiot, but a dangerous idiot, one of the people she'd meant when she'd told Grant that some people would kill for the Sphinx. The Maned Sphinx of Sesostris III had been a lightning rod for true believers, lost souls, and avaricious charlatans of all stripes for over a century, with immortality as the prize. People got a little crazy when life everlasting was put on the auction block, especially people who were a little crazy to begin with—like Esteban Ponce.

Both Ponce and Asher had been noted and highlighted in the DIA files she'd read on the plane, along with half a dozen other collectors and dealers, some of whom she knew, some she didn't. The DIA Moonrise team had compiled quite a number of lists concerning the Memphis Sphinx, not least of which were the things she shouldn't do if by chance she actually got her hands on it: *Do not hold the statue up into the moonlight on the night of the third full moon in the year of Horus, as immortality may be imparted to the holder. Do not drench the statue in blood on the night of the third full moon in the year of Horus and set it on a corpse, as resurrection may result. Do not take the statue apart.*

Easy enough, she'd figured, especially the blood and corpse part—but she could see why some people would get excited about that particular power.

She didn't imagine she'd be holding it up in the moonlight either, and she would definitely be doing her damnedest not to accidentally take the thing apart, but she knew the Sphinx had parts, the gold death mask for one, apparently removable crystal eyes for another, and the pièce de résistance, an RFID, a radio-frequency identification tag. The scanner for that nearly invisible piece of technological wizardry had been in her briefing packet and was now in her purse, a pen-shaped gadget that fit neatly in the palm of her hand. If she got within three meters of the DIA's Sphinx, the scanner would light up and register the location via its built-in GPS. Three meters was an amazing range for an RFID powder chip with an internal antenna, and the DIA was rightly proud.

"You know whom I represent," she said to Ruiz, keeping her voice very low, very cold. "Are these Señors Asher and Ponce more important than my client?"

It was a trick question.

She was in Paraguay for only one reason—Buck Grant had asked her to be—but Jimmy Ruiz had been led to believe she was on a buying spree for a certain congressman from Illinois, the kind of man who could exert his influence to get the U.S. government off Jimmy's back, if things went well in Ciudad del Este, if perhaps Ms. Royal came home with a few particularly prized pieces.

Ruiz's gaze slid to hers again.

"There must be someone you can call," she said coolly. "If not, there's certainly someone I can call."

That did the trick.

With a furtive glance back at Esteban Ponce's henchmen, Ruiz pulled his phone out of his pocket and hit a speed-dial number. He lowered his chin and turned away as he spoke—a few quick words.

In a matter of seconds, one of the henchmen's phones rang, and in less than another half a minute, both of the bodyguards stepped aside, allowing Ruiz to escort her into the Old Gallery with the 9mm pistol Ruiz had reluctantly supplied her with safely concealed in a shoulder rig under her suit jacket.

And there she goes, Dax thought, into the lion's den. *Dammit.*

His plan had been to cross the street and head down toward the gallery to get within useful range. Useful for what, he hadn't precisely determined. He supposed there was an off chance that Ms. Toussi had no clue about the Old Gallery's less-than-kosher reputation—but he doubted it. She hadn't struck him as the kind of girl who didn't have all the angles figured before she got out of bed in the morning. Every angle, every morning.

No, she knew what was going down in there, and

she was part of it. The biggest surprise here was that she hadn't shown up anywhere in his investigation of the Sphinx. Hell, he'd been investigating her at the same damn time. Somewhere, somehow, some kind of connection should have shown up between her and the Egyptian statue. That it hadn't meant one of two things. He'd either missed something big, and his answer to that was "Not very damned likely." Or she was working for one of the other players on his list, which didn't make a damn lick of sense, not considering her avocation. The list was one scumbag after another: guys like Esteban Ponce, who had too much money and a sense of entitlement to match; an overwrought and highstrung dealer like Levi Asher, whose sexual proclivities ran the gamut from lurid to illegal; and by far the worst of the lot, Erich Warner, his handler on this damn thing, who played hard and fast and under the table for millions of dollars on every deal, running drugs and guns and women and children and stolen art and anything else he could turn for a profit, which included some pretty damn strange things. Half a dozen other world-class con artists and criminals were all in his files as having also been actively pursuing the Memphis Sphinx since it had first started getting some play in the underworld market, and Suzi Toussi's name had not been attached to any of them.

"Mademoiselle, how kind of you to come to my small shop," he heard Remy Beranger again through his handset. The man's voice wasn't quite as effusive as when he'd been speaking with Ponce,

but an American woman looking to make a score in Ciudad del Este was enough to put anyone on edge.

It sure as hell put him on edge.

"*Mr. Beranger,*" Suzi Toussi said, and there wasn't a damn thing about the sound of her voice that didn't make Dax's gut churn just a little bit. He was in the right place at the right time, but she wasn't, not by a long shot. She had no business being here, not according to everything he knew about her, and he knew plenty. He knew the tragedy of her first marriage. He knew about the girls she brought back from Eastern Europe, and he knew about the one in Ukraine who hadn't made it three months ago. And really, he had to wonder if the violence and loss of that failure had given her some kind of guilt-induced death wish, because, baby, this was the place, and this was the deal, for people who wanted the odds stacked overwhelmingly against them.

"*Jimmy tells me you are in the market for Incan gold,*" Beranger said. "*You and your client, a man, I hear, who is placed very highly up in your government.*"

"*Incan gold, yes, the congressman is very fond of all the ancient cultures of the world and the artifacts they left behind,*" the in-it-up-to-her-neck Ms. Toussi replied. "*He's especially in the market for something unique, a rare and powerful piece perhaps, not necessarily Incan, if you have anything currently in your shop that would qualify.*"

A significant pause ensued, and Dax could just

imagine the sweat breaking out on Remy Beranger's brow. The word "congressman" was making him sweat a little, too, along with that not-so-coy allusion to the damn Memphis Sphinx. *Geezus.* What in the hell was a U.S. congressman doing in the middle of this deal? And if Suzi Toussi was representing a congressman, he'd sure as hell like to know why and which one.

"*If you'd like to come with me,*" Beranger spoke again, "*I believe I have a few things that might be of interest. Jimmy, here, take my bag, please, and see to the men in the viewing room.*"

Viewing room?

Now which, Dax wondered, of all the dozens of squirrel-sized rooms in the gallery was the viewing room? And why in the hell hadn't he figured that out yesterday morning and gotten a transmitter in there? And what was in the bag Beranger had just handed off?

"*Mademoiselle Royal, if you please.*"

Dax had emplaced four transmitters in the gallery—one each in the entrance, the main ground-floor room, Beranger's office, and in a junk room full of broken artifacts. He didn't know where Remy Beranger was "if you pleasing" Suzi Toussi, but after fifteen seconds of silence, and then another twenty, he knew they'd left the entrance, skipped the main gallery room, and hadn't ended up in Beranger's office, all the places Levi Asher and Esteban Ponce weren't either.

As a matter of fact, of the thirteen people in the gallery, Beranger, Suzi, Ruiz, Ponce, Asher, and enough bodyguards between them to fill every-body's dance card, he currently had a bead on ex-actly two—the guys standing outside the front door. Everyone else had disappeared off his grid. *Dammit.*

CHAPTER THREE

Suzi knew junk when she saw it, and she was following Remy Beranger through aisle after aisle of junk, looking at junk from one end of the Old Gallery to the other, nothing but piles of junk and stacks of Galeria Viejo T-shirts. She slipped her sunglasses off and dropped them into her purse, which didn't do a damn thing to improve the view.

No one looking for anything of value would come to this place. She'd owned a few galleries, and Beranger's Old Gallery wouldn't have made her "B" list on its best day.

Hell, it wouldn't have made her "D" list.

Maybe not even her "Z" list.

There were plastic blowguns and rubber knives on the shelves.

"I have recently acquired a few unique items, including a small quantity of very nice Moche pottery," Beranger said, stopping in front of a heavy wood door and taking a moment to wipe his face with a crumpled-up handkerchief. The man's cream-colored linen suit hung off his thin frame and had definitely seen better days. His shoes were scuffed, his shirt stained, his face deathly pale with sweat running down the sides. This outfit, combined with his slow, shuffling gait made him look more like a homeless derelict than a businessman, even a shady businessman, and yet the finest intelligence-gathering agency on the face of the earth had sent her here to deal with him, a man whose Rolex all but screamed "knockoff," who was wearing half a dozen tarnished "goldtone" bracelets on his left wrist and half a dozen chains loaded down with all kinds of religious medals around his neck. He clinked and jangled with every sliding, limping step he took.

Using a set of keys hanging from a retractable fob off his belt, he undid the locks on the door, then let the fob snap back to his waistband, before leading the way into a long, narrow, poorly lit room.

"The Chapel Room," he said in an aside over his shoulder, with obvious pride. "My reliquary, so to speak. The Sacred Heart of the gallery, *Sacré-Coeur*."

Reliquary? As in plastic saints' bones, and rubber splinters of the Holy Cross? she wondered.

Well, that would be damned uninteresting.

Suzi followed him in, the 9mm automatic pistol snugged up against her body under her jacket, and her willingness to use it, keeping her from having any particular concerns about being alone with the

Frenchman or about following him into the depths
of his odd Old Gallery.

"The Moche is very rare," he continued, closing
the door behind her and giving his face another
quick mopping. His longish dark hair hung down
over the collar of his suit in damp, curling locks.
"Quite explicit, if your client is truly interested
in owning something, shall we say...unusual...
something perhaps not to everyone's taste. Though
I must warn you, I do have another buyer."

Rare and unusual Moche meant erotica, and
Suzi figured Beranger might possibly have a shipment of it, because at first glance, the quality of the
Frenchman's sales goods in the Chapel Room were
nominally better than in his main gallery.

That was the good news.

The bad news was unnervingly obvious. Despite
the comfort of her 9mm, she was now closed in
a small, dusty room with a sick little man selling
pornography.

Buck Grant was going to owe her for this—big-
time.

Beranger shuffled on, and she followed, being
careful to stay close to him, without getting too
close. They passed a heavy oak table covered in
dust with an iron cross nailed to its top. Smaller
crosses—some iron, some tin, some painted, some
bare metal or wood—were haphazardly stacked
down the table's length along with an intricate, if
doubtfully ancient, array of Mughal boxes, carved
soapstone ankhs, leather flasks, and all-around junk.
He even had a pile of small, gold-painted Buddhas,

every one of them smiling, all in a jumble with about a gross of neon-bright, pink and blue yin-yang key chains at the end of the table—which, in her book, made Remy Beranger the undisputed king of religious kitsch. He had it all.

But did he have the Memphis Sphinx?

That was the day's question.

Opening the clasp on her purse, she glanced down and checked inside to see if the light on the RFID scanner was on—and it wasn't.

Now, why wasn't she surprised? *Dammit.* That would have been easy—and nothing was ever easy, not when she worked for General Grant. Nobody pushed her like Buck Grant pushed her, except herself, to her limit and then some. But Buck always gave as good as he got. She didn't fail him, and he didn't fail her. He'd been there every time she'd called in one of her favors—every single time, even though she knew he thought she was playing a losing game.

Truth was, she thought so, too, but that wasn't going to stop her. Losing or not, it was the only game in town, the only protection she'd found against the pain.

Her mouth tightened in fleeting remembrance, and in the same breath, she forced herself to move on, to think about the heat, the job, the need to stay on red alert, anything. It was the only way to keep going, to never remember.

In front of her, Beranger came to a stop next to a large, darkened case and reached for a small switch on the side. When the light came on, she knew that the DIA's intel was getting closer to the mark. She'd been sent to the right place, even if she hadn't yet been within three meters of the exact right place.

Chavín, Incan, Lambayeque, Aztec, Mayan— carefully inked signs were set in amongst the hodge-podge collection of pre-Columbian artifacts filling the long case from end to end. A lot of what she was seeing was in bits and chunks, but there were a few whole pieces of at least "ancient-looking" goods.

"So will it be the Moche?" the Frenchman asked, mopping at his face again.

The Moche. Sure. And she had a feeling his Moche would look exactly like his Incan, and his Lambayeque—crumbles. He did have one good piece that wasn't too damaged, a stone Mamacona, a mother figurine in pretty damn good shape, possibly even auction worthy, and where there was one pretty damn good antiquity, there might well be another even better one—within three meters of the case.

She looked in her purse again and felt the sudden surprise and satisfaction of the perfect score. The scanner was glowing.

And then it wasn't.

And then it was . . . and then it wasn't, and wasn't, and wasn't.

What the hell? Two blinks? What was that? The DIA file on the RFD scanner specifically noted two modes of response: light on, with the GPS locking in on a position and signaling completion of the data transfer with a beep; and dead quiet with no light on. There was no "silently blinking" option—and yet the thing had just blinked at her twice.

Dammit.

Clearing her throat, she shifted her attention back to Beranger.

"Perhaps," she said, keeping her voice perfectly neutral, not registering her disappointment in the monumental equipment failure she'd just experienced. Without the scanner, she had only one way of knowing if the Sphinx was in Ciudad del Este—eyeball-to-rock-crystal-eyeball. She'd have to see the damn thing.

"Perhaps?" he questioned, looking at her through his dark, rheumy eyes, and bringing his handkerchief back up to wipe the sweat off his face.

"Yes," she said, discreetly turning away from the smell of him as if she were taking in the rest of the room. Damn it all, faulty equipment was a hurdle, a big one, and she hated damn hurdles when she was in Third World countries with a crime ratio bigger than the bond yields in her portfolio.

She glanced around the room on the off chance that Beranger might have the statue displayed on one of the open shelving units or in another case, maybe with one of his hand-lettered signs with the words *Twelfth Dynasty Egyptian Sphinx* taped below it.

No such luck.

Nothing was ever that easy.

Behind her, Beranger coughed, a small, choking sound, and she hoped to hell whatever jungle fever he had wasn't contagious.

A little distance couldn't hurt.

She took another few steps down the side of the case, perusing the contents.

"This is all very nice," she continued, deciding to play her hand. She was on a schedule here, and she'd just lost one of her major advantages. "But my client is possibly... well, actually... more interested in acquiring something older than Moche pottery, if you have any artifacts that are two to three thousand years older perhaps, or..." She paused, her gaze caught by a set of narrow, rickety stairs winding up from the far end of the room into total darkness. That was interesting, definitely creepy, and maybe even a little ominous. "The congressman is currently quite taken with the ancient Near East. It's a new area of interest for him, a new arena for him to explore. Perhaps if you have something Egyptian, something from the Twelfth Dynasty?"

Beranger looked at her for a moment, meeting her gaze, and a small, discerning half smile slowly curved his lips.

"Egyptian," he finally said, drawing the word out, his gaze still on her. "It's true, then... yes... yes, I had wondered, had thought as much when Jimmy called me, if indeed my benefactor had sent someone to check on my progress."

Benefactor?

Now he had her interest.

"Egyptian, yes," she said. "Twelfth Dynasty."

"So you are here to see if I have done my job?" He stood there, in front of her, so small and bent and damp and sick, and yet a light had come on in his eyes.

"Yes," she said, tamping down a small surge of excitement—but this was good, very good. No one believed Remy Beranger had come up with the Sphinx on his own. No one believed he had the skills, the cash, or the balls to have stolen it from the DIA's laboratory, and he didn't look like he could "teleport" a gnat's ass, let alone a granite statue. He was a third-rate broker of low-end junk, and after the Sphinx, the number two item on the DIA's Christmas list was the name of Beranger's contact. With that name, they'd go looking for the next name, on up the chain, until they found someone who conceivably could have teleported the damn thing out from under their very noses, some telepathic freakazoid psychic. The DIA had a long list of them. "Thief" was General Grant's preferred term, and inside job was what he had conjectured, and he'd conjectured it loudly and repeatedly on the way to the airport last night, assuring her that the spooks need look no further than their own to find whoever had "hands-on" stolen their statue.

Realistically, he was probably right, no matter how many times the folks at the DIA used the word "teleported."

"Sent by a congressman, then," Beranger said, his smile widening for a brief moment. "A congressman from . . ."

"Illinois," she filled in when his voice trailed off, her excitement dampening all on its own. *Damn*. Beranger didn't know who he was representing on this deal. It had been a blind contact, maybe even a double-blind. But he'd dealt with someone somewhere, and he'd all but confessed to having the Sphinx.

"Ah, Illinois," he said. "A very rich state."

"Have you been there?" she asked, angling for a clue.

"No," he shook his head. "I was in Miami once, a few months ago, and as you might...ah, know, I do have a piece from the Near East, perhaps as ancient as you wish."

"Excellent," she said. "I'd like to see it."

"Of course...of course." His gaze went to the door leading back into the main gallery. "You can tell your congressman that I have other very interested buyers for the Egyptian piece, and the sale should—" The ringing of his phone stopped him in mid-sentence. "Excuse me."

He pulled his phone out of his pants pocket, checked the number, then answered it.

While Beranger spoke softly into the receiver, she did her best to listen in.

"*Policía?*" he said, his voice suddenly growing sharp.

The police? That couldn't be good. Oh, hell no, not good at all.

She leaned in a little closer, but didn't get much out of his half-Spanish, half-French inquisition of whoever was on the other end of the phone.

But she did get the sound of sirens, loud and clear, coming from the street side of the building.

Dammit.

Beranger was getting busted.

She looked around to see which was the best way to go, if things started to go downhill, when a soft, muffled beep coming from inside her purse all but riveted her to the floor.

Good Lord, the GPS had kicked in.

CHAPTER FOUR

At a hundred feet from the gallery and closing, Dax's day took another serious dive.

Fuck. A Paraguayan police vehicle, its siren wailing, was approaching the gallery, which could mean nothing or everything, but Dax's money was on everything. When the squad car pulled to a stop next to Ponce's Range Rover, he slowed his pace.

Fucking perfect. Beranger was getting busted—and there wasn't a doubt in Dax's mind that it had something to do with the Sphinx and the people who had come to buy it. The Old Gallery was available to the cops 365 days a year if they wanted to shut it down. It was no coincidence that they'd showed up today, less than ten minutes after Esteban Ponce and Levi Asher. Or maybe Suzi Toussi was the guest of honor.

God, he hoped not.

He glanced up toward the rooftops, wondering if

the police had overwatch on the gallery, some sniper team primed and ready. They'd obviously been getting their information in a damned timely fashion. He didn't see anybody, but that meant nothing. There were a thousand hiding places in this block alone—multistory buildings on both sides of the street, dozens of canopied shop stalls on the ground floor, signs everywhere, some handwritten, some giant neon extravaganzas crawling up the fronts of the stores and warehouses.

His only consolation was in knowing he didn't particularly stand out. He'd bought his clothes in the market yesterday, all local stuff, a pair of beige cargo pants, a dark gray short-sleeved shirt and a white T-shirt, a brown ball cap embroidered with the words *Santa Cruz,* and a pair of knockoff Nike trail boots making him look like everyone else in Ciudad del Este. Someone would have to be looking for him in order to see him.

Which, he realized, was never out of the question.

Two armed and uniformed policemen exited the police car with lockstep precision, weapons at the ready, both of them carrying Steyr AUG assault rifles. Another police vehicle turned onto the block and hit its lights, clearing a path through the crowds and making a beeline for the gallery.

There was only one thing to do, only one thing that made any sense at all—keep moving, cross back over to the other side of the street, and walk on by. Beranger's place had turned into an unmitigated disaster. A smart guy would melt into the scenery and let the disaster unfold without him.

Two things kept Dax from being a smart guy—the Memphis Sphinx, and the long-legged redhead in the navy blue dress. He wasn't going to let the police have either one—so he didn't cross the street. Oh, hell no. If Suzi Toussi really was working for a United States congressman, there were some pretty damn big gaps in his information—scary gaps, the kind that could deep-six a guy. He needed to fill those gaps, and he needed her to do it. Failure was not an option. The Sphinx was his, one way or the other.

Another armed policeman with a Steyr AUG piled out of the second car, bringing the squad up to three, a little thin for a bust by anybody's standards, but the police were well-trained, damned serious guys with enough firepower to take down half the block. If it came to a shoot-out, he was putting his money on the police, not the gallery full of gangsters, who were already down by two. The guys guarding the door had been quickly spun out by the first pair of cops and forced to sprawl face-down on the hood of the police car, with one cop cuffing them while the other covered them with his assault rifle.

In the grand scheme of Ciudad del Este, a bust in the market wasn't going to make the news, and Dax knew that on any given night, the guys busting Beranger might be moonlighting in the smuggling trade, providing security for someone moving a container full of electronics or whiskey, or transporting stolen cars from Brazil into Paraguay, or exporting automatic weapons in the other direction.

Paraguay was that kind of country, and Ciudad del Este was that kind of city—up for grabs.

Three policemen, though, that really wasn't enough for a bust, not when Esteban Ponce's daddy could have them all shanghaied, never to be seen or heard from again. Ten or fifteen cops disappearing was one thing; three was just too damn easy.

Walking along, looking like a guy minding his own business and not like a guy cataloguing the scene taking place at the Old Gallery's front door, he ran through the frequencies on his receiver again and came up empty. He hoped to hell Beranger had someone on the inside giving a warning, but he sure wasn't hearing one, and he hoped to God the dealer had more sense than to let the cops get ahold of the Sphinx. Dax did not want to have to go up against the official Paraguayan anything to accomplish his mission. It wasn't a matter of scruples. He'd do whatever it took to get the Egyptian statue, but there were only so many hours left on this gig, and the clock was ticking. He didn't have time to take on the Paraguayan police force.

Of course, truth be told, if he was going to have to take them on, he'd rather take on three of them in the market than the whole organization at their headquarters and be trying to steal the Sphinx out of their evidence locker.

Three cops.

It didn't make sense. If they'd been staking out the gallery, they knew how many men were inside.

Hell, this wasn't a bust. It was a shakedown, and if Suzi Toussi was the target, he needed to get to her first. The Old Gallery was big, but not so big that he couldn't find her pretty damn quickly.

Yeah, he'd play it straight. Grab the girl, shake her down himself. Tough guy, all the way.

He turned into the alley bordering the gallery and lengthened his stride, speeding up. Halfway down the narrow opening, the same pile of junk and garbage containers he'd used two days in a row was still in place, still granting him easy access to Beranger's second story. He quickly climbed to the top of the containers and swung himself up onto the roof, and in less than a minute was slipping through the window he'd jimmied open his first night in town.

The room he entered was dark, dusty, and sweltering. If it had been a hundred and one in the shade at the cantina, it was easily a hundred and ten in the upstairs room. Below him, he could hear the commotion of the police entering the gallery: raised voices, barked orders, and shelves of Beranger's tourist junk, the cheap stuff he kept by the front door, crashing. Guerrilla tactics—this was definitely a shakedown. Behind him, he heard the sound of someone running across the roof.

He leaned back and took a quick look through the window, just in time to see Jimmy Ruiz skid to a stop at the edge of the building and lower himself over the side, into the alley. He had a messenger bag slung over his shoulder that he had not been carrying when he'd entered the gallery with Suzi. Dax was guessing Beranger's.

Well, hell, so much for Suzi Toussi's partner, and

whatever anyone else thought, Jimmy Ruiz was obviously convinced that the cops were after him. Dax hoped the guy was right, and for the second time, he wondered what in the hell was in the bag.

Crossing the room, he put his ear to the door and heard someone heading his way, someone wearing blue-and-white-striped, handmade, leather spectator peep-toe pumps—he was putting the bank on it. He'd know the sound of a woman running in high heels anywhere, and this woman was running up the stairs at breakneck speed.

He was impressed.

He was also ready when she reached the top of the stairs and started to dash down the hall. With one smooth move, he opened the door, caught her hard into his arms, and swung her inside the dark and dusty room. While she still had the breath startled out of her, he clamped his hand over her mouth—not that she was likely to scream for help. She had definitely been running away.

She immediately started fighting him, squirming this way and that, her body twisting in his grip. When she tried to impale his foot with her spike heel, he lifted her partway off her feet.

Kee-rist. He tightened his hold on her, squeezing her hard enough to get her attention.

"I'm not going to hurt you, Ms. Toussi," he said close to her ear. "So don't fight me."

She jerked her head around, trying to see him, but he doubted if she could see much in the gloomy room.

"Yeah, I know who you are, Suzanna Royale

Toussi, fresh off the boat from Denver, Colorado. If Ruiz was your partner, you're on your own," he continued, his voice low and hard. "He took a powder about thirty seconds ago and disappeared into the alley, so I strongly advise that you take my help in getting out of here."

At that, she said something from under his hand, something short and vehement, and he didn't blame her. Then she started to squirm again, really putting herself into it. Up against anyone except a trained commando, she might have had a chance. She was that good, pretty tricky with the moves— but she didn't have a chance, not one. She was packing a pistol in a shoulder rig, though. At least that's what in the hell it felt like, and nothing could have surprised him more, or pleased him better, except her not being here at all. Pistol or not, his standard operating procedure on a snatch and grab was to not give the snatchee a chance to bring any kind of a weapon into play, and he'd followed procedure. She was securely restrained, her arms pinned to her sides. He could have had her on the floor in less than a second, or slammed her up against the wall and knocked her senseless in less than that, but he didn't want her on the floor, and he was too good at his job to have to knock her senseless.

So he struggled with her, let her wear herself out, and he kept tightening his grip on her, keeping her a little off balance, making her work to stay on her feet. It didn't take long in the hundred-plus heat for her to need a break.

When she went limp in his arms, breathing hard, her chest rising and falling, her shoulders slumped, he didn't loosen his grip, not an ounce. He couldn't take the chance.

Down in the main gallery, Beranger's junk was still crashing to the floor, voices were still raised, but no one else was pounding up the stairs. In between the shouted orders and interrogation, Dax could hear Beranger whining and wheedling, doing his best to placate the police. Pointedly, he didn't hear anyone else. Beranger, Ruiz, and the bodacious Suzi Toussi hadn't been that far from the entrance when the police had busted in. Ruiz had fled, Toussi had fled, albeit in different directions, and Beranger was holding the fort. The big bad boys on the deal were either still sequestered in the "viewing room," or they'd found another way out of the rabbit warren of the Old Gallery—the plan currently holding the top spot on his own "To Do" list.

"If you're ready to cooperate, we need to get out of here," he said close to her ear again.

She shook her head *no*, the gesture absolutely adamant.

"You want to stay?" That didn't make sense, but she nodded.

Well, hell.

"Not an option," he said, and he meant it. She could hear what was going on downstairs as well as he could. "Come on."

He was doing her a favor, and she had to know it, but when he started half carrying her, half plain old moving her along across the room, she began struggling again and trying to dig in her heels.

All well and good, he didn't give a damn. She was the piece that didn't fit here. She had information he needed, and he was taking her with him through the window and across the roof.

"Bull," he said, when she mumbled something against his hand.

She repeated her threat, enunciating fairly damn well for someone with a hand clamped over her mouth—and he got the message. He got it loud and clear:

"I'm with Ponce...he'll hunt you down...kill you, if you kidnap me."

"Bull," he said again, and he meant it.

It was a good threat, though, given her current circumstances, very imaginative, very quick, guaranteed to get a guy's attention and possibly his cooperation, maybe the only thing guaranteed to get a guy's attention. Esteban was a lightweight, but his father wasn't, and nobody fucked with Arturo Ponce's family, not without a very careful calculation of the odds.

Dax had calculated the odds long before he'd gotten to Paraguay, and Esteban Ponce, Levi Asher, Beranger, and anyone else who wanted the Sphinx, including any U.S. congressman or any long-legged redhead, were hell-and-gone out of luck.

He stopped at the window and looked out, holding her to one side, checking in both directions, his one arm still tight around her, his other hand still over her mouth. The coast was clear, but he was going to need her working with him to get to the alley. From there, it would be easy to disappear into the chaos and crowds of the market. Caveman tactics were a last resort, if only because they increased the risk of being noticed. Still, there was something about gagging her, tying her up, and just throwing her over his shoulder that appealed to him, probably the part about taking charge and getting the job done.

Yeah, that was probably it.

It probably didn't have anything to do with getting his hands halfway up her skirt.

Nah, he wasn't that kind of a guy.

He turned to tell her cooperation was really in her best interest, and maybe do a little placating of his own if the sheer common sense of his plan hadn't yet sunk in—but the look on her face told him anything he had to say was completely beside the point.

Shock. Disbelief. Confusion. And recognition with a capital "R." She had it all, and it was all in the stunned gaze locked onto his face.

Sure, he got it. He was feeling a little stunned himself—okay, a lot stunned.

Damn, he'd forgotten how beautiful she was. He truly had, but with the light coming in from the window, and him being real up close and personal with her, the cosmic freight train that had run over his heart the first time he'd seen her had instantly powered up and was taking him for another ride, at light speed. She was fucking luminous, her skin like satin, the curve of her nose so exquisitely elegant, her cheeks flushed with the heat, her mascara melting a bit, giving her a sultry, woman-coming-undone look. She'd lost her hat in the struggle at the door, and taken her sunglasses off somewhere between the entrance and the second floor, which left him face-to-face with the world's most gee-fucking-gorgeous, whiskey-colored eyes—exotic, dark-lashed, a deep warm brown shot through with lighter streaks of amber, like sunlight streaming through a glass of single malt.

He was taken.

He was smitten.

Yeah, she knew who he was. It was written all over her face. And he sure as hell knew who she was—it was carved in his goddamn heart.

This was crazy. He was a man on a mission, not some callow nineteen-year-old boy—and she was the woman who had haunted his dreams for six long months.

He lifted his hand away from her mouth and loosened his hold, easing up on her a bit.

"*You,*" she breathed.

Yeah, him.

"What are *you* doing here?" she asked.

Great question, the obvious question, but the answer was totally unacceptable, something he'd be damned if he admitted to anyone, because suddenly, for just a brief moment in time, with her in his arms and his brain out to lunch, the answer sounded a lot more like "falling in love" than "stealing a sphinx."

CHAPTER FIVE

Dax Killian. Oh . . . my . . . God.

The shock sent Suzi's thoughts reeling. Suddenly, she was unmoored.

Daniel Axel Killian. *Good God.* Scruffier than when she'd met him in Denver, his hair short and tousled. Beard stubble darkened his jaw, and he was dressed on the sloppy side of casual, but it was him. She would recognize him anywhere, the angles of his face damn near perfect, the little bit of slope on a nose that bordered on cute, a firm, sensuous mouth with the imperfect scar marking his chin—and those eyes, pale gray under dark lashes, absolutely clear, absolutely unwavering . . . absolutely locked onto hers.

Soulful, that's what she'd thought of his eyes six months ago, when he'd been pouring on the charm and hitting on her at the Toussi Gallery, but the description didn't fit here, not now, not in the Galeria

Viejo. Far from soulful, his gaze was piercing, fierce, and unnerving the hell out of her.

Geezus. Her heart thudded in her chest. Killian. What in the ever-loving world was *he* doing here?

And, oh, God—there was an answer to that question, only one, and it had to be the Memphis Sphinx, but why? She knew who he was and what he'd been, and she knew the U.S. government hadn't sent him. The U.S. government had sent her, which only left the nongovernmental routes open for him, and all of those routes were illegal as hell, absolutely gridlocked with black-market players like Esteban Ponce, Levi Asher, Jimmy Ruiz, and Remy Beranger.

Ruiz sure as hell hadn't mentioned an American buyer, a *norteamericano*, let alone dropped a name like Dax Killian.

Cripes, she was in so much trouble here, and geezus, was it hard to breathe in this dusty, cramped, sweltering dungeon of a room. Her head should have been reeling just from that—but no, it had taken Dax Killian to throw her off her stride.

And, oh, God, he'd thrown her.

She needed to get her bearings back, take a breath, get a frickin' grip, think things through. Dax Killian, good God, no way in hell should he be here, not for any good reason, which only left the bad reasons, and the bad reasons were very bad.

Impossibly bad. She couldn't have been that wrong about him.

"What *are* you doing here?" she asked again, confused as hell. She'd spent the last six months checking the guy out from one end to the other. With a little help from the chop-shop boys at Steele Street, she'd compiled a big fat file on his escapades, and Daniel Axel Killian was a private investigator, an ex–Special Forces operator of damn near legendary proportions, and a former juvenile delinquent of damn near equal infamy—one of Lieutenant Loretta's wild boys. He was not a black-market criminal.

Or was he?

He wouldn't be the first highly trained military operative to skirt the edges of the underworld in order to stay in the game.

Cripes.

"Getting out of here," he said, sounding damned sure of himself. "And so are you."

"No, I'm not," she said, shaking her head. "Oh, no ... no, no. I'm not leaving, not yet."

"Oh, yes, yes, yes, you are," he growled. "Come on." He started moving her toward the window, but she dug in her heels, the only part of her he didn't have in lockdown.

Dammit. She had a plan, a mission to execute, and it didn't include "cut and run," not until she'd had a chance to verify the location of the Sphinx. Two malfunctioning blinks and a beep didn't quite do the trick. Wait it out—that's what she was going to do. Wait for the police to leave, and then take another shot at the gallery with the scanner in her hand.

Another loud crash shook the walls, bigger than the others, as if the cops had turned over a whole bank of shelves, a real rumbling that made the floor tremble and sent a veil of dust drifting out of the woodwork. Dax tightened his hold on her—good Lord, as if they weren't already close enough. Now they were practically laminated, with her trying to get her feet under her and regain her balance and him holding her in a way that made damn sure she couldn't.

"You . . . you . . ."

"Bastard?" he offered.

"Bastard" worked for her, and she was just about to tell him so, when the *pop-pop-pop* of gunfire downstairs changed her whole attitude.

From one instant to the next, they transformed from adversaries with completely opposite agendas into a single, well-oiled machine with two moving parts and one goal—get the hell out of the Galeria Viejo. They reached the window, and he was boosting her up and through even as she was pushing it open. The drop on the other side was about five feet, just enough to give her a second's pause.

"Uh . . ." Geez, it looked like a long way down, the distance made exponentially more difficult by high heels, a tight dress, and a large purse.

"Do it," came his gruff command.

He was right.

She dropped her purse and threw her shoes after it, one after the other, pulling them off and tossing them onto the roof, doing some sort of squirming rumba while he was holding her, his hands simply all over her, cupping her ass, one hand gripping her thigh, pressing her up against the wall.

She swore under her breath and, as best she could, shimmied her dress up and over her hips, hitched her knee over the sill, and scrambled the rest of the way out of the window. Her feet barely touched the roof before he landed beside her.

Geezus. What was he? she wondered. Spring-loaded?

"Rocket boy," she muttered, jerking her dress back down.

Damn. This had *not* been her plan.

"White cotton?" was his only reply, his tone slightly disparaging...or maybe that was disappointment she was hearing.

Tough, she thought, leaning over and quickly slipping back into her shoes. Her underwear wasn't any of his business.

When she wobbled a little, his hands were there, one on her arm, one on her waist, steadying her, hurrying her up.

Besides, everyone knew white cotton was best next to the skin.

"They're organic." It wasn't any of his business, but there wasn't anything plain about her underwear. Quite the contrary, they cost a small fortune, the cotton grown on a farm in Alabama, the panties delicately stitched by hand in Tuscaloosa and shipped to a specialty shop in San Francisco.

He muttered something she didn't quite hear, which was probably just as well, so she ignored him, and by the time another loud crash sounded from inside the building, they were on the far side of the rooftop, with him helping her drop into the safety of the alley—a steaming, reeking, disgustingly garbage-strewn alley.

"Oh." The little gust of sound escaped her on a gasp. The stench was overwhelming, and she'd landed on something soft, and rotten, and squishy, something that oozed up over the sides of her peep-toe pumps.

He didn't give her much time to worry about her shoes, though, only about a second and a half before he took her arm and started hustling her along, heading down the alley and away from the gallery.

"Dammit," she swore under her breath, and it wasn't because of her damn shoes. Everything going to hell in a handbasket was unacceptable, especially when somebody else was suddenly and unexpectedly doing the driving.

All she could guarantee was that he wasn't going to be doing it for very damn long—oh, hell no.

Yeah, Dax was swearing, too, because he was an idiot—a stone-cold, no-excuses idiot.

This woman . . .

He swore again.

This woman, the one he had his hand wrapped around like he wasn't going to let go, the one wearing freakin' organic panties, she was trouble. He needed to take her to her hotel, pack her and her white cotton undies up, and put her on a plane out of here. Whatever she thought she was doing, and whoever in the hell she was working for, they'd all been wrong.

Wrong to send her to fucking Ciudad del Este.

Wrong to hook her up with a loser like Jimmy Ruiz.

Wrong to put her within a hundred miles of Esteban Ponce, Levi Asher, and fucking Erich Warner.

And damn wrong to put her up against a guy like him, and in this kind of game, there was always a guy like him.

He tightened his hold on her, which was ridiculous. She didn't need him holding on to her. He knew it. She'd been getting around on her own for thirty-two years, most of it in three-inch heels, and as far as he'd been able to tell from his investigation, she'd never even scraped a knee, let alone broken a bone.

And yet, for reasons that were damned annoying and had nothing to do with anything even remotely resembling logic, he'd suddenly decided it was his damn job to keep her that way.

From his vantage point in a rented room high up on the seventh floor of the Pioneros Building, the shooter watched the bust go down at the Galeria Viejo.

Christ. He checked his watch. That hadn't taken long to go straight to hell, and his target, Erich Warner, hadn't even shown up. Esteban Ponce had, though, which meant that the rumors, and the intel, and the trail, had run true. Remy Beranger had the Maned Sphinx of Sesostris III. The fuckup youngest son of Arturo Ponce wouldn't have shown up for anything less, not at some dive gallery in Ciudad del Este.

A four-thousand-year-old statue with the power to grant everlasting life, that was the prize on the block, and with his old man croaking out the last few weeks of terminal cancer, Esteban must have figured he could save the day—and it was that kind of thinking that made him the fuckup son.

The other players in Beranger's were unknowns, but he'd taken their pictures and, with a little luck, would have them identified by tonight, the sooner the better. If one of them was acting as a proxy for Warner, he needed to pick them up and shake them down. The bodyguards were unimportant and easy to pick out, but that still left a short fat guy in a pale blue suit; the taller, solidly built guy who'd been watching the gallery from the Mercado for the last couple of hours; and most intriguingly, the woman that guy had just hustled out of the building and down the alley.

She was stunningly beautiful, but that wasn't what had caught his interest, at least not initially. He'd been watching her through his rifle scope when she'd lowered her sunglasses to glare at one of the men Ponce had left at the gallery's front door, and for an instant, when he'd first seen her face, she'd actually stolen his breath, stopped it cold in his chest.

It was about the only damn thing in the world that unnerved him, having his breath stop cold in his chest—for obvious reasons.

He checked back through his scope, and for a

moment just enjoyed the easy roll and sway of her hips as she walked down the alley.

She had, by anybody's measure, a world-class ass.

But she was headed out of there, and he needed to head in, find out what was going on, and if the situation was as it appeared, take the damn Sphinx and get the hell back out. Rumors of the statue's appearance on the world stage had been percolating for four months and then spread like wildfire over the last couple of days, when it had supposedly arrived in Ciudad del Este, sporting a price tag of a million dollars cash just to get into the party. The auction would start from there. Anyone who was listening knew it was here.

Warner was listening, guaranteed, listening hard, getting desperate, and rightly so—the German's days were numbered.

Leaning forward, he snapped the lens covers closed on the scope, and in under a minute, well under, he had his M91 BDR .308 broken down and stowed, each piece of the rifle placed snugly into the foam core of a hard case. Next, he checked the charge on his TacVector, a nonlethal weapon of his own design that he carried in an extra-long holster rig under his right arm. Under his left arm, he was packing a .45, a Springfield 1911-A1, cocked, locked, loaded, and by anybody's measure, supremely lethal, especially in his hands.

The Memphis Sphinx.

Sonuvabitch.

That bastard in Washington, the spymaster, the shooter's nemesis par excellence, had actually done it: concocted a trap of near-Machiavellian dimensions and baited it with the one thing guaranteed to draw Erich Warner out into the open, the promise of everlasting life—and that was a real bad deal for old Warner, the cool million aside, because in this game, the German was just another piece of bait.

CHAPTER SIX

São Paulo, Brazil

Erich Warner read the text message on his phone, then settled back into his chair and shifted his attention to the young iguana tethered next to him. With an absentminded grace, he slowly ran his finger down the reptile's comblike spine. They were on the wide front porch of an exquisitely restored plantation house, overlooking a cerulean ocean. A jeweled leather collar encircled the beast's thick neck, with a linked chain running from the collar to the railing where the animal basked in the sun. It wasn't much of a chain, not quite a meter in length, not quite enough to keep the youngster from hanging himself if he fell off the rail.

Erich liked keeping his possessions on a short leash—like the golden-skinned woman sleeping naked on a low bed at the far end of the porch. Her name was Shoko, and she, too, wore a jeweled collar. Like the iguana's, her collar had come from Tiffany's. Unlike the iguana's, hers was made of platinum and encrusted with diamonds, an inch-wide band of icy clarity resting on sun-warmed skin.

She'd chosen it herself, the same way she'd chosen the tattoo gracing her left hip, a swastika radiating out of a kanji, a Japanese character for "hero." *Nazi Hero*—a personal calling card his beautiful slave girl tended to leave in the most surprising places, usually cut into somebody's flesh.

In recent memory, the tattoo and the necklace had been the only choices he'd allowed her, the Blade Queen of Bangkok, for slave she'd been born, and slave she was, forever and always his, a gift...of sorts, a twisted beauty from a twisted place, received in payment for an overdue debt from a very, very twisted little man.

He ran his finger down the length of the iguana's spine again.

Dr. Souk had been so brilliant, except in his choice of associates, but the man hadn't been the first or the last overindulged, slightly deranged scientist to fall prey to Hamzah Negara, an Indonesian warlord whose base of operations had been on the island of Sumba in the Sabu Sea. Souk had simply been the first and last of Erich's overindulged, slightly deranged scientists to defect to Negara. They were both dead now, unfortunately not by Erich's own hand.

Negara had been such a fool, allowing himself to

be used by the United States Central Intelligence Agency, and for his foolishness, he'd ended up splattered across the living room of his house on Sumba, his brains blown out by a sniper's bullet. Before all the foolishness, though, before Negara had seduced Souk away, there had been years of research and a burgeoning business in psychopharmaceuticals. There had been the lab Erich had built for the demented Dr. Souk in Bangkok. There had been deals in the millions of dollars. And there had been freaks of nature like Shoko, lab experiments gone awry—like so many of Souk's experiments had gone awry. Some days, the lab had resembled a charnel house of destroyed human and barely human beings. But the drugs had been beautiful, cutting-edge pharmaceuticals with names like XT7, XXG2, NG4, and the notorious BBE5, all of them razor sharp at the molecular level, capable of reshaping the landscape of the human brain with remarkable results—like Shoko, a woman so sleek and strong, so capable, so ruthless, so unfathomably unique. She had no heart, not in the metaphorical sense, no compassion, no empathy. No sense of mercy or justice.

She was perfect, and perfectly self-sufficient, except in one small area, and therein lay Erich's short leash. She needed him as much as she needed air, water, and food. Without him, she would simply cease to exist, her potential demise so gruesome, she dared not cross him—ever, not in this world.

He reached into his shirt pocket and withdrew a small silver canister, then rocked it back and forth, listening to the gentle slide of the multicolored gel-caps inside. Pills for life, pills for death, pills for pain, pills for peace—he knew what she needed, and he knew when to give it to her, and always, he made her wait until she felt the need. It kept her always on edge.

Holding the canister up to the sun, he let the reflection off the shiny metal flash on the sleeping woman's body, elusive moments of bright light touching her here and there, warming her skin an undetectable degree, undetectable to anyone except her—and slowly, she began to rouse, stretching with languid grace, her legs sliding over rose-colored sheets, the long silky fall of her raven black hair slipping across her breasts and pooling on the bed.

She never left his side, not ever.

"Have you heard from Killian?" she asked, her voice liquid and warm from sleep. It was a deception, the warmth. Pure ice ran through her veins.

And the added shade of darkness in her eyes told him she was quickly approaching the edge of her need.

"Yes," he told her. "He's at the gallery now, and says the news is good. We should hear something more tonight, after his meeting with Beranger."

This new guy he'd taken on, this Dax Killian, was proving to be a real bargain compared to the other men Erich had targeted for special mission recruitment over the years. "Exceptionally skilled," "reliable," and "cheap" weren't words that normally went together in Erich's world. But Killian had been his for the small price of a woman's life, a savvy piece of work named Esmee Alden, and for an additional bit of information Erich had been able to dangle—both of which he'd had no problem putting on the bargaining table.

Not so for Shoko. His silken-haired beauty had been forced to relinquish the American girl almost before she'd even begun to torture the brave little thing. A couple of cuts, that's all the Blade Queen had managed before Erich had taken her toy away.

He'd made it up to his lover, much to the horror of those he'd eventually sacrificed to Shoko's knives, but it wasn't as though he'd precisely had another option. He'd had a use for Killian. In his business, he always had a use for men like Dax Killian, highly adaptable, superbly trained, elite former warriors from the sovereign nations of the world, and Killian had demanded the release of his partner in return for his cooperation, for being put on retainer, so to speak.

A bargain indeed, for when the day had come, when the rumors had begun to run and Erich had deployed his team of mercenaries, Killian had been the one to track down the Memphis Sphinx. Or so Erich hoped, and so he prayed. Time was running out, and failure was unacceptable. He needed the Sphinx, felt the need of it deep in his gut where fear lay in an ever-tightening knot, sapping what little joy he'd ever felt in life. He needed the Sphinx's protection of immortality; nothing else could save him from the shadow he felt breathing death upon him at every turn.

Shadow—there was no better name for what haunted his steps, another failed experiment Dr. Souk had left behind in Bangkok when he'd defected to Negara, not a gift, but a curse, a man who had been sent to them through avenues so black, they hadn't even known his nationality. There had been a CIA connection to that beast, too, an agent named Tony Royce. But by that point in his career, Royce had been working both sides of the fence for half a dozen governments, and least of all for his own.

Royce, too, was dead now, and again unfortunately not by Erich's hand.

But the beast was alive, long since escaped from the Bangkok lab instead of dying as had been expected, desired, and decreed by Souk himself. The beast should have died from the last injection the good doctor had given him.

Should have died and had not. He was loose in the world and deadly, gathering strength all these years, readying for a killing strike. Fiercely predatory and on the hunt for the instrument of his destruction, which of course was Dr. Souk, first and always Dr. Souk—but the beast didn't seem to understand that, and in every way, in every day, Erich felt the creature on his trail, sniffing close to the edges of his life, lying in wait, killing deals and allies in equal measure, reaching out and touching Erich's existence and most assuredly determined to destroy him.

Erich wasn't going to allow it—so he kept Shoko close. If the beast should rise up in front of him some night, or make his lunge from behind, Shoko would be there to deflect the blow, or to take it herself. It mattered not which—not to Erich. She was a tool he used to sate his needs and grant him what little sleep he dared, and when she was gone, he'd make another.

Of course, the Sphinx could change the game... perhaps.

Cocking his wrist, he sent the gel-caps sliding to the other end of the canister again.

"Come here, baby," he said softly. "Come get your medicine."

With all the power and ease of a superbly fit and barely tamed animal, the Asian beauty crossed the porch and knelt before him. Eyes closed, mouth open, she tilted her head back and waited.

He never failed her.

Opening the canister, he chose a red pill out of the jeweled array, each saturated hue denoting a different Souk Special.

"Wider," he said.

When she complied, opening her mouth wider, he dropped the gel-cap onto the back of her tongue and reached down to stroke her throat until she swallowed. She never knew what he gave her, and he kept things that way, purposely, definitively.

Without moving another muscle, she slowly opened her eyes. He knew what she saw—her lord and master, matching her in elegance in every way, a long, narrow nose over a firm mouth, a shock of thick blond hair bluntly cut and casually swept to one side, blue eyes the color of a summer sky. She'd once told him that she thought he was beautiful, which he'd found so very odd. Not the opinion, but that she'd had one. She usually didn't. What she did have, and she had it in abundance, was obedience and chemically induced youth.

She was older than him, fifty-six to his forty-two, but she looked no more than thirty, her skin smooth and flawless, her body a sleek expanse of hard muscle overlaid with soft feminine curves. She didn't look like she could break a man's neck, but she could—in a heartbeat.

"We should go, Warner, today. Now," she said, still on her knees in front of him. "To Ciudad del Este. We should be there when this Killian makes his deal with the Frenchman. I don't trust him."

That last bit was superfluous, almost laughably so. She didn't trust anyone, ever. Neither did he, but there was always an extra component of risk to be weighed when venturing out into the unguarded world, a component of exposure he'd become less and less inclined to entertain over the last four years, which was why he hadn't already taken over from Killian.

"He won't cheat me." Not for any reason. Erich knew that much about the man. "If the Sphinx is in Paraguay, as he's told me, then he'll get it and bring it to me."

Killian, unlike some of the other men he'd hired, was motivated down to his core, and not by the substantial reward Erich had posted for the finding of the statue. Far more than the money, Killian wanted the information Erich had used to coerce him into finding the Memphis Sphinx, an utterly priceless piece of intelligence Shoko had tortured out of a Pakistani general who had betrayed him.

Sleeper cells of terrorists in the heartland of America—the fears were justified, and Erich had the name of a man who nurtured and presided over such a cell. He also had the name of a town in the state of Texas where this deadly cell slept, biding its time for the call to martyrdom.

Killian was a patriot.

"He won't cheat me," Erich repeated, utterly convinced.

Shoko continued to hold his gaze, her eyes growing flatter and deader with each passing moment, as if he wasn't worthy of even her lowest contempt.

He knew that look—the bitch—and it never boded well.

"What?" he asked, his voice sharp. He didn't like her in this mood. She was quite capable of killing him, and the day she decided she could face her own death, he had no doubt that she would break him into a dozen pieces and then rip him apart into a dozen more—bare-handed and with her teeth, if it came to that.

"There's a woman, Warner. I can smell her."

A woman.

Erich's own mood grew suddenly grimmer.

He didn't claim to know how Shoko sometimes knew things, though he doubted if it was actually by scent, but he'd learned not to doubt her—and if she said there was a woman involved in the Ciudad del Este deal, then he didn't doubt that there were all manner of unforeseen catastrophes on the horizon. Women, in and of themselves, had often been catalysts of catastrophe in his life, starting with his mother—who also, unfortunately, had not died at Erich's hands. A woman's mere presence, he'd learned at a young age, was often enough to skew a paradigm, which was why he didn't keep one around—present company excluded, except Shoko was not like any other woman on the face of the earth.

"A woman?" he repeated.

"Yes, Warner. It's not good."

No, it wasn't. Realistically, the odds of one woman ruining his chances at immortality were on the slim side, a possible, but not wholly probable, catastrophe.

And yet if there was a woman suddenly involved with the Sphinx, she was a new player.

Erich didn't like new players—not at this late a date, not when the Gates of Time were destined to open Sunday night and bestow life everlasting upon the person who held the Sphinx in their hands, the refracted moonlight from its crystalline eyes washing the supplicant in immortality.

That person would be him. He was the supplicant, and after Sunday night, he would be immortal.

Let the beast strike at him then and be broken.

He looked down at Shoko where she still knelt at his feet, at the warm color of her skin, the erotic perfection of her every curve, the soft pink of her mouth—and the black, dead flatness of her eyes.

No, there was not another like her, not anywhere.

"Can you be ready to leave in an hour?" he asked. The flight from the coast of Brazil to Ciudad del Este, Paraguay, was no more than three hours.

She nodded, and he smiled. They would be in the City of the East before nightfall.

CHAPTER SEVEN

Left—right—left—right—left—right...one long-legged stride after another.

Left—right—left—right...hips swaying in rhythm with her steps.

Out of the alley and onto the sidewalk, past an old Kawasaki up on its kickstand and chained to a handcart, skirting a line of plastic garbage bags spilling trash onto the pavement—*left—right—left—right*. All Dax could do was keep up. Suzi Toussi walked like she owned this godforsaken street in Ciudad del Este, and as long as she kept heading in the right direction, Dax was going to let her revel in that illusion. He had a Wilson Combat .45 tucked under his right arm in a shoulder holster, with two extra eight-shot mags and one in the pipe backing him up, enough to command a fair amount of personal space, even in this hellhole.

And Suzi had whatever she was carrying in her holster and him, whether she wanted him or not.

His money was definitely on the "or not" side of the equation.

She sure seemed to know where she wanted to go. His room at the Posada Plaza was only two blocks away, and she'd nearly covered the first one—but he seriously doubted if that's where she was headed.

Tough.

That's where she was going.

When she veered at the corner, he tightened his hold on her arm again. Possibly a risky move, but he was a risk-taking kind of guy.

"This way, Ms. Toussi," he said, redirecting her without slowing down.

"I thought we could catch a taxi up at the next corner," she said, responding to the change without breaking stride.

We? He liked that—and the way she stuck with him. He liked that a lot. It was just plain good thinking on her part not to try to ditch him.

"We don't need a taxi." Not where they were going.

"You have a car?" Regardless of how easily she'd taken the change in direction, the look she leveled at him from over the tops of the perfectly round, small gold and tortoiseshell sunglasses she'd taken from out of her purse should have stopped him in his tracks.

It didn't.

"Yes," he said. "But we don't need it either, not yet."

He glanced over his shoulder and was relieved to see the coast was clear. They weren't being followed.

"Why not?" she asked. It was a legitimate question, for which he had a quasi-legitimate answer, which she could either buy or not. It didn't matter to him one way or the other.

"Give me a chance here," he said, "and I'll get you back to your hotel in due time."

"Due?"

"Due."

He kept hustling her along, and to his surprise, she kept letting him. He'd been expecting insurrection since they'd gotten off the roof.

"So where are we going?" she asked, her tone the only cool thing in the tropical city, and he meant cool like ice, but she still had the "we" thing going, which worked for him.

"I have a room at the Posada Plaza."

Her gaze went unerringly to the decrepit five-story building partway down the next block, and he was impressed. She'd either done a lot of homework before showing up in Ciudad del Este, or she was paying very close attention to her surroundings. The sign for the Posada Plaza was damn near indistinguishable from the dozens of others tacked onto the building. At one time, the hotel had been stylish. Hints of its former glory remained in the building's pink stucco and the ornate shutters still hanging next to a few of the windows, but there was no disguising what it had become—a dive, pure and simple.

"The Posada," she said, her heels click-clicking in an unbroken rhythm as they crossed the street. "I almost booked in there."

"No kidding?" Right, and tomorrow the sun was rising in the west.

"No kidding, but I changed my mind at the last minute, something about the roach count."

"It's pretty high," he admitted, and that was no lie.

"Then what are you doing there?" she asked, sounding more curious than smart-mouthed about it. "You could have afforded better."

"Location, location, location," he said dryly, keeping her moving. They weren't nearly far enough away from the unfolding disaster at the Old Gallery to suit him, no more than a hundred meters. He knew, because his radio signal was guaranteed to a hundred and fifty, and he'd wanted to leave himself a cushion—thus the Posada. "Where are you staying? The Gran Chaco, or El Caribe?" It was one or the other. There were only two ultra-luxury hotels in the city.

And wasn't it sweet, this little conversation they were having, with the deal of the day blown all to hell behind them—and that pushed him. That pushed him hard. No matter how many times it blew up, this deal wasn't done until he walked away with the prize.

"Gran Chaco," she confirmed.

Well, she was in for a bit of a letdown then. The

lobby of the Gran Chaco was a tropical paradise, a garden courtyard of exotic flowers and bubbling fountains with mosaic columns spiraling up two floors to flank a first-class Asian fusion restaurant and a bar famous for their Singapore Slings.

The lobby at the Posada Plaza had a grill across the check-in window to protect the night clerk, one dead plant in a pot at the bottom of the stairs, and a restaurant specializing in ptomaine.

Lucky for her, he wasn't planning on keeping her very long—just long enough to shake a little information out of her and get her out of town. There wouldn't be time for a meal.

Or anything else, for that matter, and he was pretty disappointed in himself for even thinking about anything else. But there it was, jump-starting his imagination with every roll of her hips, with every glance he slanted in her direction.

She was drop-dead gorgeous, silky auburn hair swept up into a sleek French twist, except for the strands that had slipped out and were brushing across her shoulders, pale skin, almond-shaped eyes, exotic and richly, deeply brown shot through with streaks of green and amber. They knocked him out every time she lowered her sunglasses and gave him one of those looks. And man, oh, man, did she have a mouth on her—in every sense of the word. Smart, like he'd said, damnably imperious, and lush, her lips slicked with some cinnamon-colored sugar-and-spice lipstick he wanted to lick off.

Yeah, that's what he was thinking about, kissing her crazy while he got his hands up her dress.

He usually had more sense, but her whole "can't touch that" attitude was enough to make any guy want to rise to the challenge.

And he meant rise.

A fleeting grin crossed his mouth. That's what came from six months of fantasizing about a woman—a short fuse.

"The Posada isn't so bad," he said. "No worse than most of what's down here, as long as you stay out of the elevators."

She cast him another one of those whiskey-on-the-rocks looks from over the tops of her sunglasses, and his grin widened. Yeah, a knockout, just like he'd said.

"They've got a tag team running the lifts and working the clientele between floors, Marcella and Marceline," he explained. "The night clerk gets fifteen percent on the action between the first stop and the lobby, and the day clerk is taking ten on floors two through five, and everybody is shelling out five to the cops." She needed to know how bad it was here, bad everywhere, on every corner, in every shop, not just Beranger's when he was carrying hot goods. Ciudad del Este was a cesspool of violence and misery, the police included. She needed to know she needed to get out.

"Just a regular little home away from home," she said, her heels still hitting the street, one step after another. No matter how bad it looked—and even from a fair distance, the Posada looked like rough trade in a bad dress—Suzanna Royale Toussi kept walking like she wasn't in over her head.

So maybe he hadn't made his point—not yet.

"They've got a few amenities," he said. "Damn few."

"You could have sold that Plymouth of yours and checked into the Gran Chaco. The suite next to mine is available, and no, that's not an invitation."

He let out a short laugh. If she knew about his 1971 Hemi 'Cuda, a blue fish he'd named Charo, it was only because she'd gone looking to find out. A classic, Suzi Toussi was right, Charo was worth more than a few nights' worth of suite living at the Gran Chaco.

"Have you been checking me out, Ms. Toussi?" He gave her an even more assessing look.

"You failed calculus," she said.

So did you, he could have told her, but refrained.

"You were looking good, too, like you had it in the bag," she continued, "up until you bombed the final and completely tanked your grade. You were smart, just not smart enough at seventeen to think your way around—"

"Consolata—"

"Rodriguez," she finished for him. "Consolata wrecked your grade point and your Galaxie."

"The '65 Ford, yeah, that was a car." *Geezus.* More of his automotive history.

"Women seem to be a recurring weak point in your life, Mr. Killian."

Right. Like he needed reminding in that department, especially from her. *Geezus.*

"You've been talking to Esmee." Talking to Esmee a lot.

"She adores you."

Yeah, he knew it.

"Have you seen the scrapbook she made about you?" the divine Ms. Toussi asked, thankfully without giving him another of those looks, without giving him any kind of look.

Yeah, he'd seen his little cousin's scrapbook. She'd started it young, when he'd been a big hero to her. He just wished she'd stopped young.

"Sounds like you've been busy." Unnervingly busy, but he wasn't going to let that show—no way in hell, no matter how many of his report cards she'd seen, or how many of his pink slips she'd tracked down.

"And you've been lucky, starting with the night you didn't show up at the chop shop on Steele Street when the rest of the boys got busted."

"Are you talking about Dylan—"

"Hart, Hawkins, the whole crew ended up in juvie that night, and you ended up—"

"Knowing better." *Geezus again.* Was there anything the woman didn't know about him?

Yeah, of course there was. Guys in his line of work always had secrets, and unless you'd been there, part of the team, or were in the chain of command, you'd never know what had gone down in some of the places he'd been, would never know some of the things he'd done. It's what separated the big bad boys from all the rest.

"Which is how you ended up Airborne, Ranger-qualified, and at Fort Bragg," she said.

Okay, well, this was all damned interesting, but

she couldn't have gotten all that out of him in a month of Sundays, and for the record, she couldn't have gotten the piece about the bust out of Esmee. His hero-worshipping cousin didn't know about his car-stealing days. Ms. Suzi Toussi could only have gotten that little tidbit from one of Steele Street's original chop-shop boys. He knew the crew was still alive and well and running hard out of Denver, but for the U.S. government, not for grand theft auto—and yeah, Suzi knew them. She'd known them for years, quite a few of them, he'd discovered in the course of his investigation, which was something he usually tried not to dwell on for too long—women's pasts.

In her case, he'd made an exception. He'd been dwelling, plenty.

"None of which explains how you ended up in Ciudad del Este at the Galeria Viejo today," she said with a smile, stopping at the front door of the Posada Plaza and pulling it open. "After you, Sergeant Killian."

Oh, he got it. Oh, hell, did he suddenly get it. She thought *she* was in charge. Amazing. No wonder she was so generous with the "we" thing.

"That's 'former sergeant,'" he said with a smile, reaching above her on the door and gesturing for her to enter first. "You're going to like my room— I've got a private bath, a hot plate, and a window that opens."

The look she gave him might have felled a lesser man, but Dax just grinned—and followed her inside.

CHAPTER EIGHT

Well, another new low, Suzi thought, glancing around the lobby of the Posada Plaza. If the entrance to the Old Gallery had been the dumpiest, dirtiest, most squalid place she'd ever seen in her life, what with the mounds of garbage that seemed to simply pile up and spill over everywhere in Ciudad del Este, then the lobby of the Posada Plaza was the dumpiest, dirtiest, most squalid place she'd ever actually been inside.

Hands down.

The smell alone was a physical assault. She didn't want to even begin to know what mix of jungle rot and bodily fluids it took to make that smell.

Fortunately, she was a professional. She had a job to do, and she wasn't going to be dissuaded by...a small cough escaped her. Then another.

Good God.

"This is the worst of it," he assured her, taking

her arm again when she turned toward the elevators. "We're taking the stairs, remember?"

The stairs, of course. She glanced back at the
lifts and saw two rough-looking women, very rough
looking. Then she realized Marcella and Marceline
weren't women.

One of the "girls," the shorter, younger one with
a Joan Jett hairstyle, smiled shyly and waggled her
fingers in a hello.

It was sweet, unexpected, and Suzi automatically
lifted her hand in return, giving the girl a wave.

"Don't get too attached," he said next to her, and
she gave him a droll glance.

"It's just girls being girls, sisters under the skin
and all that."

"Sisters." He let out a short laugh. "Right."

Her gaze slid over the two "women" again. Transvestite tag team, Latin style—oh, yes, she was staying the hell out of the elevators. As a matter of fact,
professional or not, job to do or not, she wished
she'd stayed the hell out of the Posada Plaza. It
reeked.

Fortunately, after the first landing, the air did
seem to clear a bit.

"So you know Superman," he said.

"Christian Hawkins, yes." And, good Lord, Dax
Killian—she still could hardly believe it, and what
in the hell had happened back there with the police? God, her job had just gotten so much harder.

They made the second floor, headed up toward
the third, and she started breathing a little easier.

"And Creed? You dated him, too, right?"

Dated?

Too?

She shot him a quick glance. What in the world?

"Everybody dates somebody sometime. My social life is hardly the issue here."

"Did you ever go out with Dylan?"

She wasn't going to answer that.

"I'll take that as a yes, and frankly, I'm surprised. He doesn't seem like your type."

As if he would know her type. They'd hardly exchanged a hundred words the night they'd met at the gallery.

"How about Quinn?" he asked.

Twice.

And Dylan once—the boss really hadn't been her type.

"My point," she began, thoroughly annoyed and trying not to let it show, "was that I know quite a bit about you, Mr. Killian, and in case you missed it, the issue we're currently dealing with is what you're doing here. This thing with Remy Beranger isn't your kind of gig."

"No?"

"No. Besides the normal course of your investigations, what you and Esmee specialize in is recovering fine art, paintings in particular, not the kind of catchall crap Beranger shills."

"I didn't notice you specializing in catchall crap, either."

He had a point.

"I'm here for a client."

"The congressman from Illinois?"

She nearly stumbled on the stairs, but he caught her, his hand almost instantly wrapping around her upper arm, steadying her.

"Uh, thank you." Good God. He couldn't possibly know about the congressman from Illinois, because there was no congressman from Illinois. She and Grant had concocted the story between them just last night. No one else even knew about their plan.

Except the guy they were squeezing with it, Jimmy Ruiz, and, obviously, Daniel Axel Killian, which led her straight to the question of *How in the hell?*

"Are you okay?" Killian asked, very solicitous.

"Yes, quite, thank you." *Dammit.* Jimmy must have told him what was going on, which meant they were partners.

Cripes. She hadn't seen that coming.

"My room is just down the hall," he said, when they reached the fifth floor. "I've got a balcony with a pretty good view of the gallery."

"How...uh, convenient." Of course a tactical genius with Killian's reputation would have picked an operating base where he could keep a watch on things.

"Hopefully, we'll be able to see if the cops are still at Beranger's, and what they're doing."

"Good." Great. Wonderful. *Crap.* Ruiz and Killian, now there was a match to ruin her day and put her back up against a wall.

Dammit. The Memphis Sphinx was hers. She was finding it tonight, calling in Dylan and whoever was with him to steal it, and she was personally going to be there when the damn thing landed on Buck Grant's desk.

They stopped at the door to room 519, and Suzi's phone rang from inside her purse.

She pulled it out and answered, "Yes."

"Do you know who this is?" a man's voice said.

Well, well, well, she thought. As a matter of fact she did know who it was.

"Yes."

"I have what you want."

And that would certainly work for her. That would work very well, indeed. She glanced at Killian, and he was busy getting the key in the lock, but she didn't doubt for a second that he was hanging on her every word.

"Are you sure you know what that is?"

The caller let out a short laugh. "Everybody in Ciudad del Este wants what you want, starting with Esteban Ponce and Levi Asher, the men at Remy Beranger's this afternoon."

Okay, they were definitely on the same page.

"Meet me at your hotel in an hour," he said.

"Certainly."

"I want cash, U.S. dollars, five hundred thousand, and guarantees."

"Yes." Fat chance. She wasn't authorized to grant guarantees, and Grant hadn't sent her down here with half a million in cash, but she knew how to work an antiquities deal long enough to get what she needed out of it—money or no money.

"One hour." The call ended, and when she looked up, Killian was looking at her.

"Anybody I know?" he asked, opening the door.

"No." She shook her head, allowing herself a small measure of relief, very small. No deal was done until Grant said "Good," but this one at least wasn't dead in the water, not yet.

He finished jimmying his key out of the lock, and then, without missing a beat, took the phone out of her hand.

She started to bluster, but even one look was enough for him to see Jimmy's number, and with one press of a key, he was dialing it.

She could shoot him, but somehow she thought, in the long run at least, that wasn't to her advantage.

Short run was up for grabs.

Dammit. She hoped Jimmy was smart enough not to answer with a full introduction, or to have left his name on his voice mail. She'd be back to square one in a damn hurry either way.

After a moment, with the phone to his ear, Dax said, *"Quién es este?"*

And not so surprisingly, it looked like Jimmy hung up on him.

"Happy now?"

He didn't answer her question, and she gave up with an annoyed sigh when she realized he was putting a number into the phone's memory.

"Ciudad del Este is a rough town," he said, punching the last few keys. "If you get into any more trouble while you're here, call me. Okay?" He handed the phone back to her, and after a moment, she took it and dropped it back in her purse.

"Okay." Fat chance. She was back in play with a fairly strong hand, and apparently Killian wasn't in cahoots with half the black-market miscreants she was up against, not with Jimmy Ruiz calling and offering to sell the Sphinx to her. She'd be out of this hellhole long before she got into any more trouble.

She discreetly checked her watch. She had one hour to get her butt back over to the Gran Chaco.

"After you," he gestured for her to precede him inside, and with just the slightest hesitation, she led the way. A couple of questions wouldn't be amiss, especially if she got a couple of answers, maybe add a little chitchat, sort of an "imagine running into you in Paraguay" thing, and she was out of here. She wasn't looking for help on this deal, or, God forbid, a partner, no matter how many people she and Dax Killian both knew. She worked better alone.

Story of my life, she thought, looking around his room. It was huge, the ceilings at least twelve feet high, the wood floor wide-planked and much used and abused. There were two windows, one on each side of the shutter-type wooden doors leading to the balcony, and one of them was open, just like he'd promised. The other looked painted shut. The room was a dump, but it was kind of an exotic dump, with a big bed covered in muted gold, rose, and sage green bedding—sheets and blankets.

O-kay, she thought, *so much for the bed.* She checked to the right, and sure enough, there was the promised hot plate sitting on a dresser. She bet he was having a lot of fun with that. She also noted an ice bucket, a couple of fruity-looking bottled soft drinks, a computer up and running on a table with a pair of binoculars close by, a medium-sized duffel bag and a telephone on a console next to the bed, and an olive drab backpack with extra pouches on the outside sitting next to the duffel.

"How do you keep the elevator girls and the desk clerk from coming in here and stealing your stuff?" she asked.

In answer, he lifted his left hand and rubbed his thumb back and forth over the tips of his finger. Money, she got it.

"Go ahead and have a seat," he said, walking over and tapping a few keys on his laptop. She looked around one more time. She could sit on the bed—not likely. She couldn't remember the last time she'd sat on a man's bed, or had one sitting on hers, or doing anything else on hers—and now was not the time to be trying to remember. Or she could squeeze by him and sit at the table where he had his computer set up. Or she could do what she darn well liked, which was stand.

"I'm fine. This won't take long," she said, taking charge and setting the tone.

He glanced back at her from where he'd been watching the computer screen and smiled as if he knew exactly what she was trying to do.

Actually, there was no "try" about it. She was doing it, and she told him so with a return smile— a small smile, a smile that said he needn't bother to get too friendly. This little association they'd had for the last fifteen to twenty minutes or so was just about ready to come to an end.

"So how did you know about the congressman?" she asked. Now that she knew it hadn't been Jimmy Ruiz telling him, she was damned curious. She was also damned impressed with Ruiz. While Remy Beranger had been pleading with the police, and she'd been getting the hell out of Dodge, Jimmy had snatched the prize.

"I heard you tell Beranger, when you were inside the gallery," he said. The computer beeped, and he turned his attention back to the screen and tapped a couple more keys before picking up the binoculars and heading toward the balcony. "I bugged the place yesterday morning."

Okay, *now* she was impressed.

He opened the wooden doors but didn't step outside. Instead, he checked the streets from the shadowy safety of the room.

While he looked over the City of the East, she looked him over, letting her gaze drop down the length of him, then wishing she hadn't. He was trouble of the worst kind, even dressed in a pair of baggy khaki pants and a nondescript shirt. His clothes were sloppy, but he was built like a slab of granite underneath them. *Geezo cripes.* He was standing on the edge of the light, doing nothing more than holding the set of optics up to his eyes, and his flexed arms were literally roped with muscle. It was enough to make a girl's throat go dry, if a girl were exceedingly foolish, which, luckily, she wasn't. He was in good shape, that was all, incredibly good shape, just like all the operators she knew, the ones whose lives depended on them always being smarter, faster, stronger every time, all the time. His face was boyish, despite the hardened edges of his features, but no one would ever mistake him for a boy, not in any sense. She'd memorized his résumé, and every hard-won year showed in the way he held himself, in the way he moved.

"I also heard you tell Beranger that the congressman was interested in acquiring a rare and powerful artifact," he continued, scanning the market through his binoculars. "Something not necessarily Incan in origin, you said, which this week, in this city, means a piece of ancient Near East statuary from the Twelfth Dynasty of Egypt's Middle Kingdom known as the Memphis Sphinx."

Well. She took a breath and let it out.

Walking over to the open balcony door, she pulled a small pair of binoculars out of her purse. When she stopped just off his left side, she set them to her eyes.

Well, she thought again. She hadn't expected that, to have everything just thrown out on the table. She certainly wasn't planning on spilling her guts; she never did.

Not ever.

Not to anyone.

Looked like a bit of a commotion over at the gallery, she decided, like maybe the police had scared everybody off and now even they were leaving. *No problema* for her. The gallery was old news. This thing was going down at the Gran Chaco.

"And what I want to know is the name of your congressman," he said, lowering the binoculars, then doing a small double take when he realized how close she was. "Got your own glass."

"Everywhere I go," she said, lowering her binoculars and meeting his gaze.

He cleared his throat and headed back to the computer. "What I want to know is how you got involved in this situation, and how long it's going to take you to pack up your things and get back on a plane, because this deal, Ms. Toussi"—he finished a series of keystrokes and turned back around with an "I'm telling you this for your own good" expression on his face, a very guy-type expression—"this deal has very damn little to do with art, and a whole lot to do with the kind of people you shouldn't let get within a hundred miles of wherever you're at. This isn't a sortie to San Francisco, or a Sotheby's auction. This is nothing but bad news full of the kind of cutthroats who actually cut throats."

Great soliloquy, she thought, really great, but not precisely correct. Levi Asher was a Grade-A cutthroat, true, but only in the financial sense. The pompous little pervert squirreled his way through the art world, wheeling and dealing and throwing his weight around to get what he wanted, and he usually succeeded. He had his failings and foibles, mostly sexual, but he'd never cut a throat. Suzi would bet her favorite Nikki McKinney angel on it—and she wasn't parting with her Christian Hawkins dark angel painting for love or money.

Esteban Ponce hadn't cut any throats either, not that were on the record. His father, Arturo, was a different story, but Arturo Ponce had far better things to do with his time than chase around after the ancient artifacts of a four-thousand-year-old religion, unlike his son, who didn't have anything better to do than juggle his numerous girlfriends and distract himself with occult objects.

As for Remy Beranger, he didn't look strong enough to cut the strings on a kite, let alone a throat, and Jimmy Ruiz, arguably the most criminal guy in the group, was sitting in the palm of her hand, held in place by a shot at five hundred thousand dollars and a threat the U.S. government wouldn't hesitate to deliver on if he didn't hold up his end of the bargain.

No, she wasn't down here dealing with cutthroats.

But maybe Dax Killian was.

She ran her gaze over him and the room again.

There was definitely evidence of a holster under his right arm, a band of leather she caught a glimpse of running over the shoulder of his T-shirt and under his other shirt, and the large duffel bag on the console appeared to have gear in it rather than clothing. The sides of the bag were poked out in places, and upon closer inspection, the curved edge of metal she saw in one of the outside pouches on his backpack could be a thirty-round magazine, like one used for an AR-15.

Wonderful.

The man was well armed, after the Memphis Sphinx, and wanted her out of his way. Fine. She could accommodate that request.

"Cutthroats?" she said, letting the first thread of doubt slip into her voice, readying him for the boatload of disinformation heading his way. She didn't need him thinking about her or what she was up to from here on out. She wanted him to think she was out of the picture. "I was sent down here to complete the transaction on an antiquities deal. Skip didn't mention anything about cutthroats."

"Skip?" he repeated. "You mean Lester "Skip" Leonard? He's your client?"

"Yes." She nodded, and my oh my, he certainly hadn't disappointed her with picking up on the Illinois politician's name. There were two "Skips" in Congress. The other was a representative from New Hampshire. "He made all the arrangements, set up the deal. My job was to meet with Remy Beranger and verify the authenticity of the statue. If Beranger is selling the real thing, then I call Skip, and funds are released into Beranger's account."

"And you take the statue with you back to Illinois?"

"Well...yes," she said, standing up a little straighter, looking like a woman who was back on firm ground, like she knew exactly what she was doing—and knew what she was doing wasn't exactly right.

"Skip Leonard should have known better than to

send a woman down here." He voiced the opinion as cold fact. "Especially after contraband."

Suzi had a talent, a small one, for blushing on cue. She did it now. Looking him straight in the eye, she braved her way through his icy accusation, while letting a soft wash of color bloom on her cheeks as a clear admission of guilt.

Yes, she was silently telling him, *I know I'm skirting the edge of the law here.*

Aloud, she brazenly played the party line. "We're doing the world a favor." Screw contraband. "I only wish I'd gotten here earlier. You saw what happened back there. Nothing is sacred to these people. A piece as important as the Maned Sphinx of Sesostris III should be in more capable hands— hands capable of keeping it safe. I'm on a rescue mission here, Mr. Killian."

Both of his eyebrows lifted, letting her know he'd heard that line before—probably dozens of times in dozens of places. It wasn't an original defense, far from it.

"I'm sure you are," he said, but in a way that called her a liar.

She couldn't fault him for that. She was lying through her teeth.

"If you know anything about me, you know my reputation. It's impeccable." At least in the art world. Among a certain contingent of her ex-husbands and ex-boyfriends, the words "high maintenance" and "coldhearted" were bandied about with damning regularity. She couldn't fault them, not really. If she could have frozen her heart solid, she would have done it in a nanosecond and never, ever looked back. Hearts broke. Sometimes in ways that couldn't ever be put back together.

"On all counts," he agreed.

"So who are *you* working for?" That's what General Grant and the DIA would want to know—who the hell else was in on this game?

"Myself."

"Interesting." And as much a lie as half of what she'd been feeding him. She glanced around the room again and let out a brief sigh before bringing her gaze back to him. She didn't have to look at her watch to know it was time to go. "You're right. I didn't sign on to this deal to get shot at or to get involved with the police. It was supposed to be a straightforward authentication and pickup job. I get to keep my retainer whether I deliver the Sphinx or not. I'll miss out on the commission, of course, but quite honestly, I didn't expect this place, Ciudad del Este. I've never seen anything like it." Except for the dozen or more times she'd been to Eastern Europe these last five years, since Christian Hawkins had taken her under his wing and told her he had a use for her.

That's what Christian did, find a use for people, and if they were broken, he put them back together. She'd seen it work. Personally, she didn't think she would live long enough for Superman's magic to take hold on her. But she was still here, still on the planet, and she had a job to do. It kept her going.

"I have," he said, "and these kinds of cities don't improve over time. You're not safe here, especially down in the market, trying to do business with the likes of Remy Beranger."

She conceded the fact with a short nod of her head.

"Do you mind if I call myself a cab?" she said, walking over to the phone on the console, not waiting for him to answer.

"That won't be necessary. I'll take you."

"No," she said, picking up the receiver and dialing the front desk. "I appreciate your help at the gallery, but I can handle the rest of this. I can get myself back to the hotel."

"Not just your hotel," he said. "All the way home."

She glanced over at him, the receiver to her ear, and he was giving her "the look," the look men gave women who they thought needed a little help in their decision-making process.

It took an effort of will not to roll her eyes, but she managed.

"All those guys I dated from Steele Street?" she said. "They made sure I could take care of myself. Don't worry, Mr. Killian, I can get myself home."

For once, he looked satisfied with her answer.

"Senator Leonard, right?" he asked.

She nodded, and he smiled—like a wolf. And she noted, with all due respect, that there was nothing in that look that made her want to roll her eyes. Quite the contrary. No doubt, Skip Leonard was in for a very interesting conversation somewhere down the line.

"Yes," she said into the phone when the clerk

answered. "I need a...oh...*un momento, por favor.*" She handed him the phone, having used up her whole supply of Spanish. "This isn't the Gran Chaco."

At the Gran Chaco, the desk clerks spoke English, or at least a version of English that included limo service.

It took Killian about ten seconds to arrange her cab, before he hung up. "I'll walk you down."

"Thank you." It didn't hurt to be polite, and it didn't matter if he put her in the cab, as long as he wasn't going with her. "Curious, wasn't it? The police showing up like that? I hope to God they didn't actually shoot anybody."

"Probably just a shakedown," he said, opening the door for her, and when she was through, he locked it back up behind them. "They've got to make their lunch money somehow. I may just mosey over there, see what the damages are."

"You mean see if there's still a deal." That's what she would have done, if the deal weren't already headed her way.

He just smiled, that slow wolfish smile, and she smiled back, a sweet and easy curve of her lips.

CHAPTER NINE

She was working him. God, was she working him. Dax knew it, and he was still taking the bait. She could melt a brick wall with that smile.

"I'm tempted to go with you," she said, and all he wanted to say was, *No, baby. This one's not for you.*

What he said instead was, "How about if I take you out to dinner the next time I'm in Denver?"

The words were no sooner out of his mouth than he realized that might not have been his wisest course—to ask her out on a date.

Yes, he thought, *unbelievably, that's exactly what you just did, boyo. You asked her out on a date when you know she's done nothing but lie to you since you grabbed her in the Old Gallery.*

He was fucking brilliant.

But she was fucking gorgeous. It was bound to go to a guy's head.

"Denver, then," she said, laying on another smile gee-fricking-guaranteed to slay him.

She knew it.

He knew it.

And she knew he knew it.

He had no defense, but he wasn't getting sidetracked, not even close. He was multitasking. That was all. Guys did that sometimes, multitasked about some really important issue, like, say, the fate of the world . . . and sex. It was always sex, that second task, just humming away in the back of a guy's brain.

And yes, he was well aware of the inherent contradiction of trying to get rid of a woman and get in her pants at the same time, especially, somehow, if the pants were white cotton undies.

They rounded the third-floor landing and headed down to the second. He was keeping her moving, hopefully without being obvious enough to rouse her curiosity. Curious women were dangerous women.

Unless they were naked and in your bed.

Right. He was all for curiosity in bed—or out of bed, or anywhere, actually, when a woman was naked, and if she was naked and dangerous, all the better.

More multitasking. *Geezus.*

His point being that he'd lied, too. That had been no shakedown at the Old Gallery. Before she'd gotten her optics out, the dust had been going up in rooster tails, the whole lot of them, police included, piling out of the building and burning rubber to get away—from what the hell what, is what he wanted to know. Ponce, his crew, and, for whatever reason, one of the cops, had been going one way, Asher the other, and that damned Jimmy Ruiz had circled back to get the Land Cruiser. The only person he hadn't seen come out the front door had been Remy Beranger. The sick little Frenchman hadn't been anywhere in sight.

"So when did you get interested in ancient Near Eastern artifacts?" she asked.

"A couple of years ago," he said, giving her as good an answer as any. He took hold of her arm for the next few steps, because the carpet was lifted in places and torn in others. It was an instinctive gesture—three-inch heels, steep stairs, bad carpeting, hold on. He didn't even think about doing it. "How about you?"

"My interest isn't personal," she said. "It never is, not with antiquities, and a piece like this Memphis Sphinx, a statue with no known provenance or verifiable authentication, has a good probability of being something other than what all these buyers have been told."

"You mean it's a fake."

"There's a good possibility of that, yes." They reached the last flight of stairs, and he made sure they got down them and through the lobby as quickly as possible. He didn't have a problem with the place, it suited his needs, but he understood why she did, and he'd noticed Marcella and Marceline over by the elevators get all but riveted to the floor by the sight of a real girl.

He didn't blame them. Even in the great pantheon of real girls, Suzanna Royale Toussi was realer and girlier than most. Anyone who wanted to know how it was done would have been staring their eyeballs out—like Marcella and Marceline.

He hated to tell them, but it didn't matter how hard they stared, or how hard they tried, even with a trowel and forty yards of spandex, they couldn't get within spitting distance of the super-hot Ms. Toussi. Not on his Curve-o-Meter.

"Beranger could have the real deal," he said, opening the hotel's main door onto the street. The Posada Plaza didn't have the world's best air-conditioning system, but it was a damn sight better than the straight heat of the city. It was still a hundred and one outside, and the sidewalk was steaming.

"Yes, it's a possibility," she conceded.

"Do you believe in it, the Sphinx? The whole immortality thing, that it has mystical powers?"

The question seemed pretty straightforward to him, but he felt her stiffen, her body making a subtle shift from acquiescence to defense.

"No," she said, reaching up and adjusting her sunglasses, settling them more firmly on her face, her voice coolly adamant. "Absolutely not."

He'd hit a nerve, unintentionally, and it didn't take him more than a moment to realize which one.

Hell. Under other circumstances, he would apologize, but he didn't think her knowing he'd been investigating her would improve the situation, and this most certainly wasn't the time to be bringing up the subject of her dead daughter.

He'd given her loss a lot of thought over the last few months, remembering how she'd looked that night in the gallery, so gorgeous it hurt, and absolutely untouchable, like she did now. More than once, he'd wished he could reach out over the miles and offer her some comfort, usually about the second glass of Scotch, sure, but the intent had been pure. She was cool, all right, firmly in control, and he'd bet that was exactly the way she needed to keep things.

Well, she had a lot better chance of doing that if she got out of Ciudad del Este *inmediatamente*.

A cab pulled up at the curb, and she started forward.

He matched her stride for stride, and when they reached the taxi, he opened the door for her, then stood by while she moved past him to get in. At the last moment, he reached for her arm again, stopping her with a light touch.

She turned to face him, the obvious question on her lips, but he beat her to the punch.

"You're making the right decision here," he said. "I'll let you know how it all turns out when I get to Denver."

Classic strategy, reinforce the goal, which idiotically seemed to be that damned dinner date, once he wrapped up his whole trading-the-ancient-Egyptian-statue-for-the-intel-on-a-terrorist-sleeper-cell-in-the-heartland-of-America mission.

"I'll hold my breath," she said, her eyes unmistakably focused on him through the amber lenses of her sunglasses.

Cool, cool Suzi Toussi—he just shook his head and stood back as she finished getting in the cab, and he closed the door for her when she was settled.

Reaching in his pants pocket, he pulled out a roll of bills and thumbed off a few, then leaned down into the passenger side window of the front seat and handed the bills across to the driver.

"Gran Chaco," he said. There was only one.

"*Está bien,*" the driver replied with a broad smile, noticing the healthy tip Dax had added to the fare. "*Muy bien.*"

Turning to look in the back seat, Dax had only one word for her. "Home," he said, and he meant it. He didn't want to see her in Ciudad del Este again. The congressman was out of luck on this deal—and really, when he thought about it, few things were scarier than the thought of a congressman looking for immortality.

She glanced at him over the tops of her sunglasses, and he figured that was as good as he was going to get. The message had gotten through. That's all he wanted. He stepped back on the curb, and even after the cab pulled away, he stayed there, watching her leave.

Home—it's what he'd said. It's what he expected.

What he didn't expect was to see a goddamn blue Land Cruiser with Jimmy frickin' Ruiz at the wheel pull out of a side street and take off after Suzi's cab.

Geezus. He was starting to feel like he was in the middle of a beehive, with all the worker bees buzzing around trying to steal the honey and snatch the queen.

Dammit.

Suzi or the Sphinx—it wasn't really a contest, but one of those prizes was going one way, and the other—he hoped to hell—was still at Beranger's. Or if it wasn't, that's at least where the trail would start.

Again, dammit.

He pulled his radio receiver out of the cargo pocket on his pants and started down the street at a fast walk, heading for his rent-a-Jeep, and trying not to draw any attention to himself. Ciudad del Este was the shopping capital of Paraguay, racking up billions of dollars' worth of merchandise sales every year, most of it illegal. In the market, the streets were always packed, not just with shoppers, fruit sellers, guys hawking all kinds of crap out of handcarts, armed security guards for the big stores, and the occasional, oddly open-market drug dealer selling his goods off the hood of his car, but with hundreds of *hormiguitas,* "little ants," men who made their living smuggling goods across the border on their backs.

Walking along, weaving his way through the crowd, Dax ran through the frequencies of the transmitters he'd hidden in the gallery. The one in the entrance was silent, which was to be expected, considering that everyone had already left the damn place. He checked Beranger's office, where

Ponce's men had been discussing the new whores at the Colony Club, and got nothing but static; the same as in the junk room—so who knew what in the hell had happened in those two places. The last transmitter was in the main gallery room, what might be left of it anyway, after the police had trashed and crashed their way through it. He dialed in the frequency and listened, then came to a stop in the middle of the sidewalk.

There was something coming through, something very human-sounding.

Checking both directions, he waited for a break in the stream of shoppers, then made his way into the doorway of an electronics store to stand next to a burly security guard holding a pistol-gripped 12-gauge—and he listened.

Breathing, that's what he was hearing, heavy breathing coming through the receiver, like someone was right against the transmitter. He was getting it all, a whole chorus of the raspy, rattling struggle, an inhalation of infinite, pained complexity. It could be Beranger. The man was not well.

The guy with the 12-gauge gave him a dark look, like he was taking up important space, and Dax gave him a half-assed smile and shrugged.

"Mi mujer," he whispered, *my woman,* like there was just no help for this little moment of togetherness in the doorway. The security guy was not his fight.

He hoped the guy was nobody's fight, not with him carrying a shotgun for curbside security. The streets and sidewalks were jam-packed full of people. If some *cholo* decided to steal something, the only safe place for a hundred yards was going to be behind the guard. Nothing in the wild, wild West back home could hold a candle to this place. There were no rules in Ciudad del Este.

Another sound came through the receiver, commanding his attention, a scraping noise echoing in rhythm with the breathing, like someone was getting dragged, like . . . like he didn't know the hell who, but the visual he got was of somebody dragging Remy Beranger, who was breathing loudly, across the main gallery room to do . . . well, something horrible—that was the visual he got from the raspy, pained sound. He wasn't an alarmist, far from it, but the gallery had been coming down around the Frenchman's ears when Dax and Suzi had bailed off the roof.

Geezus. Whatever he thought of Remy Beranger, he needed the guy.

He looked down the street. The cab and the Land Cruiser were gone, but he knew where they were going—the Gran Chaco, and honestly, he didn't doubt that Suzi could take care of herself at a luxury hotel, especially when she was packing a pistol, and most especially since it had been the SDF guys who had taught her how to use it. He knew guys like that. He was a guy like that, and guys like him not only would have taught her how to shoot, they would have taught her when to shoot, which in the case of self-defense was well and often, and quickly—very, very quickly. A couple of shots in a second and a half would do the trick nicely. Hawkins would have taught her that.

Beranger, though, he'd been about half done in every time Dax had seen him, and if that really was him breathing like that and getting dragged across the floor—well, then Dax had to do something, or he was going to lose the only person he knew who might have actually seen the Memphis Sphinx.

He looked up the street again, then swore under his breath. Half an hour, that's all it would take for him to check on Beranger, get the damn Sphinx out of him if it was there to be gotten, and then get back on the road to the Gran Chaco.

CHAPTER TEN

Shot and crushed. Oh, God, he hurt. He hurt so badly...everywhere. They'd shot him, the bastards, and then pulled a bank of shelving over on top of him.

Remy sucked another breath into his lungs, felt it rattle out in a bad way, then sucked in another, painfully, almost unbearably, and with each one he prayed it wasn't his last.

There was blood all over him, all over his clothes, all over his hands, pooling on the floor where his savior had pulled him out from under a pile of broken shelves—sweet, sweet Jesus, my Lord *Jesucristo,* savior of the world.

Jesus Christ in blue jeans, kneeling down beside him in a Jimi Hendrix T-shirt and a snakeskin belt. Jesus with a gaze of holy compassion seeing all the way through him to his soul.

"I...I have...have sinned," he said, his voice a

bare breath of sound, the need to confess compelling him to speak.

"We're all sinners," Jesus said, his voice so matter-of-fact that Remy felt he'd been absolved—such was the Lord's grace. Everyone sinned, everyone could be granted salvation, if they repented.

Lying in his own blood, lying in pain, Remy repented—oh, God, did he repent—and he forgave those who had sinned against him, everyone, even the damn *policía* for shooting him, the bastards, and tearing his gallery apart.

He dragged another breath into his lungs, felt the pain of it from beginning to end—and then he coughed . . . *Jesusjesusjesus*, the pain racked him, and the blood flowed.

"Open your eyes, Remy, look at me," Jesus said, his voice deep and smooth and compelling.

Remy forced his eyes open, knowing what he'd see—his Lord Christ with his dark hair short and standing half on end, his saintly face a study in chiseled angles and perfection, his jaw strong, his cheekbones high, his gaze narrow beneath thick, straight eyebrows. Jesus was a hard, hard man, his arms powerful, his chest and shoulders broad beneath his dark T-shirt and the silky green shirt he wore open over the top of the T-shirt. The muscular length of his legs was visible beneath the worn denim of his jeans. Remy had never realized Jesus was so tall, six feet or more of power and grace, like an archangel, his body honed like granite. He had known his Lord was a warrior, and it was in his warrior guise that Jesus had come to Galeria Viejo tonight, to vanquish Remy's enemies and save his soul. The air still thrummed with the power of his presence, the echo of it matching the rhythm of Remy's heartbeat, and like his heartbeat, growing ever fainter.

But it was Jesus. Remy had seen the marks, and no one else could have saved him from the violence and chaos. The *policía* had fled at his entrance, but the savior had caught one of Asher's men and hauled him up by the scruff of his neck against the wall. Eye to eye, no one could resist the Lord, and harsh words had been spoken before Jesus had released the man. All was quiet now, with nothing but the sound of his own labored breaths filling the cavernous room.

"You have a statue," Jesus said, looking through the pockets on Remy's jacket. He was so gentle, all his movements so smooth, so fluid, laying back the front of his coat, frisking him, checking his pants pockets. Remy didn't mind. His savior was barely jostling him at all.

Jesus pulled a piece of paper out of his front pants pocket and unfolded it. Remy knew what it was, the lading document for the Sphinx, though, of course, it didn't say "Maned Sphinx of Sesostris III" anywhere on it.

Jesus read the paper, then refolded it and returned it to the pocket where he'd gotten it.

"You do have a statue, Remy," he said, very calm, very sure.

Yes, yes. Remy nodded. He still had a statue. He looked around himself and felt another wave of

pain. The police had broken everything, his bookcases, the lights, the furniture, they'd broken down
doors, smashed paintings and pottery, and the bastards had probably stolen him blind.

But they wouldn't have found the Sphinx. They
would never find it, and Remy wished to God he
hadn't either, found it in a plain wooden shipping
crate addressed to him, a small crate banded in
metal.

The death of him—that's what he'd thought
when he'd opened the crate and lifted the top half
of the foam packing container off to reveal the
Sphinx.

He'd known exactly what it was; he'd been expecting it, while at the same time never expecting
that it would really come to him and his small shop,
a dangerous gift with too few strings attached, only
that he let it be known that he had it to sell, the
profits to be his—the Memphis Sphinx, a mystery
of the ages, its very existence a battleground of con-
jecture, its expounded history rife with riddles and
theories. For a brief moment when he'd first seen
it, his heart had soared, then had come the fore-
boding of doom, crashing down on him—*the death
of him*.

And so it had come to pass. Death delivered to
him upon the word of a white-haired stranger with
a cultured American accent and lofty ties to the
United States government. Bait, the man had said,
to lure a shark home. For the million-dollar profit
Remy had known he could make on the deal, he'd

thought he could survive any shark who would come to feed on the fabled idol.

He had not.

Instead, he'd become the center of a maelstrom.

"The statue, Remy, the Sphinx," Jesus said. "Where is it?"

Hidden, Remy thought, in a place where nobody could have come along and taken the thing away from him.

He wasn't a fool, but Esteban Ponce was, a dangerous fool. Remy had taken precautions, knowing there could be trouble, but look at him—murdered in his own gallery.

He gritted his teeth against the pain. Ponce had brought this upon him. The cops in the city were easily bought, and they'd only been minutes behind the Brazilian. Ponce could have signaled them from the viewing room, thinking the Sphinx could be had for the price of three crooked cops instead of the opening bid of a million dollars.

Poor fool Ponce—he'd called his dogs in without even seeing the real statue. Remy and Jimmy Ruiz had gone to great effort to make the buyers think the gorgeous plaster and composite reproduction they'd had made, with cut-glass eyes and a "gold" mane, the lapis lazuli embellishments made of plastic, was the four-thousand-year-old artifact. No one knew fakes better than Remy Beranger. He specialized in the crap—and now he was going to die for it.

Stupid Ponce wouldn't even have gotten the fake statue for his trouble. Remy had taken it with him when he'd left the viewing room and handed it off to Jimmy. No sense letting the marks get too close a look at it. When he'd seen their cash, he would have shown them the true Sphinx.

He swore it by the blood of Christ.

He had never wanted to keep the damn thing—too dangerous, too heavy for his spirit, too deadly.

"Remy, Remy, Remy," Jesus was saying, reaching down and sliding his hand across Remy's brow, smoothing his hair back off his face, his palm cool, his voice hitting a tone of comforting compassion. "Don't go yet. Tell me where you put the Memphis Sphinx."

It was the gentlest of caresses, made with a saintly hand—a hand made powerful by suffering and redemption, a hand of salvation. Remy knew. He'd seen. Jesus had made no attempt to hide his wrists, and in the center of each was a scar from the holy cross.

Scars and the frightful power of his presence. From where Remy had lain beneath the broken shelving, he'd felt the power of Jesus entering the gallery, heard the resonant command of his voice, and all Remy's enemies had fled.

Who but the Lord could have vanquished them all?

He drew in another rattling, pained breath, hating the sound of it, knowing it meant the end was near.

"*Dans la cage,*" he said, using his last ounce of strength. *In the cage.* "Hidden in the . . . the cistern . . . " He wanted to say more, ask Jesus about

Heaven, but the words wouldn't come to him. Not now. Not on his last breath.

He lifted his eyes to his Lord, and Jesus spoke to him then, the words soft and consoling, a blessed comfort as the light and the darkness drifted into an endless blanket of gray.

CHAPTER ELEVEN

Outskirts of Ciudad del Este

"Yes," Creed answered, sitting at a table in a dingy riverside bungalow on the southern edge of Ciudad del Este—mission central for this goatfuck.

Dylan Hart threw another question at him, and again he answered.

"Yes."

Christian Hawkins's voice this time, but again a question, in two parts and both parts like knives in his heart.

"Yes," he said. "Yes."

A third voice joined the first two, Zach Prade's, and as they all conferred, Creed kept his gaze locked on the photographs spread out across the kitchen table—Cesar Raoul Eduardo Rivera, Creed.

The man who'd shortened Creed's name for him

twenty years ago on the streets of Denver sat opposite him, on the other side of the table, looking
rode hard, and that, more than anything else, had
warned Creed that he was in for one of those bad,
bad times that everybody had to get through sometimes. He'd never seen Dylan look so tapped out.

Still, when he and his partner on the mission,
Zach Prade, had arrived at the bungalow an hour
ago with the supplies Dylan had ordered, he hadn't
expected what he was looking at on the table.

No one would have expected it, not after six
years, not ever.

He took a breath and settled deeper into the
ladder-back chair he'd been offered, settled deep
and heavy, more to keep himself steady and in one
piece than to get comfortable.

There was no comfort to be had, not in this
place, not with those photographs on the table.

Shit.

Dylan, the head honcho of 738 Steele Street,
the brains behind Special Defense Force, was un-
shaven, his hair long and pulled back in a pony
band, his clothes sweat-stained and dirty. On
Creed's right, Hawkins, the heart of SDF, didn't
look any better. The other SDF operators, men and
women alike, called him Superman for a reason,
for a lot of reasons, but Superman looked like he'd
run the length of South America to get to this hellhole in Paraguay.

"One more time," Dylan said, and Creed cow-
boyed up, swallowing the hard ball of rage sticking

in his throat like a forty-pound weight, ignoring the edge of fear licking at his emotions.

Carefully, his movements slow and controlled, he stacked the photographs back in order and started at the top.

"First day in camp," he said, sliding a photograph off the stack. It showed him and a dark-haired man, J. T. Chronopolous, bound, blindfolded, and gagged, bloody and beaten, lying on the ground in the Colombian jungle, with five huts in the background and a cooking fire and open-air kitchen in the foreground.

"Where was the camp?" Dylan asked.

"Northern Colombia. We were three days out from the town of Coveñas on the coast, when we were ambushed. From there, we were four days on the trail, gaining altitude, before we reached the NRF outpost." Six years ago, he and his teammate, J.T., had been captured and held by a group of Colombian guerrillas, the National Revolutionary Forces. He'd lived through the ordeal. J.T. had not.

"Who was your connection in Coveñas?" Hawkins asked.

"It was a CIA setup, at least the guy in charge was CIA." This was all old news. He'd been debriefed a hundred times a hundred different ways on the mission that had cost J.T. his life, but no one had ever mentioned photographs. Whoever in the hell had taken them, Creed hoped they were long dead.

"Who else was in Coveñas?" Dylan asked.

"A security guy from Occidental Petroleum," he

said, "and four shooters and looters who were running their own game out of there."

"Had you ever seen any of them before you and J.T. got to Coveñas?"

He shook his head. "Not before or since." And he'd been looking. He and J.T. had been set up for that ambush, but by whom and why remained a mystery. Creed had always wanted to have a chat with those other boys who'd been at Coveñas that summer, but that whole crew seemed to have vanished off the face of the earth. The last Creed had known was the four of them heading up toward the Darien Gap in the northern Choco region of Colombia, on the border with Panama. An agent named Tony Royce had been high on Dylan's list of suspects for the ambush, but like so many of Royce's treacherous deeds, the confirming details had never surfaced, and Royce was dead now, killed by Hawkins.

"Do you remember the drugs you were given by the NRF guerrillas?"

Creed shook his head. "Only that there were a lot of them."

"Hallucinogenic?" Dylan asked, and Creed gave him a hard look.

"I know what I saw, Dylan." It was branded on his soul.

"Tell me . . . again."

Creed reached for the second photograph and pushed it across the table. "I saw Pablo Castano torture and beat both of us." A close-up photo showed a man with a flattened, broken nose and a pockmarked face grinning for the camera. "For the record, for the hundredth time, I personally slit Castano's throat in Peru, sent him straight to hell. I heard there were photos taken of the body."

Skeeter had told him.

"Did you ever see Ruperto Conseco?"

Creed looked down at the stack of photographs and spread them out again. "This guy," he said, choosing one of the pictures and sliding it out of the stack. "I remember him coming twice, always treated like a VIP, looking things over, giving...orders." A dull pain came to life in his gut.

Kid, J.T.'s brother, and Hawkins and Creed had killed all the bastards in that camp, their mission sanctioned by three sovereign nations. Tracked them down over the course of a continent and a year and killed them—the guerrillas, the drug cartel boys like the Consecos, and one rogue CIA agent, Tony Royce, who had gone down in Denver in an alley, in the rain, one shot to the back of the head delivered by a steady hand—Superman's.

Guns and drugs and thugs—all over the world, those three things were twined together tighter than the knots on a dropped noose.

Creed took another breath, keeping it slow and easy.

This was going to get worse. He could tell, and a part of him wished Dylan would just get to his point—and a part of him prayed Dylan would never get to the point.

"What else did you see?" the boss asked.

With only the slightest hesitation, Creed reached

for the pile of photographs and cut to the chase. The bottom picture was the one he needed, and he dragged it out from under all the others and pushed it squarely into the center of the table.

It was horrifying.

Unbearable.

But he bore it, the way he'd borne the deed while it had been happening, bearing witness.

"He's dead, Dylan." He shouldn't have had to say it, and in no small way, he hated Dylan for making him voice the horror aloud. "He's dead. He died on that cross, in the fucking jungle, crucified for reasons I'll never understand."

He lived with brutality. He was more than capable of his own brutality—but watching the NRF crucify J.T. and cut him open had damn near broken his brain.

Or maybe there was no "damn near" about it. He knew, no matter how he kept going, that he'd never been the same, that as J.T. had left his life and his blood and his screams on that cross in the jungle, Creed had left part of himself, the best part, in the blood and mud at J.T.'s feet. He knew his screams had echoed along with J.T.'s, and that they'd made no difference. None. He had not been able to save John Thomas Chronopolous.

Yes, he'd been drugged, and sick, and beaten, and tortured, but he knew J.T. was dead. He knew what he'd seen, what he'd witnessed.

"There are doubts," Dylan said.

No, there weren't.

He cut his gaze to Dylan's and held it hard.

He could take the boss. He knew it. Dylan knew it, too, and Creed wasn't shy about letting it show in his eyes.

"There's a compound upriver, Costa del Rey," Dylan said, his voice strong and calm, his words clipped, delivering information in a steady stream—holding Creed to a line he couldn't afford to cross, ever. "It's isolated, at the end of a nearly impassable track, formidably protected. Seven months ago, the CIA got a team up there who sent back photographs. They haven't been heard from since."

Half a dozen heartbeats passed during Dylan's news flash—but Creed hadn't moved, not so much as a muscle.

He was looking at the boss, but he could see the folder lying under Dylan's right hand. The seals on the folder had been broken, telling him the boss had seen the contents, probably Hawkins, too.

"I'm not going to tell you what's in here," Dylan said, sliding the folder across the table. "But I want you to tell me what you see."

Easy enough.

He didn't hesitate to reach for the folder, to take control of it, he didn't dare. It looked like a viper coming toward him across the table, sliding, coiling, ready, and bottom line, he wasn't going to be beaten by a goddamn folder full of photographs.

Dylan removed his hand, and Creed flipped to the first picture.

It was enough.

Just the one.

He knew what Dylan wanted, what the boss expected, what the job took, and he gave it to him—endurance. Second by second, moment by moment, he gave the photograph his undivided attention, scanning it from top to bottom, cataloguing the face, and with the utmost deliberation he kept his hands loose, his left palm resting lightly on the folder's cover, his right resting equally lightly on his thigh.

There was no one in this room to blame for what he was seeing.

There was no one to fight.

There was no motherfucking explanation for the photograph on the table, a photograph taken seven months ago.

"Grant tagged us for an assassination six months ago," Dylan said. "This man is our target, a rogue CIA agent they think is holed up at Costa del Rey. Hawkins and I believe the same thing. We've been on this guy's trail for six months, and he's finally come home to roost. His name is Conroy Farrel."

No, it wasn't, and Dylan knew it as well as Creed did.

Nobody was named Conroy Farrel.

The name and the identity had been one of J.T.'s covers, and this man looked exactly like him—except J.T. was dead.

Goddamn CIA. What the fuck had they done?

CHAPTER TWELVE

Ciudad del Este

Dax stood in the front door of the Old Gallery, holding it open, looking in, but not crossing the threshold.

Geezus. The place was a wreck, but that's not what held him where he stood.

Something had happened here, something beyond the obvious destruction. The police had done a number on the place, broken just about every damn thing Dax could see, and that was no shakedown. That was violence of a different character. He could smell it. Nothing moved in the shadows of the main gallery. Dust motes drifted, but there was no sign of life in the room—only the scent of death rising to taint the air, familiar and unmistakable.

The unfamiliar was harder to catalogue, being

no more than a faint, oddly electrical quality in the atmosphere, the aftermath of some kind of disturbance, but he didn't know what.

Well, hell. He drew his pistol and crossed into the gallery, keeping the gun at a low ready position, just in case there was another "unexplainable" disturbance in his immediate future.

Step by step, he cleared the entrance and moved into the main room, into a deeper silence. It took his eyes a few moments to adjust to the low light, but when they did, he very quickly located the source of death.

Remy Beranger, his small body crumpled on the floor in a pool of blood, the right side of his chest a ragged mess.

Geezus, the cops had killed him.

Pistol raised to the ready, Dax moved forward, but there was nothing, no threat and nobody else on the main floor of the gallery—only Beranger lying on a pile of rubber knives and Galeria Viejo T-shirts.

Dax knelt by the body. He didn't need to check. The guy was dead. No pulse. No life. Three shots—two in the chest, and one in the gut.

Geezus. Beranger hadn't been such a bad guy.

Dax let out a breath and checked the gallery again, listening carefully, looking into corners. He didn't mind being one-on-one with the dead, but to the best of his ability, he was never getting involved in anything that would require coming back to this hellhole called Ciudad del Este.

Immortality, *Christ*. The damn Sphinx sure hadn't granted Remy Beranger any immortality.

He checked his watch. It had been twenty minutes since he'd put Suzi in the cab, and in another twenty-five to thirty, he could be at the Gran Chaco.

But first he needed to search the gallery, and the best place to start was with the Frenchman, even if chances were that the Sphinx had been snatch-and-grabbed by somebody on their way out the door, maybe even one of the policemen. If he could confirm that the cops had taken it, maybe Colonel Hanson, the man he'd contracted with for this job, could bring some pressure to bear on the good people of Paraguay and get them to loan him the damn thing until he got the information on the sleeper cell in Texas out of Erich Warner. But unlikely. In Ciudad del Este, the terrorists were up on the cops about two to one any day of the week.

So, hell.

He finished searching Remy's jacket pockets, coming up with a few scraps of paper, a couple of pens, a little cash. He kept the paper scraps, putting them in one of his cargo pockets, before moving on to Remy's pants pockets. He hit pay dirt on the front right, a lading document from an import-export business in Virginia dated two weeks previous, addressed to *Remy Beranger, Galeria Viejo*, one item listed simply as *Orthostat relief. Basalt. h. 20 cm*.

Right. It didn't say *Occult Statuette, Maned*

Sphinx of Sesostris III, a.k.a. Memphis Sphinx, grantor of everlasting life. Granite. h. 17.5 cm., but somehow it was close.

Close enough.

And coming out of Virginia, well, hell, that was damned curious.

For whatever reason, and there were probably more than a few good ones, he flashed on Jimmy Ruiz hightailing it off the roof of the Old Gallery with that messenger bag slung over his shoulder just as all the commotion had started. Jimmy swinging back around to pick up his damn Land Cruiser. Jimmy Ruiz who had arrived with the lush and lovely Suzi Toussi and who was currently chasing the lovely Ms. Toussi back to her hotel.

Yeah, there were a lot of coincidences in that little series of events.

Hell, no wonder she'd been so quick to get out the door of the Posada Plaza and insisting that he not accompany her. While he was standing in the Old Gallery with a dead body, a curious-as-hell lading document, and his you-know-what in his hand, she was collecting her contraband and getting ready to go wheels-up back to the States and Senator Leonard. She was going for the win here. She was taking the Memphis Sphinx to Illinois.

The hell she was.

Dax left the gallery at a fast walk, and by the time he hit the alley, he'd busted into an easy run.

Three or four minutes was all it took for him to be sliding in behind the wheel of his Jeep, firing her up, and leaning over to pop open the glove box. He needed two things to get onto the grounds of the heavily guarded Gran Chaco Hotel—a Cuban panatela, just because, and the press pass he never traveled without, from *The Daily Inquirer*.

CHAPTER THIRTEEN

All Suzi wanted was to get the hell out of Ciudad del Este, but from what she was looking at, she wasn't going to be getting what she wanted anytime soon.

Jimmy Ruiz must think she was a total idiot.

"Twelfth Dynasty, you say?" She looked up from the "Memphis Sphinx" he'd set on the coffee table in her suite, the one he'd taken out of a padded leather bag and carefully arranged next to a thick stack of papers he'd also taken out of the bag. For the record, he looked like hell, even more frazzled than when she'd last seen him at the gallery.

For the record, she knew she didn't look much better. She'd torn her skirt, lost a button off her jacket, and scratched her face, up high on her cheek, all while getting out of the gallery window. She'd also broken a nail and had barely had time to wash God knew what off her feet before Ruiz had come knocking on her door.

"That must make it . . . how old?" she asked.

Her beautiful peep-toe pumps, needless to say, had been ruined by their immersion in Paraguayan garbage. She'd lost her hat, and her hair had all but completely fallen out of her French twist.

She felt absolutely straggly. *Cripes.*

"Hundreds and hundreds of years old," the young man said with amazingly misplaced confidence.

Try four thousand years old, she thought, refraining from a weary sigh. She'd had a long day, coming off a long night and a long flight, and for a few brief moments, before Ruiz had unveiled his fake statue, she'd hoped her job here was done, and not only done, but done exceptionally well. She wouldn't have simply located the darn Sphinx, she would have had it in hand, saving Dylan, and Hawkins, and any other wild boy down here running around Paraguay the trouble of stealing it, and from what Dylan had told her when he'd contacted her this morning, she knew there were a couple extra SDF boys in country and headed her way, maybe already in the city, and it was a good chance the two of them would be tagged for the snatch—if she could verify the Sphinx's location.

Which she had not done.

Dammit.

So much for her moment of mission glory. Ruiz's fake had sealed her fate. She was doomed to at least one night in Ciudad del Este, and from what she'd seen so far, that was about as sketchy a situation as she'd ever encountered. She was damn glad to have a 9mm. Ruiz at least hadn't let her down in that department.

"It's beautiful," she said, looking at the statue, and that was the truth. The artful amalgamation of plaster, composite something-or-another, paint, and plastic was very sleek, very well executed—except for the flat-out dead giveaway of the bottom of the statue. Anyone who turned it upside down was bound to notice the letters and numbers written in black marker on an unpainted patch of white plaster on the base. This one said *GV 3/5*, which she was sure meant that Galeria Viejo had ordered five of these babies made. She had to admit that the blue stamp of the Great Sphinx of Giza next to the numbers made the whole thing look very official—if four thousand years ago Sesostris III had commissioned a plaster sphinx.

He had not.

The legend of the Memphis Sphinx, and Howard Carter's notes, distinctly described a granite statue.

Granite. Not plaster.

"You have the money?" Ruiz asked.

God, he really did think she was an idiot.

"Half a million American? Right?"

"*Así es.* This is correct."

"It can be arranged." Not that she was going to bother. "I'll need a couple of days to authenticate the statue, and also a bank account for the deposit."

"No," he said adamantly, shaking his head and

leaning over to pick up the papers he'd laid on the table next to the Sphinx. "No. There is no time for waiting. The documents for the statue are all in order, and the money, it can be transferred through my *cambista*. Everything *inmediatamente*."

He handed the papers over with a small lift of his head, as if to say, *Read them, read them now. This is all very perfect.*

She accepted the documents with a brief smile and quickly glanced through them, duly noting that they appeared very authentic, very official, complete with tea-stained edges and lots of rubber stampings in various colors of ink. He and Beranger must have been busy as a couple of beavers getting their scam together.

And Ruiz's plan with the *cambista*, well, that would definitely speed things up, to use the underworld freeway of cash transactions. Bags of cash given to a *cambista* entered the *cambio* pipeline in one country and, with a few phone calls, would be matched by the same amount of cash in another country, minus a sizable commission.

"I don't believe the congressman will be willing to deal with..." Hmmm, with a moment's reflection, she revised her original thought of *a bottom-feeding, scum-sucking, money-laundering lowlife* to something with a bit more cachet. "With anyone who might be running afoul of the law. He wants the Sphinx, not a scandal."

She also didn't know where in the world Ruiz thought a United States congressman would come up with half a million dollars in cash *inmediata-mente*. That kind of money was always dirty.

He looked at her with a dubious expression on his face, as if he couldn't believe whom he'd been stuck with on this deal.

She knew the feeling.

"You do know that this statue is worthless after Sunday night?" he asked.

Actually, the statue on the coffee table was worthless now, despite the little batch of provenance papers he'd given her, but she went ahead and nodded. "Yes, I understand that some people believe a certain alignment of cosmic forces on Sunday night can be channeled through the Sphinx."

"And you don't believe?" For the first time since they'd met at lunch, he sounded impressed.

"I believe in acquiring for my clients whatever they hire me to find, Señor Ruiz, and I let them believe whatever they want, as long as I get my cut of the deal."

He held her gaze for a long moment, and she could practically see the gears turning in his mind.

"I have the same beliefs, Señora Royal," he finally said. "And I have a lot of connections for finding these sorts of mystical objects."

She just bet he did—starting with Remy Beranger and whoever had manufactured the knock-off Sphinx sitting on her table.

"What I no longer have is a partner with connections to buyers in the United States."

Well, that was damned interesting. General

Grant hadn't mentioned that the U.S. Treasury agent currently in custody for tax evasion and treason had also been hustling antiquities—talk about a mixed bag of felonies.

"Perhaps if we can negotiate an . . . arrangement," he concluded.

An arrangement. Sure. She could do that, if it enabled her current mission to go forward to a satisfactory conclusion—which it just might. She sure as hell didn't have the Memphis Sphinx yet, and all signs pointed to the real thing being in this damn town somewhere, despite the fake Ruiz had delivered.

"An arrangement could be negotiated," she said.

"Then you should call your congressman. I can give you the name of someone he can deal with in Illinois, someone who can accept the cash. Chicago or Springfield, his choice."

She shouldn't have been surprised. Given the size of the world's black-market economy, which was huge, every state in the Union was probably knee-deep in *cambistas* shoveling drug money in and out of the country, and her getting the name of one of them from Jimmy Ruiz was not such a bad idea. Half of what she always got for General Grant was somebody's name, but Jimmy Ruiz getting any money simply wasn't going to happen. She could make a phone call, though. She could always make a phone call.

She walked over to the suite's bar to get her cell phone out of her purse, when the room phone rang, its soft beep and discreet blinking giving her a moment's pause.

Present company excluded, to her knowledge, only four people knew where she was: whoever was manning the front desk at the Gran Chaco, General Grant and Dylan Hart, neither of whom would be calling her on the hotel phone, and the man who had put her in the cab in front of the Posada Plaza.

Dammit.

"Excuse me," she said to Ruiz.

Taking her purse with her, she walked past him and the Sphinx to take the call more privately in the suite's bedroom. She closed the heavy doors behind her and threw the bolt before going over to the bedside table to answer the phone.

"Yes?"

"Señora Royal," a softly spoken, very officious man said. "This is Rodrigo at the front desk. A reporter from *The Daily Inquirer* is here to interview you. Should I have the guards pass him through?"

A discomfiting mix of curiosity and alarm held her firmly in place—a reporter? Here in Ciudad del Este? She couldn't possibly have screwed up that badly.

For one, she hadn't had time to screw up that badly. She'd only left Washington late last night. She hadn't even been gone twenty-four hours yet.

"Oh... ah, yes, the interview, I'd almost forgotten," she said, stalling for a moment, thinking. "Tell me, Rodrigo, what is the reporter's name again?"

"Danny Kane, señora. He said to remind you that the interview was arranged through a Señor

Duffy in Denver, Colorado, the United States. The guards have him detained at the main gate. Should I have them pass him through?"

Danny Kane, Dax Killian—the names were fairly obvious, and if they weren't enough to clue her in, Duffy in Denver sealed the deal. Duffy's had been the bar where she and Dax had almost had a date six months ago. So what in the world was he up to, and what did she want to do here? He'd been on his way to see Beranger, hoping to score the Memphis Sphinx, at the same time that she'd been zipping back to the Gran Chaco, hoping to score the same damn thing.

Was it possible that he'd gotten lucky, while she'd tanked? If so, why come to see her?

No, she decided. If he'd gotten the Sphinx, he wouldn't be here—that's what the smart money said.

And if she'd gotten it, she'd be on her way out, too, one way or the other. So the question became—

"Señora?"

No question at all, she decided. If Killian had dragged his butt all the way out to the Gran Chaco to see her after seeing Beranger, she wanted to know why.

She checked her watch. She had at least ten minutes before he would get through the mandatory vehicle search. Explosives—that's what the armed guards were looking for, which said plenty about Ciudad del Este.

"Yes, Rodrigo," she said. "Have the guards pass

him through, and call me when he arrives at the lobby."

"*Sí, señora.*"

She ended the call and dialed another number. When the phone was answered, she keyed in a code and waited until General Grant's machine picked up.

"Hi, Buck. This is Suzi. The party was a disaster. We got raided by the police. No confirmation on the item. Others in attendance were Levi Asher and Esteban Ponce, both of whom were on the guest list you gave me, so the intel is good. The guy who wasn't on the list used to be one of yours, in a manner of speaking, Daniel Axel Killian. Check that out for me, will you? What's Dax Killian doing here? I'll call when I have more."

She hung up the phone and headed into the bathroom, her mission clear—get rid of Jimmy Ruiz and his fake Sphinx, but keep him dangling, in case it turned out she needed him for something, like to help her set up a meeting with Esteban Ponce. She could find Levi Asher on her own. He was never more than a couple of phone calls away. Ponce, on the other hand, could easily be holed up at some local hacienda or estancia, or at someone's big house near the country club.

In the bathroom, she quickly stripped out of her ruined suit and slipped into a pair of olive green cargo pants and a white T-shirt with her shoulder holster fitted snugly over the top. She finished the outfit with a black camp shirt printed with white and yellow orchids to conceal and camouflage the pistol and holster rig. The RFID scanner went into a pocket on her pants, along with her phone, some cash, and her identification. A few other necessities came out of her purse and went into a canvas fanny pack she buckled around her waist. Then she pulled a pair of low-heeled, brown leather boots out of the satchel.

With her boots tied, she was ready to face whatever the night brought on, including Dax Killian, she hoped.

Dinner in Denver?

And in the middle of a top secret mission she'd said yes? Good Lord, she didn't know what in the world either of them had been thinking, or at least she wasn't about to admit to anything, not even the obvious, not here.

A couple minutes later, when she opened the doors from the bedroom to the living room, ready to shoo Jimmy Ruiz out of her suite, she realized she'd been wrong about the night ahead, dead wrong— and Jimmy had not been fast enough.

He'd been shot, over and over again.

There was blood everywhere.

She clenched the doorknob, her knuckles white, her pulse suddenly pounding, her gaze riveted to the body on the floor for a long, endless, gut-wrenching moment before her brain and her training kicked in.

Geezus. Sweet geezus. She took a breath and drew her pistol, and began clearing the suite, just like Superman had taught her, starting with the bar area and moving to the patio. Coming back through the living room, she avoided looking at Jimmy and walked to the main door. It had been left open, and she quickly checked the veranda overlooking the lobby. It was empty. Whoever had killed Ruiz was gone.

They'd also stolen the Sphinx.

Geezus. She looked back toward the body and felt her breath catch in her throat, felt her chest tighten. Jimmy Ruiz had been killed for a hunk of plaster, shot multiple times in the torso—and the whole game had changed.

She started to close the door, then stopped with it still partway open. She couldn't do it, couldn't close herself in a room with a massacred body lying in a pool of blood. Not even Christian Hawkins, Superman, could teach her how to do that.

Good God. A wave of heat rose in her face, and she felt an edge of panic skitter across the base of her brain. Sweat broke out on her upper lip.

She took a breath, then another.

Jimmy Ruiz.

Dead. He was so still, so torn up, lying there with his blood and his insides spilling out of him, his blank eyes staring off into nothing.

He had a gun, and he'd drawn it, but he hadn't used it. The .45 lying next to him on the floor didn't have a silencer, and if he'd gotten a shot off, she would have heard it, even in the bathroom behind two sets of closed doors. The deed had been fast and effective, and she hadn't heard a damn thing, no struggle, no cry for help, no shots, which meant that whoever had killed him had been using a suppressed weapon, and to her that meant one thing—professional killer, somebody who killed as part of their job or for hire, a gangster or somebody's thug, which was just about everyone in the whole goddamn country.

She honest to God didn't think it had been Dax Killian, and yet...and yet she knew he was more than capable of killing as brutally as necessary. He'd been trained for violence of a very high order. He was one of the world's warriors, the one in a hundred who ruled in combat, the one in a hundred who did what had to be done—dispassionately, professionally.

But this wasn't combat.

At least it hadn't been until now.

So help me...so help me, God. Her gun hand started to shake, and her breath grew shorter, and she stood there, second after second, frozen in place, looking at Jimmy, at what was left of him.

It had been a long time since she'd seen a dead body, but not long enough. It would never be long enough.

Oh, Christ, please. She couldn't do this.

A sob left her, and she clamped her mouth shut, holding everything inside. She couldn't afford to fall apart, not here, not now.

A fake Memphis Sphinx.

Somebody was going to be very unhappy when they looked at the bottom of the statue and figured out they'd gotten exactly nothing for their trouble, and that very unhappy person might just decide to come back.

With the realization came a fresh wash of fear, born in panic and running like a streak of wildfire down her spine, all of it leading to one undeniable conclusion: She needed to get the hell out of the Gran Chaco.

CHAPTER FOURTEEN

Dax saw the bad news the minute he pulled into the parking lot of the Gran Chaco—Esteban Ponce's Range Rover parked in front of the hotel's grand entrance with one of his boys standing guard.

Fuck. This was a party, and he most definitely should not have been late. *Goddamn.*

He braked to a stop and pulled the Jeep into first gear. Jimmy Ruiz's Land Cruiser was sitting a few rows over, and he bet that guy wasn't too damn happy to have Ponce show up at his afternoon soiree.

Guaranteed, nobody was going to be happy to see him either. There was nothing like bad odds and a dead body to put him into Don't Fuck with Me mode, and while the Frenchman was going cold on the floor of his shop, Ruiz and Suzi's odds at the Gran Chaco had laid out at two to one against.

He crossed the lot and the hotel's drive, entered the lobby, and headed straight to the front desk.

Halfway there, he changed his mind and his direction, heading instead toward Esteban Ponce. The guy was crossing the lobby in his white sports coat and red silk shirt, with one of his bodyguards and one of the cops from the gallery, complete with carbine. To top the bad scene off, Esteban had Beranger's damn messenger bag slung over his shoulder.

Sonuvabitch. The Sphinx. Somehow, some way, he was getting played on this deal every which way from Sunday, and just who in the hell was Suzi Toussi really working for here? The bulge in the bag was the right size, the right shape, and Esteban had the world's most satisfied expression on his face, the asshole, but Dax was just going to have to let it go.

Because everything that had happened this afternoon had happened way too damn fast to suit him, and he had this little problem. This little doubt eating at him, chewing him up in chunks and spitting him out with the last of his common sense and every step he took, and that little problem was all legs, slinky curves, and auburn hair, tearing him up and whispering her name in his ear—*Suzanna Royale Toussi.*

Truth was, he didn't give a damn who she was working for in Ciudad del Este, a state of affairs he was not going to be analyzing anytime soon. She hadn't gotten out of the middle of this thing, not by a long shot, and he needed to make that happen ASAP. Yeah, that was the smart move, go find the girl, the Sphinx be damned. Sweat out the deal for two years, bust his ass for four months, and then just walk on by and let the damn thing take a hike out the door.

Hell. It wouldn't get far. Dax swore it.

But Suzi, *dammit*, if the Memphis Sphinx was heading one way, and she was heading the other, then chances were that things had not gone her way, and in Ciudad del Este that was a damn good way to get killed.

Another Ponce boy was standing on the wide, curving staircase that led up to the second floor. The guy was talking on his phone, but his attention was on his boss, and as soon as he closed his phone, he hurried the rest of the way down the stairs and caught up to the group.

Second floor, Dax thought, without slowing his stride, his gaze raking the veranda, looking for something...anything. The Gran Chaco had a glass elevator servicing the other seven floors of the hotel, but the courtyard stairs ended at the second-floor veranda. There were only five room doors on that level, on the side opposite the restaurant, and the door in the middle was ajar, which gave Dax a very cold feeling in the pit of his stomach.

Panic was against his nature, so he didn't know what the fuck to call that cold feeling, but it definitely kicked his alert system up to code red.

He kept moving across the courtyard, passing by

Ponce and crew and giving them a casual glance, before he headed up the stairs. When he turned to walk down the veranda, he checked the Brazilians' location. They were heading toward the hotel entrance, their intent clear, and the best Dax could hope for was that they would leave with the prize. He could pick those pieces up later, including the statue and every single one of the bastards if he needed them. He had a license plate and photographs in his computer, and even in the short time that he'd been in his room at the Posada with Suzi, a couple of names had come up on his screen, matching up with the photos, and he'd sent it all to Colonel Hanson, the same way he would those scraps of paper and the lading document.

No, the Brazilians wouldn't be hard to track, no matter how fast or how far they went with the Memphis Sphinx, but what he needed right now, right here, was to get his hands on little Miss Suzi Q—literally hands on, physical contact, under his control, and most importantly, under his protection.

This was not mission protocol, and he didn't give a damn.

At the open door, he walked straight in, drawing his pistol as he entered, his strides long, his weapon up, his gaze cataloguing everything in the suite, searching for targets—clearing, moving—searching for Suzi.

Jimmy Ruiz dead.

Multiple shots to the chest and abdomen.

Dax kept moving, out of the living area, into the bedroom.

Bed a little rumpled, but still made.

Closet door open. Closet empty.

He didn't hit pay dirt until the bathroom.

Peep-toe pumps drying on a towel.

Her suit lying on the vanity next to a brown leather satchel. Makeup, toothpaste, hairbrush.

But no Suzi.

He kept moving, straight through the bedroom to the French doors leading to the outside. On the patio, he stopped, his gaze quartering the gardens and pool area below. The pool was a gem, like an opal sparkling in the sunlight, set down in a jungle of green—and walking quickly through the jungle, following the path paralleling the pool deck, was the gazelle he was hunting.

The relief he felt was damn near overwhelming.

Geezus.

He cleared the stairs and took out after her. She was almost to the bougainvillea-covered wall separating the gardens from the parking lot. Ponce and his boys would be hitting that lot any time now, and whatever had happened in the hotel room, he didn't think it was a good idea for her to cross Ponce's path—unless she really was in cahoots with the Brazilian and not here working for the congressman.

Sure. Splitting up and everybody going their own way after the commission of a crime, especially one as heinous as cold-blooded murder, was always a good idea.

Shit.

He hated being so goddamned clueless.

She stopped for a moment at an ironwork gate in the wall and pulled a ball cap out of a fanny pack clipped around her waist. Her hair went up under the ball cap with a quick twist, and then she was gone. With one step, she passed through the gate and disappeared from view.

Goddammit.

He sped up, pushing himself harder, and ran through the gate in time to see her slip into the driver's side seat of Jimmy Ruiz's Land Cruiser, and he kept running, not stopping for a second.

Gazelle had been an understatement. She was moving with all the precision and efficiency of a cheetah, smooth and sleek, the fastest land animal on earth—but not faster than him.

With his heart pumping up into overdrive, and his adrenaline hitting on fight *and* flight, he came abreast of the Cruiser just as she started to pull out of the parking spot. He slammed his open palm down on the hood of the SUV, giving her only two choices, gas or brake, and brake won.

He didn't second-guess his luck, and he didn't give her a chance to change her mind. He jerked open the passenger door, jumped in, slammed the door shut, and gave a quick glance back behind him. Ponce and crew were just exiting the hotel.

Perfect. There were half a dozen Land Cruisers in the parking lot, and no reason to be noticing this one.

He turned to face her, and her moment of open-mouthed shock wore off the instant she realized who he was—not that recognizing him seemed to improve the situation. She did not look happy to see him.

Tough.

"Y-you—y-you . . ." She stopped cold and pressed her lips together, as if that could stop her trembling.

And the girl was trembling, one hand over her heart, the other clenching the steering wheel.

"Geezus, Dax," she started in again. "You scared the hell out of me."

Well, he was on familiar ground now—a beautiful, angry woman swearing at him.

"Hi," he said, picking up the closest water bottle in the console cup holders. "This yours?"

She tightened her hand on the steering wheel and swallowed a hard breath before answering.

"Yes," she said, still a little breathless, still obviously dealing with a pulse that must have red-lined at a hundred miles an hour.

"Good," he said, unscrewing the lid on the bottle, looking her over a little more carefully—and then he grinned. "Practice will improve your draw."

"No doubt." She lowered her hand from her chest, where she'd been going for the pistol in her shoulder holster, not, as he'd first thought, simply holding her heart in her chest. Another split second of speed, and she could have gotten the drop on him.

"Put the car in park," he said. "Sit back, relax."

"Park?" She didn't sound like she thought that was a very good idea. "I'm not...*p-parking*. I'm leaving."

"Oh, no." He reached over and held the wheel. "Not yet, sweetheart. Give it a minute, let the dust clear, then we'll go."

Her "you're crazy" expression didn't change, not an iota, but after a moment and a short, exasperated sigh, she put the car in park.

"Thank you," he said.

Geezus. There was nothing like running in ninety-nine percent humidity at a hundred degrees to make a guy feel like somebody's old beach towel—and she didn't look much better, with tendrils of hair curling out from under her ball cap and clinging to her cheeks and brow, her pale skin flushed with the heat, even with the air-conditioning blasting away.

Glancing in the side rearview mirror, he lifted the edge of his shirt and used it to wipe off his face. The Brazilians were getting in the Range Rover.

"When Ponce and his guys pull out, we'll switch places. I'll take over the driving."

He saw her look past him, through the passenger side window, toward the entrance where the Range Rover was parked. She would recognize it from the gallery. It was unmistakable with all its bristling antennas, like the guy was the second coming or something.

"Ponce." The name fell from her lips, her face paling even more. She looked plenty scared, despite the pistol and her willingness to draw it, and he couldn't blame her for that. People were dropping like flies on this deal. "D-did you...were you—you must have seen...have—"

He took a quick drink of water and lowered the bottle.

"Yeah, I did," he said, wiping the back of his hand across his mouth. "Were you hurt?"

She squeezed her eyes shut for a second and shook her head, like she was trying not to see whatever image had popped up—and it didn't take a rocket scientist to figure out what that had been. Ruiz had been a mess.

"So how did it go down in there? Ruiz brings you the Sphinx. Ponce crashes the party, kills Ruiz, steals the Sphinx, and you...what? Magically get away?"

"N-no," she said. "I was in the other room, taking a phone call. When I came out, Ruiz was dead, and...and the Sphinx was gone."

"I'm sorry you had to see that." And he was. Terminal ballistics were kind of a specialty of his, of any soldier's, and they were never anything less than gruesome in action.

He handed her the water bottle, and after a second, she took it and took a swallow.

"Cripes," she said softly, letting her gaze drop to her lap. After a long moment, her hand came up to cover her face, and for the space of a breath or two, she sat very still—except for the trembling she didn't quite have under control. "I thought you were going back to the gallery. What are you doing here?"

"I got worried."

"That I'd run off with the Sphinx and aced you out?" She looked up at him from over the top of her fingers.

"No, just about you...in general." Honesty wasn't always his strong suit, but she'd just gotten it. Funny how that wasn't making her look any happier. He understood, though. The truth wasn't making him any damn happier either.

"Where's your car?" she said. "I'll drop you off."

"No." That wasn't the way it was going to work. "We're going to tail Ponce, see where he ends up, then I'm going to stash you back at the Posada and go get the Sphinx."

She made a short, dismissive sound that clearly said he was living in a dreamworld.

He didn't think so, not on his worst day.

"You are not in charge here, Killian."

And they were back to "Killian."

"Yes, I am," he said. "Ruiz was blasted to hell in your hotel room. That makes me in charge of everything and most especially of you, Ms. Toussi."

He was good at being in charge, and if she would just let him do what he was good at, she could save herself a lot of problems.

But count on a woman not to be all that interested in the "problem-solving" business.

"I don't know what you think you need the Memphis Sphinx for—money, personal glory, or—"

"No," he said, cutting her off. "None of those."

"Then what?"

To save the free world, he could have told her, if

he could have figured out a way to say it without sounding delusional. That was the job he'd contracted for with Colonel Hanson this time, the same kind of job he always did for the man, the same kind he'd done when they'd both been in Special Forces. When Dax had realized what Erich Warner was putting on the block in exchange for an occult artifact, he'd known exactly where to go for backup, exactly where the information would do the most good.

"I have my reasons" was all he was able to offer, and that didn't get him very far.

"Reasons?" One of her eyebrows lifted, and she gave him a considering look. "Right, well, you'll have to get in line with your reasons...preferably behind me and my reasons." She sounded pretty sure of herself for someone who looked frazzled right down to her synapses.

Yeah, she was scared, all right. She was sweating with being scared, but she wasn't scared enough to get out of the game—and she should be. She should be begging him for his help. At the very least, she should be running hell-bent for leather for the airport. An art dealer picking up an ancient artifact for a buyer, even a wealthy, influential buyer like Senator Leonard, would not be sticking it out, no way, not after somebody had massacred their connection. She was up to something else, which meant she'd flat-out lied to him about what she was doing in Paraguay. He was impressed. He never told people his business either.

He shifted his attention back to the passenger

side mirror. "Okay. They're pulling out behind us."
He twisted around and looked out the rear window.
"And...they're...heading out of the lot. When I
get out, you scoot over."

"No," she said, giving her head another shake.

No?

She was, he decided, a real piece of work. He
had to admire her grit, but he wasn't going to let it
get her killed.

"We're going after Ponce together now," he said
clearly. "Up until the hard part, and I'll do that
alone."

"Just because we know each other, and have
some mutual friends, doesn't mean—"

"Yes, it does." And it did.

She let out another exasperated sigh and swore
under her breath, way under, but he heard her.
Then she dropped her head down onto the steering
wheel, burying it in the crook of her arms, and after
a moment, mumbled something.

"Excuse me?" He thought he'd heard what she
said, but he didn't want there to be any doubts, not
about this.

"We don't need to bother going after Ponce," she
spoke up a little louder.

"It's no bother." Really. Getting the Sphinx was
pretty much his whole reason for being in
Paraguay.

She gave her head a little shake.

"Ponce doesn't have the Memphis Sphinx," she
said. "Ruiz was selling me a plaster and resin
knockoff."

Aha, and ah, hell, he thought, wincing. That was rough. The guy had been killed for a hunk of plaster—and he had to wonder, really, how long she would have kept that from him.

Damn.

"So where's the real statue?"

From where she was draped over the steering wheel, she rolled her head to one side and caught his gaze.

Yeah, he understood. If he'd known, he'd be there, too, but he didn't, and she didn't, and that only left one place to go.

"Beranger's," he said.

She nodded and slipped her sunglasses out of her shirt pocket and back on her face.

"Beranger's."

CHAPTER FIFTEEN

"Oye, listillo." The words, softly drawled by a sloe-eyed beauty in a red tank top and a miniskirt so small he could have used it for a glove, brought half a grin to Conroy Farrel's face. *Hey, slick.*

Yeah, he was slick all right. Slick enough to get what he'd come for, slick enough to win this game—the way he always won.

Always.

He tossed a blue pill into his mouth and kept walking, carrying his breakdown rifle case and watching the traffic, watching the people, watching the corners of the buildings, watching the windows, watching the rooflines. He always watched. He couldn't not be aware ... so intensely aware of everything. He did it instinctively, viscerally.

He was always watching for someone, and guaranteed, someone was always watching for him.

In any city, anywhere in the world, there'd be

some guy with his picture taped to their dash, someone with his photograph paper-clipped to the top of their "retirement" list, someone with a deep-six computer file for Conroy Farrel, and a whole helluva lot of those guys would be working for a clandestine group of operators buried deep in the Central Intelligence Agency of the United States of America, a private army to the spymaster who ran it. They'd been Con's homeboys.

Ex-homeboys now.

They wanted him dead so badly.

But the guys they'd sent after him had all gone down, leaving him up by four. Hell, you'd think they'd learn. They knew what he was, the assholes.

"Hey, gringo," the next whore said hello. "*Adónde vas?*"

Where was he going? A good question, with one good answer—*Home, sweetheart,* he was always going home.

He'd been traveling these last few months, chasing his nightmares the way other people chased their dreams, and lo and behold, his nightmares had brought him here.

Night was coming on, and the girls and the trash were coming out on the streets of Ciudad del Este. The town was full of movers and shakers and big bad ball breakers. Remy Beranger must have known it, and he should have known better than to let himself get killed.

"Jeemee," the next girl said with a short laugh, standing hipshot next to a blue door. "Jeemee Hendrix."

"*Sí, cariño.*" He smiled back. *Yeah, darlin'*—that was the voodoo child on his T-shirt.

And he kept walking. He'd spent over an hour at Beranger's, almost two, trying to find the Memphis Sphinx, before he'd finally located the prize inside a well-hidden wooden crate. The lading document he'd found in Remy's pocket had been a fake, but he hadn't needed a lading document. He knew who had sent Beranger the Sphinx, and he knew why— bait.

To catch him.

The last of his grin faded.

It was no accident that the Memphis Sphinx had ended up in his backyard. He'd returned to Paraguay four years ago and made Ciudad del Este his home base, and without a doubt, the statue had been deliberately placed here by a knowing hand— a hand compelled by hope, by the hope that it could reach across the waters and the continents and close so very tightly around his throat, tighter and tighter, holding him down and letting him thrash and convulse, to hold him hard to the ground and strangle him, breath by missing breath, until he was dead.

Fat fucking chance. In this game, the spymaster had bet on the wrong boy.

But the bait was good—the Memphis Sphinx to lure Erich Warner to Ciudad del Este, and Erich Warner to lure Conroy Farrel back to his Paraguayan lair. Talk about chumming the waters. It all worked for Con, even with the rest of the high- class riffraff coming out of the woodwork for a chance at the ancient statue. Levi Asher, the fat man in the blue suit, and Suzanna Toussi, the auburn-haired woman, were definitely people of interest. He needed to find out about them. And the guy from the Mercado who'd gone in the back, off the second floor, and hauled her over to the Posada Plaza? The man Con had grabbed inside the gallery hadn't known his name, but the Mercado guy was no street gangster. That guy had been trained to the breaking point. It showed in every move he made. It made him worth watching. But all any of them were ever going to find at the Old Gallery was the crate.

For what they really wanted, they were going to have to come to him now. He could feel the weight of the statue in the backpack hanging from his right shoulder, all four thousand years of it, and beneath his green shirt, he could feel his .45 on one side, and on the other the long, battery-packed composite barrel of his TacVector, ten pounds of Molecular Amplification by Stimulated Emission of Radiation, a maser, a virtual death ray he kept locked on stun, unless he needed it locked into "fry mofo" mode.

In most cases, if he wanted somebody dead, the .45 more than sufficed.

Immortality.

People needed to be more careful with what they wished for, not that he thought anybody was going to get immortality off a hunk of granite and gold with quartz-crystal eyes. No, that's not the way it worked. Immortality, or damn close to it, came in a syringe these days, a lot of syringes and a pile of pretty pills, and nobody with half a goddamn brain would have asked for it, let alone chased it halfway around the world to Ciudad del Este.

Except for Erich Warner, who'd seen the syringe method up close and personal and had decided to bet his everlasting ass on the occult.

Con wished him good luck with that, the best, and given that he hadn't gotten a shot at the bastard this afternoon, he was going to go all out to make sure Herr Warner had a chance to bask in the moonlit glow of the Sphinx's rock-crystal eyes tomorrow night. The German needed protection, desperately, hopelessly, but Warner was looking for it in all the wrong places, and frankly, there were no right places. Nothing could protect him from Con, not the German's whore, no matter how many knives she was wielding or pills she was popping, and not an Egyptian Middle Kingdom statue with a reputation. Quite the opposite. With the Memphis Sphinx baiting Con's trap, Erich Warner was a shoo-in for catch of the day.

"*Hola, chico,*" the next girl in front of the Colony Club said. "*Qué sucede?*" *What's up?*

Con smiled and shook his head. There was nothing about a fourteen-year-old whore in a Little Mermaid T-shirt and too much lipstick that did anything but make him move on.

People thought Ciudad del Este was such a hole—and they were right. But he'd seen worse places. He'd been in worse places, inside and out, and he could thank his enemies for that.

No shortages in that category, including the very cagey bastard in Washington, D.C., who'd sent the Sphinx to Beranger. Without a doubt, he'd stolen it from the Defense Intelligence Agency, because that's where it had been for the last decade or two, a very ballsy move. Con had seen it there, and he was impressed, though he knew damn well that the spymaster wouldn't have done it himself. The guy had a legion of pawns to do his bidding, some with that pitch-black CIA group out to kill Con this year, and last year, and next year, if he didn't get to them first, and other guys with another acronymed group out of the Department of Defense.

Hell, Con had been one of those pawns once, along with a lot of other good men...good men who...

Yeah, *good men who*—that was as far as that thought ever went. He had a lot of thoughts like that, the kind that only went so far and never reached any sort of satisfactory conclusion. He'd learned to let them go, and like everything else, he'd learned it the hard way. It could be his middle name—Conroy Hard Way Farrel.

Lucky for him, most of his thoughts went the distance these days. Yeah, he was a lucky boy, especially this week. He had the Sphinx—which he knew played precisely into the spymaster's grasping hand, to get him out of the shadows and into the open.

Girl Scout at two o'clock, holding up a BMW, all long legs, slim hips, and a serious green-eyed gaze.

"Con." The girl pushed off the Beemer she'd been leaning against and fell in beside him.

"Scout."

"You get him?" Her whole life was wound up in those three words, but she didn't let it show. The question was casual, tossed off.

"He didn't come to the gallery."

She nodded once, not letting her disappointment show either, and that was just like his girl.

"What about the Sphinx?" she asked, easily keeping up with him, matching him stride for stride in a pair of camouflage BDUs and a white T-shirt.

"Got it," he said.

She smiled at his news, a bright, wide grin that always did his heart good. The girl didn't have enough of those.

"So what do we do now?" she asked.

"Does Miller have anything for us yet?" Miller was a guy in Nevada, a wounded vet with spooky computer skills. He could not only hack, he could chop, slice, dice, and, when needed, puree databases, all kinds of databases. Four months ago, when word of the Sphinx had first started hitting the streets, Con had tagged him to find and follow Warner's private jet, to get locations and flight plans.

Scout checked her watch. "Last time I talked to him, he said to give him another hour, and we're close to that now." She pulled a phone out of a cargo pocket on her pants and speed-dialed a number.

The girl was twenty-two, lanky, brilliant, and

tough enough, with café-au-lait skin and a head full of wild dark curls that nothing could tame.

"Scout," she said, after a few moments. "You know what I need.... Yes.... Yes.... Good.... Yes. I'll get back to you on that." She hung up and met his gaze. "Miller's got a lock on Warner's location."

"Where?"

"Just about where you said he'd be, within a couple of hours' range—São Paulo, Brazil."

For a second, Con had to work to contain the sharp thrill that ran through him. The monster was close—but not close enough, and there was no victory until Warner was dead.

"Then he had somebody at Beranger's," he said, handing her his camera from out of his pocket. "Send the last group of photos to Miller along with these names—Levi Asher, the fat man in the blue suit; Suzanna Toussi is the woman; and I've got one unknown, one other guy in the photos. Tell Miller we'll get him a name, and tell him we want dossiers, as much intel as he can find."

"On it," she said, taking the camera and fishing a small cord out of her back pocket.

"Call Jo-Jo, have him find out what he can about every gringo staying at the Posada Plaza—one of them will be our guy—and find out where Asher and Toussi are staying. Those two flew in from somewhere. I want to get to them before they fly back out."

"*De acuerdo.*" *Okay.* She speed-dialed another number. "Jo-Jo, it's Scout. I need you on the horn. Two *norteamericanos* looking to buy some stolen art arrived in the city sometime in the last couple of days, four days at the most, Levi Asher and Suzanna Toussi....Yeah, Toussi. I need to know where they're staying and—"

"Tell Jo-Jo the woman arrived at Beranger's with Jimmy Ruiz," Con interrupted.

Scout nodded.

"The woman was with Jimmy Ruiz today, this afternoon....Yeah, that Ruiz, and...Yeah...You sure?" She shot him a worried look. "*Jesus*...Sure, sure. I'll send you photos. Tell all your guys to be on the lookout—and Jo-Jo...yeah...I need the names and 411 on all the gringos staying at the Posada....Yeah."

"What?" he asked, when she ended the call.

"Ruiz," she said, using the cord to connect her phone to his camera. "He's dead. Multiple gunshot wounds in a suite at the Gran Chaco. The room was registered to a Suzanna Royal."

Shit.

"This is getting interesting, Con," she said.

Oh, hell yeah.

"Where's the woman now?"

"Not at the Gran Chaco, but the cops are there and asking the same question." With half a dozen keystrokes, she started downloading the photos and sending them to Miller and Jo-Jo.

"Have Jo-Jo check the Posada for her. If she's there, or shows up anywhere on his radar, tell him to put somebody on her and to call *inmediatamente*."

"Roger that." She watched the screen on her

phone, and after a couple of seconds passed, she hit a few more keys. "Miller said the information cost him double the usual price, and he wants three times the agreed-upon amount."

Two times the cost meant three times the price? Sure, that made sense.

"What do you think?" he asked.

"I think his girlfriend is pregnant again and—"

"And that makes what, four? Five kids?" he interrupted.

"Five, and Paul Detty, that jerk, screwed him on his last deal, and I think we could buy a lot of Miller's loyalty right now for just a few more dollars."

Con thought it over for a second, but no longer. It was that kind of game, and Miller actually had quite a bit of loyalty that could be bought for not very damn much cash, and Scout wasn't really asking. She knew the score on all their deals, sometimes better than he did, especially with the stringers, and she had a soft spot for Miller's brood of sniveling brats.

Christ. Scout had a soft spot for every sniveling brat on the planet—and he had a soft spot for Scout. If he had a sniveling brat, she was it.

And if that wild-ass boy on Con's payroll who was chasing her from one side of the globe to the other didn't watch himself, Con was going to put his butt in a sling. Scout could do better than some red-haired, freckle-faced heathen with more balls than brains. Jack Traeger was running on pure testosterone, which was fine on the job, but not when it came to Scout.

"Your call," he said to her, and saw a small smile of satisfaction curve her lips. Pretty soon, she'd be the one giving the orders. He could see the writing on the wall. He could see a lot of writing on the wall, and sometimes it unnerved him, especially when it concerned her and their mission.

"Are you sure you want to do this?" he asked. It wasn't too late for her to walk away. Her part of the mission had only one target, Erich Warner. But the mission had gotten complicated, and in Con's experience, each added layer of complication increased the possibility of failure, and failure was a dangerous commodity.

The look she gave him would have quelled a lesser man.

"Don't go there, Con," she said. "I've got as much right to this as you do . . . almost."

Yeah, but the almost was a big one. He was locked in, every chemical in his body irrevocably changed by the drugs he'd been given—and the scars, hell, from the looks of them, he was damn lucky to even be alive. As bugged as he sometimes got with his memory situation, he was glad he couldn't remember being tortured, but he'd been cut, that was for damn sure, deep and often. Given the array of "tools" available to the good doctors in Bangkok, it didn't take much figuring to figure out who'd carved him up.

Scout had not been touched by the brutality or the drugs, but her father had been in that charnel house in Bangkok with him, and the Girl Scout's father had not made it out alive.

"So how does it look?" she asked, slanting him a curious glance. "Cool? Like it's magic or something?"

"Really cool," he said and grinned. At heart, Scout was still a kid, and to the best of his ability, he tried to keep it that way. "But no magic."

"It's worth a fortune, though, right?"

"Millions, easy." To everyone else. For Con, the statue had only one value, the same value it had to the spymaster—bait. Keep it or lose it—he didn't care, not after Erich Warner was dead, and to that end, he wanted to get the statue to *Costa del Rey,* King's Coast, the compound he'd taken over upriver. Given the tricky time frame on the transference of immortality—brief and nonnegotiable with the rise of the full moon at sunset, with all necessary astral conjunctions in place, the whole shebang destined to happen in just a little over twenty-four hours—Warner had to have his sights locked onto Ciudad del Este and be waiting for the call.

Con was going to do his damnedest to oblige.

It wasn't revenge. It was justice. Dr. Souk was dead, Tony Royce, Con's initial contact into the blackest operations ever run out of the underbelly of the U.S. government, the same, long dead. Scout had only one name left on her Christmas list— Erich Warner, the man who had supported and nurtured Dr. Souk's demented mind and twisted science. The man who'd turned Souk's research and experiments into a worldwide, multimillion-dollar industry in psychopharmaceuticals, the kind of drugs Con couldn't live without. None of the pills made him high. They just kept him alive, and his life was only one of thousands Warner had touched and destroyed. The German's operations extended far beyond what had gone on in Bangkok. The man had constructed an empire of misery and suffering, of dragging people under with the dirtiest and darkest of crimes—and someone had to hold him accountable. Someone had to stop him.

If the world needed a defender, a guardian angel to stand between it and hell, it was Warner's dark deeds that had made one, and so the man would be killed by his own creation. Scout saw a hard, karmic balance in the completion of such a brutal circle.

Con only saw necessity.

CHAPTER SIXTEEN

Traffico jammo at the guardhouse with the main exit gate closed. *Hell,* Dax thought. This sucked.

Even worse, it was dangerous.

Things had been crawling along, up until about thirty seconds ago, when the gate had come down, and in less time than it took to say "sonuvabitch," a traffic jam had been born, everyone jamming up, getting cattywampus on the road, ready to push through, practically parking on top of one another. Some people were getting out of their cars, walking, talking, starting to get in the guards' way, slowing things down even more.

Geezus.

He and Suzi weren't nearly far enough behind Esteban Ponce's Range Rover, not for this kind of crap. It was eight or so cars ahead of them, bristling with antennas, unmistakable, and they had another dozen piled up behind them.

"This could get dicey." And it wasn't just Ponce. Something had happened to get that gate closed off, to change their protocols, and the biggest thing he could think of was the bloody corpse in room 205. Someone had found it and the cops had been called. "We need to change places—discreetly."

She immediately undid her seat belt and started over the console, for once not arguing. He was appropriately grateful. If they needed to make an escape, he needed to be the one driving—that is, if he survived the seat exchange.

Good God. In a matter of seconds, she went from being the untouchably divine Ms. Suzanna Royale Toussi, to being Suzi, Girl on Top. And for the record, even sweaty and wrung out, she was so drop-dead gorgeous, it almost defied description. Nobody looked like her in real life, except Suzi Toussi, sleek and sophisticated, her makeup so bare it was barely there, her skin pure peaches and cream. The softness of her cheek, the sweet, elegant lines of her face, the winged arches of her eyebrows, every angle and curve on her conspiring to create beauty.

Fortunately, he was a very cool guy who was more than able to keep a level head in the proximity of female physical perfection.

Right.

"Excuse me," she said, using his shoulder to steady herself.

"S'okay." *Geezus.*

"*Oh* . . . sorry." She kept moving over him, around him, next to him.

"Yeah, uh . . ." Fine, everything was fine, but her hair was brushing his cheek, and the inside of her arm was up against his neck, and . . .

"If you'll—"

"Yeah, right." She was right. He needed to slip out from under her.

He managed, somehow, to maneuver into the driver's seat, he hoped without giving himself away—that he'd kinda stopped breathing there for a second or two to keep from inhaling her.

But he was okay now. All systems go.

Right.

And then his phone rang.

He took a look at the number, and hell, he didn't dare not pick up.

"Yes," he said into the receiver.

"I have a friend in Paraguay," Erich Warner said. "A few miles from your location, and he is offering his services, to send armed men into Ciudad del Este to help secure the Sphinx, if you are having trouble meeting my expectations."

Yeah, yeah, the guy was just full of fricking expectations, the biggest turning out to be almost impossible. One damn statue, Dax had thought four months ago when Warner had set out the bait—one damn statue in exchange for the kind of information agencies of the U.S. government spent months and years searching out.

"No, sir, that won't be necessary." That's the last damn thing he needed, a private army spooking everybody into next week. "We should stick to the plan. The statue is here, in the city, and I have the deal set. When I have it in my hands, I'll call for the transfer of funds. Do you want me to use this number?"

"When you have the Sphinx, yes."

And that was the whole damn trick, now, wasn't it?

"Yes, sir."

"Oh, hell," Suzi said softly, leaning forward in her seat, her gaze fixed out the windshield.

Oh, crap.

"Who is that?" Warner asked, his voice sharp, and just the thought of the bastard knowing about Suzi made Dax's blood run cold. "What's her name?"

"Some girl. Hey, honey, what's your name?" he asked, then briefly put his finger to his lips, warning her not to speak.

He waited a beat.

"She says for ten thousand guaranis I can call her *Azúcar,* Sugar."

And he still wasn't happy. *Dammit.* Not about her speaking, not about Warner hearing her, and for sure as hell not about what was happening up ahead. Ponce's guys were piling out of the Range Rover, burly and armed.

"Don't make any mistakes, Killian. I'm not in the mood."

Finally, he and Erich Warner had something in common. Dax wasn't in the mood for any mistakes either.

"Yes, sir." And not for the first time, it crossed his mind that there were fifty good ways to kill the bastard—and maybe a hundred good ways to use him, if Dax could keep his hands in the cookie jar. Colonel Hanson had suggested very strongly that he should try. If Warner's information turned out to be operable, if there was a sleeper cell in Texas with a viable plan for an act of terrorism, and if they were stopped because of what Dax was able to do in Ciudad del Este—then it was no contest. Erich Warner would live to fight another day. As a matter of fact, Colonel Hanson had strongly suggested that Dax make it so. Hanson wanted to mine the vein for as long as possible.

"I'll expect your call soon, very soon." It was a threat.

When the call disconnected, Dax slipped his phone back into his pocket, and all the while, he watched the action up ahead.

There was plenty—with drawn guns to add to the suspense.

"Oh, hell," she said again, and *oh, hell* was right.

Ponce's bought cop was striding up toward the guardhouse, undoubtedly to throw his weight around and get Ponce's car through the gate, the rest of the idiots trapped at a standstill on the road be damned.

Two of the Brazilian's goons were walking down the haphazard line of cars, gesturing and yelling, telling everyone to move, move, move. *Vamos!* Get out of the way. Back off. Make room for the most important and expensive Range Rover to turn around.

One way or the other, Esteban Ponce wanted out of this roadblock.

For Dax, it was a classic rock and a hard place—start doing the bumper car thing to get out of there, too, and draw a lot of unwanted attention. Or stay put and take the chance that these guys wouldn't recognize Suzi from earlier at Beranger's.

It took him about a tenth of a second to calculate the odds on a guy not remembering Suzi. He cranked the wheel hard and threw the Land Cruiser into reverse.

"Oh, hell," she said again, and he didn't doubt her for a moment.

He looked back up the line of cars, and Esteban Ponce himself was getting out with the Sphinx in his hand, looking extremely agitated and very unhappy. The driver who got out with him appeared to be trying to calm him down, but the spoiled youngest son of Arturo Ponce refused to be consoled. He was throwing a fit, a temper tantrum, and any second, he was going to break something. Dax could see it coming.

Holding the Sphinx by the top, Ponce shoved the bottom of the statue in the driver's face, his other arm swinging wildly.

"Is there something wrong with the bottom of the statue?"

"That's where the plaster shows through," she said, both of them watching damn near breathlessly through the windshield. Sunlight was glinting on the fake creature's eyes. The gold mane was catching the light. From a distance, the thing looked good.

"Then this is it," he said.

"I think so."

In the next moment, it was a done deal. With a final grand gesture of unprecedented, undeserved, monumental disappointment, Ponce smashed the statue to the ground.

They couldn't see what happened to it, but the way Ponce was kicking around at the road, and still waving his arms about, and practically frothing at the mouth, Dax had a good idea that the thing had been smashed into smithereens.

"You're sure that was a fake."

"Absolutely positive. One hundred percent."

"Then we're out of here." Whatever it took.

And it was going to take a lot.

He stepped on the gas and bumped into the car behind him, moving it about six inches. Then he cranked the wheel hard to the left and bumped into the car in front of him.

He noticed Ponce's goons notice the Land Cruiser.

"The next time you're coming up on a guard-house, Sugar, or really, anytime, even just for a stoplight"—he cranked right and stepped on the gas again, bumped into the car behind him, heard all the cussing going on, and just kept gunning the motor, *really* moving the car behind him—"it's a good idea to keep enough distance between you and the car in front of you that you can see their tires."

"I'll remember that."

"Good girl."

He cranked left one more time, stepped on the gas, took the Cruiser over the median, into the southbound lane, and headed back to the Gran Chaco.

"I think there's another road out of here," he said, remembering the maps of the city he'd downloaded and studied.

"One of the service roads on the golf course goes all the way down to the river. If you follow it long enough, it'll empty out on Calle Palma." *Palm Street.*

Okay, he was impressed.

"Ponce is going to head back to Beranger's, same as us," she said, turning in her seat and looking out the back windshield.

He heard it, too, the sound of sirens approaching from the north. Hell.

"We'll never get ahead of him taking the river road," she said. "Do you hear those sirens?"

"Yeah, and we don't need to get ahead of him. We just need to get in place. He can have first shot at Beranger's. If he walks out of there with anything, I'll go after it." He speeded up—quite a bit. "How far is this service road into the golf course?"

She looked out each side window. "About a quarter mile."

He speeded up a helluva lot more. The best way for this to work would be to get off the road before the cops even knew they were on it.

He was hoping a hundred miles an hour for a quarter mile would do the trick.

"Do you have a visual?" he asked, somewhat surprised by the quick pickup and good handling of the Cruiser. He wasn't an SUV kind of guy, but this thing was doing its job.

"No. We're still clear."

There was no median this far from the guardhouse, so when he saw the smudge of a dirt road peeking out of the heavy vegetation on the east side of the pavement, he slowed down just enough to take the turn without rolling the vehicle—which was quite a bit of slowing down.

Thirty yards in, he slowed down even more, and at the edge of the golf course, where the trees ended, he came to a stop. They would cross after the cops went by.

It didn't take long, about half a minute, before the sirens crested and started to wane, the police passing them on their way to the Gran Chaco.

So, this was perfect. They'd escaped the cops. Ponce was very unlikely to turn around and virtually follow the police to the scene of where he and his men had committed murder. Even in Ciudad del Este, that was bound to go over very poorly. Of course, the cops would be looking for Suzi. Everyone was going to be looking for Suzi, and all of them for no good reason.

He needed to get her out of this country, and he needed to keep her with him until he could do it.

Yeah, that's the way it was going to be from here

on out, him and Suzi Q joined at the hip, until he put her on a plane, whether she liked it or not.

And yeah, he knew exactly where he was headed with the whole joined-at-the-hip plan—trouble.

Which didn't stop him from making his play.

"We need to cut a deal, you and I, together."

She buried her head in her arms on the dash and swore under her breath, way under, but he heard her, and he waited until he got what he wanted.

"Fifty-fifty," the word finally came out.

"Sure. Great. I can work with that." Not really. She was lying, but he didn't care. He was lying, too. He didn't need a deal with her to get what he wanted. He just somehow, in a very real macho caveman way, needed to be in charge of her for a while, until she really did leave the country.

It wasn't about sex.

Not all of it. Really. Not even most of it.

It was more about... *more about*...

He let his gaze drift up the length of her to where she was draped over the dash like she didn't have an ounce of energy or gumption left. No, it really wasn't about sex. The sun was coming in through the windshield, dappled with the shadows of the palm fronds above them, dappling her. She had a line of sweat running down her side from under her arm, and one down the middle of her back, turning her black shirt even darker. The telltale print of her holster showed across her shoulders in another damp trail, and he could see the grip of a semi-automatic pistol where her shirt had been pushed back, a Beretta M9 to be exact, a 9mm, and yes, he recognized it just by the frame and magazine.

She actually looked kind of tough, wearing a pair of lace-up boots and tactical pants with cargo pockets, like maybe she could kick a little butt. Of course, she'd be kicking it in a silk camp shirt and butter-soft Italian leather boots, so soft the tops folded down. Her tactical pants weren't heavy cotton twill like his, either. They looked like a linen and cotton blend, expensive, tailored to within an inch of their lives for some long-legged, curvy-hipped, small-waisted, all-girl female like Suzi Q . . . Sugar . . . *Shu-gah*.

Sweet.

Her hair was coming out of her Spa Monterey ball cap in kind of a tangle, but he could still see the nape of her neck—and when he did, he knew that was it. The whole caveman thing was about the nape of her neck, the sheer tenderness of that soft expanse of satiny skin, the silken strands of auburn hair curled damply across it, the delicacy of her nape, the vulnerability of it.

The way he wanted to get his mouth on it.

Yeah, that was the situation—the kiss-the-back-of-Suzi-Toussi's-neck situation. Talk about tough.

Tough luck, because he sure as hell wasn't going to be fulfilling that little fantasy anytime soon.

As if to prove his point, off in the distance, coming from the north, he heard the rise and fall of police sirens again.

Suzi lifted her head at the sound, her eyes meeting his across the console and the bucket seats.

"More cops?"

"Oh, yeah," he said. "Gang-style slaying at the Gran Chaco is going to trump a lot of street crime. It doesn't even matter that the dead guy is Jimmy Ruiz. What matters is that he was killed in the *gringa*'s room."

Even behind her amber tinted glasses, he could see the sudden edge of panic in her gaze, and man, did he understand. In about ten minutes or less, she was going to own the top slot on the cops' suspect list, and ending up in a Paraguayan prison was simply not on the menu—ever.

Then she went for the slam dunk. For the barest instant, as their gazes met, she did something so unexpected, so ingenuous, so purely female, that all he could think was *Fuck it.* She bit her lower lip, her teeth gently pressing into that plump curve of super soft, cinnamon-lipstick-slicked skin—and it was a done deal.

The whole thing was over.

Without another thought, he leaned across the Land Cruiser and took her mouth with his, his hand sliding around the back of her neck, over her soft, satiny nape, his fingers tunneling up into her hair, holding her, his tongue sliding into the warm, honeyed depths of her mouth.

And sliding again, exploring, taking her with a kiss, again and again, holding her tighter, kissing her harder, his heart starting to pound—because she let him. She more than let him. *Geezus*, for such a piece of work, she was so sweet, turning into him, her lips so soft, her tongue sliding over his teeth. She made a small sound deep in her throat, and he knew he was in trouble, hands down, no holds barred—and he loved it, the heated thrill of it, the chase, anticipating the hot, hot sex of discovering a woman for the first time, the excitement of taking her clothes off—the way he wanted to take Suzi's clothes off and just get into her.

Yeah.

He slanted his mouth over hers more fully, taking more of her, taking everything he could get, all the sweet surrender and every soft sigh.

Oh, yeah.

She was so wonderfully dangerous, turning him on. Six months of nonstop fantasizing had brought him to this, their first kiss and wanting to just "do it" and keep on "doing it" in the front seat of a stolen Land Cruiser, with a dead body behind them, a dead body ahead of them, the cops getting closer, second after second, and him getting hard.

Perfect.

Oh, God, his kiss.

Suzi just gave herself up to it, to the taste and the heat of it. He was rock solid up against her, the muscles in his arms flexing around her, the gentle strength of his hand on the back of her neck, the sensual thrill of having his tongue pushing into her mouth again and again, the erotic rhythm of it melting her brain. He was insistent and tender at the same time, turning her on with every move of his lips over hers, with every thrust into her mouth, making her want to give him more.

Oh, God, she usually had more sense.

And she wasn't fooling herself. This didn't have anything to do with being scared half to death by Jimmy Ruiz getting massacred in her room or by the police descending on the hotel.

This was all about Killian the Konqueror, "Konk" to the guys with their boots on the ground, or sometimes K.C., to those who could spell, she guessed. Rumor had it that it was tattooed on his ass in Chinese—"Conqueror," his nom de guerre, his war name.

God, she believed it. There was enough "boy" left in the Boy Scout to pull a stunt like that. And so help her, she wanted to find out, to get him out of his clothes and just get so damn close to him.

She slid her fingers up into his hair and kissed him like her life depended on it, slow and deep, teasing him with her tongue, breathing him in and tasting him—and it was all so impossibly good, so impossible.

"Konk"—geezus, who in the world let themselves be called Konk?

She sighed and moved against him, pressing herself against his chest. God, he was built like a slab of granite, and she loved it, and yes, she knew what kind of guy let himself be called Konk, the kind of guy who'd earned the name the hard way from the kind of guys who'd been up there on the ridge with him in Afghanistan seven years ago and innumerable times since.

She'd had to dig deep for that information, for the story of the ambush, of the overwhelming enemy forces, and of the deeds that had brought him and his guys home that long-ago night. Dax's cousin Esmee Ramos didn't have access to those facts, but her husband, Johnny, did, and so did the other SDF guys. They knew Dax was a legend in the wasteland, and Johnny hadn't been shy about telling that story and all the others. Before joining SDF, Johnny had been a U.S. Army Ranger, one of the bad boys who hoped to end up with the big bad boys like Dax and the A teams.

But this kiss... this kiss was crazy and had no place to go.

No place, she told herself.

Off in the distance, but getting closer at an accelerating rate of speed, the wail of sirens cut through the air—trouble and nothing but, just like Daniel Axel Killian, and heading their way.

Somebody needed to show an ounce of sense, and considering the way his hand was sliding up her side and heading toward her breasts, she figured if there was going to be any sense in this front seat, it was going to have to come from her.

Damn.

With a monumental effort, because he tasted and felt so good, and because it had been so, so long since she'd been kissed, she broke away from him—and there they sat, still wrapped up so close, their noses touching, his breath soft on her skin, the temperature in the Land Cruiser heading for the deep freeze with the air conditioner going full blast, and her still absolutely melting inside.

"Hey," he said, his voice rough.

Yeah, that was about all she had left, too.

"Hey." She needed her head examined, and they were still so damn close, one of his hands still in her hair, rubbing the back of her neck, the other no more than an inch away from her breast, their foreheads still touching.

Behind them, the second flank of police cars screamed by, their sirens descending in the other direction.

"We need to . . ."

"Yeah." The quicker the better, and still she didn't move away from him.

Who the hell was he to affect her this way? Some guy who'd walked into the Toussi Gallery one night and looked too good to be true. Some guy who'd smiled at her and with one unabashed, come-on curve of his mouth had told her that he knew all about her, everything—and for a moment, she'd believed that he had.

But he didn't. No one did, except for Buck, and probably Hawkins, maybe Dylan, her family, and the few people who had been involved. An accident, it had been termed, and rightly so, a violent accident covered up by the money and power of one of Australia's most prominent families, the records sealed, the rumors squelched, the story barely heard. The Weymouth clan was synonymous with the Northern Territory, be it cattle stations, gold, or uranium, and by their choice, a life had been nearly wiped off the slate of the world, nearly forgotten.

Nearly, but not quite.

Suzi would never forget. She couldn't, no matter how many years passed.

She pulled away from him and was so disappointed by the effort it took. She was usually smarter. He was an unnecessary complication, the competition, the guy to beat, not the guy to be kissing.

"That was a mistake," she said. Unacceptable. Dangerous territory.

"Yeah."

"We have a job to do." She had unfinished business, and she couldn't afford to fail, not in the work she did for Buck, and never again in the work she did in Eastern Europe. She wasn't trying to save the world, or even every poor woman who fell into prostitution—but the younger girls, the ones who were trafficked from the U.S. to the Balkans, the Czech Republic, and the one she'd found in Ukraine, in Odessa on the Black Sea—with the SDF crew's help, and Buck Grant's documents, she'd returned six of those girls, almost seven.

It was the "almost" that kept her going. The "almost" she hadn't forgiven herself for. The last thing she'd needed was another black mark on her soul, but there it was now, and like the first one, it had a sweet name—Lily Anne Thompson, but at least she could voice that name. The other one, the one she felt with every breath, that one she couldn't speak.

Hell, sometimes she wondered if she was going

to live long enough to make up for her failings and wash away her sins.

"Which one next, Warner?"

Inside the luxury cabin of his Learjet, flying high over the western edge of southern Brazil, Erich Warner closed his SAT phone and returned to watching his mistress roll half a dozen pretty pills around a small silver bowl—blue, red, green, orange, yellow, purple, all gelcaps, bright and shiny.

She was fascinated by her pills, as well she should be. He'd only let her go a minute too long without medication half a dozen times. Each time had been a punishment, a lesson taught. Each time had been a lesson learned.

Sometimes he wondered if he would ever let her go longer. Two minutes, possibly. The pain, he knew, was excruciating. He'd spent enough time in Dr. Souk's lab to have seen human suffering on a truly epic scale—not in quantity, but epic in the quality and the depthless wonder of the suffering.

Pain had been Dr. Souk's stock in trade. No mere torturer, he'd been a medical genius, a chemist, and Shoko was one of his finer creations. Erich knew why she cut people to ribbons, literally, with her knives. She was sick. Her mind twisted by the pain of her countless near deaths and rebirths in Souk's laboratory.

Poor, bitter little thing. He'd been known to give her prizes as well as punishments, and today, he'd decided, would be a prize day. Maybe his generosity would bring him luck. His faith in Killian was being tested.

Tonight, the man had said. He'd have the Memphis Sphinx tonight.

If he didn't, Dallas, Texas, was in for a very bloody Monday morning the first week in April. Heroin made for predictable bedfellows, drug lords and warlords, and nobody had more heroin to transport than a man who was both, Akram Jamal in southern Paktika, Afghanistan. For the favor of piggybacking one of the Afghan's loads into Marseilles in one of Erich's cargo ships, and for facilitating the land transportation of a shipment of surface-to-air missiles, SAMs, across Tajikistan, Jamal had given him the name of a restless Saudi deep in the heart of Texas.

Erich had more power and money than half the countries he did business in, and yet neither power nor money was enough to save him from Souk's shadow beast. The creature had an uncanny ability to reach into Erich's business and make his presence known. Two of Jamal's lieutenants had been killed during the transport of the surface-to-air missiles, and the missiles had arrived in Jamal's warehouse irreparably disabled. Erich hadn't supplied the missiles. He'd only transported them—and yet it was clear to him that the shadow beast had been involved. He left things for Erich, marks. There had been a mark on one of the SAM crates—XT7, Dr. Souk's code for a particularly effective drug he'd created. It was the only mark Erich had needed to know the beast had been involved. Always it was like this, the silent, evasive threat of him. The creature lurking around Erich's deals, breathing on them, ruining them, then disappearing for months.

He was alive, he knew too much, and Erich had not been able to stop him in any way. The situation was untenable, and the solution was the Sphinx. With the shield of immortality upon him, he could track the beast down and kill him—or bring him to heel.

The thought was a recurring one and never failed to make his blood race, to control that much power, to chain the beast to him the way he'd chained Shoko.

"The woman, Warner," Shoko said, looking up at him from where she sat at his feet, gently rolling her pills around and around in the silver bowl, the iguana resting along her hip and thigh. "I heard her on the phone, while you were talking with Killian."

"What about her?" As if he didn't know.

"I want her, Warner. I told you there was a woman, and I want her for my own. No interference."

"So be it," he said, granting the unknown "Sugar" a death unlike anything she ever could have imagined.

Shoko smiled, and that truly was a lovely sight.

"Purple, my dear," he said, and she all but purred, taking the purple pill out of the bowl and putting it in her pocket for later, when she needed it.

For the next few hours, she was free of him, free to roam as she willed, and he had no doubt that when they landed, some poor sap in Ciudad del Este would pay for her freedom with his life.

CHAPTER SEVENTEEN

Stakeout—Suzi had never been on a stakeout, but surprisingly, the scene in front of her was very familiar—half a dozen prostitutes congregating on their strip of turf in front of Galeria Viejo, gearing up for the night shift.

"Coffee?" Dax asked, offering his cup.

She'd opted for bottled water when he'd made his recon stroll past the Old Gallery and then slipped into a dive called El Mercado for a few supplies, but a little coffee wasn't a bad idea. She'd stayed in the Land Cruiser, parked a ways down the street, but in a place where they had full view of the main door and Ponce's Range Rover parked out front.

"Thanks." She took the cup and held it to her mouth, blowing first before taking a sip. "So what do you think? Is that the world's oldest profession?"

"Nah," he said. "War is the world's oldest profession, by a long shot, and then comes tax collecting, and *then* the trick turners showed up to give everybody some relief from the other two."

She grinned, and when he glanced over, he did, too.

Yes, sir, that was them, just a couple of fun-loving kids with murder and mayhem behind them, and a four-thousand-year-old occult statue in front of them—hopefully.

Ponce hadn't even left a guard on the Range Rover. All five of his crew, himself included, were in the gallery. Suzi almost hoped he did find it. At least they'd know where it was then, and she didn't doubt that Dylan and the boys could steal it back, maybe even before Dax could get his hands on it.

"What are his chances, you think, of them finding anything in there?"

"Slim to none, about the same as ours. The place is really torn up inside. As a matter of fact, you might want to reconsider this plan and let me just take you to the airport." He held a cookie out for her, from out of a bag he'd bought, and she took it.

They'd been an hour on the river road, getting back into town, and were an hour into watching the gallery, and that was the third or fourth time he'd suggested taking her to the airport.

"No," she said. "I need to get inside, look around for myself."

She still had the scanner, her ace in the hole, and yes, he was bound to notice when she pulled it out, but until she was in the gallery, she was keeping her technical advantage to herself.

He had caveman tendencies. It wouldn't be beyond him to just take the damn scanner and try to ship her out. He wouldn't get far with getting rid of her, but she could save them both the wear and tear of him finding that out by just keeping her secret to herself.

"Senator Leonard must be paying you one helluva commission."

"Top-notch," she agreed.

"Bull," he said.

"Whatever."

He held an open bag of chips out, and she reached in and got a handful.

Sharing coffee, eating chips and cookies, they both watched the gallery and the Range Rover and the whores.

"I could pay you more."

That's all he said, sitting over there dangling bait, and yes, she knew he could. General Grant was paying her twenty plus tactical support, and Dax had both those and more to offer. He'd done well in his business, whatever his business was—which she was guessing was more than the art-recovery-type investigations he'd done with Esmee. The guy had money.

Without biting on his offer, she handed the coffee back to him and reached for her bottle of water.

"And here we go," he said, leaning slightly forward in his seat, picking up the binoculars she'd donated to the cause.

Ponce and his boys were coming out.

She looked at each man, carefully cataloguing what she saw, and knew he was doing the same. Neither one of them said a word, until the Range Rover pulled away from the gallery and drove off.

He lowered the binoculars and looked over at her. "What did you get?"

"Nothing." She shook her head.

"Nothing," he agreed. "They came out empty-handed. Let's go."

Three minutes later, back in the alley behind Beranger's, Dax started prying open the makeshift security gate someone had attached to the Old Gallery's delivery door. The sun was going down, the alley was still piled with garbage, and Suzi, Dax noticed, was taking a pen-shaped object out of her fanny pack. After getting a look at it, he lifted his gaze to her face.

Geezus, she was beautiful. Beautiful and, he was sure, guilty as hell—of something, standing there holding the small piece of equipment like it was a wand, pen-shaped, yes, but with a readout display and a couple of pressure switches.

"What is that?" he asked, leaning into the length of rebar he was using as a lever on the iron bars. Walking in the front door, where Ponce and his men had come out, would have been nominally easier, but Suzi probably had the top spot on Ciudad del Este's Most Wanted list for another couple of hours at least. By midnight, for certain, some other horrendous crime, or probably half a dozen, would have taken place and knocked her into yesterday's old news. Until then, parading her through the lineup of Colony Club whores and pimps taking over the block and congregating in front of the gallery was not in their best interest, and besides, it just wasn't all that difficult to get into Beranger's Old Gallery.

"Well, actually," the beautiful redhead said, "it's a scanner... for an, uh, RFID tag."

To her credit, she dropped that bomb without stumbling around too much, and it was one helluva bomb. Right. A scanner.

He stopped with the rebar in his hands, just holding it between the bars of the gate, and looked at her.

Looked at her hard.

"You've been holding out on me."

"A little," she admitted.

Sonuva-gee-fricking-bitch. There was only one thing in Beranger's damn gallery worth tagging with a radio frequency identification chip, the Memphis Sphinx, and sure as hell that was the only damn thing she was searching for in this dump—and the lucky girl just happened to have a scanner for it in her pocket?

Oh, baby, that was a huge can of worms.

"So where's the chip?" As if he didn't know.

"On the Sphinx."

Yeah, she said it with a straight face.

"Excellent. Great." He pushed on the rebar again, giving it his all, and the rusted-out lock on the gate gave in and busted apart. "So we'll be able to find this thing in record time and get the hell back out of here, right?"

Her answer to that was an elongated pause.

"Theoretically," she finally said.

Theoretically.

Absofuckinglutely amazing, and geezus, what a cool piece of action she really was—all this time, in possession of a freaking scanner to pick up the signal off a chip someone had adhered to or embedded in the statue.

And wasn't that suddenly the biggest mystery in the whole damn day—who?

No art dealer, no antiquities smuggler, that was for damn sure, and he was betting no senator from Illinois either. He'd known she was lying about a few things, but the sheer scope of her subterfuge had just hit cosmic proportions.

And she'd been good at it, damn good. She made him look like an amateur. A smart guy would pay attention to a fact like that, but somehow, he knew he'd been smarter earlier in the day, before she'd shown up—and wasn't that just the damn way of it.

He pulled a pair of lockpicks out of his shirt pocket and went to work on the main delivery door.

"Theoretically?" he repeated. "What's the matter? Doesn't it work?"

"I'm not sure. I got a hit when I was in here with Remy," she said, and he heard her unzip something—and hell, yes, that was enough to get him to turn around and look.

"Do you want some light on that?" She was pulling a flashlight out of her fanny pack.

Fanny pack, not her pants. Right. He needed his head examined—and he was starting to get real impressed with her kit, what she'd brought, and what she'd not. Everything she'd pulled out had been damn useful.

"Yes." *Geezus.* "A hit?" And he was filing that under the day's nearly empty category called "Good News," about a hundred steps down from where he'd filed "First Kiss."

She turned the flashlight on and held the beam on the door's lock while he slid the picks into the mechanism.

"More like half a hit," she said. "We were in his Chapel Room, at the bottom of the stairs where you were on the second floor. I thought the scanner was malfunctioning, that it didn't work, and then just as the cops were coming in, it signaled a GPS location."

"GPS," he repeated, and felt the locking mechanism release.

She nodded.

And he swore.

RFID scanners, chips, and GPS, hell, she was light-years ahead of him on this deal.

He opened the door and then just stopped for a second, waiting for the first wave of heat and stench to wash over him. It was bad, old Remy cooking in the heat for a few hours, and if Suzi didn't lose her lunch in the place, he was going to get her a gold star or something.

"An RFID tag on a four-thousand-year-old Egyptian statue," he said, pulling his own flashlight out. "I didn't realize the ancient Egyptians had that kind of technology." It wasn't a question, but he sure as hell expected an answer.

"They were very advanced."

No shit.

"Not that advanced, Sugar." He slid the beam of his flashlight down the inside wall, found a light switch, and gave it a flip. Nothing happened, which racked up another *el perfecto* in his day. This wasn't going to work. "Why don't you give me the scanner and just wait outside." Sometimes he didn't know much about women, and sometimes he knew even less, but he knew she'd be happier if she didn't go inside the gallery. It was dark, dangerously haphazard with broken everything all over the floor, and it reeked.

The only answer he got was a short laugh, very short.

Okay, she could have it her way—almost.

He looked over his shoulder and met her gaze.

"Remy's dead, Suzi. The cops killed him when they busted in the gallery this afternoon, and from the smell, I'm pretty sure he's still in here. Are you sure you're up for this?"

"Ah, hell," she said, closing her eyes and suddenly looking very weary.

Yeah, it had been a long day, and poor dead Remy was just one more hurdle—but it wasn't enough to send her packing, and she should have been running the other way the minute the cops had first busted into Galeria Viejo.

"Who are you really working for, Suzi?"

He needed to know, not just for his sake, but for hers. He hadn't seen anybody in this damn city trying to save her butt except him, but there was somebody out there somewhere who was responsible for her being in this mess, the same somebody who had tagged the Memphis Sphinx and lost it, and of all the damn things, they'd sent Suzi Toussi to Ciudad del Este to get it.

Well, that somebody needed to know that the job had gone south.

"One name," he tried again. "Just give me a name."

That was a question, straight out, and the girl straight-out ignored it, opening her eyes and looking at him, but not moving her lips—*geezus*, as cool and collected as a cube of dry ice, even in the ninety-plus heat.

So he put it another way.

"That name isn't Skip Leonard, is it? You're working for somebody else, aren't you?" he asked, and sweet thing, she ignored him again.

Actually, she did more than ignore him. She shook her head, like he should know better than to ask.

"All right, sugar. Have it your way, but the deal we have is fifty-fifty." No matter who was holding her leash.

And he was going to find out, guaranteed.

"Fifty-fifty," she said, not sounding any more

convincing than he probably did. Fifty-fifty on the finding was one thing. Fifty-fifty on the keeping was where their deal was going to get sticky.

But fine. He was going to let her have it her way for now. He just hoped to hell she was ready.

"Stay close" was all he said.

CHAPTER EIGHTEEN

Outskirts of Ciudad del Este

From where he was working out of the back of the Jeep he and Zach had rented, checking his gear, Creed heard footsteps and looked up. The boss was heading his way.

Yeah, they needed to talk.

They'd loaded the Jeep and the vehicle Dylan and Hawkins had been using for the last six months, getting ready for their morning recon on Costa del Rey, or maybe it would turn out to be a raid, or a snatch and grab.

It wasn't going to be an assassination. He knew that damn much.

The photograph in the folder had shown a man who looked like J.T., with J.T.'s face, but just a little skewed, not quite right. The basic body build had been J.T.'s, but J.T.'s on steroids. The guy in the photo was big, over six feet and two hundred pounds of ripped muscle and raw power.

The CIA wanted an assassination, and Dylan and Hawkins had decided to go another way, and that was the kind of independent thinking that got them in trouble and, more often than not, got the job done.

Creed would have made the same decision. No way in hell could he pull a trigger on that face—not without knowing one of two things: that it wasn't J.T., or that J.T. had turned, and the only way to figure either of those out was to talk to the guy. No one at SDF was going to take the CIA's word for who the man was, not on a bet, especially not Creed, who would have sworn on his grandmother's grave that J.T. had died in the Colombian jungle.

But that face . . . that face was almost enough to make him doubt what he'd seen—almost, but not quite.

Dylan stopped next to the vehicle and pulled a cigar out of his pocket.

"You could have told me," Creed said, loosening the straps on his rucksack.

Dylan lit the cigar and got it going before handing it over.

"Command decision" was all he said.

"Bullshit." Creed took a long draw on the cigar, letting the smoke fill his mouth. Dylan always had the best cigars.

"Throwing that information, and that photograph, down in front of the whole team would have started a riot, and you know it. I still haven't figured out how to tell Kid."

"Bull," he said again, then blew out a cloud of smoke. "You give the 'telling Kid' part to Superman." That's what any of them would have done.

"Yeah," the boss said, wiping his hand over his face, sounding as weary and worn out as the dump they were using for mission headquarters looked. "But we need better facts than we've got."

"I figure that's why you brought me and Zach down here, boss." He pulled five empty pistol magazines out of one of the pockets on his ruck and started loading them. "Fact. Finding. Mission."

"The CIA has those four dead agents on this thing already, and that's if they're telling us the truth."

"Which they probably aren't." And that was a fact he would take to the bank.

"Yeah, that's what I figure, too."

Taking one last long draw, Creed gave him the cigar back and started in on his second magazine.

Dylan took a short puff and kept the cigar clenched in his teeth. "The spooks were also saying there's a girl up there at Costa del Rey. That she's been seen with Farrel in Bangkok and Berlin."

"That's convenient." Damned convenient.

"Hawkins and I thought so, too, and the third time we went up there to run our recon, Hawkins saw her checking the compound's perimeter. She does that real regular-like."

"And?"

"She's good in the woods, and she takes Costa del Rey's security damned seriously."

So they were going to grab the girl. Creed was fine with that, whatever it took.

"I put in a request a couple of weeks ago," Dylan said, then paused for a moment. "I've asked Grant to have the body exhumed for DNA testing."

Fuck. He kept on loading, sliding one cartridge in on top of the last, kept on breathing.

"Body?" he said, when he figured he could do it without chewing up the damn word. "What *body*, Dylan? We buried bones, burned bones. There was no *body*."

Butchered and burned—that's what the NRF had done to John Thomas Chronopolous. It had been overkill, none of it making sense, except to some twisted cocaine bastard out of Colombia named Juan Conseco trying to make a point, trying to send a message to the U.S. government.

Message received and returned in kind. None of them had been left alive. Not kingpin Juan, not his nephew Ruperto, who had delivered the death order, not the fucking guerrillas who had carried it out.

"Grant's been working on this thing and coming up with nothing. The file on Conroy Farrel is buried in the Mariana Trench. We've got one damn lousy photograph and no corroborating evidence that he even exists. I need some facts, either of who he is or who he isn't."

"Whoever he is, it's a dirty deal, Dylan." And

there wasn't a man jack of them who hadn't
thought it, who didn't know it.

"That's why we're going to bring Farrel in alive."

Dylan was right, they needed to capture Conroy
Farrel. They needed to talk to the man up close and
personal, whatever it took. Nothing else would do.
Creed didn't know what had gone wrong for those
four CIA agents, but he didn't have a doubt in his
mind that SDF could bring the guy in.

"What about this snatch on some antique Suzi
Toussi was going to tag for the DIA?" he said. "You
said Grant had that mission on his priority list."

"Against his will," Dylan admitted. "Suzi is in
Ciudad del Este. She arrived earlier today and is
staying at the Gran Chaco, a luxury hotel near the
country club. We were in contact this morning, and
she had a meeting set for this afternoon with the
gallery owner, a man named Remy Beranger, who is
supposed to be selling an Egyptian statue, a sphinx
with some kind of special powers that was stolen
from the spooks over at DIA."

Geezus. Creed gave him a look that said he had
to be kidding. Dylan just shrugged.

All right, then. He wasn't going to ask what in
the hell the Defense Intelligence Agency had been
doing with a magical Egyptian statue, or how in the
hell it was important enough to involve General
Grant and SDF, but DIA, CIA, hell, yeah, they
were definitely on sinking sand everywhere they
stepped in this hellhole.

"Suzi's good," he said. "She'll get the job done. I

helped her and Cody bring one of her girls out of Bulgaria last year. She had everything set up just so."

"Yeah, but she lost that one in Ukraine, and I think she took it real personal."

She had. Creed knew it for a fact. His wife, Cody, did a lot of footwork for Suzi on the girls, and more often than not provided tactical support. But Cody hadn't been able to get into Ukraine three months ago, some problems with her passport, the Ukrainians had said. Some problems with her past, was what she and Creed and Suzi had figured, and maybe some trouble with what she and Suzi had been doing the last couple of years in that part of the world. Cody and Suzi had decided to abort the mission—but the girl, some little southern chick, had not been able to keep her cool, and her house of cards had tumbled down on her real hard. She'd ended up dead, and Suzi had ended up finding her, and it was just a big mess, with everybody feeling guilty, except Viktor Kravchuk, the guy who had killed the girl. Creed could guarantee Viktor had not lost a wink of sleep over the murder. There was nothing weighing on that guy's conscience.

Suzi, though, she'd gotten herself all locked up over Lily Anne Thompson. She was tough, though, he'd known that about her for a long time. She'd work it out.

"I don't like it," Dylan said, looking at the cigar before putting it back in his mouth and puffing on it quietly, looking around, thinking. That's what the boss did best, thinking.

After a few moments, he took the cigar out of his mouth and blew out a large cloud of smoke.

"I'm changing the lineup," the boss said. "I don't care how good she is, I want her out of here. Grant gave her an RFID scanner to pick up a signal off the statue, and I want you to go get the scanner, get Suzi on a plane out of Paraguay, and get back here. We'll do what we can with the DIA's magic sphinx business, but Farrel is here, right now, and he is our priority mission." That was a set of orders, not a string of suppositions, and Creed didn't misunderstand for a second.

"Yes, sir," he said.

And that was the right answer, the only answer Creed had, no matter what Dylan asked him to do.

Suzi followed Dax into the gloomy interior of the Galeria Viejo. She knew she'd shown her hand by taking out the scanner, but she hadn't had a choice. The day's events had narrowed her options at a dramatic rate, and she wasn't about to search this damn place by herself in the dark, even packing a pistol. Oh, hell no, but she still needed a solid hit on the scanner. From there, one phone call would complete her mission—maybe. If the SDF operators wanted eyes-on, she'd give them eyes-on, if she could, but if it got to eyes-on, it was going to be hands-on, and one set of those hands was going to belong to Dax, and her money said he wasn't going to play nice and let the girl have it, even if he had kissed her.

Fifty-fifty. Right. He'd been lying, too. Nobody cut a fifty-fifty deal on immortality—and that's what everything was about. Not the inherent value of an ancient antiquity. Not its historical significance. And not its price on the open market.

Everyone was in Paraguay because of what the statue was supposed to be able to do tomorrow night.

Carefully picking her way across the floor behind him, she really did wish she was anywhere else in the world. The stench was awful, and she could hear the loud buzzing of flies in the dark.

God, she didn't even want to imagine what they were doing.

Ahead of her, Dax swung the beam of his flashlight around the room, and for a second, it followed along the edge of Remy Beranger's body.

Oh...my...God. A wave of heat washed through her, and she was afraid she might be sick.

Dax had warned her. So help her God, he'd warned her.

Beranger, that skinny, sick little man, was dead on the floor, his body covered in a flying, buzzing, crawling cloud of flies.

General Grant was going to owe her tactical support for a year for this.

"I'm...uh, going to go search the office," she said, backing away from the body, trying to talk and not breathe.

"Good idea. If you hear or see anything you don't like, call out. When we're done on this floor, we'll head for the basement."

Oh, hell. A basement. She didn't even want to think about a damn basement.

CHAPTER NINETEEN

There oughta be a law, Dax thought two hours later, tilting his head slightly to one side.

"You're shining your flashlight on my ass," Suzi said, bent over a stack of crates in Beranger's basement.

Yes.

He was.

"No, I'm not. I'm looking for the Sphinx. Are you sure you don't want to tell me where you got this scanner?" he said. "Because I think we should file a complaint."

"I *told* you I thought it might be broken." She sounded even more frazzled than she looked, which was plenty, and yes, she'd given him her opinion on the scanner, but the more he looked around, the more he was beginning to think it was another problem at work here.

He sure as hell hoped so, because there were

hundreds of crates in Beranger's basement, a lot of them sitting in water, and he'd be damned if he wanted to be down here long enough to look through all of them.

"Dammit," she muttered, sorting, and bitching, and griping, and moaning.

She was on the edge.

He was, too, actually. The day was getting too damn long to be trying to get through it on what he'd had for breakfast and a bag of chips.

She tossed another piece of junk off to the side, and he got hit with the splash—not that it made any difference, not at this point.

On its lowest level, the Old Gallery had turned out to be a swamp. He and Suzi had been sloshing their way through floating junk and whatnot for half an hour, after spending two hours searching the upper floors, and in his book it was all starting to be about two and a half hours too long.

He slid the beam of his flashlight off her lovely backside and up to the ceiling. It took effort. Looking at her ass was the closest thing to a pick-me-up he'd had since they'd gotten here.

"Tell me again the sequence of events when you were standing next to Beranger in the Chapel Room." There was something here, something niggling at him.

Three meters, that's what she'd given him as the scanner's range—nine feet, ten inches.

"It blinked twice, then I took a couple more steps, stopped, and after a minute or so, the GPS locked in a position."

He swung his flashlight back to her. She was standing outside one of two floor-to-ceiling wire mesh cages in the basement, one cage for each concrete cistern built into the floor—the overflowing cisterns. Both of the cages had stacks of crates and boxes and junk piled around the outside and nothing inside besides the cisterns. When he shone his flashlight down on them, he could see the pumps that should have been emptying the water out. Of course, if those things had been working, his boots would be dry.

Still, it was the wire cages that finally clicked into place.

"Well, Sugar, it could be that the statue was here when you first arrived." He sloshed over to where she was standing and stepped inside the open door of the first cage with the scanner in his hand.

Nothing registered, and he waded over to the other cage. The mesh was too fine for him to stick the scanner through, so he swung that wire door open as well and checked to see if the scanner registered anything inside.

It didn't.

He looked back up at the ceiling. It was low, seven feet maximum, which when she'd been standing next to Remy had given her a range from the floor of the basement to almost three feet above the floor of the Chapel Room. He swung his flashlight beam back to where she was standing, plenty of room to catch a signal, and the door on the cage she was next to had been open when they'd entered the basement.

"You got mixed signals, because when you first arrived at the gallery, the Sphinx was inside the cage where you're standing now," he said very matter-of-factly, even though he was impressed as hell with himself.

She'd left her Spa Monterey ball cap in Ruiz's Land Cruiser, and her hair was a mess, fallen down around her shoulders and starting to curl in the oppressive humidity of the basement. It gave her kind of a wild-woman look, very erotic, very nice.

He liked it, the same way he liked watching her bend over something—anything.

"Well, that's a brilliant piece of deduction, Sherlock." She straightened up from the crate she was looking through and stretched her back. "Or should I be calling you Karnak?"

Without giving him a glance, she leaned over the crate again and went back to work sorting through the rest of the junk inside—obviously not impressed at all, but he was sure that was just because he hadn't explained all the science to her yet.

"Sherlock Holmes," he said confidently. "You're standing next to a Faraday cage, and your scanner would have picked up the electromagnetic signal off the chip as you walked across the floor upstairs. At a certain angle over the open cage door, the signal wouldn't have been blocked by the wire cage." He sloshed back over to her side of the basement, using his flashlight like a laser pointer, happy to be giving her this little primer on radio signals. "At the next angle, your next step, the signal would be blocked. Any enclosed metal cage, even mesh, depending on the gauge and the wavelength of the frequency, will shield electromagnetic radiation, in this instance the radio signal sent by the transponder on the Sphinx. That's why you got blinks instead of the steady light you were expecting. It's why when you stood still for a moment, directly above the open cage door, the scanner's GPS kicked in. But I think the Sphinx is gone now."

"Gone?" she asked, sounding like she wanted to believe him, if for no other reason than to get the hell out of the slimy water and the grim basement.

"Positi—"

He stopped, cut off in mid-word by a loud clanging, and the quickly subsequent thumping, straining, running-up sound of the cisterns' pumps kicking into gear. All the crates and junk started to shimmy and shake, and the water to ripple.

"Oh, my, God," she gasped. "What was...what was—"

He swung his light back on her.

"*Geez, oh, geezo, cripes.*" She was scrambling, high-stepping, trying to get through the water, moving away from the cage. "*Ohmigod—*"

"It's okay, Suzi. It's okay," he said, forging forward. "It's just the pumps to drain the water out of the cisterns."

"*No, no, no, no,* not that, not—*ahhh!*" She jumped. "*That!*"

He swept the flashlight beam around her, but didn't see anything.

"*That...that...snake!*" She jumped again, sideways this time, her voice rising in panic.

He followed her gaze to the top of the water, and thought, *Oh.*

"*Ahh!*" She squealed again, loud enough to be heard above the horrendous racket—and then she let out a yelp and in a flash had drawn down on a piece of rubber tubing, her 9mm firmly in hand, her gaze raking the water, her jaw tight. Her right arm was straight, her left hand cupping her right on the grip, her left elbow pulled in.

Geezus, he was impressed. The girl was fast, damn fast, and she was solid on her gun, her draw needing no improvement whatsoever. She looked good, deadly, like that piece of rubber tubing floating around had better be saying its prayers. She looked like she knew exactly what she was doing, except for the fact that they were in a rather cramped space, and she'd be shooting into a couple of feet of water onto a concrete floor.

"Uh . . . no, no, sugar," he said, slogging forward, talking fast. "Don't shoot. I got it. Everything's okay. It's just a length of tubing."

"Where is it?" she asked, her gaze glued to the top of the water. "It was moving."

"Everything down here is moving," he pointed out. The water was rippling and streaming, and starting to eddy up against stuff, and all around them was the echoing clang and thump of the pumps and the gurgling, rushing sound of the swamp draining away down through the cisterns.

As a first date, he had to admit that this one had pretty much sucked, except for the kiss. They'd gotten that right, and for a moment, as he came up next to her and quietly but firmly told her to holster her weapon, he got to thinking about a better date, something with cold beer, fresh limes, and expensive tequila. Something with live, sultry music, spicy food, and a warm evening breeze.

Something that didn't involve mud, blood, and other people's guts spilling out all over would be a real step up. Something they could negotiate without a flashlight or a .45 would be a huge improvement.

Not that he ever went anywhere without a .45.

The sound of water rushing down the cisterns eventually started to slow, until it was no more than a trickle, the last few gallons of the overflow sliding toward the openings in the floor and getting pumped into the main line, and as soon as the water was gone, the great clanging and thumping of the pumps stuttered and clanked to a halt.

He shifted his gaze and the beam of his flashlight back to the cage, to see if they'd missed something while the place had been underwater.

And lo and behold, he'd be damned. There it was, the prize, a small wooden packing crate tucked up under the iron grate on the cistern, the perfect size for the Memphis Sphinx, and the perfect hiding place for something of inestimable value. With the cistern flooded, no one would ever know it was there, and the smell and looks of the place made it obvious that it flooded quite regularly.

"Do you see something?"

"No." He kept the beam of his flashlight moving,

swinging it across the floor and up to her. He'd only been on the crate for a second, but he knew what he'd seen.

She slid her hand back through her hair. She had mud on her arms, a streak of mud on her face, mud on her clothes. God, she looked like hell, like he'd put her through the wringer.

"Come on, let's get back to the Posada. I'll go get us something to eat, and we can come up with a Plan B." He took her by the arm and headed for the stairs.

Yeah, he had a conscience, but fifty-fifty was never going to work. Erich Warner wanted the Sphinx, and it wasn't a cash deal. Whoever Suzi was working for was just plain out of luck.

He'd make it up to her, if he got the chance. But first he needed the name of some asshole in Texas who thought he was going to take his shot at the U.S.A.

CHAPTER TWENTY

Costa del Rey

Con loved this time of night.

Crickets chirping, tree frogs singing, and Scout's pretty patio lights illuminating the Costa del Rey compound. The river was running dark and deep, heading toward Argentina and the Iguazú Falls. A soft wind soughed through the trees.

Leaning back against the cool stone wall of the house, looking out over the deck to the water and the jungle beyond, he took a heavy draw off his cigar. For a long time, he held the smoke deep in his lungs, longer and longer, until slowly, he began to let it out.

Softly, he opened his mouth in an O and blew smoke rings, one after the other, each more perfect than the last, and he watched as, ring by ring, the smoke settled like the loops of a necklace around the statue he held in his hand. A small fortune in gold was draped in a headdress from the Sphinx's brow to its leonine shoulders, slivers of regal lapis lazuli decorated the frontispiece of the crown, and rock-crystal eyes caught the light of the waxing moon and reflected a glittering shimmer deep into the beast's granite skull.

Tomorrow night the deed would be done.

He took another draw off the cigar and felt a subsiding flicker of pain in his arm.

He was running out of time. He felt it with each passing day, and he wanted Erich Warner dead. The fact would bring him a small measure of peace, and if he should triumph over the spymaster as well, he could die a happier man. It was the only doubt he had, that he could get to the man in Washington, D.C.

He held his last inhalation of smoke in his lungs—longer, and longer, and longer, seconds passing one after another. At a minute, the smoke started drifting out of his nostrils.

He certainly didn't doubt that he would die—probably badly, considering what he'd seen in Bangkok, considering how Scout's father, Garrett, had died.

Hopeless.

Hopeless.

Helpless.

If Con could have reached him, he'd have slid a knife up into the back of Garrett's skull and severed his brain stem, would have given him instant death, anything rather than watch the slow, twisting dev-astation that had allowed Garrett Leesom to linger and suffer.

But they'd been more than a cage apart, and the man in the cage between them had been dead for days by the time Garrett's meds had started to fail.

Fuck.

It could just as easily have been him.

Since then, Con had learned how to control his situation, but not without some failures of his own—and the failures weren't worth the living it took to get to them. So he kept his meds close, and he kept his supplier very close, and he kept his .45 closest of all. The fools who touted "no pain, no gain" didn't have a fucking clue what pain was all about, or how long it could last.

Long enough to make a man fear that even death wouldn't stop it—and, baby, that was taking fear right down to the soul. *What if . . . what if even death won't stop it?*

What then, *kemo sabe?* What then.

Religion, of course.

Con loved religion. It was so damned fearless, not only answering his biggest, scariest question about life but throwing it right back at him, utterly fearless. Pain, *pendejo?* it said. Live right, or we'll show you pain, guaranteed everlasting pain, Pro-methean pain.

No matter what he sometimes thought, pain had not been invented in Bangkok by Dr. Souk.

But it could be alleviated by the pills and by the *brujo* in Danlí, Honduras, who hand-rolled the ci-

gars for him. A *brujo,* a shaman, a witch doctor—
God only knew what the man put in the things.
Con didn't, but neither did he care. The long filler
was dark, almost oily, and the wrappers were faintly
green, and whatever blessings Mario Sauza Or-
lando chanted over the cigars, they worked.

He let the rest of the smoke drift out of his
mouth and took another long draw, feeling the
sounds of the night wash over him.

Tobacco was a drug—his favorite.

"Con?"

He'd heard her coming, the soft tread of slip-
pered feet on the cool tile floor.

"Scout."

"I've got those names for you from Jo-Jo, the
gringos staying at the Posada Plaza, and the intel
you wanted on Levi Asher and Suzanna Toussi."
She was standing in the light of the doorway onto
the deck, and there wasn't a thing about her that
didn't fill him with pride. He wasn't sure how it had
happened, this love he had for her, that her welfare
was so important to him, sometimes even more important than the justice he sought—and that was
saying a lot.

She'd been such a lost little wild thing when he'd
finally found her, living on the streets of Bangkok,
seventeen years old and looking about twelve, but
most definitely Garrett's daughter, with her father's
warrior spirit running true. It was the only thing
that had saved her.

Jack Traeger wasn't good enough for her, but
Con had a feeling Scout was of a different mind.

What she saw in the hellion was beyond him, except Jack was a lot like he used to be—before Bangkok.

He needed to talk to the boy, set him straight about a few things, let him know that once Scout was his, there'd be no more riding the edges of the rails. And as for all those wild oats Jack had been sowing—well, that was going to come to a screeching halt.

Or maybe not.

Con had a feeling that was the only reason Scout hadn't given in to the boy yet, and he was all for Scout not giving in to the boy.

"Start with Levi Asher," he said.

"A well-known dealer in the art world," she began. "Famous, or infamous, depending on a person's perspective, for brokering substantially profitable sales. Buyers love him because he knows where all the good stuff is and who's willing or being forced to sell, and the collectors love him because he always has access to people with money to spend. He works mostly out of Europe and has run some major pieces through Sotheby's, London."

"Not our guy. Too high-profile for Warner."

"More than that," she said. "Asher has given three pieces of sculpture to Yad Vashem, for their grounds."

He understood, and she was right. Even if Warner had contacted Asher about the Memphis Sphinx, anyone who donated works of art to the Holocaust museum in Jerusalem, Yad Vashem, would not work for a man like Erich Warner, a man whose political views were decidedly anti-Semitic along with being anti–everything else.

So Levi Asher was off the hook.

"What about the woman?"

"Suzanna Toussi, a very wealthy American art dealer, also known for brokering major deals and for finding the rarest of antiquities for her clients, but she likes to keep her deals private and doesn't work through the auction houses. She's been to Eastern Europe a number of times over the last few years, most notably in and out of Bulgaria."

A damning résumé in this game, and why in the hell that would demoralize him was beyond Con. Beautiful women could be as bad as anybody else on the planet, sometimes worse.

She was definitely still on the hook.

"And the gringos at the Posada?" One of the out-of-towners was Warner's proxy on the deal. The German had somebody here.

"There are three," Scout began. "George Teller, a tire salesman from Detroit. The description Jo-Jo got from the concierge—

"Wait a minute." Concierge? There was no concierge at the Posada Plaza. "Do you mean that pimp behind the front desk?"

"He prefers the term 'concierge.' " She gave him a look. "And he says Mr. Teller weighs in at two-fifty and about five foot eight inches."

"Not our guy." The asshole probably was a tire salesman, down here for the whores.

"Victor Bradley from Savannah," she continued with the list. "He bills himself as an investment broker, and he's connected in Ciudad del Este, doing business with Lorenzo Mamoré, trying to score a container of high-end electronics."

"No." Mamoré's customers weren't in the same league as Erich Warner. The German wouldn't have trusted some low-end hustler to represent him at an auction for the Memphis Sphinx.

"Last, we've got Daniel Killian. Jo-Jo says he's just another gringo looking for a deal and a whore, but Miller says otherwise."

Con's money was on Miller.

"What's the wizard got to say?" he asked.

Scout was still backlit in the doorway, reading from her notes.

"Miller says he's definitely the guy in the photos you took at Beranger's. When he slapped the name Jo-Jo got from the Posada onto that picture, he came up with a former U.S. Army soldier, Special Forces, highly decorated. His last couple of tours were in Afghanistan. And Miller wants ten times the normal price for that bit of information. As you can well imagine, he says, tagging an SF guy took a Herculean effort on his part and every favor he ever had coming to him."

"Ten times?"

"Ten," she confirmed.

And the wizard was still a bargain.

Con nodded, glad to have the information and highly doubting that Daniel Killian was Warner's mule. Nobody who'd bled for the flag would roll over and hustle contraband for the likes of Erich Warner, not for something as New Age hocus-pocus as a magic statue. Those SF boys were grounded in the real world with a vengeance.

No, Con's money said somebody else had sent the former Special Forces operator.

"So the DIA wants their statue back," he said, giving in to a slight grin. They definitely would have sent somebody when they'd picked up the chatter on Beranger's auction, and they would have definitely picked up the chatter. Hell, everybody else had, and Killian was just the kind of guy they liked—skilled and connected to the community. Nobody would have suspected someone of the spymaster's standing and privilege of having stolen the thing. Certainly no one had yet figured out that the spymaster had been underhandedly dealing them all a stacked and marked deck for years, and in the process lining his pockets with boatloads of money and the kind of power that shook Third World countries like a paint mixer.

"Sure looks that way." Scout knew as much about the Memphis Sphinx as he did. He'd made sure of it. She knew where it had come from, and she'd know what kind of guy the Defense Intelligence Agency would send to get it back.

Former Special Forces was perfect for the job, less easily held accountable than an active-duty soldier. The deal would be a private contract, and Con doubted if the other two gringos at the Posada were on his team. They didn't fit the profile.

"Killian's got good intel," he added. "The kind of information the DIA would have. He certainly showed up at Beranger's right on cue. If he becomes a problem, let's do our best not to kill him." Garrett had been SF, and there were other ways to get people out of the picture, at least for a while. "He gets a pass on this job."

"Roger that," Scout said.

DIA, CIA, Con didn't give a damn who wanted what. He'd killed every assassin the spymaster had thrown at him, no matter what agency he'd culled for his hit men, and he wasn't planning on changing his standard operating procedure anytime soon. But Killian appeared to be a different story. He was a soldier, and for his own sake, he needed to fail in his mission.

Whereas Ms. Suzanna Toussi, he'd concluded, needed to succeed, brilliantly. She needed to find the Sphinx, get her hands on it, and report back to Erich Warner, telling him exactly where it was being kept, and extend an open invitation for him to come and get it.

Con, for one, was only too glad to help her, though he doubted if she would much like his methods.

"Did Jo-Jo get a line on the woman yet?" he asked.

"No." Scout shook her head. "But she hasn't been listed on any flights out of here, so she's lying low somewhere."

"Unless she headed out on the roads."

"Maybe," Scout said. "But that's the long shot, Con. Traffic on the bridge is backed up halfway to Asunción, and heading into the interior isn't her best bet for escaping the Paraguayans. And most of all, if she's working for Warner, she's still got twenty hours to pull this thing off, and if she's working for Warner, she knows better than to fail."

Con agreed. He'd be doing the woman a favor by bringing her to Costa del Rey and putting her under house arrest, whether she appreciated the fact or not—but he needed to get her first.

He stuck the cigar between his teeth and stretched his arm all the way out, then stretched his fingers. There was no pain. Good.

He pushed off the stone wall and handed the statue to Scout.

"I'm going to go get Ms. Toussi." If she hadn't flown the coop, then his money said she was going to end up at the Posada Plaza sometime tonight. If not, Daniel Killian was a good place to start looking for her. She sure as hell wasn't going to go back to the Gran Chaco.

Scout nodded, holding the gold and granite sphinx close to her chest. She was worried, he could tell, but there wasn't a damn thing she could do to save him—tonight or any other night.

"I should go with you," she said.

"No. I might need to cover a lot of ground. Relay any information Jo-Jo comes up with. I'm heading back to the Posada Plaza."

"What you need is somebody to watch your back." She stood her ground. "You're not alone out there, and you know it."

Yeah, they both knew it. Two guys had been on his ass for months, staying out of sight, just on the edge of his radar, moving through the shadows, moving like he moved, following him, but keeping their distance. He didn't know who in the hell they were, but he knew they were here, in Ciudad del Este. He could almost smell them.

They hadn't been at Beranger's, though. They didn't give a damn about the Memphis Sphinx. They were in Paraguay for one reason—to kill him, like the others before—and like the others, they didn't have a clue what they were up against.

And like the others, he'd bury them in this damn country.

CHAPTER *TWENTY-ONE*

Ciudad del Este

Oh, God. Suzi hurt everywhere.

She followed Dax up the stairs to his room in the Posada, dragging her feet, every muscle in her body aching. Three hours of moving junk around in the gallery had taken its toll. She was tired, hungry, wet, and far from done for the night.

Hell, five frickin' flights, and then she had to ditch him. It wasn't going to be easy. The boy was in full-out rescue-the-woman mode. Under any other circumstances, she'd be charmed senseless, but she had only one card left in her deck of tricks, and she would need to be on her game and alone to play it—the Levi Asher card. Levi was the only piece of live bait left in this town, if he even was still in this town.

It wouldn't take her long to find out, no more than a couple of phone calls.

Oh, yes, she had her Plan B all mapped out, the sexual pervert plan. The thought alone was enough to exhaust her.

At the fifth landing, they stumbled onto the Posada Plaza's welcoming committee, the Latino transvestite tag team of Marcella and Marceline, which was about the only thing to go her way all day. The two elevator specialists played right into her one-card hand, and there they were, coming down the hall, front and center, dressed to kill in buckles, snaps, and bustiers, fake white lace and tight black polyester, flowered scarves and stiletto heels.

Beautiful.

"Hola, chico," one of the "girls" called out to Dax.

"Marceline," he said with a short nod.

"Chica, cariño..." the other "girl," Marcella, crooned, her warm amber-colored eyes rimmed in thick black eyeliner and sweeping over Suzi from her head to her toes.

"Hola," she said, a little uncertain, then turned to Dax. "What did she say? I didn't get that last word."

"Hey, darling," he translated.

"Cómo estás, chiquita?" Marceline added.

Suzi gave Dax a little poke in the side.

"How you doing, baby?" he said, reaching back and taking her hand, keeping them moving forward.

"Can you tell her I'm fine?"

"Liar," he said, tightening his hold on her as they passed the Latinos in the hall.

"Bueno," she said, looking back over her shoulder. *Good.* She was doing good.

Marcella shook her head, tsk-tsking, then rattled off a few comments.

"He's calling you a liar, too," Dax said, "and he wants you to know that you can tell him everything. He's your new best friend."

"I could use a friend," Suzi said, barely keeping up with him, stride for stride.

"Not that one, babe. Marcella would just as soon sell you as hold your hand."

Actually, Marcella was exactly the friend she needed, once she ditched Dax, and yes, she had a plan. She was a girl, she needed things, and he was a guy, he'd go get them. She wasn't going to be an idiot about it, but it was simple, and simple plans usually worked.

The two "girls" had turned to follow them and were catching back up. In a couple of steps, Marceline slid in next to Suzi and started making conversation, smiling and obviously asking questions, her heavily made-up eyes alight, her head cocked slightly to one side, her tone deeply inquiring— and, well, just deep all around.

"What should I say to her, help me out here," she said, giving Dax's hand a squeeze.

"He," he used the gender pointedly, "wants to know what...uh, happened to you. Why you look so...disheveled, when you left here looking like a

princess on a, uh, cake, or something to that effect."

"Princess?" Suzi said.

"On a cake," he repeated. "And he thinks I'm a real jerk for letting you get in this condition. *Cálmate,* Marceline."

He tightened his grip on her hand when they stopped at his door, and with his other hand, he dug in his pocket for the key.

"*Gringo?*" Marcella said.

"*Sí?*" He jimmied the key into the lock and got the door open without bothering to look up.

Before Suzi stepped inside, the "girl" rattled something off in Spanish and blew her a kiss—and oh, my God, just like that she racked up another new low, getting hit on by a guy in a miniskirt wearing eyeliner.

Dax closed the room door behind them, then locked it, bolted it, and used the worthless chain, and throughout the whole security procedure, such as it was, he held on to her hand.

More telling, she held on to his—and at this point in the day, that was about all the encouragement he needed, for all the good it was going to do him right now.

"I don't suppose you've got something to drink?" she asked.

"Sodas? Water?" He had a few things.

"Gin martini?"

He grinned. "Kentucky gold."

He let go of her hand and walked over to the small duffel bag he'd set on the bedside table. Behind him, he heard her cross the room and open the balcony doors. When he found his flask, he unscrewed the top and walked over to where she was standing, looking out onto the street.

He handed her the flask, and she took a small sip, holding it in her mouth for a moment before swallowing.

"Bourbon," she said.

Whiskey, neat.

He took a bigger swallow when she handed it back, and then he gave her the flask—and my, wasn't this cozy, just the two of them, having a drink. He had a plan, and in a minute or two, he was going to put it in motion.

But for a minute or two, he was just going to enjoy the view.

"What did Marcella say?" the view asked. "There at the last, when she was running on?"

He could have made up half a dozen things, but went ahead and told her the truth.

"First, Marcella is a 'he,' not a 'she,' and he goes both ways, and if there were three ways to go, he'd go that way, too, for a price, and he said you have the most perfect ass he's ever seen."

Dax tended to agree, but he didn't think this was the time or the place for his opinion on the subject, not when she was close enough for him to see the amber highlights in her eyes, the sheen of dampness on her skin—and something he shouldn't have missed.

His brow furrowed.

"When did this happen?" he asked, turning her face into the light. She'd been scratched, high up on her cheek, almost into her hairline.

He carefully smoothed the auburn strands of her hair away from her face.

"When we came out of that window at Beranger's."

"Hell," he muttered, sliding his thumb across her cheek, just below the injury. "I thought I was more careful with you than that."

"It's just a...uh, scratch," she said, her voice breaking just a little, and yeah, he understood. They were alone, and safe, and suddenly close enough to make something happen, and he was touching her.

Sex.

That's what he was thinking could happen.

"I've got some antibiotic cream in my pack." Geezus, she was beautiful. It just wrecked him, the way she looked.

"I already put some on, at the hotel."

Sex.

Just sex.

"Good," he said, nodding his head like a little antibiotic cream on a scratch was rocket science.

Just soft mouths and soft...

"I had a tube in my suitcase—*ah, hell.*"

Yeah, her luggage. He'd kind of forgotten about that. Actually, he was having a little trouble remembering a lot of things, like his plan, the one where he walked out of here and left her all by her lonesome in this room while he scooted back to Beranger's to get sopping wet in one of those basement cisterns.

That plan was losing its appeal faster than a lightning strike.

"I think I can get your stuff back—your suitcase, your shoes, everything you left at the Gran Chaco." It was a long shot, but not impossible. "I know some guys ... some guys who can ... uh ... "

The thought ran out, because she was looking up at him, her gaze softening into a languid, mesmerizing stare.

"Thank goodness," she said, her voice sweetly sincere. "Dax?"

"Yes?" When she sounded like that, the answer was bound to be yes.

"I'm hungry, and really tired. Could you go get us something to eat?"

And there was his plan, the solution, his exit strategy, all laid out for him—except he wasn't all that interested in going now.

Hold on, boy—his brain kicked in—*let reason be your guide*.

He was all for reason. Right.

"There's a restaurant down the street," he said. "A *churrascaria,* a lot of grilled meat, some different kinds of bread, fruit. I could head down there."

He started to turn away, but she stopped him with her hand on his waist.

"Thanks."

That's all she said, just "Thanks," but that's all he'd needed, just one more moment of hesitation.

Hell.

He was such a fool. He knew it, dammit, but he went ahead and did it anyway, slid his hand around the back of her neck and lowered his mouth to hers.

Big mistake—he was so instantly lost in the warm, lovely taste of her mouth, the mindless pleasure of her kiss, so sweet, so hot, so softly, erotically female.

She melted up against him, her body yielding in all the right places, and it was such a turn-on—but at some point, she was going to realize he'd cut her out of the deal, and if she'd already gone to bed with him when she discovered his betrayal, she was going to think he was the world's biggest bastard, or even worse—and she'd be right. She'd feel used, and he'd feel like hell, and it would be damn hard work to come back from a dirty trick like that and maybe make a go of it, make some kind of relationship—the kind that had a chance at lasting.

Lasting relationship? Now there were two words that didn't go together in his vocabulary very often—let alone in his life.

Okay, this kiss wasn't nearly mindless enough. He was thinking, a lot, and even with this exquisitely hot and beautiful woman in his arms, he was thinking he needed to get the hell out of the room, before he did something he was going to love and she sure as hell was going to hold against him.

Damn. Talk about bad timing for an attack of conscience.

But then she opened her mouth wider, pressed

herself closer, and his conscience did a nosedive. He slid his hand down over the curve of her perfect ass and pulled her in close, where he could feel her up against him, cradling him, and he deepened the kiss.

Oh, yes, he was going to go straight to hell for this and love every minute.

Unless he stopped.

And did the right thing.

"Suzi," he whispered, pulling back from the kiss just enough to get his brain working again, and he immediately wished he hadn't.

She stiffened in his embrace, then turned her back to him and leaned up against the balcony door.

"I'll just go ... get us something to eat." And with those few words, he won the Lame-Ass Idiot of the Year award, hands down, no competition in sight. "I won't be gone very long," he promised, but he figured she pretty much didn't give a damn how long he was gone. Like maybe forever might be too soon for him to come back with a plate of barbecued meat and some nameless piece of fruit.

Well, perfect. Turning women down was not exactly his forte, so no wonder he'd blown it. *Geezus*.

He went and got a couple of tools out of his duffel bag and slipped them into the cargo pocket on his pants. He had some connections, still knew a few guys who could pull all kinds of strings, even as far south as Paraguay, and when he had the statue secured, if it was even in that damn crate hidden inside the cistern, and got back with the food, he was going to do his damnedest to get her out of Ciudad del Este—tonight, before sunrise and another day of disasters. For the kinds of guys he knew, it wouldn't matter that the police were looking for her. Evading all and every law enforcement entity on the planet was their modus operandi—and they were the good guys.

But first, he had to get back to the gallery, before the damn basement flooded again.

CHAPTER TWENTY-TWO

Suzi stood just inside the door to the balcony and watched as Dax crossed the street below. Once he disappeared into the crowd, she took the phone General Grant had given her out of her fanny pack and headed across the room, toward the door to the hall.

Within a minute, she had her assistant on the phone.

"Jane?" she said. "It's Suzi."

Jane Linden had been with her, on and off, for almost five years, working at different galleries Suzi had either owned or managed.

"Hey, Suz," Jane answered. "What's up? Where are you?"

"In a room with a view," she said, being deliberately obscure, and with an answer like that, Jane knew not to pry. "I need a cell phone number for

Levi Asher. Can you look in the dealer files on your computer?"

It wasn't really a question. Between Suzi and Katya Hawkins, they'd nearly created the girl, taking her from being a half-wild street urchin with a few years of reform school on her résumé, to a sophisticated art aficionada with superlative job skills and exquisite taste. Between the two of them, she and Katya had given quite a few girls a second chance, including a couple of the Eastern European women.

"Sure. I'm at my desk, so just give me a... minute or so... and I'll... Got it." Jane gave her the number, then repeated it for good measure.

"Thanks." When she reached the door, she stopped for a second and took a breath. God, that kiss. It had almost been her undoing. She had to stop kissing Dax Killian, but good Lord, it had felt like heaven. No man had affected her like that since—since too long to remember.

"So what's up, Suz?" Jane said. "It's not like you to call Asher. What's he working on that you can't resist?"

Levi Asher's reputation for art was impeccable. He was one of the world's master dealers. But his reputation with women was nothing but bad. Suzi wasn't one to deny anyone their fantasy world, but to date, she'd declined becoming part of Levi Asher's entourage. To date, she'd declined him about an even twenty times.

Tonight, Levi's ship was coming in, or at least Suzi was going to do her best to convince him of the fact. If he knew anything at all about where the Memphis Sphinx was, she was going to get it out of him. Something had happened in the Galeria Viejo, while she and Dax had been bailing out the second-floor window, and she wanted to know what. If someone, anyone, had gotten their hands on the statue, she wanted to know who. If Levi had actually seen it—and Levi would know if he had—she wanted to know that, too.

"He's got a piece he's working on that I'm interested in, yes," she admitted, opening the door and checking the hall in both directions. It was empty, but she knew where to find what she needed. "At the least I'm hoping he's got some information I can use."

"Do you want me to do some research on this end?"

"No, but thanks, Jane," she said, heading down the hall to the elevator. "I've got plenty of research." Half a ream of it, compliments of Buck Grant. "When I get back, we'll put the finishing touches on next week's Solano opening. See you in a couple of days."

She ended the call and dialed in Levi Asher's number. He let it go to message, just as she figured he would for an unknown number.

"Levi," she said. "It's Suzi Toussi. I'm in Ciudad del Este tonight, I think for the same reason you are, and I was hoping we could get together over drinks and see what we can come up with on this deal."

She didn't even get the phone back in her fanny pack before it was ringing.

"Hello?" she said, and she kept walking. "Oh, hello, Levi. Thanks for returning my call.... Yes, how thoughtful, dinner would be wonderful.... At the El Caribe, of course.... Of course.... Yes... and, Levi? Send a car, please. I'm at the Posada Plaza, and I'll be out front in twenty minutes. Don't be late."

She hung up the phone and kept walking, all the way down to the elevator before she came to a stop. Then she let out a long breath and pushed the call button. The old elevator kicked in and started to grind its way up to the fifth floor, and Suzi stood there and waited—waited for what she needed, Marcella and Marceline, the Latino transvestite elevator tag team, the girls with the goods.

Thirty minutes, Dax thought, his jaw tight. He hadn't left her alone for more than half an hour, and she was gone.

He walked through his room at the Posada one more time, checking the bathroom and the balcony again, and the girl was gone, just like the Memphis Sphinx.

Sonuvabitch.

He dropped the small wooden crate on the closest table, where it rolled and fell open. The lock on the crate had been broken long before he'd pried the damn thing out of the cistern in Beranger's basement—all for nothing. It was empty, with only an indentation in the foam packing container to show where the statue had been, and the indentation was perfect, like a fricking lost wax cast of the Maned Sphinx of Sesostris III, the damn Memphis Sphinx.

Dammit! It had been here, in Ciudad del Este, in Beranger's, and somebody had beaten him to it. How in the hell had that happened?

And where in the hell had Suzi gone? He couldn't think of a single safe place for her to be, other than with him. If she'd gone after the Sphinx, she'd had fresh intel since he'd left, because when they'd been in that basement together, she'd been tearing through that garbage hoping to find it.

He set the bag of food he'd bought on the table next to the crate and ran down the options. It didn't take much running. Beranger was dead. Ruiz was dead. She wouldn't have contacted Esteban Ponce, not after the mess he'd made of Jimmy. That only left Levi Asher.

It was time to pay the big-name art dealer a call, and maybe, probably, Suzi had come up with the same idea.

He pulled his phone out to make some calls, to find Asher. If he wasn't at the Gran Chaco or the El Caribe, he could be at one of the resorts near Iguazú Falls. Or he could be in Asunción.

Or he could have gotten the Sphinx and be hell-and-gone out of Ciudad del Este.

Dax still had the number for the Gran Chaco in his call list and was about to hit it, when something on the table caught his eye—a padded red bra with rhinestones on the straps, a very padded bra.

It wasn't Suzi's. He'd been pressed up against all girl when he'd kissed her. He knew that much, and from the size of it, he was going to say Marcella instead of Marceline, and how in the hell had Marcella's bra gotten into his room?

He walked back to the bathroom and turned on the light. All of Suzi's toiletries had been left at the Gran Chaco. When she'd run out of her room at the hotel, she'd left with what she'd had on her.

But there were toiletries in his bathroom, girl stuff—two barrettes, a twist-up tube of bronzer, and half a dozen bobby pins.

He turned on his heel and dropped his phone in his pocket. He didn't need to make phone calls to find Suzi. He just needed to go hit the call button on the elevator and shake down whoever came out first.

Night on the river was a beautiful thing, the wind in his face, the stars above, the cool dark water below, and the roar of the twin Mercs off the back of the boat.

Up ahead, Con could see the lights of the city just starting to break the darkness at the edge of the world. He didn't have a doubt in his mind that he would find Suzanna Toussi in Ciudad del Este. Something about the woman had sunk into him, triggered something, and now she was there, deep inside him, elusive but there, like a scent on the wind.

Reaching down to the controls, he throttled up the engines, doubling his speed, and the shoreline stretched out on his port side, slipping away mile after mile into shadows and darkness.

CHAPTER TWENTY-THREE

Dax didn't have any trouble picking Suzi out of the crush of people playing and paying in El Caribe's casino. She was the tallest redhead in the room. She had the tightest skirt, a cheap little black polyester number with a zipper all the way up the side he'd last seen on Marcella—but Suzi made it look like Gucci. She had the biggest hair, all ratted, sprayed, swirled up on top of her head and held in place with a sparkly barrette. She had the biggest earrings, gold hoops, and the tightest bustier, red with little black ribbons running through it, her breasts all but spilling out of the top, the tiny black lace straps going up over the tops of her shoulders.

By any stretch of the imagination, she had the silkiest, palest skin, and there was just so much of it on display, all bare legs, bare arms, those lovely shoulders, the death-defying décolletage—*geezus*.

Her eyes were made up with a barely restrained

hand. He was guessing Marceline's—eyeliner, shadow, and bronzer all set on Sultry and Stun.

He recognized her, yes, but he didn't think anybody else would. The girl was in disguise, and as outrageous as she looked, she fit right in with the rest of the casino crowd. In El Caribe, bare skin was camouflage, wild hair was de rigueur, and cleavage was the answer, no matter what the question.

And the shoes. There was nothing like a pair of trashy, black patent leather platform heels with lots of buckles and straps to really slut-up an outfit.

Talk about overkill.

She looked so freakin' hot.

And that jerk Asher kept trying to put his hand on her ass, which Dax figured might be the whole point of the exhibition and her costume, but it still pissed him off.

He needed a life, one like he used to have, before he'd walked into the Toussi Gallery in Denver six months ago and been hit by a cosmic freight train, and he was going to get one, he swore it, right after he took charge of this little get-together and rearranged the dynamics a bit.

He started forward into the casino, working his way through the crowd, trailing Suzi and her new, fat, old boyfriend. Cutting him out, that's what she was doing, and to think he'd had a couple more pangs of conscience when he'd been down in Beranger's basement, slopping around in the cistern, trying to get his hands on that crate.

Well, no more. He could see her chatting Asher

up, doing all the little things guaranteed to get a guy's attention—the leaning in close, the touching his arm, the sweet smiles, doing her damnedest to soften the old buzzard up.

In that outfit, she looked like she needed paddling, and Dax was thinking he was just the guy to do it. He could sure as hell see Asher was thinking he was the guy, the way he kept trying to pat her ass. The jerk finally did get one in, and man, if the buzzard had missed the flash of Suzi's smile turning downright tight and dangerous, then Asher was a bigger fool than he thought.

The girl obviously did have some sort of plan, and, he hoped to hell, her 9mm in the fanny pack clipped around her waist, and Dax was going to let her work her mojo up to a point. Maybe she'd get what she'd come for, which, despite the gloating expression on Asher's face, wasn't a good time. Dax was betting his peace of mind on it.

So he followed along, trailing in their wake, stopping when they stopped. Suzi got on a roll at the craps table, and just about started a riot shaking the dice. Asher was eating it up, being so close to the center of so much attention. He didn't really look like a guy who was going to lose a lot of sleep over the Memphis Sphinx tonight, which made Dax think the old man had a reason not to be too worried.

Suzi's winning streak came to an end, and the party moved on. Besides Suzi and Asher, Asher's two bodyguards were moving along with them, and after the win at the craps table, they'd picked up another couple of girls, with drinks and champagne all around.

Yes, this was going to get interesting. Dax could tell.

Hell.

The group moved into El Caribe's ritzy dining room, a conservatory with a domed glass roof and a jungle's worth of plants and trees. The staff had a table set up in a grove of trees that offered some seclusion, and Dax noticed Asher dismissing the others with a wave of his hand as he and Suzi were seated.

Wouldn't have been Dax's first choice, but he appreciated the strategy on both their parts. Asher wanted privacy for something he didn't have a chance in hell of getting, Dax hoped, and for Suzi, it could be damn hard to pump somebody for information with a passel of party girls in close proximity. He knew it from personal experience. Party girls had a way of distracting a guy—all kinds of ways.

The dining room was a beehive of activity, packed, and fifty dollars was the only reason Dax didn't have any trouble finding a place to sit where he could keep an eye on their table.

And so he sat through the first course, biding his time, watching her flirt her way into more trouble than he thought she could handle, especially with Asher's hand permanently affixed to her knee.

Sure, the girl knew what she was doing. That's what he kept telling himself.

When his phone vibrated in his pocket and he checked the incoming number, he reminded himself that he knew what he was doing, too. He flipped the phone open and put it to his ear.

Now all he had to do was convince Erich Warner and do his best to keep that private army idea on the back burner.

"Buscando una mujer, la gringa," Con said, leaning on the night clerk's counter at the Posada Plaza. *I'm looking for a woman, the American*. He had a 100,000-guarani banknote in his hand, about twenty bucks' worth of Paraguayan cash.

The "concierge," a greasy-haired guy with bad teeth wearing a stained T-shirt, looked up, took the money, and picked up the house phone. The conversation with whoever answered the call quickly veered into uncharted, domestic territory. Con could hear the yelling coming from the other end of the phone even on his side of the counter.

He didn't have any sympathy. Pimps running transvestites shouldn't have it any easier than the guys running women, and the Posada was known for their elevator crew.

After a minute of listening to the argument escalate, he leaned farther over the counter. He had plenty of patience, a lifetime's supply, but the situation called for impatience, so he delivered it.

"Oye, pendejo!" he said, slamming his fist down. *"Apúrate!" Come on, asshole. Hurry up*.

The man glanced up from the phone and gave him a dark look, then said, "El Caribe."

"Bueno." Good, that's what he'd needed.

"*Espera,*" the pimp said, and Con turned back. "*Quieres un nombre?*"

A name? Absolutely. Con peeled another 100,000 note off his roll and slid it over the counter.

The man smiled a rotten-toothed smile, well pleased with himself.

"Leevee Asha," he said.

Levi Asher. *Perfecto.*

CHAPTER *TWENTY-FOUR*

Levi Asher's palm was sweaty.

His face was sweaty.

His neck was sweaty.

Even his eyeballs looked sweaty.

And the more he drank, the sweatier he got.

Suzi reminded herself that she'd asked for this opportunity. She'd called him, knowing what she was getting herself into, but the possibility of being groped paled in comparison to the actuality of having Levi Asher trying to get his sweaty hand up her skirt.

Well, Marcella's skirt.

"Suzi, Suzi Toussi," the old man murmured for about the thousandth time since she'd shown up looking like Barbie Gone Wild, and the more he drank, the more he liked saying her name. "You are here. Thank God, we're finally alone. This is wonderful. Champagne, yes?" He signaled to the waiter, then returned his full attention to her. "We must talk, Suzi. The day has been so... well, when my man, Gervais, told me you had come to Beranger's this afternoon, I was astounded. Not in a hundred years would I have dreamed to see Suzanna Royale Toussi in Ciudad del Este... or, my dear"—he lowered his voice intimately, let out a soft burp, and continued—"that you would ever come to me so... so delightfully *en déshabillé*. You look lovely."

Or like a cheap hooker, she thought, as the case may be, but actually, not so cheap. Besides the Get Out of Jail card she'd had to pony up for, Marceline had bargained hard for every piece of fashion she'd dragged out of her and Marcella's closet. Suzi had never been afraid of a short skirt or a tight top in her life, but she didn't have any illusions about how she looked.

Or any illusions about Levi Asher. He was rich for a reason, disgusting by nature, older than he appeared to realize, and getting drunker by the minute.

Just as well. She was hoping to catch him off his guard, get him to babble a bit, instead of just drool. If the old slimeball knew something, she wanted to know what.

She smiled. "Levi, we're both a long way from London or New York right now."

The waiter stepped forward to pour more champagne, while another refreshed the first course, bringing a second round of tapas.

Levi reached for a couple of bacon-wrapped dates and popped them in his mouth.

"Yes, a long way," he said, chewing and leaning closer, his pale blue suit clinging to him in a dozen bad, sweaty ways. His hair was gray and very sparse across the top, his full face flushed with the heat, but his watery eyes were alight with excitement. "It's the Sphinx, Suzi, she brought us here. She *exists*. She wasn't just a figment of Howard Carter's imagination. She is *here. Now.*"

"Where?" she asked bluntly. That was the damn question of the day, and by her count, that was the third time she had successfully brought the conversation around to it, so far without much luck in getting an answer. "I was with Remy when the police came to the gallery. He told me you were in the viewing room with Esteban Ponce. We were headed that way, but when the police started destroying everything and the shooting started, I ran out the back."

"You were very wise to do so, my dear, very wise." For once, he patted her hand instead of her ass or her knee, then he picked up his glass of champagne, drained it in one go, signaled to the waiter again, and popped another bacon-wrapped date in his mouth.

The man was a consumption machine.

"What happened in there, Levi? Did you see it? Was it there? The Sphinx?"

"No," he said, shaking his head, and another burp escaped him. "Beranger showed us a fake in the viewing room." His gaze moved impatiently over the fresh plates of tapas, going from one to the other. "I knew what it was, of course, but Ponce thought it was authentic. Beranger took the fake with him, when he went to greet you, I'm guessing. Then the shooting started. Good God, the service in Third World countries is usually better." Spotting a waiter across the way, he snapped his fingers in the air. "Why don't we have any tapenade?" he muttered. "There's always tapenade on a tapas tray."

"So where's the real statue?" And that made four times.

Levi opened his mouth to say something but then seemed to think better of it and smiled instead, which was a shame, because Levi Asher had very gray, crooked teeth.

He obviously needed another glass of champagne, or two, or three, whatever it took to keep loosening his tongue.

"Well, that's the million-dollar question, now isn't it?" he did say, sounding like a jerk for a reason. "Fortunately, I have a lead I'm following, and I'm guessing you do not?"

He was always easy to hate.

"I've got a couple of things I'm working." *Like you.*

For a moment, he looked at her, measuring her, chewing away with a chomping, swaying roll of his jaw. She didn't have a clue what he was thinking— and that was not good.

"It's been a difficult day," he eventually said, then swallowed. "Stressful."

He had that right.

Suzi leaned in closer, resting her hand on his leg and giving him a comforting little pat.

"Would you like some help, Levi? I'm very good at following leads and finding things," she said, and under the table, she rubbed her strappy platform heel up and down his calf.

And that's when she felt all the little hairs on the back of her neck start to rise.

Noticeably so.

Unavoidably so.

With her hand still on Levi's leg, she glanced across the dining room, and ran smack-dab into an iron-gray gaze locked onto her like a tractor beam.

She considered herself very cool under pressure and oblivious to the unsolicited demands of men, and she was—except, it seemed, when it came to this man.

Her pulse instantly picked up in speed, and she quickly broke the contact between her shoe and Levi's calf. She straightened up, sitting back in her chair and loosely linking her fingers around her champagne glass.

"Absolutely, Suzi dear," Levi said, and she dragged her attention back to him. "No question about it. We should be working together on this. I've been thinking about it all day, ever since I heard you were here. Partners, yes, that would be best."

Suzi stared at him for a moment, surprised—and wary. His offer appeared generous at most, and benign at the least, but she could guarantee it was neither. Levi Asher made his money by knowing other people's business and knowing how to work it for his own gain. He was calculating and ruthless, and not anybody's friend—least of all hers.

None of which dissuaded her, not at this point.

"I'm in," she said unequivocally. "What did you have in mind?"

So she'd run out on Dax. So what. She refused to feel guilty. The whole fifty-fifty deal would never have worked—and yet she did feel a little twinge of guilt. He had gotten her out of Beranger's, and considering what had happened in there, it was a damn good thing. He'd come after her at the Gran Chaco, and kept on coming, even after seeing what had happened to Jimmy Ruiz. He'd tried to protect her from going back into the gallery, and he'd paid Marcella and Marceline a hundred dollars to watch over her while he'd gone out to get her some dinner. She knew, because it had cost her another hundred to get them to sell her some clothes and let her out of the Posada.

He was practically a saint, and she'd run out on him.

Guilt, that's what drew her gaze back across the dining room, and oh, hell, he looked good.

He'd changed clothes, cleaned himself up from the sludge and mud of the day's misadventures. Unlike her, he looked very elegant, and yet still very tough, in a black polo shirt and a pair of dark gray slacks. She noticed he was still wearing his trail boots.

You can take the boy out of the jungle, she thought, *but you can't take the jungle out of the boy.*

The polo shirt was almost a crime, really, the way it hugged his shoulders and how the material stretched around his biceps. He'd gotten the mud off his face and combed his hair, but it was sticking up a little in front. His jaw was hard and still stubbled with beard, and he was relaxed back in his chair with all the barely leashed power and grace of every big bad boy who'd ever been at the top of the food chain.

Long legs, strong hands, oh, yes, there was a reason she'd been kissing on him all day.

"There's a place up the river," Levi said, leaning in closer, taking up the slack of her retreat. "And a man there who is . . . *involved* with the Sphinx."

Her gaze shot back to Levi.

Her first score had netted her two points: a place up the river and an *involved* man. Maybe this was all going to be easier than she'd thought—but probably not.

She put her hand over Levi's where he had it on her knee and gave him a little squeeze—a promising type of squeeze.

"What's his name? Is he someone you know?" That's all she needed, a name—the guy's name or the place's name. She didn't care which, she just needed somewhere to start looking again, and she'd be out of El Caribe in a heartbeat.

"I don't know his name, but I can guarantee he's worth talking to." Levi's smile returned, all toothy and gray and maybe starting to get just a little bit wobbly, and she gave his hand another encouraging squeeze. "He was...uh, at Beranger's today, after the damage was done. We were all scrambling around, trying to find the statue in the wreckage, and Remy was dying on the spot, shot up by the police, and not talking to anybody, though everyone tried to rush over and help."

Yes, she just bet they had. Probably more like rush over and try to shake the location of the Sphinx out of him before he expired.

"That must have been terrible for you, Levi," she said, leaning over again, letting her personal concern for his safety put a catch in her soft, soft voice.

He popped a tiny empanada in his mouth as his gaze slowly fell to her cleavage and got stuck there.

"It was a...a, uh, free-for-all in the gallery, absolutely crazy, Ponce and the cops with a whole damn platoon of bodyguards trying to take charge, which my men and I simply weren't going to allow—and then this man came in the back door, just one man, and we all got *hit*." He stopped, and reached for a toothpick with deep-fried baby squid on the end of it.

"Hit?" she prompted after a few seconds of dead silence.

"Uh, yes, Suzi dear." He lifted his bloodshot eyes to meet hers and used his teeth to drag the bit of squid off the toothpick and into his mouth. "Zapped with some *force*," he said around the tapa, "something unlike anything I've ever known, something hot. It was everywhere, all over us, making our skin crawl, and we all ran, but Gervais got caught by this man, right by the throat, and of all things, my dear, he wanted to know your name."

A bolt of alarm skittered down her spine. That was the last thing she'd expected to hear.

"*My* name?" she asked.

"Yes," Levi confirmed, still chewing. "And mine."

"Wh-why?" This was not good, some guy zapping people in Beranger's wanting to know her name.

"Because we're the *dealers* here," Levi said. "You and me. This man said he would have the Sphinx at this place up the river tomorrow, and he wants to sell, and who else is he going to contact in this town to unload something as valuable as the Maned Sphinx of Sesostris III besides you and me? Beranger is dead."

Precisely, and Beranger was the last guy who'd tried to unload the Sphinx.

"Aren't you jumping to conclusions? Just because this guy says he has the Sphinx doesn't mean he actually has it."

He looked at her like she'd missed the whole point—which she undoubtedly had.

"Nobody is *jumping* to anything," he assured her, sounding thoroughly exasperated and annoyed and frustrated and like all the champagne and the four shots of vodka he'd had at the craps table were finally, suddenly, starting to kick in. "I have been *ch-chasing* this piece of Egyptian *junk* for the last damn four months, and that's not counting all the years when I merely *thought* it might be out there somewhere, and the one thing I can guarantee you, *Suzanna*, is that *somebody* has it—in their hands, in their keeping, right now, in this damn city. *Everything* points to it being *here*."

"But anybody could have it."

"No." He shook his head, adamant. "It's not just anybody. It is this man who was at Beranger's, who is now up the river, and...and you need to go up there and get the damn thing for me...for *us*."

Oh, right. And that's what this was all about? Levi welcoming her with open arms, not because she looked like a guttersnipe, but because he thought he could order her around?

Good God, the man was delusional.

"So where am I supposed to go?" Really, it couldn't be this easy, but he looked so relieved when she asked that for a moment she thought it *was* going to be this easy.

"You don't need to know that."

The hell she didn't, but she could let it ride for a minute or two.

"You'll be going with Gervais, and he knows the name of the place and where it is."

"Uh, what about you?" she asked. "Where are you going to be?"

He slumped back in his chair and squinted up at her from under his bushy gray eyebrows—and he burped.

"Suzi, you know I'm not a well man." He reached for more champagne and filled his glass.

No, she didn't. Overweight, old, and out of shape, yes, flat-out cowardly, yes, but not unwell.

"Actually, you look great, Levi," she lied.

He beamed for just a second or two at the compliment. "So do you, my dear. You know, you've always been one of my favorites."

"Thank you."

"We *need* to work together on this," he continued, taking a short gulp of wine before he continued. "Gervais wouldn't know an authentic artifact if it hit him in the head, but you will, and if we present a solid front, this other man can't play us off against each other." He was making the hard sell and proving once again that for a real player, money trumped sex every time. "The piece starts at a million, we both know that, and he will, too, but working together, maybe we can keep the price from going to five, which means we both make money, profits to be split fifty-fifty."

He had a buyer. She could see it in his watery gaze, and he was offering her a cut of the money, which told her exactly what he thought about this whole "up the river" plan—sketchy at best, dangerous at worst.

"What's your client willing to pay?" All she needed was a name, and he'd have to give her one before she got on a boat heading anywhere.

He hedged for a minute, then said, "Eight."

Which meant ten.

"Who is it?" she asked, even knowing he wouldn't say. Push, shove, push back, pull—it was the game they played.

"He's Japanese."

"Ahh," she said. All the good stuff was going to Japan these days.

"What about you?" he asked. "What's your client willing to pay?"

"Twenty." Twenty thousand, not million, but that was a minor difference in this situation.

His eyes widened for the briefest moment, and she knew he was hooked.

"Twenty? Well, yes, then, I think we go with your client on the Sphinx, and I'll find my Japanese friend some other exquisite Middle Kingdom artifact."

And there she was, making another fifty-fifty deal on something no one she knew had ever laid eyes on.

"Your buyer isn't interested in a chance at immortality?"

"Suzi, please." Levi gave her a long-suffering look. "The stories are good for increasing the price. If I had a dollar for every four-thousand-year-old magic statue I've handled, I'd be retired in the south of France by now."

She, too, but she'd never handled a magic statue endorsed by the Defense Intelligence Agency of the United States of America.

"So where am I going tomorrow morning?" she asked again.

He just stared at her, blinking owlishly, silently perturbed. She knew he didn't like being pushed once, let alone twice—but neither did she, so she stared right back.

"You'll have to shrust me on this," he said, starting to slur his words.

Trust, she was sure, was what he meant, and the hell she did.

She scooted her chair back and started to rise, but he caught her arm with his hand and held her in place.

"*Sit* back down, S-uzi," he whined. "Pul-lease, you need to—"

That's as far as he got.

"Mr. Asher," a strong masculine voice interrupted with a tone of command she instantly recognized.

Dax.

She turned and found him closing in on her and Levi.

The old man quickly released her, then immediately looked for his men.

"They went back into the casino," Dax informed him, pulling up a chair from the next table. "We need to talk."

"And you...are?" Levi asked, trying to draw himself up into a figure with some authority—and failing. Despite his effort, he was still slumped in his chair, all sweaty and drunk.

"Danny Kane, from *The Daily Inquirer,*" Dax said, flashing his press pass. "I'm down here following a story, and—"

"I'm, uh, *sure* that I don't talk to reporters," Levi said, not actually sounding too sure of anything. "And, Suzi dear"—he turned to her and started to rise shakily out of his chair—"I don't think you should talk to any, uh, reporters either."

"No, Levi," she agreed, being careful not to look

over at Dax. She stood, too. "Do you want me to walk you up to your room?" He wasn't very stable on his feet

"No. No, my dear." He was holding on to the table. "It's been a frightful day, truly frightful, and I'm not feeling all that well."

After four shots, numerous glasses of champagne, and a couple of pounds of deep-fried squid and bacon-wrapped dates, Suzi wasn't sure that she'd be feeling very well either.

"Yes, Levi, I understand, but—"

"Ah, Gervais." His gaze shifted to somewhere behind her, and his face brightened. He lifted his hand and beckoned the man over, then returned his attention to her. "You *will* be here in the morning, right? We have a deal?"

"Yes, but it would be best if you told me—"

He let out a short laugh. "Oh, no, Suzi. No, no. I'm not that drunk. In the morning. You can go with Gervais."

Dammit.

The burly Frenchman hurried to Levi's side, took him by the arm, and the two of them started off.

Dammit. Watching him leave just took it out of her, her last ounce of strength. The day had been too long, too brutal, too awful. Frightful, just like Levi had said. All she'd wanted was one damn name to make it all worthwhile, and she hadn't been able to get it.

She turned to Dax, but before she could say anything, Levi called her name.

"Suzi...dear?"

She shifted her attention back to where he was standing a few feet away, Gervais by his side, still holding on to him, a small, pudgy old man in a very damp and wrinkled pale blue suit.

"Yes," she said.

"I never got the sh-chance to, well, because..." He paused for a second, his brow furrowing as he looked at her. "Well, because we haven't really run into each other lately, but I'm sorry."

Sorry about something and drunk. She turned back to Dax, hoping to come up with something to say, because the "sorry" word wasn't going to work for her, not with him. She was on a mission, not a social outing.

"About the girl in Ukraine," Levi said from behind her back, his voice suddenly sounding painfully clear. "The one you'd set up with Pierre Dulcine in New York, to work in Dulcine's gallery. He told me the girl was killed in Odessa, on vacation or something, such a terrible tragedy."

Yes, a terrible tragedy, and poor old Levi didn't know the half of it.

She took a breath but couldn't quite find the strength to turn around and face him. It was too much at the end of a bad day, the same way the girl's death had been too much three months ago. An eighteen-year-old Alabama girl who'd thought she was heading for a life of adventure in Europe, to work at a first-class resort. Instead, she'd ended up at a fourth-rate brothel on the shores of the Black Sea, a grim existence full of brutality and meagerness, and she'd died there.

"Pierre was shocked, of course, quite dis-traught," Levi was going on. "And we were both so concerned for you, my dear, that somehow the whole awful-awful thing would bring back memories of your own terrible tragedy, what with the similarities. You know, the girl for Dulcine's getting shot, and your daughter getting shot."

Her heart stopped for a beat, and in that short, intense interval, all the pain she always barely held at bay came washing into her.

"How old was she again?" Levi asked. "Your little girl? Three?"

Three, and Suzi could hardly breathe, *her little girl.*

God, it had been so long—and would never be long enough.

Levi was still yammering away behind her, and the thought crossed her mind to just take her whole damn day out on him.

Her baby, her little girl, how dare he bring that much heartache back to life, how dare he be so casually destructive.

She started to rise from the table, her hands closing, tightening. Christian had taught her how to fight, and she could take Levi any day of the week—except before she could make a move, she was caught from behind and hauled up close to a very solid body. Dax, *dammit.*

"No" was all he said, very softly, very close to her ear, his grip like iron around her waist.

"Let go of—" She started to struggle, just letting herself get wound up to go after Levi and teach him a damn lesson, and maybe get her hands around his throat and just shake him until he gave her the damn name of the place on the river, just throttle the bastard, just get the information out of him— just get him to shut up.

"Not here, not now," Dax said, his voice still so very calm, his words still for her ears only.

"You don't understand," she gritted from between her teeth, tensing against him, ready to fight him, too.

She felt movement around the table, heard the sound of footsteps, but her attention, every atom of her being, was focused on Levi Asher, on the dawning stupefaction spreading across his face that Suzanna Royale Toussi wanted to slug him.

"Back off," she heard Dax say to someone coming up behind them. "I said *back off*. I've got her. We're leaving." He was angry, protective, his voice on edge.

Tension was pulsing around her, Levi babbling, his bodyguard steadying him, and Dax was taking charge, giving clear directions and walking away with her in his arms, getting them out of El Caribe.

CHAPTER TWENTY-FIVE

"Dylan, we've got a mess at the Gran Chaco," Creed said, walking out of the hotel's main entrance.

"Explain."

"Suzi's AWOL, and the contact she told you about, Jimmy Ruiz? He's dead. Shot to death in her room. Rumors are running wild out here, but it sounds like the police have all her luggage, and she is definitely *numero uno* on their suspect list. I thought we should—"

"I'm on it. Stay on the line," Dylan said, then Creed heard him talking to someone else, giving an order—*Get Grant on the horn.*

He stopped with his back to one of the portico's marble columns and lit up a cigar he'd bummed off the boss, holding the phone between his shoulder and ear while he bent his head over the lighter cupped in his hands. He puffed until he got the cigar going, then he closed the lighter and took the phone back in his hand.

Sucking in a mouthful of smoke, he leaned back against the column and visually quartered the area, from the parking lot, to the entrance, to the valet stand and the doormen, and back again to the parking lot.

And he waited, letting the smoke slowly drift out of his mouth.

Fucking twilight zone, that's where they'd landed with this Sphinx business. He'd seen it coming, and Suzi was in the middle of it. *Dammit.* That just coddled his balls.

One of the first things he'd seen when he'd walked into the Gran Chaco was the police security on her room, and it hadn't taken more than two minutes of hanging around in the lobby to find out why. Jimmy Ruiz had been massacred in there. By all accounts, and there were a hundred available, the deed had been a lovers' quarrel, with the Paraguayan man killed by the beautiful *gringa* in a jealous rage. Creed could guarantee there hadn't been any lovers' quarrel, but that didn't mean Suzi hadn't shot Jimmy Ruiz.

Somebody sure had, and Suzi was gone.

"Beranger's gallery is on Carlos Lopez Avenue, Galeria Viejo," Dylan came back on the line. "He lives up on the second floor, so he shouldn't be too hard to find. And I've got a confirmed location for one of the dealers short-listed by the DIA as a potential buyer for the Sphinx—Levi Asher. He's at El Caribe."

"Got it," he said, pushing off the marble column and crossing the street to the parking lot.

"One more thing," Dylan said.

"Yeah?"

"Suzi told Grant that Dax Killian was at the gallery this afternoon. Apparently there was a run-in with the police, and he got her out of there."

Dax Killian?

"I don't believe in coincidence, boss. What the fuck do you think is going on?"

"I don't know, and Grant hasn't been able to find out, so we'll play it as it comes."

"Roger that," he said, heading back to his car. "I'll let you know what I find at the gallery."

Women, Levi thought.

There was just no telling what got into them sometimes. Suzi Toussi had looked a little murderous there, a state of affairs that was absolutely beyond his ability to comprehend.

Suzanna Toussi, ready to pounce on him—and not in a good way. Oh, no.

He hoped she bounced back to her normal, coolheaded self by tomorrow morning. It simply wouldn't do to send a half-deranged woman up the river.

He shuffled around in his luxury suite, dropping clothes everywhere he went—his jacket in the hall, his tie on the table, a shoe here, a shoe there, his shirt over the back of the couch, his pants on the floor. He'd dismissed Gervais at the door. He felt terrible and simply needed to be alone.

He'd eaten too much, drunk too much, was too hot, feeling light-headed, and his stomach was in distress.

He padded into the bathroom to get a towel to mop his brow, and while leaning over the sink, took stock of himself.

He wasn't a bad man, but he'd done a bad thing, involving her, and felt very remorseful. Not so much remorse that he would change the course of events, but he felt remorse.

Suzi would be fine, he told himself. It would be an adventure for her to go up the river and meet with this crazy dangerous man with the hot-crawly weapon who was not quite right.

Levi considered himself a very astute judge of people, and this man from Beranger's who had grabbed Gervais, asked questions, and then invited them all up the river to get the Sphinx—well, he was quite dangerous.

Quite.

Big, strong, determined, fierce—Gervais had said the man's arms were marked, scarred, and that there had been other scars on his face and neck.

Honestly, Levi had been in a perfect quandary. He wanted the Sphinx, or rather he wanted his Japanese buyer's money for the Sphinx, but he didn't care for the company of men under the best of circumstances, and he didn't care for the company of dangerous men under any circumstances.

He hadn't known what he was going to do, until Suzi Toussi had called.

She was perfect.

The fifty-fifty part, the percentages could be manipulated later, if she actually made it back with the statue.

He reached up and combed his fingers through his hair, arranging it a bit. He wished he hadn't mentioned that girl in Ukraine and her daughter again, poor little thing. He'd just been trying to be nice, but all that should have waited until after the deal. It wasn't good to have Suzi upset. He needed her on her game. He needed an expert up there to deal with this man from Costa del Rey. That's the place where he'd told Gervais to come, Costa del Rey, King's Coast, and if the Memphis Sphinx was truly there, then it was a king's coast indeed. Levi hadn't come all this way to pay a million dollars for a fake, and Suzanna Royale Toussi could smell a fake from a hundred miles. She was so very talented, a superb negotiator, her instincts impeccable when it came to art and artifacts—but not when it came to men, and Levi didn't think she'd done any better for herself this time.

"Danny Kane," he muttered. Suzi always went for brawn instead of brains. It's why she never went for him, though she'd come close tonight, up until she'd gotten so unreasonably upset.

But up until then, she'd definitely been on track for his bed.

He smiled at himself in the mirror—and something caught his eye and held his beady little orbs like they were in a vise. His smile froze in a moment of stark and utter terror, his lips stuck to his teeth, his arms trembling on either side of the sink.

A shadow, that's what he'd thought, if he'd given the dark reflection in the mirror any thought at all, which he hadn't—not until he'd smiled and the shadow had smiled back.

It was him, the crazy dangerous man from Costa del Rey, in the suite's living room, standing quietly against a wall, and for an odd, confusing second, Levi wondered if he'd walked right past him while he'd been taking off his clothes, not even aware that he hadn't been alone.

"The woman," the man said. He was big, just like Gervais had said, with short dark hair and very well defined features, chiseled, high cheekbones, a strong jaw, firm mouth, arms like pile drivers. "The redhead, Suzanna Toussi, where is she?"

Now, this was shameful, truly it was, but Levi didn't hesitate for a second to give the girl away. There was no thought to it at all, let alone a second thought.

"I-I picked her up at th-the Po-po-po—"

"Posada Plaza?" the man asked.

"Y-yes."

"Where is she now?" For a crazy man, his voice was very calm, very measured, and somehow, very reassuring.

"On h-her way back, I th-think, w-with a m-m-m-m-m—"

"Take a breath, Levi. Everything is fine."

He did exactly as he was told. That was his new plan, to do everything exactly as he was told, to not cause this man any trouble, so he took a breath.

"A m-man," he finished. "D-danny Kane, a repor-porter."

"How well do you know her, Suzanna Toussi?"

Oh, God, a trick question. Levi's panic skyrocketed again. He didn't know what to say. If he didn't know her very well, would the man leave? Or would it be best to admit that he did know her very well, and leave himself wide open for God only knew what?

He was frozen in indecision, nearly crushed senseless by the weight of the question. He couldn't afford to make a mistake. The truth? Or a lie?

God, he shouldn't have had so much champagne.

In the end, with the seconds ticking away and his indecision spiraling out of control, the heat and the booze and the fear got the best of him—and he crumpled in a faint to the floor.

"One dead body rotting in the heat," Creed said into the phone, talking to Dylan. "The place was torn apart. No sign of any priceless statue, that's for damn sure."

"Who's the body?"

"Remy Beranger," Creed said, making a right-hand turn in the Jeep. "I checked his wallet. He'd been moved around a little since he died, and I moved him a little more, but I don't think anybody really much cares about old Remy."

"Why not?"

"Well, boss, he's been there for a while, all day I'd say, and if the police did this, like Suzi told Grant, then I'd say nobody gives a hill of beans for this guy and his gallery."

"So you think the statue is gone."

"Hell and gone."

"And who the hell has it?" Dylan asked.

Creed took the next left and shifted up into third. "I think we need to ask Suzi. I'm headed over to El Caribe and this Levi Asher guy, and if I come up empty-handed there, then we've got a real problem on our hands."

"Suzi can handle herself."

Creed wasn't so sure, but he kept his mouth shut. Dylan had more faith in the girl than he did. Oh, he adored her, all right, but he had to say, despite Hawkins's stellar success with Skeeter and Red Dog—okay, *astounding* success—Creed thought Superman had pushed his luck with Suzi. The girl was just too girly, too hothouse orchid.

Hawkins, though, hell, he thought every girl could be toughened up with PT, physical training, and a .45—and he was right, of course. Creed just didn't think that made them tough enough for Ciudad del Este, especially with dead bodies piling up all around—except, of course, for Skeeter and Red Dog. Those two were tough enough, period.

"I'm almost to the hotel," he said. "I'll call you after I talk to Asher."

He ended the call and pocketed his phone.

Talk. Right. Suzi Toussi had gone missing off a damn "pink" op that should have been a cakewalk—and Creed was damn well going to find her.

CHAPTER TWENTY-SIX

Well, that had gone well, Dax thought, pulling up in front of the Posada Plaza and throwing the Land Cruiser into park.

He looked over at Suzi, who was just sitting there in the passenger seat. She hadn't said a word, not one word since he'd kept her from jumping Levi Asher and hauled her out of El Caribe.

Geezus.

The girl had been ready to rumble. She actually had a little muscle action in her arms, some biceps business, and some deltoid business. He didn't doubt for a minute that she could have done some damage.

Of course, he would have had to take Gervais out, and then the other bodyguard would have shown up, and on and on. In a social situation like that, the best fight was no fight, every time.

He put his hand over his mouth and looked out

the windshield, thinking, but all he could think was *Three years old.*

He'd known—he was damn good at his job—but reading it in a pile of documents and hearing it bandied about in a damn casino restaurant by some drunk were two different things, and he couldn't let it stand, not like it was, with her shell-shocked and silent, and definitely exhausted, emotionally and physically.

Geezus. Levi Asher might be the stupidest bastard on the planet.

"Tell me your daughter's name." It wasn't a request, no matter how careful he was to keep his tone neutral.

When she didn't answer, he slanted his gaze across the front seat. There weren't many streetlights in Ciudad del Este, but the Posada Plaza had a big pink neon sign on the front of the building, and the light shone down on her, limning her profile, softening the garish colors of her bustier, and turning her skin into a silken wash of rose and pale peach.

Her eyes were dark, the downward cast of her gaze making it hard to discern her mood. She was so quiet.

Too quiet.

"Your daughter's name," he said. "I need to know."

And he waited, watching the slow rise and fall of her chest.

"Here," he said, opening one of the bottles of

water they'd left in the Cruiser and handing it over. "Take a drink."

He was being very deliberate with his words, keeping everything simple and direct.

With the water bottle half in her lap, she went ahead and took it from his hand. A small drink later, she gave him what he'd asked for.

"Adriana," she said, her voice not very loud but very distinct. "Adriana Louise Weymouth."

"Thank you." It hurt hearing it, because he hurt for her. He wasn't going to tell her he was sorry, though. There wasn't enough sorry in the world to cover this.

"It was an accident," she said, and he nodded silently over on his side of the car.

An accidental shooting. Man, that was a nightmare.

"It wasn't me who had the gun," she said, "and sometimes I think if I went back and shot Nathan, killed him, like he killed our baby, that maybe it would help."

Nathan had been her first husband, back when she'd been in her early twenties.

"Probably not." He told her the truth. He wasn't against revenge for people who had the stomach for it, but he knew it was a dangerous indulgence for those who didn't. "Come on. Let's get you inside."

She let him help her out of the car and hold on to her through the whole elevator ride. He hadn't thought either of them had the strength for the stairs, and it didn't take more than one look at her for Marcella and Marceline to call a temporary truce on the action in the lift.

Inside the room, he turned the radio on low to have something to break the quiet, and he opened the doors onto the balcony to let the moonlight and the sounds of the city night in.

While he set out the food he'd gotten for her before he'd gone to El Caribe, she stayed next to the closed door to the hall, her back literally up against the wall.

"Do you want to eat something?" he asked.

She shook her head, standing in Marcella's too-high platform heels, looking like she could either collapse or bolt—and he'd be damned if he let her bolt.

"You might feel better." He opened the room's small refrigerator again and pulled out a beer.

She let out a short laugh. "You don't know anything about it."

"So tell me." He sat down at the table and popped the top off the beer.

He saw her sigh, and he took a drink—and from across the room, she met his gaze.

"That's a nice wooden shipping crate you've got there on the table."

Yes, it was, or it would have been if it had still had its contents.

"Thank you." He wasn't going to deny anything.

"It wasn't in the room when I left for El Caribe."

"No," he agreed. "At that point, it was still hidden in the cistern at Beranger's." He reached inside, took out the top half of the foam core, and showed it to her. The cut-out area for the Sphinx was very clear. "And for all the trouble I went to, I got nothing."

Suzi tilted her head back against the wall, exposing the slender column of her throat, and he felt the first coiling promise of desire come to life deep inside his body. Inappropriate, yeah, but undeniable. She was the most beautiful thing he'd ever seen, and he'd been chasing her for six long months, even if it had only been the facts of her life he'd been getting.

Denver—that's where he'd been heading as soon as he'd finished his business with Erich Warner. He would have been there a long time before now if this deal hadn't come up.

"As bad as it's been for me, as bad as it *is*," she said, her voice so low he could barely hear her, "I know it's worse for Nathan, and...sometimes... that's the only thing that keeps me going, knowing he's suffering even more than me and still living, day after day."

He took another long swallow off his beer. Suzanna Royale Toussi, Suzi Q with her lush body and sophisticated style, with her designer clothes and highbrow art, living in the wasteland. He knew what it was like. He'd seen it. He'd felt it. He'd been there.

But he'd never lost a child, and he knew that place was different from all the others.

Inconsolable.

She started to tremble over on her side of the room. He saw it in her shoulders and in the way she wrapped her arms around herself, like she was trying to hold herself together.

Before the first sob broke free from her lips, he was there, holding her.

"No," she said, covering her face with her hand. "Don't touch me."

She was still backed up against the wall, her body so stiff, and yet shaking—everywhere, all over.

"D-don't," she repeated, not looking at him, keeping her hand over her face.

"Suzi," he said, wanting to help and yet feeling so helpless.

"No." Another sob broke free, and then another, and she dropped her hand, looking at him, everything awful showing in her stricken gaze.

He moved in closer. This was going bad fast, and there wasn't any help for it.

Tears started running down her face in dark tracks of smudged makeup, and inch by inch, he felt her crumple and begin to slide down the wall, her knees weakening. He tightened his grip, with predictable results.

She sobbed and slapped him, and he let it happen. He could have stopped her. He'd seen it coming.

Oh, hell yeah. He'd seen it coming from a mile off, the flash of fear and anger and anguish in her eyes, the tension holding her on the edge of an abyss. Hell, for what she needed, he'd have let her hit him twice.

Not that it didn't hurt. The side of his face stung like hell, but he couldn't have cared less about getting his face slapped. Not when everything was welling up inside her and getting ready to break her the hard way.

"You... y-you bastard."

That's right, baby. That was him, the bastard.

He kept her backed up against the wall, and he didn't have a regret in the world about using his physical advantage against her.

She lifted her hand again, but instead of slapping him, she made a fist and hit him on the shoulder—and he let her.

Life was complicated, a real fucking mess most of the time.

She hit him again. *"How dare y-you... you..."*

He had his hands on her waist, holding on to her, but she wasn't fighting to get away from him. She was fighting for the sake of it, and she was fighting herself far more than she was fighting him. She was hitting him, yeah, but she was the one who was hurting. Oh, baby, she was hurting bad.

"You sonuvabitching bastard."

All day, every day. She could count on it.

She twisted against him, but not to get away, just to twist and squirm and ache with the pain.

He was no rocket scientist, never had been. He'd been damn lucky to have even graduated from good old East High in Denver. School had not been his strong suit, despite his half a moment of brilliance in calculus, before it had all gone to hell. He'd never actually seen a point in it, not from kindergarten on, not until he'd joined the Army and started learning stuff that counted. So, yeah, the sheer, cosmic expanse of all the things he didn't know was pretty damn vast—but give him a compass, a map, a weapon, and a target, and he was the fucking valedictorian of that class. It didn't matter how complex the problem was, how many countries he had to cross, how many enemies he had to vanquish, he knew how to come out on top—and he knew her. He knew this, where she was in her head, what was driving her, and where she was going to end up, which was the abyss—and he knew how to save her. He knew what she needed, and he knew he was the only guy in the whole world who did—because what she needed was him.

No one else.

Only him.

He pressed closer to her and lowered his head to hers, resting his forehead on her brow, and he let her rant at him, let her vent her anger and her pain, let her pound on his chest until she was clutching his shirt in her hands and just holding on.

"Dax..." she whispered his name, burying her face in the curve of his neck. *"Oh, Dax."*

Yeah, baby. Oh, Dax was here for her.

He kissed the top of her head, let his lips slide over the silken strands of her hair—and he pulled her closer. Even at midnight, it was a hundred degrees in this town, but he was offering her his warmth. He was the man for her.

"Dax..." She gripped him tighter, buried herself deeper, clinging to him. *"Dax. Oh, Dax."* She loosened her hold on his shirt, and her arms came up and around his neck.

Yeah, that was right—and so were the tears. She wasn't sobbing. She was just crying silently, nearly immobile in his arms now. He felt the wetness on his neck, and it broke his heart. God, life could be so fucking hard, harder than a person could bear.

And yet it had to be borne, every day, in every way, over and over again until the end, and if a guy was lucky, every now and then, he'd end up with a complicated woman in his arms, somebody who could turn him inside out.

"Suzi," he spoke her name, grounding her with it, bringing her back to him.

She slid her arms farther around his neck, and he kissed her cheek.

"I'm sorry, so sorry, sugar," he whispered in her ear and kissed her again, and he felt her soften against him.

Sex was a funny thing, and he was thinking about it, but it was all up to her. He wanted to make love with her, to ease her pain, to remind her there was life, always, the flame of it burning deep inside, to give her pleasure and ease her mind.

Yeah, he was such a great, selfless guy.

He wanted to fuck her so sweet, to make her come apart in his arms, to make her his. He wanted to come so deep inside her, to claim her.

Suzi, Suzi Q . . . *sugar baby*—he wanted to taste her, make her.

He opened his mouth on her neck and slid one hand down over the curve of her hip to pull her closer, to bring her up against him, and she turned her face into his neck and softly brushed her lips across the skin she'd made wet with her tears.

It was enough.

He kissed her neck, using his teeth so gently, licking her with his tongue and then sliding his mouth to hers and kissing her deep, angling his head to get more of her. Handful by handful, he dragged her skirt up over her ass, giving himself the access he needed. When he had the skirt up around her waist, he slid his hand underneath her white organic cotton panties, over the softest skin he'd ever touched, over the perfect curves of her derriere.

And he fell in love all over again, with the sweet softness between her legs, with the promise of her body.

You and me, babe. Just the two of us in the whole world. Right here. Right now.

Her hands were on his belt, but before he shucked out of his pants, he knelt down and un-laced his boots. Then he reached up, one-handed, and pulled her panties down around her ankles and helped her step out of them.

Moonlight had never looked so pretty as it did on her bare skin and the soft curls between her legs.

He was smitten, the scent and loveliness of her going straight to his head and messing with it. Nothing was better. Leaning forward, he pressed his tongue to the hot, sweet center of her desire, and he teased her, licked her, felt her softly grind her hips against him and tunnel her fingers through his hair.

"Dax..." His name was a sigh on her lips, her body a silken, tangible force in his arms.

She spread her legs wider, and he slipped his fingers up inside her. She was so soft, so wet, such a gift—electrifying, turning him on, getting him so hot and hard. He plied her with his tongue, loving the taste of her, the little catches in her breath, and the way she was holding him to her, tighter and tighter.

"Dax..."

Come for me, baby. He wanted it so badly, to make her come undone, to make her feel so good. He wanted her to know he was her man, the one she needed, the one who could take her higher.

Her sighs grew rougher, more guttural, and he kept on—on and on and on, endlessly pleasuring her—sliding his fingers in and out of her, teasing her with his tongue, over and over again, until her soft cries became a moan, until she pressed herself against his mouth and held herself there, until he felt the contractions of her release rippling through her.

When she collapsed against the wall, he rose to his feet and shoved his pants to the floor. Taking her mouth with his, he fitted himself to her and pushed up inside. No hesitation. No thoughts. It was mind-bending. She was so hot and slick, taking all of him on his first thrust, to the hilt.

Her mouth was soft and wet, sucking on him, sucking on his tongue, then deepening the kiss. Between them, he felt her undoing the bustier, and he did his best to help. Slowly, the thing opened up, one loosened lace at a time. He ran the tiny black straps off her shoulders, letting them fall to the sides, and then there she was, her breasts so soft and full and filling his hand even as he filled her, again and again, getting lost in her, mindlessly, so easily, following the heated warmth of her skin into a pleasure so deep he never wanted it to end.

All he wanted was to be with her.

To be like this, driving into her, holding her to him. He had his tongue in her mouth, his hand on her breast, and his other hand wrapped under her thigh, lifting her leg around his waist, letting him go deep and deeper. He thrust into her, and she took him every time, all the way, moving her hips with his, until the heat and the rhythm and the seductive softness of her body took him straight over the edge.

He pinned her up against the wall, his body rigid with the pleasure pulsing through him, her soft gasps of breath hot against his mouth. Women. *Geezus.*

So perfect. Especially her. Hot, and soft, and wet, and silky, turning him on and setting him off.

He pushed into her one last time, keeping himself deep inside, just to feel her as he finished off, just to hear the small sound of pleasure she made. God, he could do her all night long, but she didn't feel like she had the strength left to get to the bed.

So he held her, and he stayed inside her, just loving the way she felt, his heart still pounding.

She was so dangerous.

God.

"You okay?" he asked after a few more moments had passed, brushing his mouth across her cheek.

"*Mmm-hmmm.*" She rocked against him, ever so slightly, and his eyes damn near crossed—it felt so good.

He smiled and kissed the side of her neck.

"I wanted to do this the night we met," he whispered against her skin, "from the minute I walked into the gallery and saw you."

"*Mmmmm.*" She was still pulsing around him, soft, latent ripples.

He tightened his arms around her and buried his face in her neck, and he breathed her in, filled himself with the warm and lovely scent of her skin. "You feel *so* damn good."

"Oh, Dax," she murmured, softening against him and running her fingers up through his hair—and he kissed her, moved his mouth to hers and just played with her, sucking on her tongue, gently biting her lips, just trying to get more of her.

She was so responsive, teasing him, giving of herself—he felt it with every move she made.

Carefully, slowly, he pulled out of her, and he kissed her while he did it, softly, on her mouth, on her cheek, on the side of her neck. Then he lifted her into his arms and carried her to the bed.

He wanted her naked.

CHAPTER TWENTY-SEVEN

Suzi felt satiated with his lovemaking, yet she knew she wanted more.

Sitting on the bed in her birthday suit, bustier on one side of her, Marcella's skirt on the floor, she watched Dax where he was bent over her shoes, unbuckling every tiny strap.

"I could help you with your shirt," she said. It was the only piece of clothing he still had on.

"Got it." With her foot still in his lap, he reached up behind his neck and pulled the shirt off over his head.

He tossed it off to the side and went back to getting her out of the platform heels. The boy was concentrating on the job, his hair all tousled from her fingers, a smudge of lipstick on his cheek, his gaze intent.

God, he was beautiful, dark hair covering his

chest, delineating his abs, his legs so strong and muscular, his fingers nimble.

She didn't want to think about anything else, not about earlier, when she'd been crying in his arms, and not about the loss that would forever haunt her days, not right now. The ache was always with her. It never went completely away.

But with Dax, she had a chance for a small reprieve, and she wanted it, just a little more time with him, time to be held and cared for, and to get lost in his loving. It was crazy, something of the moment, intense and vital, sex and solace and salvation all wrapped up in Dax Killian's arms.

The sheets were clean on his bed, and they'd pushed the blankets and covers down to the end. He had a lot of pillows, and while he worked on the tiny straps, she rested back on them.

He didn't look up from his task, but she saw him smile, and when he got the shoes off, he lifted her leg over his shoulder and kissed the inside of her knee.

"That's a good start," she murmured, and he grinned wider—and then he kissed the inside of her knee again.

Inch by inch, he worked his way up her leg, stretching himself out on the bed, until his mouth was back at the hot sweet center of her desire.

She lifted her hips against him in rhythm with the forays of his tongue, and she let herself sink into the loveliness of how he made her feel.

And so it went, on and on, his mouth on her everywhere and then coming up to take her in a kiss, hot and soft and deep, claiming her as he pushed up inside her. Everywhere she held him, she could feel the sleek, powerful movements of his muscles beneath his skin.

The world disappeared, time and again, every moment in his arms drawing them closer—*hot mouth, soft skin, hard body, lush breasts, the curves of her hips, the angles of his, warmth, eroticism, tenderness, falling...falling...falling into lust, into taste, and sight, and scent, and sensation.*

On his next thrust, he pushed up harder into her and held himself deep, and there he stayed, his breathing slow, and even, and sure, his body like iron.

He leaned down and kissed her, a fleeting touch of his mouth.

"You're hot, sugar," he said, smoothing her hair back off her forehead.

They both were. There was no fan in the room, and the heat rolling up from the street was a palpable force, even at midnight. Their bodies were slick with sweat, the room like a steam bath, and he was teasing her, holding himself so still, second after endless second, until even the slightest movement nearly sent her over the edge.

"Dax...*please.*"

He pulled out and pushed back in so slowly, she thought she might lose her mind.

"Please..."

She strained against him, wanting him to take her there, to make her come, to give her the release he promised with every thrust.

"Please...oh, Dax."

He leaned down and kissed her again, and his next thrust came harder, and the one after that faster, each one stoking a banked fire deep in her core, until it caught and flashed into flame.

She clung to him, riding wave after wave of pleasure, hearing him groan on top of her, a guttural sound of need and satiation that echoed in her heart.

Dax Killian had come undone, and oh, how she loved it.

Slowly, their bodies relaxed as they breathed together, still locked in each other's arms, and dear God, he smelled good—all overheated male.

Dax Killian with the car named Charo. He was so smooth. He was so slick, such a tough piece of work on the street at sixteen, and twenty years later, that toughness had been tempered into steel. In the last six months, she'd wondered hundreds of times what might have come of them, if she hadn't missed him that morning at Duffy's Bar in Denver. Lord, she'd never dragged herself out of bed for a man at six o'clock in the morning—until he'd asked her to meet him for coffee.

Now she knew why she'd raced around like a maniac on less than four hours' sleep just to see him. It wasn't that his smile could melt bricks, or the easy confidence of his gaze. It was for this. That for whatever reason the universe worked the way it did, Dax Killian was a haven for her, a place to rest. She'd felt it instinctively then. She felt it in every cell of her body now. He was here, by her, with her, and she was safe.

She let her breath out on a soft, easy sigh, and he brought his forehead down to rest on hers.

"You okay?" he asked.

"Mmm-hmm." She stretched beneath him, and he grinned.

"Good," he said, resettling himself next to her and sliding his nose down the side of hers.

Oh, geez. She could get used to this. She could get used to it in a heartbeat.

Wrapping his arm around her, he slowly rolled them to their sides, and he kept her close. He stuffed a pillow under his head and one behind her back, and then he kissed her, slanting his mouth over hers and sliding his tongue in deep.

It was a hot kiss, lazy, thorough, missing nothing. Breaking off, he gently bit her lower lip, then licked her, then kissed her again, taking her mouth with his own. It wasn't a "turn you on until I turn you inside out" kiss. It was a "hello" kiss, a "now that we're both not so crazed maybe we can explore each other" kiss, and he was exploring her the same way she was exploring him, not just his mouth, but the taste of him, the angle of his jaw, the weight of him up against her, the hard muscles in the arm around her.

She smoothed her palm over the broad curve of his shoulder and continued upward, tunneling her fingers into his hair—and she kissed him, one long moment after another, luxuriating in the sensuality of having him naked and close, and in the comfort she felt—even the way he smelled made her feel safe.

She snuggled in closer to him and kissed his chest and breathed him in, and after a moment, she confessed.

"I've got a deal with Levi."

"Yeah, I heard him mention that on his way out. You're meeting him in the morning. Right?"

"Right."

"Going after the Memphis Sphinx?"

"The one and only," she admitted.

"But there's a catch."

She nodded, and he waited, smoothing his hand down over the curve of her hip and slowly back up again.

"He wants me to go upriver with Gervais to meet a man with some kind of force field or something. He says this guy was at Beranger's earlier, and that he has the Sphinx."

"Force field?"

"Yes." That was a major tactical consideration, and she wasn't surprised he'd latched on to it.

"Sounds a little sketchy," he said.

"For a girl with nothing but a nine millimeter."

He stretched out on his back, keeping his arm around her, and looked up at the ceiling. After a while, he seemed to come to a decision.

"If you like, I could go with you, watch your back. Take on the force field, that sort of thing."

"Ya think?"

A brief grin flashed across his face. "Well, we've already got that fifty-fifty deal in place. If you trusted me, I could just go up there by myself, pick up the statue, bring it back here—piece of cake."

A sweet offer, but it was a no-go. "Even if I had the name of the place, I wouldn't let you go up there alone."

"Levi didn't tell you where you were going?"

She shook her head.

Another grin curved his mouth—the wolfish one.

"I can change that," he said. "Come on, let's get some food in you."

He reached over the side of the bed and grabbed his shirt, and then, to her surprise, he turned to her and said, "Lift your arms, babe."

She did, and he slipped the shirt over her head. Then he found her undies.

By the time he got her seated at the table, Dax was about half dressed himself and was feeling better than he had in months—six months to be exact.

This woman—she worked on him, and bedding her wasn't even half of what he wanted.

Okay, it was half, maybe even more than half. It wasn't negotiable. He knew that much. Taking her to bed had just shot to the number two slot on his hit parade, right after keeping her out of trouble— and he had a plan. It started with Levi Asher, and ended somewhere upriver, and when it was over, he'd tell her all about it.

After the fact.

She was checking her phone, probably for messages, which he really needed to do, too—check her phone for messages.

"Um, what did you say this was again?" she asked when she was finished, zipping her phone back into her fanny pack and giving the paper plate of roasted meats and white rice, with its straggly bit of overcooked green something-or-another vegetable a very dubious look.

He kissed her on top of her head.

"It's fine, Suzi. I've been eating at that particular restaurant all week and doing great."

"You sure?" She glanced up at him, and even with her hair all wildly sticking out and her makeup smudged beneath her eyes, her beauty struck him hard.

He lifted his hand to her face and smoothed his thumb across her cheek. *Geezus*, she was soft and so incredibly lovely, and he hoped to hell he never ran into Nathan Weymouth. He wasn't sure he trusted himself with the details of the accident that had killed their child, but he was damn sure he didn't trust himself with the man who had done it.

"You're safe," he said and gave her another kiss. "Go ahead and eat. I'll be right back."

He headed into the bathroom for a minute, and when he came back out, she was gone.

CHAPTER TWENTY-EIGHT

Creed had the right room, a luxury suite at El Caribe, and the right mountain of booze-soaked flab, Levi Asher, but not the right answer, not yet, so he tried again.

"Mr. Asher, Levi," he said calmly. "Have you seen Suzanna Toussi since you arrived in Ciudad del Este?"

The man was face-down on the bathroom floor in his underwear, silk boxers and a wifebeater, pretending to be passed out or asleep, but not doing a very good job of either. He was breathing hard and fast, and folks in drunken stupors were usually, well, too damn drunk to have the brains to be afraid, and people who were asleep didn't open their eyes every few seconds, look around real quick, and then squeeze them shut again real tight.

It was ridiculous.

Old Levi was wide-awake and very afraid, and in

about thirty seconds, he was going to wish he'd done a better job of playing possum.

"Levi, here's the truth," he said, sitting down on the edge of the suite's huge jetted tub. "Every time you open your eyes, I know you're looking to see if there's a way out"—he paused for a second and thumbed open his folding knife—"and there isn't, not unless you can get through me, and you can't."

Levi's eyes popped open again at the sound of the knife blade locking into place. It was just a small snick, but the knife wasn't small. The knife was big, the blade sharp and serrated down the back side, and the sight of it was enough to cause the mountain to quake. Creed had seen a lot of things in his life, but he'd never seen that much wrinkly, old chubbiness tremble on cue.

Given a choice, he would have taken a pass.

"So I'm going to ask you one more time, and you will give me an answer."

Geezus. The guy had been on his hands and knees, crawling out of the bathroom, when Creed had let himself in the suite. Asher had actually made eye contact with him before he'd collapsed back down and taken, without a doubt, the stupidest defensive posture Creed had ever seen—the old curl-up-and-die defense.

Anyone could have killed him.

And in this town, someone would, but it wasn't going to be Creed.

"Mr. Asher, have you seen Suzanna Toussi since you arrived in Ciudad del Este?"

His nod was hesitant but unmistakable.

"Where?"

"H-here." He gasped the word out, his voice trembling as badly as the rest of him.

"In the hotel?"

The old guy nodded again.

"When?"

To Creed's amazement, Levi opened one eye and checked his watch.

"An-n hour ago," he said. "Maybe an hour ten."

Close, Creed thought with relief. He wasn't that far behind her.

"Where is she now?"

"I p-picked her up at the Posada Plaza."

That was good information, but it didn't tell him what he needed to know.

"But where is she now? Why isn't she still with you? Where did she go?" Personally, Creed could think of about a hundred and eight reasons why Suzi wasn't with this old geezer in his hotel room, but he had a feeling it was the hundred and ninth one he needed to hear.

"There w-was a man . . . well, two . . . I guess," Levi said.

Bull. There was no "guessing."

"Tell me about them. What do they have to do with Suzi?"

"She left with the first one."

And that was disturbing information.

"Do you know his name?" Always a good place to start.

"D-danny Kane. He came and got her out of the

casino. He's a reporter. Maybe they went back to the Posada. I don't know."

"So what did the second guy want? Tell me about him."

Levi's eyes closed again, and he pressed his lips shut for a moment, shaking his head. "The same as you, to know where she was. He was big. Bad. V-very bad. That man. Frightening."

And that information went into the column marked Very Disturbing. Creed didn't like big bad scary guys going after his friends.

"Do you know his name?"

"N-no," Levi said. "Only..."

"Only what?" He hardened his voice, letting the old souse know he was treading on thin ice. When he didn't get an immediate answer, he leaned down with his knife, grabbed the shoulder strap of Asher's undershirt, and slit it clean through.

The man whimpered, and Creed figured he had another Boy Scout badge coming for this one.

"Wh-where he lives," Asher confessed, a gasping, high-pitched whine in his voice. "I-I know where he lives."

Very, very good information.

"Tell me."

Levi looked up at him from where he was cringing on the floor, and despite still looking pathetic, there was a definite change in his gaze.

"W-we should make a deal. This man has a statue, a sphinx, old, priceless, worth—"

"No deal," Creed said, cutting him off. Yeah, that's what this whole damn deal was about, some damn statue. "Tell me where this guy lives while you still have a tongue in your mouth. *Comprendes?*"

"No, no. There's money, I tell you, mill—"

Creed was done with the weasel. With one move, he hauled the old man to his feet and shoved his head down into the sink. Then he turned on the water, the cold water. *Geezus.* Creed wouldn't have given somebody the time of day for running cold water on his head, but he knew his man, and old Levi Asher rolled over because his hair was getting wet.

He spluttered and choked and said something, and Creed turned off the water.

"What was that?"

"Costa," Levi repeated, spitting water into the sink. "Costa del Rey. That's where this guy lives."

And that pretty much clinched the Twilight Zone for Creed. Oh, yeah, this mission was headed there at light speed. Conroy Farrel had the magic statue and was gunning for Suzi Toussi.

Leaning heavily on the bathroom counter, barely holding himself up, Levi watched the man leave the suite. *Thank God.* He needed to call Gervais. He couldn't be alone. This was awful. The whole night was awful.

My God, his room had been broken into twice, and he'd been roughed up, and manhandled, and practically tortured.

He looked down at himself. He was drenched.

A small hiccup escaped him.

He was doomed. All his work had been for nothing.

He wiped his hand over his face. He probably needed another drink. His nerves were shot.

Step by shaky, trembling step, he eased his way out the bathroom door and toward the bedroom. He always kept a bottle of whiskey by the bed, just in case he needed a little swig in the middle of the night. He had trouble sleeping, but nobody seemed to care.

My God.

That man—with the big knife and fierce, heartless gaze, that wild man with the long blond hair and the iron grip had practically lifted him straight off his feet from the floor.

Battle of the Titans, that's what was going to happen up at Costa del Rey, with the Memphis Sphinx in the middle of it. How in the world was he supposed to come out ahead in a ruckus like that?

My God. It was going to be brutal, epic, and Suzi was going to be worthless.

And Gervais? Did he dare send him up the river in the morning as planned? Was there any hope?

Gervais didn't know about the brutes. Was it possible to send someone into a melee, completely unaware, and have them come out on top with the goods?

Perhaps.

Gervais certainly wouldn't go upriver if Levi told him about the men set to go mano a mano. The man wasn't that devoted. In fact, he wasn't devoted at all. He worked for his money, the same way Levi did, and there was a lot of money at stake in this damn country—twenty million dollars to be exact. If Levi could get the Sphinx, and if Suzi survived, it was certainly possible to squeeze the name of her buyer out of her. He had no doubts about that. He was good with women.

He finally made it to the bed and flopped down onto it. He was so exhausted, he probably didn't need the extra booze. He would probably fall asleep like a log any minute now.

Rolling over onto his back, he stared up at the ceiling and just tried to relax and catch his breath. Ciudad del Este was everything he'd been told and more, violent and crime-ridden and lawless, a cesspool. Good God, he couldn't wait to get out of here.

He'd forgotten to call Gervais, he remembered, and he would, in a minute, but he was starting to drift just a bit, and it felt so good, he decided to just keep drifting...

"Good morning, asshole."

He awoke with a start, harsh words in his ear, and a hand around his throat.

"This is your wake-up call."

Levi stared, panic-stricken and wide-eyed, into the fiercely dark-eyed gaze of the reporter.

"D-danny Kane," he stammered, feeling the man's hand squeeze tighter and tighter around his throat. "Pul-lease."

"Where is she?" the man demanded to know, and Levi didn't have to ask who.

He let out a small choking sound, and Danny Kane lightened his grip ever so slightly.

"I know you had a deal with her for this morning, and I want to know what, you sonuvabitch," Danny Kane's voice was low, and gruff, and mean, like he wanted to know *what* very much, indeed.

Levi hated this place.

And he hated this damn room.

And he suddenly felt very guilty about Suzi Toussi, but she was the one who'd begged him to get in on his deal. She was the one who'd wanted to help—and really, on second thought, it wasn't his fault that she had all these over-testosteroned brutes ready to tear him limb from limb in order to get to her. She'd gotten herself down to Ciudad del Este all on her own.

She'd done this to herself, not him, and she was dragging him down with her.

It simply had to stop.

"Costa del Rey," he said as clearly and succinctly as he could with some behemoth practically strangling him. Who *were* these guys? he wondered, and why did Suzi Toussi know *so* many of them? It was crazy. "That's where she was going for me this morning, to bargain for the Memphis Sphinx, the Maned Sphinx of Sesostris III. That's where it is." He couldn't protect her anymore. He'd done his best, but now the truth must out. "Costa del Rey is up the Paraná River, north of Ciudad del Este, on a tributary called the Rio Tambo. I don't know exactly where that is, but I'm sure it's on a map and that you can find it. You look like a guy who's good with maps." All brawny and tan from being outside. "And if you care for Suzi at all, you *will* find it, because two other guys are already trying to catch her, for God only knows what reasons, and they all seem to be heading there—Costa del Rey." He enunciated the words very carefully. He was done. He didn't want any more encounters involving the Sphinx. He was handing off the problem.

Danny Kane released him, and he fell back onto the bed.

"What two guys?" Mr. Kane's voice was still plenty mean, but Levi didn't care anymore. He was getting used to being abused.

"The last man in here had long blond hair and a big knife, and I gave him your name and suggested the Posada Plaza as a good place to look for her." His mind was so clear now that he'd made his decision. He was leaving, getting out of here, immediately, today, this morning.

"You asshole." Danny Kane looked like he could chew nails—and he probably could.

"Be that as it may." Levi was beyond being offended. "But I told the first guy the same thing, to look for her at the Posada Plaza. He was big, dark-haired, forceful, without actually *strangling* a person, and he had a nice voice—much nicer than yours—I gave him your name, too. So I'm guessing if they don't find Suzi, they'll both come looking for you." Fair game as far as Levi was concerned. His neck hurt from being squeezed and rattled around. "I'm guessing it'll be an even match, with all three of you going *hand to hand,* or whatever it is guys like you *do.*"

He didn't care. Good God, the Maned Sphinx of Sesostris III *finally* shows up on the world stage, and there was just *no* getting to it.

He was just going to have to let it go. There were other amazing artifacts out there. Thousands of them, ancient and priceless, some of them yet to be discovered, and there were paintings, his bread and butter—all of them needing to be traded and sold and shifted around, and money to be made on every trade, sale, and shift.

He sneaked a peek at his watch. Well, no wonder he felt better. He'd had just enough time to sleep off a couple of glasses of champagne.

"I wouldn't waste any time, if I were you, getting up there to save her," he suggested. He wanted Danny Kane *gone.* "You can't possibly help her by hanging around here *strangling* me." And that was the truth, and by the time *any* of these men got back to Ciudad del Este, *if* any of them got back, Levi Asher was going to be at thirty-seven thousand feet, jetting north.

TWENTY-NINE

Costa del fucking Rey.

Goddamn Levi Asher, there was no Costa del Rey on any map Dax could find, and he was a pretty damn good map finder, one of the world's best. But he'd found the Rio Tambo, and Dax was betting everything he had that Levi had told him the truth, and that Suzi was smack-dab where the Tambo flowed into the Paraná.

Because she sure as hell wasn't here.

Geezus.

He rubbed his hand across his chest, trying to ease the tightness that had taken hold of him the instant he'd realized she was gone.

Two men, Levi Asher had said, and one of them had gotten to her in a heartbeat, five floors up. The security chain on the inside of the door had still been in place when Dax had come out of the bathroom. Nobody had gone out the front door. She'd been grabbed so fast, she'd dropped her fork and the rice on it on the balcony—and not another thing had been out of place in the whole room.

That was crazy. Who could do a snatch and grab that clean, that quick, without Dax knowing it?

A few folks, maybe, he guessed, but as soon as he'd seen the chain on the door, he'd run to the balcony, and there had been no one on the street below, not with a leggy redhead in tow.

The guy had taken her fanny pack, too, so the sonuvabitch was thorough. *Hell.*

He hit a key on his computer, locking it up and shutting it down. He had a couple of calls out, to guys he still knew in the trade, but so far, no one had Costa del Rey on their radar. It wasn't a town, or a village, or even a spot in the road as far as he could tell. It was a place, a private place on the river with at least one badass knuckle dragger and one multimillion-dollar piece of stolen goods.

Geezus, he hated going in cold, but he didn't have a choice.

He glanced up at the door. The chain was hanging broken now. The frame was busted where the Posada's cheap dead bolt had gone through it, assisted, Dax had been told, by someone's heavy, booted foot, *un rubio,* according to Marcella, a blond-haired man, *un gato,* according to Marceline, a cat, a very big cat who had gotten Marceline's motor running.

The first guy in here tonight had grabbed Suzi without a trace. The second guy had been sure to leave his mark, and both those guys were on their way to Costa del Rey.

Dax hoped to hell he wasn't too far behind.

He'd changed back into his cargo pants, T-shirt, and shoulder holster, with an open shirt over the top. The 9mm he'd carried in a holster inside the back of his slacks had been transferred along with two folding knives to the cargo pants, and he had extra magazines in the pockets.

He rechecked the loads on his sidearms and the submachine gun he'd picked up the day he'd landed in Paraguay. That was one of the perks of working for a world-class criminal—easy access to plenty of armament.

He packed five extra magazines for the subgun in a duffel with a couple of bottles of water and basic survival gear. Then he loaded his tac vest with more ammo, a flashlight, and a sheath knife.

The way this had been going down all day had proved one thing to him—this was not and never had been an art auction. This damn thing had been down and dirty from the get-go, and he had a lot of bad feelings about not knowing what in the hell was really going on here.

Suzi had been kidnapped, with him not ten feet away from her. Somebody was pulling a helluva lot of strings, and when Dax found that guy, he was going down.

He put his vest in his duffel, made sure he had plenty of cash in his pocket, a big, fat roll of it, and turned to head out the door.

And stopped dead in his tracks, staring at a woman who made his blood run cold.

Ice cold.

He'd met some bad men in his life. Killed quite a few of them. But he'd never met anyone like her.

Shoko.

"Warner wants to see you," she said, her voice a lilting combination of accents and sibilant seduction, the complete opposite of the flat deadness of her eyes.

She was a machine. He believed it down to his own soul that she had none. She'd been made, pieced together somehow, like a Frankenstein, but the seams didn't show.

She was standing there in front of him in a pair of lace-up boots, all golden-skinned with her long, silky black hair draped over her shoulder, her body encased in a pair of black pants and an olive green T-shirt, and it made his cold blood curdle.

She looked tactical, like she had a plan, like she was going somewhere. She had three knives he could see, and probably half a dozen he couldn't.

"I'll call him," he said.

"No. He's waiting out front. Let's go."

It was a voice of unmitigated command in five feet three inches of pure sadism. He hated her, and she knew it. No big deal. As far as he'd been able to tell, she hated him, too, just like she did everybody else on the planet, including Warner. Dax didn't know what the German had on her, but it kept her in line. For all the murderous energy she expended on everyone else, she was never anything other than obsequious to Warner.

Which didn't solve his current problem.

Paraguayan standoff in a dive—that's what he had here, and the damnedest thing was, he knew he couldn't take her, not unless he killed her, and that would be screwing the pooch. Old Warner wouldn't be giving him anything if he killed the guy's woman—and Dax was using the term "woman" lightly, *very* lightly.

So he was going to talk to Warner, give him a minute flat, before he headed up the Paraná to where it met the Tambo.

Zipping the duffel closed, he gave Shoko a short nod.

He closed and secured the door to his room as best he could and then followed the Blade Queen of Bangkok down the stairs and out onto the street to an armored Humvee.

Con keyed a code into the boat's onboard computer, and the steel gate in the cliff wall swung slowly outward. The engine was in idle, and he could hear the waves lapping at the hull. The woman, Suzanna Toussi, was still out cold, stretched across a bench seat down the port side and wrapped in a light blanket to keep the wind off her.

He'd been careful not to hurt her, but he didn't think she'd be waking up before early afternoon. He was exceedingly skilled in the pressure points of the body, and Ms. Toussi was down for the count.

Scout would take care of her once he got her inside.

When the gates finally came fully open, Con throttled up the engine and drove the boat into the cave that sat beneath the house. It didn't take long to carry Suzanna Toussi up to a guest room, and once he was assured of her well-being, he clipped her fanny pack off from around her waist and took it with him into the living room.

Her pistol was locked and loaded, a serviceable 9mm. Her driver's license and passport both had all the requisite authentications, but it was her phone that intrigued him.

She had only two names in her contact file, and five numbers dialed in her call log, which included both her contacts—which all said one thing to him: It wasn't really her phone. It was a mission-specific phone, and it didn't take him long to figure out who she was working for. He started at the bottom of her call log, and the man who answered only said one word—"Go."

Con pressed the end key and went on to the second number on her call log. The phone was answered, but nothing was said, and then he heard a series of clicks. *Sonuvabitch,* the receiving phone was waiting for him to key in a code.

Sonuvabitch.

He couldn't believe it.

She was the DIA agent. Her phone setup was pure covert ops.

And that meant Daniel Killian was his connection to Warner. The world was definitely going to hell in a handbasket when former Special Forces operators started running contraband for the likes of a scumbag like Erich Warner—but that was the world's problem, not Con's.

He only had one problem, and fortunately, he had a phone number for the man who could solve it—Daniel Killian.

CHAPTER THIRTY

Following Shoko down the stairs at the Posada, Dax felt his phone vibrate in his pocket. He glanced at the phone's screen, and thank God, Suzi's name was at the top.

"Yes," he said into the receiver, bringing the phone to his ear.

"Killian," some guy said, and Dax's heart plummeted. "My name is Conroy Farrel, and I've got two things I think you're looking for—the Memphis Sphinx and Suzanna Toussi. For a price, you can have them both."

"Where are they?" He didn't miss a step, despite the jolt that went through him. Conroy Farrel—he would not be forgetting that name. Whatever the guy had, he definitely had Suzi's phone.

"Costa del Rey. Ten kilometers up the Paraná to where the Tambo comes in. Then another four kilometers up the Tambo. You'll see my place on the north shore. I hope you're already moving, because you're running out of time."

"What's the price?" There was always a price, and it would inevitably be something big and hard to get that was going to cost Dax something big and hard to hold on to, like maybe his life. He had plenty of enemies for the things he'd done—more than he could count.

"Erich Warner, bring him to me. I know he wants the Sphinx, and you can guarantee him he'll have it before tomorrow night, before moonrise."

Sometimes when a guy least expected it, when every damn thing except his sex life had been going wrong all damn day, he got a break.

"We'll be there." He hung up the phone, and Shoko took it out of his hand. It wasn't a pleasant experience. She was fast enough to surprise him and strong enough to get her way.

She could have asked, but he would have said "Fuck you," and she probably knew that.

She hit a couple of keys and looked at the screen.

"Su-zee," she said, a satisfied smile curving her lips. "I knew there was a woman. Who is she, this Su-zee?"

"A dealer out of New York who was at Beranger's gallery earlier. She says she's got the Sphinx, and she wants to make a deal."

Those dead black eyes slid over him, and he had to consciously check himself to keep from striking out and snapping her neck. Rumbling with the

Blade Queen was not going to get him what he wanted most, which was his girl back.

Farrel wanted Warner in exchange for Suzi? Dax could deliver.

"Where is she, this Su-zee with the Sphinx?" She made the name "Suzi" sound like something she was going to be scraping off the bottom of her shoes.

Over his dead body, he thought, and he wasn't planning on checking out anytime soon.

"That information is for Warner," he said. "When I see him, I'll tell him."

Her lips curled, and she practically hissed at him—bitch. She could hiss all she wanted. He only had one shot at doing this. He reached out and took his phone back. Yeah, he was pretty fast, too, and pretty damn strong.

When they reached the street, he was unceremoniously relegated to the front seat of the Humvee, shotgun, which was fine with him. On this job, he was working for Warner.

He glanced over at the driver, a young guy, sharply dressed in a spic-and-span black T-shirt with camouflage pants, who looked like he took himself and his job very seriously. Fine with Dax, he liked serious guys. He was kind of a serious guy himself. But it would be damn nice to know whose Humvee he was riding in, and even better to know where they were going. Regardless, he figured his "minute flat" with Warner was hell and gone.

He let out a heavy sigh and relaxed back into his seat.

"*Caray! La mujer está loca, sabes?*" he said, shaking his head. *Cripes, the woman is crazy, you know?*

The young driver kept his eyes on the road and didn't say anything, but Dax saw the small grin he couldn't control.

That's all he needed, a little something to work with, and by the time they pulled up to a walled compound an hour out of Ciudad del Este, Dax and Pedro were on a first-name basis, and Dax knew exactly where they were—Joaquin Vargas's estate, and he knew Pedro's life story and Vargas's business.

Drugs and guns—that's what made the world go around, especially on the Paraguayan frontier.

They drove past Vargas's elaborate villa and came to a stop half a mile down the drive, under a smaller house's portico. There were guards everywhere, all over the grounds, all of them armed. Dax was told to stay in the car until Pedro drove around to the garage entrance of the house.

That's right. He was the hired help, and he very much wanted to keep it that way—low-key, important but not equal, not worthy of too much notice.

Pedro led him inside, all business again, down a long marble-floored hall to a large library, where he was directed to wait.

He'd been slumming it in the market and at the Posada Plaza for three days, and been in muck up to his knees for half of today, and this place was stunning, like a museum, everything pristine and expensive from the floor-to-ceiling bookcases and rich wool carpets to the huge mahogany desk commanding attention on the far side of the room. There was a fireplace on the near wall, flanked with leather chairs and a couch, and various exquisitely inlaid tables.

Dax took up a position slightly off to one side of the fireplace, where he could see the whole room, and he kept a good hold on his duffel bag, and tried not to think too much about the phone burning a hole in his pocket, or about the last call he'd gotten.

He needed to stay cool, to play it as it lay, and somehow, without anybody knowing it, get exactly what he needed here tonight.

"Have you failed me, Mr. Killian? Or does this Suzi have what I want?" The tone was bored rather than strident, but Dax could instantly see the strain on Erich Warner's face when the man walked into the room.

Good. For what Dax needed him to do, strain was the perfect motivation.

He also saw the iguana draped on Warner's shoulder, a young one, not very big, with a jeweled collar and a linked-chain leash, an odd accoutrement for somebody who looked more like a fresh-faced German schoolboy than anyone over eighteen should. Warner's hair was very blond, thick, and bluntly cut, his features straight out of the Aryan handbook, which Dax knew was a tremendous source of pride for the man.

Dax also knew he was into some pretty strange stuff on the side, genetic research or some such, which under the best of circumstances he didn't believe belonged in the hands of an underworld kingpin. But he'd heard things about drugs and procedures, and the truth of it, in Dax's opinion, was the walking advertisement for strangeness that was always at his side.

Shoko, gliding in behind him, was neither bored nor strained. She always just was—oddly present in the moment and dangerously ready. Even considering the size of the room, he was well inside her "reach out and touch you before you can blink" perimeter again—and her boss was unhappy with him.

Sometimes he thought he needed a new job.

"I haven't failed," he said with the utmost confidence. "Do you have the information?"

No information, and Dax would kill the bastard himself.

In answer, Warner pulled an envelope out of his jacket pocket. "A terrorist cell, the names you need, just as we agreed. You sounded so sure of yourself when we spoke earlier," the German said, stepping over to the front of the desk and pouring himself a short shot in a highball glass. He downed it in one swallow and poured himself another. The envelope went back into the inside pocket on his jacket.

Nerves. Yeah, Dax understood. The night was wearing on his nerves, too. The same way the whole damn day had worn on his nerves.

"When we spoke earlier, I was headed into a meeting with one of the dealers from Beranger's. I made it clear that I was willing to beat anybody's offer on the Sphinx, and was told to wait for a phone call. The phone call came shortly after Ms. Shoko arrived." He nodded in the bitch's direction. He was a good liar, so he didn't have many qualms about Warner not buying his line.

"And Beranger is now dead, you said?"

"Yes." And probably still lying on the floor in his gallery.

Warner downed his second shot and set the glass back down.

"It makes more sense, really," he said, "him being dead, than it ever made that this unknown little Frenchman in Paraguay had acquired the Memphis Sphinx."

Dax agreed. He'd been running in the art world for a few years now, and while it wasn't unusual for some rare and wonderful thing to show up in a dump every now and then, the Memphis Sphinx was not merely a rare and wonderful artifact. It was a legend. The name of Howard Carter, its finder, attached instant cachet. That the piece had never been formally or academically displayed had created a mystery that had remained unsolved for nearly a hundred years.

"And this phone call? This Suzi, the dealer, did she give you the location of the Sphinx?" Warner's tone sounded a little frayed, and he glanced toward the Blade Queen, looking, Dax supposed, for some kind of reassurance, and for a moment Dax wished that he'd been spending a little more time at the range. Marksmanship was a frangible skill, and if that woman made any kind of a move whatsoever, his skill in that area was going to be put to the test.

"Suzi gave me the first mark. I'm to call her when I reach it, and she'll give me the second."

"And the first mark is?"

"Five kilometers up the Paraná. I was just heading out when Ms. Shoko arrived at the Posada." Mostly true. He'd cut the distance in half, not wanting to give too much away, but needing them headed in the right direction.

"You do understand the time constraint we're dealing with here, don't you, Mr. Killian?" A more frazzled edge definitely crept into Warner's voice with the question.

Of course he did. Time was the whole raison d'être of the quest. Warner was looking for immortality, actually thinking he was going to get it off a hunk of granite in the moonlight.

"Yes, sir. I do. My plan was to get up there tonight, make the deal and call for a funds transfer, just as we'd planned, and have the Sphinx back here by tomorrow afternoon, in plenty of time for the...uh, ceremony." He didn't know what else to call this unlikely transfer of immortality that had Erich Warner's boxers all in a wad. All he knew was that he'd hoped to be long gone before that moment arrived.

"That seems a bit risky now, doesn't it?" the man said, lifting the iguana off his shoulder and setting the reptile on the desk. He pulled a handkerchief out of his pants pocket and wiped at his brow.

"Not if I leave immediately. The dealer I'm meeting, Suzi, she knows the time constraints as well as we do. She knows her price drops through the floor after moonrise tomorrow night. Trust me, she is ready to sell."

Dax needed Erich to push him, not back off, but he was playing it cool, watching the man fret and hoping for the best.

"The timing will be closer than either of us anticipated or wanted, that's true," Dax continued, "but we *have* to try. I need to leave immediately." He meant that with all his heart. Again, he wasn't selling a lie. *Geezus*, Suzi was up there.

Warner tilted his head to one side, giving him a very discerning look, as if he'd come to a decision— and he had, the absolute correct decision. "You've had your *try*, Mr. Killian, and you've taken us up to the final countdown, and still don't have the Sphinx. From here on out, I'm taking over the operation, and far more drastic measures than you've been able to bring to bear must now be employed."

He could hear Warner swear under his breath before he poured himself another shot and finished it off in one swallow.

Normally, Dax was fairly wary of drastic anything, but in this case Warner was right, and the sooner they all got on board with "drastic measures," the better—not that Warner needed to hear that from him.

"Well, sir, normally I would agree, but I feel I still have a chance to pull this thing off, and the quicker I can get up there, the more quickly I can get back. If we can cut this meeting short, I—"

"Short?" Warner interrupted. "This meeting is going to go on all the way to the first mark, and then the next, until I have the Memphis Sphinx in my hand. Do you understand?"

"Yes, sir."

Warner snapped his fingers, and one of Vargas's men strode forward into the room.

"Tell Señor Vargas I need a boat with twenty armed men, immediately."

The man agreed with a nod and turned on his heel.

"You have forced the issue with your incompetence," Warner said, shifting his attention back to Dax. "We have no choice now but to go with you. I can't take the risk of not being with the Sphinx by tomorrow night."

Perfect.

CHAPTER THIRTY-ONE

Costa del Rey

Suzi woke in the night to the sound of a river running. Lying calmly in a lavender-scented bed, she slowly opened her eyes.

She didn't know where she was, but the sheets on the bed were white, and the pillows were soft. A stone fireplace on the far wall crackled and glowed, casting a soft, flickering light over the room.

The door to the outside was open, leading onto a moonlight-washed deck, and beyond the deck was the river she heard—a rippling chorus of running water, eddies, and the deeper pull of the river's flow.

She'd been kidnapped in her underwear.

She could feel the soft organic undies perfectly in place, the same with Dax's polo shirt.

She looked down at herself and felt a moment's

relief. She'd been kidnapped, rendered unconscious, and hauled off somewhere, but not molested, and nobody knew better than her what a miracle that was.

It had all happened unbelievably fast. One second, she'd been sitting at the table in the Posada Plaza, and in the next second, she'd been scooped and swooped. The last thing she remembered was being on the balcony at the hotel, being held very close against a rock-hard chest. She'd looked up, still holding her dinner fork, and...and something had happened.

She'd gasped.

She remembered now. Looking over the balcony railing, five floors up from the street, and suddenly realizing that they were going over the side—all of this in the space of a second or two. There had been that first initial sensation of being in free fall, and then nothing, until now.

Nobody could move that fast, could they?

And yet somebody had, somebody with a very expensive house.

She rolled her head a few inches, looking up at an open-beamed ceiling. Soft, subdued light spilled out of a door on the wall opposite the deck. She could see a marble floor and a pedestal sink, and thought there was probably a decadently large jetted tub to go with the sink.

Wow. Where was she?

She felt safe. Her instincts weren't clamoring for her to leap up and get out.

Quite the opposite.

Her instincts were somnolent, unconcerned about her odd dilemma.

She let her gaze drift back to the fireplace—and in the space of a heartbeat, all those somnolent instincts went screaming into action. She froze in place, her pulse skyrocketing, her attention riveted by the shadowy figure sitting in the corner of the room, a man, his shoulders broad, his countenance very still—and she knew it was him, the man who had taken her from the Posada Plaza.

"You're awake," he said.

Very awake. *Ultra* awake. Her eyes *wide* open. Her heart pounding.

He leaned forward into the light of the fire, his hands clasped together, his elbows resting on his knees, and for one long, endless second after another, she barely breathed. She opened her mouth to say something, but no words came out.

Confusion warred with perception and kept winning, over and over again. What she was seeing was impossible. There wasn't any way to comprehend him, the reality of him sitting in this room with her—*John Thomas Chronopolous, J.T.*

He rose from the chair, and if she'd had an ounce of strength, she would have leaped from the bed and run like hell—somewhere, anywhere. But she didn't. Her limbs felt heavy.

"Don't worry, *cariño*." He walked with all the lazy grace of the superbly fit, no wasted movements, no "visual noise." His strides were long, easy. "You're tired, that's all. Sleep tonight." He stopped by the side of the bed and smoothed his hand around the side of her neck to the back of her head. "You'll feel better in the morning."

She felt herself falling again, but it was sweet, a release of tension allowing her to drift back down into sleep.

Yes, sir, for a moment there at Vargas's estate, things had been going completely Dax's way, and the minute he'd stepped out of the library with Erich Warner, it had all gone to hell. They'd been at this "get the hell up the river" trip for-freaking-ever—and Dax was afraid he was going to start foaming at the mouth.

He felt pretty damn rabid, and Warner was starting to look like a deer in the headlights. This was his gig going down the drain. Hell, Dax didn't even want to live forever, especially if he couldn't save Suzi from Conroy Farrel.

Dax had been on completely FUBAR missions that had gone more smoothly than this. For starters, getting twenty armed drug runners onto a boat for an unplanned, middle-of-the-night sortie had taken an ungodly amount of time. Dax truly could have gotten his butt back into the city and down to the docks and stolen half a dozen boats and rented six more in the same amount of time— but that wouldn't have done him a damn bit of good. He needed frickin' Erich Warner with him, and Warner seemed to think he needed a small army to protect him.

He was going to need more than Vargas's twenty

goons if anything happened to Suzi—that's all Dax could guarantee him.

All the time spent at Vargas's, screwing around getting ready to go, Dax had been painfully aware that Suzi was up on the river somewhere, kidnapped and alone, and in her underwear—which was why his nerves had been sliding along a fine edge by the time they'd launched the mission in an honest-to-God gunboat with two squads' worth of hardened criminals, no intel, the man he was taking to his death, and one psycho bitch who he swore was eyeballing him like tomorrow's lunch.

CHAPTER THIRTY-TWO

Creed low-crawled into place next to Hawkins and Dylan in their observation post on the ridge above the house at Costa del Rey. Zach was five yards behind him, watching their backs. They'd come in at dawn and were prepared for the long haul, breaking into two-man teams and flanking the compound, clearing their avenues of approach, gathering intel, and waiting for the cover of darkness, when they could use thermal imaging to locate their objectives and get in closer to the house.

They'd come across the two dead CIA agents a hundred yards down the ridgeline in a ravine, or what was left of them. Seven months in the jungle hadn't left much, and even three months ago, the ravine would have been running with water. If somebody had been looking for those boys, Creed wasn't surprised they hadn't found them.

Two dead agents, Suzi Toussi a hostage in the

house below, some damn statue causing nothing but trouble, and the astral shields moving into conjunction with the meridian lines of the pre–vernal equinox high tides—the mission had gotten damned complicated. General Grant had offered up the hocus-pocus edition of their intel, and Dylan had immediately passed all of it off to Hawkins to handle.

Despite the pressure bearing down on the general, Creed knew Dylan had one objective here in the jungle this morning—Conroy Farrel. Not magic statues.

"Did you get the girl?" Dylan asked. They were all flat on their stomachs in the dirt, buried into some leaves, Hawkins bagged in behind an M40 rifle and glassing the area through the scope, with Dylan on a pair of binoculars.

Creed got out his own binoculars. He had an M4 carbine slung across his back.

"Yeah. Zach and I tranked her and hauled her down to the boat. She's secure. Now all we need is Suzi and Farrel." And then the real work would begin, the finding out who Farrel really was. "You get any more movement down there yet?"

"Not since the girl," Hawkins said.

It had been a perfect snatch. Creed and Zach had been up on the other side of the compound, their hide closer in than Hawkins and Dylan's.

Farrel's girl had exited the house and headed down a trail for one of her perimeter checks, and they'd slipped down the trail after her.

"Have you guys come up with any new ideas on why Conroy Farrel took Suzi?" he asked.

"We're getting played," Hawkins said without a second's worth of hesitation.

"What about a flash of brilliance on why these two completely unrelated operations are both coming down to the same damn place?"

"Played," Hawkins repeated.

"Played," he agreed. None of them had a doubt in the world, and getting on the horn with Grant this morning had only bogged them down with all that useless information about the astral meridians.

"*Fuck,*" Dylan said, and he said it for all of them. "We'll get answers, guaranteed, but first we have to get Farrel."

"Played," Hawkins muttered again under his breath.

Dylan looked over, and his gaze landed on Creed.

"You're bleeding. What happened out there?"

By "out there," the boss meant out there on the trail on the other side of the compound, where he and Zach had tracked down Conroy Farrel's girl and snatched her.

"When I grabbed her, she fought. Hard and well." And she'd done a fair job of kicking his ass around a little bit. He'd been impressed.

"Glad you came out on top," Dylan said, giving him a look that plainly said the day Creed couldn't come out on top up against a twenty-something girl was the day he needed to turn in his jungle boy badge. "When Farrel goes looking for her, we'll go in, make sure Suzi is okay, and have a nice surprise waiting for him when he comes home."

"If Suzi's even there," Hawkins muttered.

Superman did not like this mission. He hadn't liked it since Farrel had gotten away with one of his girls—if Conroy Farrel really had gotten to Suzi. One old man's word wasn't much to go on, but other than one cryptic call from her in the middle of the night, a phone call during which she hadn't said a word, they hadn't heard from the divine Ms. Toussi—and she sure as hell hadn't been answering any of their calls.

"Okay, we've got her," Hawkins said, sounding relieved.

Creed checked through his binoculars and saw two people exiting a door onto the deck. A woman dressed in a T-shirt and a pair of khaki pants and a big man in BDU pants, a gray T-shirt, and a ball cap crossed the deck and entered another door. The man had been holding on to her arm, moving her along.

"Positive identification. That's Suzi," Dylan said.

"And Farrel?" Hawkins asked.

"Who looks a lot like our boy," Dylan said. "A helluva lot."

Sonuvabitch, Creed thought, and he knew he was thinking it for all of them. No way should Suzi have ended up in the company of a man who'd killed four CIA agents, two of whom were still rotting in the jungle.

"We shouldn't let this play out all day," Hawkins

said, looking up from his scope at Dylan. "I say we offer this guy a deal, our girl for his girl, and hit him with the tranquilizer gun while we're talking. We get Suzi, we get this guy, and we go home."

"Aye, aye," Creed whispered, flat on his belly, watching everything in the compound and the house below. They were all keeping their voices down. "I'm with Superman."

"And you're both with me," Dylan reminded them, unnecessarily and sounding a little snappish in the heat. "We'll hold our—" The boss stopped talking and turned his head, listening. They all fell silent.

Dylan signaled for Creed to move out. They could all hear it, a boat coming up the river.

Suzi's Big Day—God, if she'd kept a diary, she would have written those words at the top of the page.

Costa del Rey, that's what he'd told her, the name of his home, King's Coast. He'd also told her his name was Conroy Farrel, but that she should call him Con.

Conroy Farrel, for the love of God.

He pulled a chair out for her, and Suzi sat down to a beautiful meal laid out on an exquisitely crafted teakwood table. Warm croissants, sliced bananas, fresh pineapple, rich coffee with cream, petite filets mignons grilled to perfection, sliced cheeses, scrambled eggs—it briefly crossed her mind that maybe she should get kidnapped more often.

It also, more than briefly, occurred to her that the gray backpack lying on the table might hold the answer to all her problems. It was so out of place on the elegant table, and without a doubt, it was there for a reason.

She took a sip of coffee and helped herself to a wafer-thin biscuit with a tiny dollop of crème fraîche topped with some kind of tropical fruit preserves on it, all while safely ensconced in a beautifully cushioned rattan armchair, under a gently wafting, slowly *whap-whap-whap*ping ceiling fan.

Heaven would be like this—quiet, subdued, wood floors, stone walls, teak paneling, slatted ceilings, white furniture, and big windows framing a tropical forest and a slow-moving river.

She'd woken up to the sound of birds singing, her room flooded with sunlight, and her window open onto a large wooden deck. There had been clothes laid out for her on the edge of the bed, a white T-shirt, khaki pants with a leather belt, and on the rug, a pair of flip-flops and a pair of canvas boots and cotton socks, none of it new, but all of it spotlessly clean, with the clothes pressed.

She'd awakened twice more in the night, and every time he had been sitting quietly in the corner of her room, next to the fire, an oddly comforting presence, and every time, she'd drifted back off to sleep, the day's exhausting cares and woes lifting off of her, becoming burdens of the past, not of the present.

He had the most soothing voice, deep and calm

and certain. The voice had not changed, not since she'd first met him.

There had been a girl in the night, too. A young woman, no more than mid-twenties, by Suzi's estimation, she'd been tall and lanky with a wild mop of curling dark hair, and Conroy had called her Scout, but Suzi hadn't seen her this morning.

"Suzi," he said, "Suzi Toussi," as if he simply liked the feel of how it rolled off his tongue.

He didn't smile much, but when he did, it was dazzling—a quick grin, a boyishly lopsided curve of white teeth accompanied by a twinkle in his eye. He had that kind of eyes, dark hazel and utterly depthless, like the stars and the cosmos were in them, and when he grinned, she felt like she could see all of it, all the way down through the ages of the universe.

"I realized last night that I had made a mistake," he continued. "And I usually don't."

She believed him. He wasn't the type to make mistakes, never had been, and yet things had happened to him, bad things, and they were easy to see—the scars on his arms, the scars on his neck and face. Interestingly, they didn't mar his looks. He was as beautiful as he'd ever been, and J. T. Chronopolous had always been a beautiful man— tall, and strong, and muscular, his face cleanly chiseled, an older, tougher-looking version of his brother, Kid Chaos.

"What mistake?" She wanted to know everything, especially what had happened to him. Just looking at him made her heart pound. He was a friend, a street runner from way back, one of the best of a crew of former juvenile car thieves who had become Special Defense Force. She and J.T. went back years, and yet not even the faintest glimmer of recognition lit his eyes when he looked at her.

"You're not the one I should have taken last night," he said.

Well, it was hard not to agree with that, but she went ahead and asked.

"Why not?" Good Lord. She'd gone to his funeral six years ago, and she'd cried her heart out with everyone else who had been at that gravesite, and if he wasn't dead, then she needed an explanation.

Everyone at Steele Street would need an explanation. She felt like a Saturday morning hero, some kind of intrepid adventurer, to have gone off into the wild jungles of Paraguay in search of an ancient Egyptian statue purported to have the power to grant everlasting life—and to return with the lost chop-shop boy risen from the dead, the one who'd changed them all.

He smiled and reached for the backpack.

Oh, yes, that was her all right, Indiana Jones and some Crystal Temple of the Covenant–type thing, except what he pulled out of the backpack was a granite and gold statue known far and wide as the Maned Sphinx of Sesostris III, the Memphis Sphinx, and he set it down on the table between the coffee urn and the butter, next to the salt and pepper.

The real deal. Just sitting there. Defying all the

death and destruction it had left in its wake in Ciudad del Este and probably everywhere else it had been for the last four thousand years. A tingling rush of excitement coursed up her spine.

She would have known it anywhere.

"Go ahead and look it over if you want to," he said. "It's lasted for millennia. I don't think it's going to fall apart on my kitchen table."

And he didn't much sound like he cared if it did.

J. T. Chronopolous and the Memphis Sphinx— Suzi's Big Day, indeed.

Geez.

She reached out and picked the statue up and immediately felt the weight of it, not just the granite, but the gravitas, the seriousness of it.

"So how long have you been working for the DIA?" he asked.

Her heart took a start, and she looked up from where she was running the tip of her finger over the Sphinx's paws.

"What in the world would make you think that?" She was shocked, truly. No one could possibly know whom she was working for in Paraguay.

He shrugged. "It's their statue. They've had it for over ten years, squirreled away in a lab, using it for experiments they and the CIA conducted in remote viewing under the code names Stargate and Moonrise. The Memphis Sphinx, in particular, was associated with the Moonrise part of the program."

Her nerves, which she thought she'd been doing an amazing job of controlling, started to fizzle and spark.

"And you know this because?"

"I think I was part of that program."

"But you don't know for sure?"

He shook his head. "I know Erich Warner, though, and I brought you here because I thought you were working for him." There was just enough question in the statement that she felt she needed to answer.

"No," she said. "I'm not working for a world-class degenerate psychopath."

"Do you know Daniel Killian?" he asked, giving her heart another start.

"Uh...yes." She returned the statue to the table.

"Is he a criminal, mob connected, cartel connected?"

"No," she said.

He gave another small shrug, as if he didn't believe her, and then he checked his watch.

"There were four buyers at Remy Beranger's yesterday afternoon. Ponce was there for his father. Levi Asher was there for himself. You were there for the DIA, at least you haven't denied it, and someone was there for Erich Warner," he said. "Daniel Killian is the only one left."

A startling conclusion, if he was right, which he wasn't. A number of the buyers on the DIA's list had not shown up at Beranger's.

"What makes you think it's not me? What changed your mind?"

"Instinct." He poured more coffee into his cup, and as the steam curled up around his right hand, she noticed a tremor run through it, strong enough to make his hand shake. Some of the coffee spilled onto the table, and he carefully put the urn back down. He was missing half of his ring finger, and she was not going to ask how, or why, but her heart just broke.

What had happened to him?

"And your phone," he finished. "You have a couple of interesting numbers in it and not much more."

Her phone, *dammit*.

"Can I have it back?" She'd looked for her fanny pack first thing when she had awakened, knowing it contained her two best chances for escape: her 9mm and her phone. But she hadn't been able to find it and would have been shocked if she had.

"No," he said. "Not yet. Not until after Erich Warner is dead. Then you can have it all, even the Sphinx."

Her eyebrows lifted as she absorbed that surprising offer.

"Thank you." It was the only appropriate thing to say. It was also exactly how she felt—*thank you very, very much, Mr. Conroy Farrel*. Erich Warner dead was a big favor to everybody.

He reached for his coffee, revealing the inside of his right arm. It was a tragedy of scars. Another tremor rippled up the inside of his forearm even as she was looking at it, and when she glanced up to his face, she saw him wince.

J.T., my God, J.T.—he'd been on a mission, like dozens of missions he'd gone on before, down into Colombia, and he'd been killed there. That's what they all thought, what they'd all thought for six years.

But here he was, his memory gone, his body a testament to the suffering he'd borne, and she was overwhelmed by it all. She didn't know where to begin to help him, or if she should even try. He didn't even know who she was, and sometimes it was better not to fix things but to let them lie—and she had no idea what would be best for John Thomas Chronopolous.

It made her feel so helpless, and when she looked at him, she wanted to tell him.

But he'd kidnapped her and was holding her hostage, and she needed to be smarter than to trust him.

CHAPTER THIRTY-THREE

Creedence Clearwater Revival, CCR, those were Creed's boys, the guys with his theme song—"Run Through the Jungle."

Like a cat.

A hundred yards from Dylan and Hawkins's OP, Creed cut down through the trees to the river. He could hear the boat getting louder, coming nearer, but he needed eyes-on ID. They'd seen two fishing boats already today, and if it was another one, all the better. If not, the boss was going to have to make a few more command decisions.

At two hundred yards, Creed knelt in the brush at the shoreline, concealed behind a dense layer of trees and vegetation, sweat running down the greasepaint camouflaging his face.

Yeah, he could see it. A gunboat had entered the

mouth of the Tambo River and was cruising along the far shore, about a hundred yards downstream and headed his way.

Creed took out his binoculars and keyed his radio.

"Cartel cowboys in an RPB," he said when he heard Dylan's beep, letting him know it was a river patrol boat. "Twenty or so, well armed. One woman, Asian, a gringo in a fedora—yeah, you heard me right—and *sonuvabitch*."

"Continue," Dylan ordered.

"I—" Creed stopped the transmission, looked harder at the boat crew. He didn't want to make any mistakes, but hell no, it wasn't a mistake. He keyed his radio again. "I found Waldo."

"Again." The order came back at him.

"Killian. He's on the boat."

Creed didn't actually hear Dylan cussing, but he knew exactly what couple of words were coming out of the boss's mouth.

In their business, surprises sucked. On the other hand, it was good to have a friend in the enemy camp. Creed had worked with Dax on the streets of Denver, stealing cars, and once in Afghanistan three years ago, and there wasn't a doubt in his mind whose side the man was on. Suzi's for sure— and he had to wonder, really, when did the art game get so damn dangerous?

He keyed his radio again. "Maybe it's time to make a trade."

"Roger. I want you and Zach back at your OP. If

Farrel wants his girl back, he'll deal with us before the boat party arrives."

"Roger."

Suzi gently turned the Sphinx on its side and looked for any marks on the bottom of the statue. There were a couple of scratches in the granite, and she duly notated them in the notebook Con had given her. Sure, he'd said she could have the ancient artifact, a mind-boggling idea, but she was a long way from home, and a lot of other people wanted this thing. Quite frankly, she wouldn't have put five bucks on the chance of her being the one to get it out of Paraguay.

Not that she wasn't going to give it her best shot.

Conroy Farrel was pacing. He was very quiet about it, walking from one door to the next, looking outside. Looking for the girl, Scout? Suzi wondered. She hadn't seen her since last night.

"There's a scanner in my fanny pack," she said. He had it clipped through a couple of belt loops on his BDU pants. "May I have it?"

He didn't hesitate to pull it out, look it over, then walk over and hand it to her.

She wished he'd give her the whole damn fanny pack, but she wasn't going to hold her breath on that. Her phone had rung three times, and each time he'd answered it and given a set of directions. Nothing more.

Somebody was coming, Erich Warner at the

least—and Suzi couldn't imagine that was going to be good for her.

She picked up the scanner and let out a short breath. If nothing else, she would at least know if the damn thing worked, and if it did, Dax's far-fetched theory about the Faraday cages in Beranger's basement would be true. She hoped to hell she got a chance to tell him.

Without further ado, she turned the scanner on, and it lit up, clear as day. So simple, and after a moment it beeped in the completion of the GPS locator function, and that was that.

Well. Somehow she felt better, like she'd done her job—found the damn thing and locked in its location.

Great.

She was sure there would be a bonus in there somewhere, if she could just get out of this damn country alive.

She set the scanner aside and went back to cataloguing every little thing there was to catalogue about the great Maned Sphinx of Sesostris III, a.k.a. the Memphis Sphinx. Howard Carter himself had discovered this thing. He'd held it in his hands. He'd drawn it—and Suzi could feel it all, the depth of the statue's history, the power of the legend. In Grant's office, she'd scoffed at the idea of the Sphinx having occult powers, but holding it in her hands was enough to make a believer out of her—almost.

The gold mane framed a regally serene face and draped down onto the black granite shoulders of a lion. The rock-crystal eyes were small and elegant, set into the granite eye sockets like a pair of stars, no bigger than the irises would have been. The thing was beautiful, the lion's paws placed firmly and squarely on the statue's base, the beast's tail curled precisely around its body, the animal emanating an innate power, an unexpected suppleness of form. It was an amazing piece of art, the golden mane luminous, the crystal eyes catching the sunlight—a magnificent sphinx.

The moment held her, and she placed both her hands on the statue, one on each side of the lion body. It was truly beautiful, conceived and created on the banks of the Nile four thousand years ago. The granite was warm against her palms, with a luster that caught the light. It wasn't pure black; there were flecks of gold and gray in the stone, which made it seem to shimmer.

Magical, indeed.

And for the moment, hers.

People had killed for this statue, possibly hundreds of times over the centuries, and suddenly what had seemed so abhorrent before made sense. This black and gold beast with the cut-crystal eyes was worthy of blood, of sacrifice.

She slid it a few inches across the table, into a stream of sunlight, and the crystalline eyes lit themselves from deep within.

Ahhh, she thought. *This is it. And when this happens in moonlight, the power of the creature is unleashed. The doors of time will open, either to give or to take—but the power is there, lying latent and heavy in the rock.*

With the sunlight catching on every facet of crystal, she reached for the left eye and slowly twisted and pulled, and hoped beyond hope that the piece would release and fall into her hand. She wanted to see inside, to touch a place of ancientness.

This Sphinx was made for Sesostris III, King of Egypt and the Nile, two thousand years before the birth of Christ.

So clearly, she heard the voice of history, of pain, and loss, of being buried in the crypt, of crying out to be released.

Released.

The rod of crystal pulled free, and Suzi's pulse began to race. She couldn't pull her gaze away from the dark abyss of the empty eye socket. She leaned closer, her heart in her throat—*so dark, like the far reaches of coldest space.* Her breath vaporized along the surface of the supremely serene, one-eyed Sphinx.

Impossible.

But she exhaled again—and again the coldness of the statue turned her breath to visible vapor.

She tilted her head slightly to one side, peering deeper into the empty socket. The stone was shot through with gold and gray flecks—and as she looked, noticing each cluster of flecks in the dark night of the eye socket...they seemed to move... in orbits. She blinked and leaned in closer, curious, enchanted...enthralled by the—

"No, Suzi. That's not for you." Con grasped the Sphinx by its head, covering the empty socket, and with his other hand, he relieved her of the crystalline eye and set it back into place.

She blinked, feeling a cold shiver trickle down her spine.

Oh, my.

Her phone rang again, and she turned to look at Con. He had the Sphinx in one of his large hands and her phone in the other.

"Go," he said when he answered.

He listened for a moment, and as he listened, she watched his face turn very grim.

"Dylan Hart. I won't forget."

Good Lord, Dylan. The relief flooding through her was palpable. Dylan would be able to find her.

"How many?" Con asked.

She thought about calling something out, but all she could think was—

"Costa del Rey!" she hollered as loudly as she could.

"No," Con said into the phone, giving her a very cold look.

It shut her up. She'd gotten her point across.

"If you hurt her in any way, I'll hunt you down, Hart. You bring her back to me, the Toussi woman is yours. If not, you can pick up the pieces when I'm gone."

And Conroy Farrel had most definitely gotten his point across.

Geezus. Dylan and Hawkins had snatched the girl. She had to get out of here. She couldn't outrun

Con, and she couldn't outgun him, but there had to be a way.

"We have no deal, Hart, except for the women. Keep your distance." He hung up the phone and put it back in her pack.

Keep your distance? Good God. Was it possible Dylan was just outside the compound? Suzi had no idea how long Scout had been missing. The girl could have driven into Ciudad del Este and gotten nabbed there for all she knew.

But her gut was telling her Dylan was close. That he and the boys had grabbed Scout right off her own front porch. That's the way the guys worked— up close and personal.

Con had moved toward the open door onto the deck. He was looking out, and after a moment, gave her an order.

"Get over here." He still had the Sphinx in his hand. "You've got a job to do. If you do it right, exactly the way I tell you to do it, and everything goes well, you'll walk away from this."

If not, she'd probably die—he didn't have to spell it out. She could see the handwriting on the wall.

Holy crap.

He handed her the Sphinx when she stopped next to him.

"There's a boat coming," he said, pointing to the river, and when she looked, she could see it, a gunboat with a .50-caliber BMG mounted on it, which did nothing to calm her fears. "Erich Warner is on the boat, and he's coming to buy the Sphinx."

"That's a lot of people on there." And every

one of them was armed with some kind of carbine slung over their shoulders. *Holy gee-fricking-crap.* There was only one way to spell firefight—B.A.D. I.D.E.A.

She did a quick look around at the interior of the house. *Too many windows* was her first thought.

"I . . . uh, need my pistol."

"I'll handle security and defense," he said. "You just do as you're told."

Oh, man, she could have belted him for that. Doing as she was told had never been her strong suit.

"We're going to let them make the first sortie. What I need is for Erich Warner to come off the boat. You're going to make that happen for me."

Oh, God. She clutched the Sphinx closer.

Down on the river, the boat was tying up at the dock, and a whole army of guys was getting off. Drug runners, that's what she was seeing, somebody's private paramilitary force—and then she saw Dax, right in the middle of all of them, with his own damn carbine slung over his shoulder.

For an instant, she doubted him.

And then she didn't. She knew Dax Killian, and if he was working for Erich Warner, he was doing it for a reason. He'd been running his end of the Sphinx business like a military campaign, not like a collector. She knew his background. She knew what kind of man he was—the kind she wanted, the kind she needed, and so help her God, the kind of man she could fall in love with.

CHAPTER THIRTY-FOUR

"Well?" Hawkins asked, watching the house and compound through his rifle scope. Dylan had made his offer, trade Farrel's girl for Suzi.

"He said he wouldn't forget my name."

"That's a start." He let out a short laugh. *Geezus Kee-rist*. "Have you decided whose side we're on? It's getting a little crowded down there."

"We're on Suzi's side. Everyone else is fair game, including Farrel, if we can't take control of him."

"*Fuck.*" He hated this damn mission.

"Jungle Boy," Dylan said into his radio. "Are you in position?"

"Affirmative."

"If Conroy Farrel takes one step onto that deck, I want you to trank him."

"Affirmative."

Dylan put the radio back into a pocket on his tac vest and lifted his binoculars back to his eyes.

"Looks like the drug runners are sending Mr. Killian up to parlay."

They both lay very quietly in the muck and the mud and the leaves, sunk into the landscape as invisibly as possible, watching the scene unfold.

"When Farrel is finished here, he'll be ready to trade," the boss said.

"Good. Then we can go back to square one and start all over. That's good, Dylan."

"Asshole."

"I wanted to wrap this thing up in Bangkok last November. We practically had him." Without a doubt, he and the boss had been at this for a while, tracking down Conroy Farrel.

"You seeing that?" Dylan asked.

"Yeah." Dax had barely stepped foot on the deck before he stopped, bent down and picked something up, then turned around and headed back toward the two squads of paramilitary forces lined up on the dock.

"I wonder what that's all about," Dylan asked.

But Hawkins, hell, he figured they were going to find out soon enough.

Conroy Farrel was one tough customer, and the Memphis Sphinx was absofuckinglutely amazing, and Suzi was safe. Dax had caught sight of her standing just inside the door, the Sphinx in her hands, with Conroy standing in the shadows behind her.

Dax had hoped to get a lot closer to both of

them, but Farrel had other plans. Actually, Conroy Farrel had only one plan—kill Erich Warner as expediently and with as little fanfare as possible.

That's the way Dax would have done it, but he wouldn't have put Suzi in the middle of it, and Farrel's plan was deeply flawed in that respect.

Dax quickly crossed the stretch of empty ground between the house and the dock, wondering if Erich Warner wanted the Sphinx badly enough to abandon common sense, leave the boat, and go up to the house to get it.

Probably, he thought with disgust.

Warner would have the illusion of cover—heavy on the "illusion" part. The German could take as many of Vargas's soldiers as he wanted, and he could take his little Oriental pit bull, Shoko, but Farrel had made it clear that the Sphinx wasn't moving without Warner personally coming up and getting it.

Dax knew for a fact that Warner wouldn't get anywhere near the house, let alone near the Sphinx. Conroy Farrel would drop him the instant he got a shot, which would be the exact instant Erich Warner poked his head out from under the canopy on the boat.

Dax knew, because that's the way he would have done it.

He made his way down the dock, through two squads of Vargas's trained militants, and stepped into the boat. Vargas's captain had remained on board, in charge of the craft.

"We've got a problem," Dax said to Warner. Actually, Dax had more than one, but the German really only had one. "The dealer wants to talk with you personally."

"Why?" Warner asked, showing a respectable amount of skepticism. "I can have the money transferred from here, she can check her accounts, and you bring me the statue. That's the deal."

It always came down to this—who had whom over the bigger barrel. On this deal, Dax figured it was a wash. Both men had already shown an obsessive amount of zeal for what they wanted.

"She wants to meet."

Warner looked disgusted.

"Some woman named *Suzi* thinks she's calling the shots here?" He said the name with such disdain that for a moment, Dax thought the man's intelligence and instincts for survival would win out.

"Yes, sir."

"She wants a million dollars for her statue, and she's running out of time. Tell her I'll make the transfer when she gives you the Sphinx."

Behind the German, Shoko said something in Japanese, something bitchy, and Dax saw Warner's mouth tighten.

"Shoko told me there was a woman involved. Call this dealer, tell her the terms of the original agreement are set."

"Actually, sir, she wants to talk with you." He handed Warner the radio Conroy had left for him on the deck.

Warner gave the thing a very skeptical look, then took it and keyed in the mike. "Yes," he snapped.

After a moment, his expression hardened. "Five million?"

Hardball on a losing game, Dax thought.

"I want to see it."

Of course he did, and Dax needed to be somewhere else.

"Sir," he interrupted, keeping his voice very low. Warner turned to him. "Tell her I'm coming up there to negotiate the terms of the meeting. You shouldn't go in there cold."

Warner dismissed him with a nod, probably having no intention of going up to the house, not if he could get what he wanted any other way, and he was a man used to getting his way.

It was all a moot point. The line of sight from the house to the boat was a straight shot at seventy yards. Conroy Farrel didn't give a damn about the money or the Sphinx, and Warner didn't have to leave the boat. All he needed to do was move about four feet, and he'd be dead, and something was telling Dax that Conroy had a plan to get Warner to move four lousy feet.

And he did.

The collective murmur of awe running through twenty calloused drug runners made Dax look up toward the house, and he wondered how in the world Erich Warner was going to resist.

Farrel had sent Suzi out onto his deck, obviously unarmed, the radio in her one hand, held up to her ear, and in the other, the Memphis Sphinx, held up high into the fading light of the late afternoon sun. The Sphinx did not fail, not in any way. The light falling on the crystal eyes shattered into a dazzling, glittering spectrum of color and brilliance. The body of the statue was luminous in sunlight, supple. It was as if Suzi were holding an incandescent creature, a living thing that was warming in her hand.

An illusion, of course, but a damned effective one.

Anthropologists had a term they used when trying to get close to indigenous peoples who had never before been contacted by the outside world—"lure and attraction." They would set glittery pieces of modern junk along riverbanks, where the tribespeople were known to come for water or to fish, and that's what Conroy was doing, luring old Warner in with a show—a beautiful woman, a stunning artifact, and lots of flash and dazzle to catch the German's eye.

Dax wouldn't have fallen for it, but he knew how little exposure was necessary for a sniper's shot to hit home. All a sniper needed was to see part of a man's head, just enough to get on target, and if Dax had been responsible for Erich Warner's safety, he would have made damn sure the German didn't go poking his head out of the boat.

Warner was doomed. Dax's problem was Suzi. When Conroy killed Warner, all those twenty drug runners could easily have a knee-jerk reaction and open fire. Or possibly, Conroy wouldn't be content with just killing Warner. Maybe he would open fire on all of them, and then it was going to be mayhem, with Suzi exposed for as long as it took her to get back in the house—a few seconds at most. But it took far less than one second to die.

So Dax made his way back down the dock, through all the armed men, and when he heard the shot, he knew Warner was already dead, that the man had stepped out of concealment to get a better look at the amazing sight of immortality blazing away in the sunlight.

Stupid bastard.

The thought was fleeting, cut short by a screeching wail of some unspeakable emotion coming out of Shoko. For a second, the twenty men on the dock were held in check by the awful, wrenching sound.

Not Dax, he was moving, breaking into a run, heading for cover, and planning his assault on the house.

Orders—Creed loved them. They gave his life a certain dimension. Performing them superbly well gave him a lot of satisfaction.

The boss had said to tranquilize Conroy Farrel if the man set one foot onto the deck, if he exposed himself for even the barest instant of time—and Creed did. He'd been watching the doorway like a hawk, and almost at the same time as Creed heard the shot, Conroy stepped out, and Creed put pressure on his trigger, darting the man.

To Creed's amazement, the guy did not go down. He kept moving.

"Tough bastard," Zach said, obviously impressed, with good reason.

"Suzi?"

"Farrel grabbed her on her way in—*geezus.*"

A screeching, banshee wail tore through the air.

"Boss?" Creed said into his radio.

"Close on the house," Dylan said. "Get Suzi and Farrel out of there."

"Geezus. You seeing that?" Zach said next to him.

"Christ." He heard Dylan in his ear.

"Who *is* that woman?" he said, but didn't get an answer. Down on the dock, the Asian woman had drawn a knife and already cut three of the soldiers trying to get back on the boat. They all had blood on their shirts. One of them had dropped to his knees, his hand holding his throat. Creed could have given him the odds on that move working out for him—zip.

The Asian woman moved like lightning—like Red Dog, was what he actually thought, sleek and smooth, and lethally efficient.

He didn't know what kind of knife the woman was wielding, but he wanted one. Hell, he wanted a dozen. Three guys sliced and diced and it still cut through the mooring rope like butter. Once she'd freed the boat, in one smooth move, she swung around and had her knife at the captain's throat.

"She's gonna..." Zach said.

"Oh, yeah," Creed agreed, and then it was over. A long arc of blood shot out of the captain's neck, and he crumpled to the deck as the woman started the gunboat's engine and headed up the Tambo River.

And so she could have had her little river cruise. She'd done SDF a favor, two dead cartel cowboys and two probably mortally wounded, and the odds were now down to about three to one.

But the girl didn't stop. She went for the .50-caliber gun mounted on the boat, and Dylan made his call.

"Take her out."

"No shot." He hated saying it, but he couldn't see her. In another two seconds, he and Zach weren't going to be able to see the boat either. She was moving upstream, past the house, and it was blocking her from their line of sight.

"Maybe you better go get one," Dylan suggested.

"Roger." He and Zach were already on the move. They knew what needed to be done.

The first guy to get hit by one of her .50-caliber rounds ended up in pieces. The same with the second, and then she started in on the house.

Ba-bam. Ba-bam.

And the whole compound turned into a melee.

CHAPTER THIRTY-FIVE

Suzi had a plan, and it was called "get the hell out of Dodge."

She had the Sphinx. Dax was somewhere close by. Conroy Farrel was—well, she didn't know what Conroy Farrel was, except that it was awful. All she and Dax needed was to rendevous and find some transportation out of this place.

Conroy Farrel needed something else. She didn't know what, but he was writhing on the floor, almost convulsive. She'd seen the dart he'd pulled out of his neck, and she didn't understand, except to think that Dylan knew who he was and hadn't wanted him dead.

She was smart enough to figure out that Conroy Farrel was SDF's Paraguayan mission.

None of which mattered if she couldn't get away from here.

Someone was shooting the house, breaking

windows, rocking it with blast after blast. Shards of rock and shingles were raining down all around, turning the place into a war zone.

Conroy Farrel still had her fanny pack with her phone and her gun, but she didn't dare get close enough to him to take her pack back. She did grab the carbine he'd dropped and moved toward the door to the deck, hoping to locate Dax.

Looking out over the deck to the river, there were men running everywhere, a lot of them shooting toward the house, some of them shooting toward the river, but she didn't see Dax. *Dammit.* Racing back to the dining room table, she felt a percussive *thump-thump-thump* shaking the house from below. Then it stopped.

Just one more damn thing.

Moving quickly, she put the Sphinx inside the gray pack, then slipped the straps onto her shoulders. She wasn't going to lose the statue. If she got out of here, she wanted to get out with her mission completed.

Chances were, though, that she wasn't going to get out of here. She checked the magazine on the carbine and headed back to the door that was still open onto the deck. Using as much cover as she could, she sidled up to the wall, raised the weapon and settled her cheek onto the stock, and then she found a target and squeezed the trigger.

Everyone in the compound was moving. It was *not* like shooting fish in a barrel. She missed more than she hit. Her adrenaline was pumping. Her small motor skills were shaky as hell. Half the time she had to hold her shot because she'd lose her focus for a second. Then she'd remind herself to breathe and aim again.

Tunnel vision—that's what happened to her. She was concentrating so hard on what was out in front of her, that she never saw what was coming up behind her.

Dax had two goals—get to Suzi, and get to Erich Warner's body, or rather, Erich Warner's jacket. Screw the Sphinx. He didn't need it for anything now that Warner was dead.

But Suzi had it, and he bet his girl had it locked down.

Another blast off the .50-cal rocked the house, shattering glass. The next round hit one of the stone walls. *Goddamn*, somebody needed to take Shoko out. She was on a rampage.

A few shots had come from the house, but they'd stopped a minute or so ago. There were shots still coming from up on the ridge, precision shots, one Vargas boy going down after another, and he'd sure like to know who was helping him out.

He made it to the house by fast-crawling along the edge of the compound, using the trees for concealment, until he could make his break for the deck. When he got there, he swung himself up, subgun ready to blast anybody who came out of the door.

But nobody did, and he ducked inside. At one time, about two minutes ago, the place had been beautiful. Shoko had turned it into a garbage heap. He didn't see Suzi anywhere. There was a carbine on the floor by the door, though, and when he reached for it, he saw something else lying on the floor—a long, faceted piece of rock crystal.

He knew what it was, and when he picked it up, he got a bad feeling. He had to find Suzi, and he was well aware of the fact that Warner's jacket was moving away from him and up the river, still wrapped around Warner's dead body, with Shoko at the wheel.

Still, if his girl was here, he had to find her.

It took him too damn long to check every room, and by the time he finished, he realized he was in danger of being overrun by the few Paraguayans that hadn't either run away into the jungle or been killed, and he didn't know where Conroy Farrel had gotten off to—the guy was nowhere.

The last door he checked opened onto a dark stairwell with a deeply dank smell coming up from out of it. He didn't hesitate. He followed the stairs down at a quick gait, feeling the air getting cooler and wetter.

"Suzi!" he called out, hoping to get an answer, and getting none.

In combat, phone calls were called communications, and though he doubted if Conroy Farrel had let her keep her phone, it was a chance.

His carbine still at the ready, he slipped his phone out of his pocket and called her number— and heard a ring. He speeded up his gait. Nobody answered the phone, but it kept ringing until he got about halfway down the stairs. Then he lost service, *dammit*.

At the bottom of the stairs, he came out into an underground boathouse, a cave lit by the fading sunlight coming in through its mouth, and a few lit lamps. The cave floor had been extended with a wide dock, and there was a go-fast boat tied up to it. The gate at the cave's opening had been blown off its hinges. The place still smelled of burned metal and pulverized rock, and all he could think was Shoko and the .50. The girl had blasted her way in here, and she'd done it for one reason only—the Sphinx. His gut was telling him she'd gotten Suzi, too, if for no reason other than he didn't think his girl would have given up the statue without a fight.

But it wouldn't have been much of a fight.

Oh, hell no.

Moving quickly, he headed toward the mouth of the cave, and at the edge of the dock came to a sudden halt. There was something, a low, grumbling growl that made the hackles rise on the back of his neck. He'd trapped something in the corner of the cave, something wild, some animal.

He took a step back from the dark form he could see huddled up against the wall, and he exchanged his phone for a flashlight he took off his tac vest. He pushed the button on the light and stopped cold.

It wasn't an animal. He didn't know what or who it was, but his first guess would be Conroy Farrel— and he took another step back. The growling deepened, the creature's wild eyes locked onto his. It was a man, purely human, but a feral human, twisted up in agony, sweat running off of it, his muscles tight, his teeth bared.

Dax had an instinct to try to help, but it was instantly overridden by his need to find Suzi, to save her.

Backing off, without taking his eyes off the guy, he made it back to the boat. He cast off and fired up the engines, and using the throttle, he reversed out of the cave. When he hit open water, he swung the prow of the boat upriver and poured on the speed.

CHAPTER THIRTY-SIX

Suzi had never dreamed in all her years that she would die in Paraguay, but the writing was on the wall. She'd made a tactical error, and she was going to die for it. She hadn't been watching her back, and she'd been caught, attacked from behind by an exceptionally strong, crazed woman with far too many knives who had all but knocked her out and dragged her down and out of the house and thrown her in the bottom of the gunboat.

This was not going to go well, and she knew it, and once again, she was trapped in far too small a space with a dead body, two this time, Erich Warner's being one of them, she presumed. The man's clothes were exceedingly expensive, even by her standards, and he'd been shot in the dead center of his face by an expert marksman, and that would have been Conroy Farrel, whose sole purpose had been to kill the German crime lord. And the other dead guy was a Paraguayan homeboy, she would guess. In a new twist for the day, he hadn't been shot. No, Suzi could see the crazed woman's handiwork from one side of his throat to the other.

If she hadn't been so scared, she would have been sick. There was blood everywhere, the bottom of the boat awash in it—the wasteful bitch.

The Asian woman was motoring them up the river, watching the shoreline, and Suzi knew exactly what she was looking for—an open space, a break in the trees where the moonlight could shine down on them. The ceremony for immortality was not that complicated—physical contact with the statue, glinting eyes, moonlight falling on the whole show—immortality. In Warner's case, considering his state, which was dead, a few pints of fresh blood needed to be poured over the granite Sphinx, and that magic combination would bring him back to life—resurrection.

The Asian Queen here obviously knew all of this, and Suzi didn't have to work too hard to see what part she played in the drama—blood donor. It was ridiculous. There was a perfectly fresh extra corpse lying in the bottom of the boat, and considering the time frame they were working with, if Knife Girl hadn't let it all run out of him, the captain's blood would have been more than fresh enough to suffice.

But no. The bitch had miscalculated, and in Suzi's opinion, was getting ready to miscalculate again.

Much to her surprise, and her chagrin, Suzi had lost one of the rock-crystal eyes out of the statue.

Somewhere on her run, from when she'd grabbed the Sphinx off the kitchen table until Psycho Girl had coldcocked her, she'd lost the left eye, the one she'd taken out earlier but had seen Conroy Farrel put back in. It must have fallen out while she'd been running around the house with the statue, before she'd had the sense to put it back in the gray pack.

And now she was paying for her lapse in logic.

She had a good-sized bruise forming on the side of her face. She could feel it, and it hurt like hell, but she had always supposed it would hurt to be pistol-whipped. It had knocked her out cold for a while—*again, dammit*—and she'd come around handcuffed to the boat, with the woman frisking her with a knife, cutting her pockets, ripping seams, obviously looking for the damn eye. She'd been cut a dozen times, small nicks and a couple of deeper cuts that all stung like hell and scared her spitless.

So, great, another crappy day of being terrified and run ragged.

This job had been unlike any job General Grant had ever sent her on—and if she wanted another, so help her God, she needed to step up. Buck Grant wanted the Memphis Sphinx, and come hell, high water, and one crazed psycho bitch, she'd gotten it. She'd won. Hands down. The Memphis Sphinx was lying right there in front of her, cushioned on the backpack and a greasy rag laid inside a box of tools.

Most of it anyway.

But not enough of it. Not in her opinion. To lose her life over a ceremony whose odds of succeeding had just dropped from "highly unlikely, babe" to "no way in hell, bitch" was untenable.

She did have a plan. It was covered in blood, but it was there in the bottom of the boat, the dead Paraguayan's pistol. All she needed to do was free herself from the handcuffs, move like a lightning bolt, wrestle the pistol out of the bloody holster belted onto the dead guy's waist, and shoot the black-haired beauty as many times as she possibly could.

Piece of cake.

But she'd had that plan for the last half an hour or so and was still handcuffed to the boat, and then suddenly she ran out of time. Just like that. The river widened, the sky opened up on a grassy inlet, and the bitch slowed the gunboat down.

"This party is over," Creed said into his radio. The woman in the gunboat had disappeared up the river, taking her .50-caliber gun with her before he'd gotten within range.

He'd lost sight of Dax in the fighting but had to consider that Suzi might still be here somewhere, and the quicker he and Zach found her, the better, and if he found Conroy Farrel, even better.

There'd been some casualties. He didn't know whose fight this had actually been, or what everybody had been fighting over, except the Sphinx thing, but a lot of boys had died for it—the man in the boat, the captain, four guys here in the compound, and he was betting a few more over on the other side of the house, down by the dock. The house looked like it had been severely damaged—just about every window was shattered, and part of the deck had been blown off.

The sun was falling fast now, the light was low, but the fight was over. He and Zach ran across the compound without meeting any resistance.

"You take the main floor," he said to Zach. "I'll check the boathouse." Or cave, such as it was. They'd all seen the big iron gate covering the opening onto the river.

It was dark going down the stairs, with only the faintest light coming up from below. He could hear the river running and smell the water.

He had his carbine safety off, his finger on the trigger, and step by silent step, he went down the stairs. He had a tac light on his weapon, but he would save it until he thought he had a target. He was good in the dark, the best, so there was no reason to give his position away.

He stopped on the last step, his hackles rising, a warning shooting straight up his spine. He wasn't alone down here.

The man came from out of nowhere, from out of the darkness with a speed Creed couldn't counter. The first hit had them both grappling on the dock, and Creed quickly realized that he wasn't in a fight. He was in a death match, and it was his death. The guy on top of him who had him in his grip was unbelievably strong, and he meant unfuckingbelievably strong. Creed could bench three hundred pounds all day long, and he couldn't budge this guy. *Geezus. Dying in fucking Paraguay.*

The guy had knocked his carbine off to the side, and it was tangling him up in its sling, making it hard to get to a knife, and then the guy just stopped, went completely mannequin on top of him, and the longer the guy held him down, pressing him into the dock, making it impossible for him to move, the better look he got at the guy's face— and he knew the guy was looking at him, too. He could feel it in the slightest lightening of his hold, he heard it in the catch of the guy's breath, and everything he felt, and saw, and heard, fueled an anger so deep, it gave him strength he hadn't known he possessed.

In one mighty lunge, he upset the balance of the guy's hold, and they were grappling again. He'd seen it, the sonuvabitch. He knew. A flash of the truth had been in the man's eyes, and Creed was going to kill him. The betrayal was an abomination.

J.T.

My God, he'd died a thousand deaths in his heart, endured a thousand nights of shame for not being able to save his partner, his friend, and J.T. was here.

Creed was going to kill him.

His rage was boundless, like the opening of a floodgate.

And in an instant it didn't matter. The guy landed one blow, and Creed's lights went out in a burst of agony.

CHAPTER THIRTY-SEVEN

Something terrible was happening to the Asian woman, something besides her being consumed by an ever-growing madness. When she'd dragged the dead German out of the bottom of the boat and hauled him up onto the shore, and then kept going, Suzi had seized her chance, using her feet to pull the dead captain closer—but she couldn't get him close enough to grab his gun, not while she was cuffed to a piece of metal bolted into the boat. *Dammit.*

She was going to die here.

The woman made another trip with the Sphinx before coming back for Suzi, and the minute she undid the cuff from the boat, Suzi lashed out, pushing hard against her chest and sweeping her leg out to kick the woman's legs out from under her—and it worked, just the way it worked in training, when she was exhausted and Superman kept pushing her harder and harder, being mean, being tough, roughing her up.

When the woman went down, Suzi kicked her hard and made her escape, leaping over the side of the boat and letting herself sink under the dark water.

Freedom.

She stroked for the bottom, trying to become as invisible as possible, but didn't get far before a hand buried itself in her hair and dragged her back up to the surface. For a second, Suzi thought she could fight the woman off, but in the next passing second she realized the Asian woman wasn't just strong—she was very strong. Stronger even than Superman.

There was no hope, no chance. The woman had her under control, her hands cuffed back together, and was hauling her up onto the shore in less than half a minute, dragging her up through the grass like a half-drowned rat.

Suzi spluttered and choked, and for good measure, the woman hit her in the face before dropping her next to Erich Warner.

Damn. Suzi didn't even care that he was dead. Dead people were not the ones beating the crap out of her. She was *never* going to be afraid of another dead person, not ever.

A cramp hit her, and she wrapped her arm tight around her middle and threw up on the ground, a whole stomachful of river water.

Geezus. She was probably going to die from that. But then she thought no, not really. She was going to die bleeding out for Erich Warner and the Memphis Sphinx—unless she could figure out a way to kill this bitch with the knives.

She threw up again, and used the back of her hand to wipe her mouth, and then she launched herself at the Asian woman, right over the top of Erich Warner's dead body, her hands going for the woman's throat. If she could just get a grip—but the woman knocked her away, and the blow left her stunned.

For a moment, she lay there, trying to catch her breath, trying to clear her head so she could think, but all she could think was that she didn't want to die—not now, not in this place, and not by this woman's hands.

Dax gunned the twin Mercs on Farrel's go-fast boat, going even faster, driving the thing in curving arcs up the winding Tambo River. He didn't know where Suzi was. He only knew the worst place for her to be, and that was with Shoko, and Shoko had gone up the river, undoubtedly not very far—unless she'd already gotten what she needed. So the farther he went, the surer he was that the Blade Queen of Bangkok had gotten the Sphinx, and probably Suzi, too. Both those things had been promised to him by Conroy Farrel, and both of those things had been missing from the house.

Shoko had a use for Suzi. He wasn't kidding himself about that. Warner was dead. The Blade Queen was either going to try for immortality for herself, which would only make sense, or she was going to try for magic trick number two, which was resurrecting the dead.

Dax had a feeling that for whatever reasons, and she probably had more than one, Shoko was going to go for magic trick number two, which required copious amounts of fresh blood.

And he had to wonder, really, who in the hell dreamed this stupid shit up? Like life wasn't complicated and mysterious enough without that crap. *Geezus.* His life was plenty complicated, and if a guy wanted mystery, well, hell, that's why God created women. All the mystery a guy ever needed was wrapped up in a soft mouth and a racetrack's worth of curves.

He throttled down for a tight turn up ahead, pointing the bow and letting the back end of the boat slide in behind before he gunned it again.

Two more winding turns in the river later, he saw the gunboat, and it was empty. Twin Mercs didn't leave any chance for a silent approach, but that hadn't been his plan. He wanted Shoko to know he'd found her. He wanted her attention on him as quickly as possible. He wanted her to be faced off with him, not Suzi—and sweet geezus, he wasn't a second too soon. There was movement in the grassy field, low and to the ground, and the furtiveness of it just about stopped his heart.

"*Shoko!*" he called out. His next move was to pull the rock-crystal eye out of his pocket and hold it high in the air. "*Shoko!*"

He didn't tie off the boat; he ran the bow up close to the shore and kept the engines running.

"*Shoko!*"

In the fading light, he saw more movement, bodies moving, but he couldn't tell which was Shoko and which was Suzi—and he was praying one of the moving bodies was Suzi. There was a small mound in the field that looked like a nonmoving body, like a dead guy—and that would most likely be Erich Warner.

Except that was Shoko up there, and knowing her, she could have killed half a dozen people by now.

"I have the eye!" he shouted.

All movement stopped, and he hoped to God that he had her attention.

"You're running out of time, Shoko. If you want the eye, you need to give me the woman now!" He was still shouting, making himself very clear. "If you shoot me, the eye goes over the side." He had very deliberately moved his hand over the river, and was leaning in that direction.

"She's hurt, Killian. If you want her, you'll have to come and get her."

Hurt.

He took a breath, tried to slow the racing of his heart.

"Show her to me, Shoko. I need to see that she's still alive."

He wasn't going to tell her again that she was running out of time. She knew it. The sun was dropping like a cannonball now, with the full moon scheduled to come into view over the eastern horizon as soon as the last rays of sunlight faded from the western sky.

"Your bitch, Killian," Shoko said, and two dark forms rose up from the ground in the deepening gloom.

He jumped off the boat and started forward.

"I want to hear her voice, Shoko." It was an old negotiator's trick, to keep using someone's name. There was nothing like a person's name to get and hold their attention.

After the last command, he stopped. He could hear the river and the rocking of the boat, hear the waves lapping against the hull, and he waited to hear Suzi's voice.

"*Dax . . . Dax . . .*"

That was his girl all right. He started across the grassy field, moving quickly but carefully.

"Let her go, Shoko, and you can have the eye. I—" His next words were cut off by a keening scream that rent the air, a wailing cry of pain, more agony than he'd ever heard.

The two women crumpled back to the ground, becoming nearly indistinguishable from each other, and he started to run.

"*Nooooo . . .*" the voice cried. "*Noooooo . . .*"

It was Shoko.

"*Which one? Warner, Warner . . . which one?*"

At twenty-five yards, he could see her clearly on her knees at Warner's side, wailing. Suzi was handcuffed, half sitting, half leaning on the ground, free from Shoko's grip but not running away.

He ran to her side and dragged her to her feet. She was nearly limp. He held her close and backed off, his gun drawn, but Shoko barely seemed aware of them.

"*Nooooo . . .*" she wailed. "*Warrrrrrner.*"

She looked to the east and grew even more frantic, her crazed eyes coming to rest on them.

"The crystal, give it to me, hurry, hurry." She reached out her hand.

Erich Warner's body had been arranged, straight and true on the ground, the Memphis Sphinx on his chest, facing him, facing east. Shoko had duct-taped his hands to the statue, and she had a pile of brightly colored pills poured out onto his handkerchief where she'd laid it on the ground.

Okay, this was weird, and oddly compelling. It was also, Dax realized, an act of utter desperation, and he wondered for a moment if it was love motivating her. Then he thought not. He tossed her the crystal eye, keeping Suzi close, and wondering what in the world Shoko was going to use for blood. Warner was covered in it, but unless he'd had a bad accident on the way up the river, Dax figured most of what he was seeing had come from rolling around in the bottom of the boat with a guy who'd had his throat slit.

He kept backing off. He could have shot her. He was more than ready, but there was this little tug of curiosity he couldn't deny, and he had a feeling that this was going to be one of those times when things just took care of themselves.

He hadn't forgotten about the envelope in

Warner's jacket, but for all the trouble he'd gone to, the months of searching, he wanted to see this thing through. He wanted to know, beyond a shadow of a doubt, that it was all a bunch of crap.

So he backed off, and he didn't take his eyes off Shoko, or his finger off the trigger of his .45, and every time she looked to the east, he wondered at the stark fear in her eyes.

She pulled a knife out of a sheath on her belt, and he took up the slack on his trigger.

She looked to the east again and placed her left hand on top of the statue. When moonlight flooded the grassy area, coming up over the tops of the trees and pouring across the wide spot in the river before flowing up the shore, she slashed her wrist, deep.

A cry left her, a cry of such pain, he nearly reached for her. But he didn't. He watched as her blood spurted out of her artery and poured over the statue, and when the moonlight struck the crystal eyes, he was held in place, enthralled by their glittering luminescence.

It was beautiful, an amazing sight to see, but it wasn't magic.

A minute passed, then half a minute more with Shoko's life pouring out of her. Next to him, he felt Suzi take more of her own weight on her feet, felt her come around a little bit, and the two of them stood quietly in the moonlit field and watched Shoko, the Blade Queen of Bangkok, die, and they watched Erich Warner stay as dead as he'd ever been.

But Dax didn't lower his pistol, not for a second, and when Shoko finally collapsed on her dead lover, he knew the world had suddenly become a better place.

"I'm taking that Sphinx," Suzi said at his side, and it was a statement, not a question.

"Yes." It was hers. She'd more than earned it. Even if he'd had a use for the damn thing, he'd have let her have it. "Are you okay?"

He stepped back up to the bodies, bent down, and pulled the envelope out of Warner's jacket. He shoved it way down deep in the cargo pocket on his pants before buttoning the pocket.

"She beat the crap out of me every time I tried to escape, and that was quite a few times."

"Good for you." *Geezus.* He didn't know a guy who could have come out ahead of Shoko, and his girl had stayed in one piece. "Turn away, Suzi, and cover your ears."

She didn't ask why, she just did it, and he put one shot in the back of Shoko's head. It was just good business.

Together, he and Suzi walked back to the boats, and they found a couple of containers to carry river water back up to where Shoko and Warner were lying with the Sphinx still sitting on Warner's chest. One container after another, they poured the water over the Sphinx, washing off all the blood. When it was clean, he pulled the duct tape off and Warner's hands fell to either side, his arms dropping to his sides.

For good measure, they splashed the rest of the river water over it, emptying both containers.

"You want me to carry it for you?" he asked, but she shook her head and bent down to pick up the statue.

What a thing, he thought, all golden and granite and crystalline, warmed by moonlight. It really was beautiful.

Suzi was careful, picking it up and holding it close in to her chest, and they started back down to the boats.

She had it cradled in her arms, facing up, and when they were ten yards from the shore, the eyes lit up like a couple of damn flashlights. Two beams. Bright as frickin' halogen, cutting through the night like a pair of lasers, and lighting her up like a Macy's parade.

And then they turned off.

Fuck, he thought.

"Geez," she said. "Did you see that?"

He let out a short, unhappy laugh.

"Oh, yeah, babe. I saw that."

Per-fricking-fecto.

Another damn mystery in his life.

"I need a drink." He was just being honest. Scotch had been invented for times like these.

CHAPTER **THIRTY-EIGHT**

Creed awoke to the sound of a ringing phone. He was lying flat on his back in the dark . . . in a cave, that was right. And he'd gotten hit by a pile driver . . . yeah, that was right.

He rolled onto his side, curled up, and pushed himself to his hands and knees. *Geezus.* He put one hand on his forehead before he got to his feet. *Geezus.*

He flipped on his flashlight, arranged his carbine so the sling wasn't all cattywampus, and then he found the phone, lying on the dock, about twenty feet away.

"Hello," he said when he answered it.

"What are you doing answering Suzi's phone?" Dylan asked. He'd recognize the boss's voice in his sleep.

"I found it in the cave under the house. The one behind the gate we could see on the river."

"You have Suzi with you?"

"No." He turned his head one way, very gently, then the other way, just as gently.

"Farrel?"

"No." He had a few kinks from rumbling with the guy, but he did not have the guy.

"So we lost him." Dylan didn't sound too glad about that bit of news.

"Maybe Zach got him." But Creed doubted it. One guy was not going to take down Conroy Farrel.

"Zach just checked in, empty-handed," Dylan said. "The house is clear, and he's headed down to you. Superman and I are coming in."

"Good." That was all good. Zach had cleared the house, while he, Creed, had gotten his clock cleaned.

Damn. He knew what he'd seen. It was all coming back in Technicolor.

"What about Killian?" Dylan asked. "We saw him take a go-fast boat out of that cave and head upriver after the gunboat. Have you—forget it. Here he comes now."

Creed heard it, too.

"Or at least that's the boat," Dylan said. "Can you see who's in it from where you are?"

"I'm in a cave, boss."

"Oh . . . right."

He heard Dylan saying something to Hawkins.

"Okay," the boss came back on the phone. "Cristo here brought along his night vision goggles, so he's up one—"

"Two," Creed heard Superman say.

"Bull, two...oh, he's taking a point for his superlative body count on the Paraguayans, and all I can say is I hope we don't read about this in the damn papers. You see a CNN reporter up there anywhere?"

"No." His head was clearing a little now.

"And we have positive identification on Suzi Toussi and Dax Killian coming out of the Tambo River, lounging comfortably in the front seats, with no one else on board, and I'm guessing heading back to Ciudad del Este," Dylan gave the report. "We're going to need to talk to him."

"Debrief him."

"Find out what he's been up to since he left the Army."

"Maybe get him on board," Creed said. It's what they'd all been thinking since Dax Killian had shown up in Denver six months ago, working a job that had ended up involving one of their own. The guy was a legend, very skilled, and they all knew for a fact that he could steal a car blindfolded with one arm tied behind his back. He had chop-shop chops.

"Yeah. I've been talking to Grant."

"Good." SDF was always running just a little shorthanded it seemed lately, at least to Creed. The world needed saving eighteen times a day some weeks.

"So what can you tell me about Farrel?"

"I saw him." Up close and personal.

"And?"

"And we need to bring him in. No assassination.

And if the CIA sends anybody else after him, we need to take them out."

There was a long silence on the other end of the phone.

"Okay then . . . got it."

Yeah, Creed knew how the boss was suddenly feeling, gut-punched, and sick, and maybe elated, except he'd be too confused to get very far with that one, and edging up behind all that, moving in fast, like a frickin' freight train, would be the anger.

Yeah, Creed knew all about it. What he didn't know was what to do with all of it—except put each overwhelming emotion in a box, and put each box someplace where none of them would get mixed in together, because man, that was one toxic brew. Compartmentalization—it was the only way.

"We've got his girl," Dylan said. "If we can't find him, he'll come to us."

And they'd sure as hell better be damn good and ready for when that happened.

"Stay where you are," Dylan continued. "We're at the boat. The package is still in good shape, and we'll be there in about five minutes. We'll check the compound, rifle through Farrel's house, steal everything we find, and then go see what happened to that gunboat."

Hell.

"Sounds like a long night, boss."

"Don't worry, sweetheart. I'll have you home before dawn."

CHAPTER THIRTY-NINE

Ciudad del Este

"Ouch."

"That's the last one." Dax smoothed a small bandage over one of Suzi's cuts. He'd paid double for super-service in this dump, so he'd had no qualms about letting her soak her heart out in the Posada Plaza's bathtub, and now she was all warm and steamy and clean, and wrapped in a towel he couldn't wait to take off of her, and this time it really wasn't about sex.

He'd been in the bathtub with her, and he knew she was as exhausted as he was, which was bordering on dangerous. They'd moored Conroy Farrel's ultra-expensive boat at the public docks, paid four kids to watch over it for the night, and eaten on the way back to the hotel.

All they had to do now was sleep.

"Come on, let's get you into bed."

Her hair was wet and stringy. Her makeup was long gone. She had a bruise the size of a pistol grip along her temple and cheekbone. She was almost trembling she was so tired and had so much emotion to work through—and she'd never been more beautiful to him in her life.

Yeah. He'd racked up a whole day and a half in her company, and somehow she was his, lock, stock, and barrel, one hundred percent, all his, the whole girl.

His.

Only his.

The rest of the world could go take a flying leap.

He'd moved furniture in front of the door, paid Marcella, Marceline, and the pimp at the front desk each a hundred bucks for security backup. He'd moved more furniture in front of the balcony doors, and he'd cocked, locked, and loaded every damn firearm they had between them.

Everything about this little oasis they were in said "Do Not Disturb." And he expected the world to respect that for at least twelve hours.

Once he got her all tucked in and comfy, he got in on the other side and pulled her in close, letting her wrap her legs in with his and rest her head on his shoulder, and breathe on him and make him feel secure.

She was his.

*　　　*　　　*

"They look pretty comfortable."

"Too damn comfortable."

"Why in the hell did you make us work all night, if everybody else got to go to bed?"

Suzi heard the voices from a long distance, like maybe she was dreaming them, but then she realized she wasn't dreaming.

She knew those voices, and with a soft groan for her aching body and her pounding head, she slowly opened her eyes to a narrow squint.

It was like old home week in room 519 of the Posada Plaza. Zach was leaning up against the open balcony door. Creed was sitting cross-legged on top of the table, eating something covered in sugar. Dylan had the chair, and Hawkins was sitting on top of the dresser closest to the bed.

"Looks like you won the fight, Suzi," he said. "Good girl."

"Thank you." He was proud of her, she could tell, and it did her heart good.

There had been a time when she'd ruled these boys just by being beautiful, and a little sad, and sometimes, in private, a lot sad, until Hawkins had found a place for her.

She'd thought he was crazy at first. Her? Do work for General Grant? But the job had been perfect for her, to wine and dine her way through a series of embassy parties in Prague and let Buck know who talked to whom.

Piece of cake.

And now look at her. Five years later, she was

getting the crap beaten out of her and still coming out on top.

"What's wrong with Killian?" Dylan wanted to know. "You slip him a Mickey, or does he always sleep like that?"

She looked over at the man sound asleep in the bed with her. He was out like a light.

"He had a big day," she said, shifting her attention back to the boss. "Two big days."

"Thought he was tougher than that," Zach said from over by the balcony.

"He's gonna *have* to be tougher than that," Creed said, and took another big bite of deep-fried doughnut.

"He'll be fine," she assured them, and for a moment, the room fell silent.

"You were with him," Dylan finally said, breaking the silence. "What do you think?"

She knew who he was talking about, and it wasn't Dax Killian.

"J.T.," she said. "His memory is gone. He's been tortured. It looks like many, many times. Half of his ring finger on his right hand is missing. He's got scars on his face, his neck, his arms . . . probably everywhere, but that's all I could see with him dressed." The memory of how he looked played in her mind as she told the guys about Conroy Farrel, John Thomas Chronopolous, and it wasn't until the tears ran down the side of her nose and pooled on her lips that she realized she was crying.

A pall had fallen over the room.

She understood. What she'd told them was

awful, maybe even more awful than what they'd believed all these years.

"We've got his girl under lock and key," Dylan
said. "We're taking her out of here with us, on a
transport plane that leaves in two hours. I expect
you and Dax to be on that plane. Got it?"

"Yes, sir." She got it. She'd just been given orders
by the boss.

"We'll debrief at Steele Street, before you go to
Washington to see General Grant. That's the way
we work. Got it?"

"Yes, sir."

He wasn't Dylan anymore; if she wanted what
she'd just earned the hard way, he was "sir."

"Then get your boyfriend up, Suzi. We'll see you
at the airfield."

"What about J.T.?" she asked. "What happens
next?" She knew her guys, and this was far from
over.

A look passed between the men.

"We left him a business card," Hawkins said.
"He'll know where to find us."

Yes, he would, Suzi thought. There was only one
business card in this group, and it said: DYLAN
HART, UPTOWN AUTOS, WE ONLY SELL THE BEST, 738
STEELE STREET, DENVER, COLORADO.

CHAPTER FORTY

Marsh Annex, Washington, D.C.

Buck Grant was impressed as hell.

He sat back in his chair, his phone to his ear, looking at Suzi and seeing his pension grow by leaps and bounds. The girl had done him good. But somebody somewhere had a whole helluva lot of answering to do, and Buck was going to damn well find out who. The Conroy Farrel mission and the Memphis Sphinx mission should never have intersected, let alone meshed like two halves of a whole—but they had, and that meant there was a connection higher up the ladder. In Buck's experience, the higher up the ladder things went, the more dangerous they became, which in this instance wasn't going to slow SDF down for a second. He and Dylan were already tearing this thing apart, event by event, line by line, and they were going to find the bastards who had turned J. T. Chronopolous into Conroy Farrel, and Buck didn't have a doubt in his mind that the search would also reveal who had stolen a top secret artifact from one of the most secure laboratories in the world.

Buck also didn't have a doubt in his mind that it was going to cost him everything—least of all the pension Suzi had just helped become a little more secure. This thing was big, and dark, and dirty, and everybody was on Buck's list of possible perpetrators, including the guy he was calling.

"Bill," he said when the phone was answered, and he meant William Davies, who'd been the assistant secretary of defense for Special Operations and Low-Intensity Conflict when SDF had first been created and put under Grant's command, William Davies who since then had been kicked so high up into the stratosphere of government that his missives and his orders came from places he most certainly wasn't at—like the Department of Labor or the Department of Education.

"Buck," Davies answered.

"I've got that item the DIA lost a few months ago, the one their buddies over at Langley asked SDF to go get back for them."

"That statue they were screaming about?"

"That's the one."

There was a slight pause on the other end of the line.

"Good job, Buck. A couple more like that, and you might actually work your way back into the Pentagon."

Buck doubted it, but it was nice to hear.

"Do you want to send somebody over to get it, or do you want my team to take it back over to DIA?"

There was no pause this time.

"I'll take care of it. No need for you and your guys to bother. I'll have some people there in half an hour."

Like Buck hadn't seen that coming.

"Good enough, Bill. The package is ready to go." He grinned. Business as usual. Don't rock the boat, not yet. Let the big boys have the glory—that was his motto. All Buck wanted was the truth.

He hung up the phone and looked over at the woman sitting on the other side of his desk.

"Rough go?" he asked. She was still beautiful, still wearing an outfit that dared him to look, but she'd been hurt. Her face was bruised and scratched, and he could see a couple of Band-Aids on her arms here and there.

"Not too bad," she said. "Nothing I couldn't handle."

Right. That's what he had Dylan Hart for—to tell him the whole truth, and his girl had been pushed to the wall on this one. They'd all been pushed to the wall, his whole team.

"Glad to hear it."

She was damn proud of herself. He could tell, no matter how cool she was playing it. She always held herself well, but her shoulders were just a little bit straighter, and he noticed.

"More than likely, given your success here, and

that you pulled this thing off in record time, they're going to want to use you again," he said.

"You mean the next time they lose something?" She gave him a very skeptical look. "I would think the DIA wouldn't go around losing things very often."

"No," he agreed. "They don't. But they do spend a fair share of their time accumulating items of interest. Are you up for it, or should I tell them to go take a flying leap?"

He meant it. If she wasn't on board, the DIA and the CIA could take their business elsewhere. It was all Grant could do to keep Bill Davies happy. SDF needed another team. He was running his operators ragged most of the time. They needed some downtime, and he was doing his damnedest to figure out how to build his unit in order to give it to them, if there was a unit by the time they finished with Conroy Farrel.

Suzi met his gaze, and he could tell she was thinking.

He liked that. She'd just come off a helluva mission, unlike anything he'd ever given her, though honest to God, he'd had no idea at the time. She needed to think, weigh the possibilities—weigh her commitment.

"Yes, sir, I'd like another go," she said, and the conviction in her voice didn't leave a doubt in his mind. His girl was ready for another go.

Well, he could pretty much damn well guarantee that she was going to get one.

CHAPTER FORTY-ONE

Nepal—eight weeks later

"Hey, sugar. How do you want your tea? Hot or cold?"

"You're hilarious," Suzi said through chattering teeth.

They were a two days' trek out of Pokhara, Nepal, staying in a flat-roofed stone house euphemistically described as a "hotel." Their room had a stone floor with a fire pit in the middle and came inclusive of a set of cooking pots. Miracle of miracles, there was a bed with plenty of blankets. The view in the mornings of the sunlight hitting the Himalayas was breathtaking—literally. By dawn, the room temperature would be hovering in the hypothermia zone, until Dax got up and stoked the fire back into a blaze.

Suzi's job at that time of day was to keep the bed warm.

She was good at her job, but this morning, the job took more than she had to give in the way of body heat.

Shivering, she watched Dax pour steaming water into two metal mugs.

"I'll take that as a 'hot' request," he said. "I think you're getting in a rut."

"I think I'm going to give Noble Faith two more days to get here with the *Paitza of Abd Hasan,* and then I'm heading back to Kathmandu and hot running water."

The Moonrise team of the Defense Intelligence Agency had gotten a line on an ancient artifact of the Golden Horde of the Eurasian Steppes—the Paitza of Abd Hasan, a gold plate from the thirteenth century—not nearly as old as the Maned Sphinx of Sesostris III, but in certain circles considered even more powerful. The Paitza purportedly granted life everlasting and untold riches. Suzi's job, if she had chosen to take it—which she had—was to meet with a man named Tam-cho, Noble Faith, in this godforsaken middle of nowhere, and cut a deal. Rumor had it that the Paitza had been discovered in the ruins of Shekar Dzong, the Shining Crystal Monastery in Tibet, somehow transported there over the centuries from Mongolia.

Dax carefully set her tea on a bedside table, then crawled under the covers with her with his own mug.

Grant had asked her who she wanted on backup for the mission, and she hadn't thought twice.

"Should we go down to the dining room later and have brown bread and cheese for breakfast?" he asked.

"How about quiche and croissants with a cappuccino?"

"And for lunch, I guess we'll go back to that little café—"

"Hovel," she interrupted.

"Café," he repeated, "and have—"

"Pea soup and rice."

"*Daal bhaat,*" he translated.

She took a sip of her tea. With the hot liquid going inside and her hands wrapped around the mug, she was warming up, and for each degree of warmth, her mood improved two degrees.

"Actually, that was pretty good," she admitted.

He leaned over and kissed her cheek.

"Do you still have your book to read?" he asked.

"Yes." There was little else to do, except hike around looking at astounding mountains that she could easily see just by going outside and turning her head in any direction. This was the Mountain Kingdom.

"Or we could hike over to that little stream again."

He meant the half-frozen, rock-filled trickle that wound its way down the village's eastern boundary.

"We could," she agreed, taking another sip of hot tea.

"Or we could do what we did yesterday," he suggested.

He looked so innocent, sitting there next to her, propped up on the pillows, drinking his tea with one hand while his other was under the covers, sliding up her leg.

She could just see the top of the tattoo running down the side of his hip, *Conqueror* in Chinese, and she couldn't help herself—a grin curved her mouth. "We do that an awful lot."

"Because we're good at it." He gave a little shrug. "Stick with your strengths, that's what I say."

"Oh, you do, do you?" Her grin broadened.

Good Lord, if anyone had ever told her she would wake up in a bed in Nepal with the man of her dreams, she would have told them they were nuts. But here she was, with Dax Killian, who was actually more man than she had dreamed she would find. He was solid, like a rock, emotionally, psychologically, physically, and he shared that strength with her. She trusted him like no person she'd ever known before. It was just there, trust down to the core, and it made her feel so safe, like she'd finally found home base.

A woman would never leave a man who made her feel like that.

"Absolutely. It's one of my rules to live by."

"Got any more of those rules?" she asked, looking at him from over the top of her mug.

"Only one," he admitted.

"And that is?" She was curious. From what she'd been able to find out, he didn't have many rules, and even fewer that he hadn't broken at one time or another.

"If you ever find yourself lying in bed with a woman in Nepal drinking hot tea at dawn, you should marry the woman."

She just looked at him, completely nonplussed.

"It's not a rule that gets invoked very often," he admitted, taking another sip of his tea before setting his mug on the bedside table. "But every time I've done it, it's worked out real well for me."

"Uh . . . every time?" She finally got a few words out. "How many times have you invoked that rule?"

"Only once," he said. "This is actually the first time, but I've got high hopes on it working out."

"Because?" she prompted him, truly out in left field. Dax Killian, unlike herself, had never been married. She would have thought "proposal rules" would have been nonexistent in his life.

"Because the woman I'm drinking tea with in bed in Nepal is crazy in love with me." He reached over and took her mug out of her hand and set it next to his on the table.

"Oh." She couldn't deny it.

"And because I can't imagine going about my life without her in it, not anymore." He slipped his arm around her waist and pulled her down into the bed with him, deeper under the pile of blankets.

"Oh," she said, loving the feel of him so close, his legs tangled up with hers, his smile meant for her alone.

"And I think we make a helluva team." He leaned down and kissed her, and it was exactly like coming home—except hotter, the kind of heat that made a girl melt in bed.

"Umm...Dax." She opened her mouth wider and let the kiss just take them away. She didn't really mean to let it take them so far away that they got off the subject of his tea-drinking proposal, but she didn't mind, not really, not when he was so ready for her, and not when he made sweet, endless love to her, his mouth and his hands all over her, his body weighing her down in the bed, hot and heavy and hard, filling her again and again, the warm, male scent of him soothing her even as he pushed her closer and closer to the edge of release.

He was so strong in her arms, the sleek power of him driving her higher and higher. She strained against him. Her body was wild for the taste and the feel of him...until she just let go, losing herself in pleasure so searing, so sweet, so incredibly binding. It tied her to him, the way every moment she'd been with him from the very first one tied her to him.

"I love you," she whispered against his mouth. *"I love you, Dax."*

He was going to take that as a yes, one hundred percent, and that was match point, and game. *Hooyah.* Suzanna Royale Toussi was his. Wife. The big "W."

He kissed her mouth and held her close. Yeah, she was his, the most beautiful woman he'd ever seen, the one who'd thrown him down hard and made him work for it.

She was tough, a hard girl, and he loved that about her. She could work him from here to eternity. He was a hard guy. He could take it. He could hold her in line, and he could hold her to him—and he could kiss her for-frickin-ever, because he'd never had a woman turn him so inside out.

He decided then and there that he liked Nepal. It was a lot like Afghanistan, except without the mortar fire—which was a huge improvement. He especially liked Nepal from under half a dozen blankets, wrapped up with the woman he loved. He loved it and was wondering maybe what he could do about it, when a knock sounded at the door.

"*O baabu,*" a small voice said, and Dax figured that was the youngest son of the woman who'd rented them the room. The boy said a few more words, none of which Dax particularly understood, except for one—"Tam-cho."

The trader was here.

"*Haas,*" he said loud enough to be heard through the door, *okay,* and that just about used up all of his Nepali.

"Noble Faith?" Suzi asked from beneath him, using the translation of *Tam-cho.*

Dax nodded. "Yeah, Noble Faith. If he's got our Paitza, we could be . . . well, we could be anywhere by this time tomorrow. Where would you like to get married?"

A grin teased her mouth.

"Short engagement?" she asked.

"Twenty-four hours, max. Where do you want to do the deed?"

"Rome."

Rome. He liked it.

"So are you ready for Noble Faith, and the Paitza of untold wealth, and life everlasting?"

She smiled up at him, her eyes all dreamy, her body so soft, and willing, and welcoming. "I think I've already got all that, Dax. All of it—the faith, and the riches, and the feeling like I could live forever, as long as I'm living with you."

Yeah. He lowered his mouth to hers for a kiss. *Oh, yeah,* he felt it, too, like they could live forever.

ABOUT THE AUTHOR

TARA JANZEN lives in Colorado, where she is working on her next novel. Of the mind that love truly is what makes the world go round, she can be contacted at www.tarajanzen.com. Happy reading!